What they're saying about...

THE LEPER

By
FREDERICK LOEB

"I truly enjoyed this book. Frederick Loeb's method of capturing the true nature of religion is amazing."

Jimmye Michal O'Connor - Boulder, Colorado

"Loeb's latest is a fun and enjoyable read that challenges both the reader's imagination and their faith in God."

Ralph Fix - Edina, Minnesota

"Once begun, 'The Leper' is hard to put down. It's imaginative and exciting storytelling, and as usual with a Loeb novel, a real page turner."

K. J. Culpepper, author of *Jewel*
St. Paul, Minnesota

"Carefully introduced characters and situations that hold your interest until the very end and you find out what happens to each of them. An enjoyable read."

Rosemary Wallner, W Creative
Minnetonka, Minnesota

Novels
by
Frederick Loeb

The Leper

The Patterson Chronicles

Gracie's Ghost – The Haunting
Gracie's Ghost – The Return
Gracie's Ghost – The Revelation

THE LEPER

FREDERICK LOEB

Copyright © 2012 by
FREDERICK LOEB

All rights reserved.
SFC Publishing Division of Write Right Ink

1210 Lillian Street
Jordan, MN 55352
1.952.239.4238

All rights reserved. No part of this publication may be reproduced, stored in a retrieval system, or transmitted, in any form or by any means, electronic, mechanical, photocopying, recording, or otherwise, without the prior written permission of the author.

Library of Congress Control Number: 2011946284
ISBN 13: 978-1-468-14263-1
ISBN 10: 1-468-14263-1

Cover Design Write Right Ink
Cover image by ShutterStock.com
Interior Set in Copperplate, Times New Roman,
Papyrus, Copperplate and Cambria True Type fonts by Write Right Ink
Editing by Rosemary Wallner of W Creative, Minneapolis, MN

Printed in the United States of America

Dedication

For Lynn because, after thirty-three amazing years, she still puts up with my foolishness; for my kids and other family members who are so supportive; for the gang at T.J.'s in Edina for never taking any of this very seriously at all; for the Richfield public school system for reasons only their graduates and James Hare understand and for Rosemary who had the courage to take this project on faith she'd actually get paid. Finally, for Jimmye and Karen, thank you for all the help and special encouragement.

F.L.

The Leper

FREDERICK LOEB

"And the angel which I saw stand upon the sea and upon the earth lifted up his hand to heaven.

"And swore by Him that lives for ever and ever, who created heaven, and the things that therein are, and the earth, and the things that therein are, and the sea, and the things which are therein, that there should be time no longer."

THE REVELATION OF SAINT JOHN THE DIVINE
Chapter 10, verses 5 and 6
King James Version

The Lake Country

Chapter 1

The Real Target

The longevity of a good automobile fascinates me. I'm not a car nut, at least not since my college days more than three decades gone, but I do have my standards.

I have one eyeball glued to the odometer's digital readout as I leave Highway 10 for Route 371 just outside St. Cloud. Two hours earlier we had left the comfortable abode of Daniel and Constance Patterson in the subdued suburb of Eagan, Minnesota. We hid in plain sight in the endless rivers of evening rush hour taillights flowing from the bowels of Minneapolis and St. Paul. Now, halfway to our destination, the mid-May sun melts into a glorious pool of orange-gold magnificence as the string of 9's on the odometer achieves a whole new level.

A grin at least as broad as that of Alice's Cheshire cat spreads across my face. "We just rolled over to 200,000 miles."

From the passenger side, my singular travel companion and sole reason for the trip, Simon Toors leans over to verify the momentous achievement displayed on the odometer. With a muddled British accent belying his darker Middle Eastern features, he says, "Congratulations, Samuel, old boy. You must be very proud."

Although I mildly resent the old boy reference, Toors is right. It's as simple as pride. Pride in a quality American-made automobile. Pride, too, because whatever it is that allows an automobile to mirror higher qualities of being human, its strength, reliability, performance or styling, it rubs off on me, too. With parts made in China, fabrics and trim from Mexico with final assembly in Ontario, Canada, my Ford Crown Victoria P71 Interceptor with a 250-horsepower 4.6-liter regular gas-powered V-8 engine, 17-inch wheels, ballistic door panels and the Street Appearance Package is an American automobile through and through. It was made by the only Big Three American automobile manufacturer that didn't cop out of the free enterprise system by taking truck loads of government bailout cash, and that makes me feel proud, too. At 200,000 miles, the car wasn't new anymore; it just looked as if it was.

I swear to God I'll never buy another car, new or used, with nameplates of those other companies for as long as I live. Then, again, if things keep going the way they're going, living longer won't be much of an issue.

"Thank you," I choose to ignore the old boy crack. "It's a six-year-old Ford Crown Vic with 200,000 miles that uses regular gas – not that flex-fuel crap – and the car runs better now than when it came off the line. And, Simon, this isn't a department vehicle – it's my car. The carpool guys butcher those MPD units. They have no respect for taxpayers' property."

Toors nods. "It's good you recognize who really owns government property – the people. Many in government service seem to lack that fundamental understanding, as if they have exclusive access to an unlimited public largesse."

I wave a wary finger at him. "Not unlimited so much anymore. Tax cuts; program cutbacks; layoffs, vacancies left unfilled and downsizing whole departments; stuff on my plate keeps getting higher and there's no relief in sight, pal."

He smiles, leans back into his seat and closes his eyes. "Thank you."

"Thanks for what?"

"It's nice to know we are, as you say, pals at last."

THE LEPER

His relaxed reflection rests in his half of the windshield.

"We're not pals," I warn him more sternly than I intend. In the glass his eyes open and I more patiently clarify my point. "We're fugitives."

Almost an hour goes by before we skirt through the Brainerd/Baxter tourist mecca. Another hour later we're just outside Hackensack where the posted speed limit falls from 55 miles per hour that no one obeys to a pathetically slow 30-mile-per-hour crawl everyone adheres to. Not wanting to attract attention, I conscientiously let the speedometer fall to a couple of ticks below the posted limit. My only passenger lowers his window a bit and curls his fingers out onto the top of the doorframe.

"It's noticeably cooler up here," he says.

"Impressive powers of observation," My sarcasm is intentional. It irks me the guy is hardly capable of taking our plight seriously.

We enter the town passing an introductory smattering of businesses on either side of the highway – Kevin's Auto Body, Hackensack Auto Value, and on the left the reassurance of the Countryside Co-op. All of the businesses are closed. The street curves; on the right the North Country Tire store/service station recedes to our rear to reveal the railed outdoor patio of a welcoming eating establishment. A long, thin, roof-peak-mounted sign that runs the entire length of the building reads River House Dining & Lounge. The lights are on and there are cars in the parking lot. They're still open.

"I'm hungry," I offer, pulling the steering wheel to the right and guiding the Crown Vic into the parking lot.

Toors nods.

"I suppose you don't have any money to help me out on this?"

Toors shakes his head. I am not surprised.

"Well, it's pre-season up here, so maybe we'll get by cheap."

I nose the car into a vacant space between two pick-ups – one Chevy and one Dodge, both late models needing a good washing and some touch-up paint. I slip the gearshift into park and shut off the engine. "There's no telling if there're any supplies at the cabin, but let's keep it light on the cash flow if we can, okay?"

Another silent nod from Toors and we exit the Crown Vic, quick-stepping it to the side door of River House.

Inside, the lounge is a cozy, low-ceiling testament to the longevity of knotty pine. A warmly lit place, there's a good-sized horseshoe-shaped bar on the left and high-tops, tables and booths to the right. There are three flat screens – one for the bar; two on opposite sides of the table and booth area – all showing the same ESPN program, muted but with closed-caption scrolling. There are now six patrons in this room, counting Toors and me: two obviously local guys at the bar, a couple sharing a quiet booth in the far corner. Beyond the bar a short hallway leads to the front dining room where I see a partial row of cloth-draped but empty tables fronting the broad expanse of windows and the outside patio and the highway beyond.

"Must be a slow night," I mutter to myself as I signal a burly looking fellow in a too-tight navy blue T-shirt behind the bar and point to the closest high-top in front of us.

"Sure is and that works," the bartender loudly replies. "You got your pick tonight!"

I thank the bartender with a wave and a smile. He arrives at our table with menus in hand almost before we take our seats. He has a genuine smile.

"Up from the Cities, are you?"

Toors nods.

I offer, "Yes, just a short little jaunt up to the cabin to check things out before Memorial Day weekend. You know, stuff's gotta get done to get things ready."

"You betcha!" The bartender's Scandi-hovian Minnesota twang fits perfectly. "Where's your cabin at?"

The corners of my mouth tighten as I silently curse myself for not thinking this through. *Why did you mention the cabin, you dumbass?*

Toors eyes meet mine and we share a cautious glance. And then, just like the dumbass I am, too quickly I go ahead and answer the man's question.

"Just outside of town," I clear my throat of a minor obstruction that wasn't there. "A couple miles up the road."

A shake of the head precedes the bartender's chuckle. "Well, I guess that narrows it down a bit, seeing how there are one hundred and twenty-seven different lakes within a ten-mile radius of Hackensack!"

Toors raises an impressed eyebrow. "That's quite a few lakes."

"You betcha!" The man laughs. "You go for a walk around here, you gotta watch where you step or you'll get your feet wet!"

I open the menu to squelch the lighter moment and return to a drier normality. "Any specials today?"

"Everything's special," the man replies reaching over and turning the page of my menu for me to the Dinners section. He points to the lead Sandwiches item. "But if you haven't had our prime rib sandwich, that's what I'd recommend. You won't regret it."

I quickly peruse the printed Prime Rib sandwich description and take the man's recommendation to speed things along. Toors chooses an obscure menu item – a Greek Salad with feta cheese – and the bartender disappears down the hall leading to the front dining room and to a kitchen somewhere nearby.

Toors leans close. "You were reluctant to tell him about the cabin. Do you think that wise?"

In a hushed voice I say, "I don't want him to know anything about us. A lot of people come in here when they hit town. He talks to them just like he talks with us. If he knows about us, who we are, where we are, he might say something to someone looking for us. Tell him nothing and he can't screw things up even unintentionally."

Another nod. "I see. That makes sense…"

"Thank you," I abruptly interject.

With a soft gesture of his open hand Toors politely tells me he has more to add.

"What you say makes sense on the face of it, assuming people who come up to the Lake Country of Northern Minnesota are typically evasive concerning their particular piece of lakeshore property, choosing not to talk about such things whenever they are asked, particularly when they are asked by proprietors of local business establishments who would have an understandable desire to cultivate positive business relationships with an owner of lakeshore property…"

Automatically I massage my temples to relieve the pressure quickly gathering behind my eyes. "You're doing it again, you know that, don't you?"

Toors shoots his silent and now familiar "I don't understand" expression at me.

"You're telling me I'm doing something wrong…"

"Not wrong; only incorrectly."

"Fine, yes, incorrectly, then. The point being, you're not a cop, Simon, so please stop telling me you know how to do my job better than I do. It really is irritating. If you have a suggestion, offer it before I do or say something you believe requires a suggestion, not after. Which, as far as I'm concerned, is never required."

"I understand, Samuel, so allow me to suggest one thing for the next time…"

My head falls with resignation. "What is it?"

"Being closed-mouth about your lake property may be suspicious to some Lake Country residents."

Of course, Simon was right; again. It was my turn for a silent nod.

Simon points to something behind me. I turn. There's an ATM machine against the wall next to the door we had just come through.

"Ah, another good suggestion," I say. I pull my wallet, retrieve the Visa card and leave the stool. I swipe the card through the reader; punch in the code and key in a four hundred dollar withdrawal. It takes the machine a few moments to process things before I hear the whir of the dispenser and the flip-flip-flip of twenty, twenty-dollar bills hitting the pay slot. They quickly join the fifty-some-odd dollars already in my wallet and I return to the high-top.

"Left the Cities in too much of a hurry," I complain, grimacing at the printed receipt before I ball it up and hold it in my fist wondering where to put it. "There's a dollar-fifty charge for the ATM to boot."

"It's not as if you had much of a choice," Toors allows. "You're in a difficult position, forced to make it up as you go. In my opinion, you're doing a bang-up job."

A hint of a smile twitches at the corner of my mouth. "You just summarized my job description. I'm just glad I've got eyes on the inside. Without Carter, we'd be completely blind."

For a long moment, Toors says nothing but I can feel the knowing glimmer his eyes offer to me.

"He's a good friend, isn't he?"

"Known him all my life; since we were kids in elementary school. When I got out of the service, ran into him by accident. After college, Carter helped me get into the department. We've been partners now for – heck – it must be a dozen years."

Toors nods. "It's good to have someone you can trust so completely. *Fidelitas*."

"Ah, *Semper Fi*!"

"Close. *Fidelitas* is from the Latin fidelis. It means 'faithful, loyal, true, trustworthy, dependable.'"

Another smile as I nod again. "Yeah, like I said: *Semper Fi*. That's Carter, alright."

"And you, too," Toors adds.

"Yeah; me, too, I guess."

The familiar warble of my cell phone ringtone interrupts us. I retrieve the phone from my jacket pocket and check the display. "Well, speak of the devil."

I answer the call. "I was just talking about you."

"How you guys doing?" Carter asks, his voice heavy with obvious concern.

"Pretty quiet. How're things down there?"

"Getting noisier," he says without humor. "James is really pissed you've dropped off the map."

I toss it off. "The police commissioner has never been a fan."

"You're not making friends with the Feds, either. Anderson's gone over the chief's head. He wants the commissioner to arrest you for aiding and abetting or conspiracy. His boss, that FBI prick from Washington…"

"Stephens?"

"Yeah, Stephens, I don't know about that guy. He's on a whole other planet or something, the way he's strong-arming Anderson and telling the governor to get the mayor in line on what he wants done about all this."

"Strong-arming Anderson? Anderson is his own section head in Minneapolis. What is it that Wayne-Baby want poor Rupert to do, anyway?"

"Besides collaring the two of you, I don't know. No one is talking to me about anything. I'm picking this stuff up as I go. I do know the FBI has tied Toors to similar deaths over the last seven years in D.C., Trenton and Chicago. Apparently, they have proof Toors was in each location during the time of the murders. They think because you and he disappeared at the same time that ties the two of you to those crimes and the others here in the Cities. Has Toors talked at all about what he knows?"

My eyes lock onto my placid tablemate with the guilt-free smile. "Oh, he talks, alright. He neither denies nor admits anything. He seems more concerned about my welfare than his own. Kinda makes you wonder who's protecting who?"

"'Whom,'" Carter suggests with certainty. "'Who's protecting whom' is grammatically correct."

"Gee, thanks. What's going on with the chief on all this?"

"Tomlinson is covering his backside as usual." Carter's response is colored by unveiled resentment of our department head. "He's supporting the FBI's push to apprehend Toors while mouthing BS about how you're innocent until proven guilty, blah, blah, blah, so he's seen as true blue to the rank and file. In short, don't count on him to get you out of this mess."

"So Mark's talking to the press about this." I wasn't asking a question.

"You better believe it. Your picture was on the six o'clock news again, side by side with Toors."

"Great. As if we weren't media stars already. You have any more good news?"

"Tomlinson wants me in Eagan. Something's happened down there and they asked for help from Homicide. I'm almost there. Where you at?"

"It's better you don't know. In fact, I'm dumping this phone and picking up another pre-paid one tomorrow. I'll give you a call by then if I'm still around."

"Okay. Later."

I return the phone to the jacket pocket and say, "The Feds are proceeding with the assumption you and I are together."

Toors nods. "You surmised as much."

"Yeah, but with the mayor and now the governor getting heat from Washington on this, it's all out of proportion. The FBI has linked you to similar killings in Chicago, New Jersey, more. I'm not surprised little pieces of evidence on you are starting to pop up here and there. They have to build their case. Apparently it's the same MO on all of it. Getting you is becoming a crusade for these people, Simon."

"I'm sorry you're involved."

"We've covered the apologies already. Things are getting worse and it won't be long now before it comes to a head. If I'm missing anything, you gotta tell me now, Simon."

"I've already told you what I can, Samuel." He leans back and asks a direct question. "Do you think I am evil, Samuel?"

My answer is immediate. "Not even a little bit. Pushed enough any man can kill, even you. Then, again, you're about the only person I've ever met who I can honestly say I don't think you have it in you. And that, more than anything, scares the hell out of me. These deaths are beyond murder, Simon, and you know more than you're saying. There's a reason why people are out to get you. You have to tell me everything."

His face is calm as he says, "Soon, Samuel, you will know."

My head falls into my hands. If I thought it would do any good, I'd beat the truth out of him. But even if I did that, I know he would do nothing to stop me, or defend himself in anyway. Even if he knew he was being killed, he'd just let it happen. I look up from my hands and shake my head. He's looking at me and I curse him.

"You're making everything impossible."

From behind I hear the door open. I turn. Two men, mid-thirties by the look of them, dressed in jeans and flannel shirts, one red plaid, one blue plaid, walk in and take seats at the bar opposite from the first two customers casually sipping beers and sharing a quiet conversation.

I turn back to Toors and with a sideways head movement toward the newcomers, say, "Business is picking up. Two lumberjacks in from the logging trails."

Toors observes the two new guys, his brow furrows noticeably and he quickly looks away.

"What?"

Toors shakes his head. "They aren't lumberjacks."

I stop myself from taking a quick glance over my shoulder and quickly return to Toors. "It's just an expression. I doubt much commercial lumbering goes on around here anymore."

"Lumberjacks in new jeans and clean, new flannel work shirts. Neither have work gloves in their back pockets and they're wearing tied walking shoes, not boots." In the same quiet voice, Simon adds a sincere warning. "Careful."

I open my mouth to respond to all this, but before I say anything, the bartender reappears from wherever he had gone carrying two food-laden platters.

"I forgot to ask," he blurts out as he places the food in front of us. "You guys want something to drink, or what?"

We both opt for waters. The bartender spins around to scurry behind the bar and retrieve two tumblers, in the process greeting the newcomers at the bar with an audible "I'll be back in a jiffy" promise as he fills the glasses first with crushed ice followed by water from a hand dispenser. He's a blur as he delivers the glasses to our table and then quickly returns to the bar and the two new customers.

A quick, hot French fry into my mouth is followed with a substantial bite from the sandwich. I'm two chews into the sandwich before I notice Simon unfold his hands, take his table knife and proceed to cut down the size of his salad pieces. He then parts the mixture in the middle and begins to nibble at the near half portion. He chews enthusiastically, looks at me and shrugs.

"You said, Samuel, you didn't know what kind of supplies were at the cabin, so maybe this second half will be useful later."

I lower my sandwich to the plate. Two-thirds of it remains.

"Good idea, Simon." I cut at the halfway point on the elongated bread roll and wolf down the trimmed, already chewed end.

I do the same economizing on the French fries, although I eat the entire dill pickle spear without a second thought. From time to time, without appearing too obvious about it, I steal a glance over my shoulder toward the two lumberjacks. Interestingly, Mr. Red Shirt is nursing a clear mixed drink on the rocks with a speared olive while Mr. Blue Shirt has a tumbler holding a carbonated beverage; no beers? Toors is right – they aren't lumberjacks. Except for a moment with the bartender, neither man seems to talk much.

Our meal progresses quickly. When we're ready to go, the friendly bartender returns with the tab and a smile. "So, you guys wanna have some dessert?"

"Thanks, but not this time," I smile back. "But we could use a couple of to-go containers. Gotta get up to the cabin before it gets too late: might get lost, you know."

"That can happen up here," agrees the bartender. "Where's your cabin, again?"

I share a quick glance with Simon and say, "Up on the northwest side of Ten Mile Lake. It's a little place, nothing special."

"Oh, just the other side of Happiness Resort?"

I nod in response and the bartender nods back in satisfaction as he leans in closer.

"That's good," he says, and then adds more quietly, "Those other guys at the bar were asking about you a little while ago. I thought you'd like to know that."

My eyes lock onto his and for some reason I see an ally. "You don't say. They locals?"

With barely perceived movement, the bartender shakes his head. "I've never seen those boys before in my life. Curious, isn't it, two guys who I ain't never seen walk in and ask if I know where two other guys I ain't never seen are headed? Gives a fella pause, don't it?"

"It do at that." I lean back as I pull out my wallet. "Well, then, just the other side of Happiness Resort it is. What's the damage tonight?"

The man looks at the tab and then hands it to me as he says, "You know we get the Cities' local newscasts up here. Got satellite, HD TV and everything. Had channel six on earlier, you know?"

"Is that a fact?" Our eyes meet again long enough for me to know there's no threat. For whatever reason, this guy is on our side. I look at the tab and nod. "Not all that bad – can't speak for the salad, but it was the best prime rib sandwich I've ever tasted. I'll be back, guaranteed."

I hand him a twenty plus another ten. He folds both and slips the cash into the front pocket behind the bar towel tucked in his belt.

"Come back, but make it soon," he says. "The same thing will be half-again as much on Memorial weekend."

I thank him for his advice as the bartender returns to his bar and Simon and I turn toward the door with our doggie bags in hand.

In the car and strapping in, I slip the gearshift into reverse and back out of the parking spot.

Simon says, "Didn't Daniel Patterson say the cabin is on Stony Lake."

I shift into drive and slowly exit the parking lot for the highway. "Yes, he did."

The Crown Vic rolls effortlessly along the main drive, unimpeded by stop signs or traffic lights. On our left, we pass by Lucette's Pizza & Pub and take a left turn on Lake Avenue. A block and a half later, we stop and the headlights illuminate an odd-looking painted statue of an extremely tall woman with a deformed hip.

I check the rearview mirror for any cars coming up from behind, or perhaps a pick-up truck with two guys in flannel shirts heading north on Highway 371. Hackensack is a small, Lake Country town of only a few hundred people and this park area seems asleep. There's no traffic.

Toors points at the painted statue. "Her name is Lucette Diana Kensack and from the monument description she's the mother of Paul Bunyan's bastard son."

The Leper

Reluctantly, I look away from the mirror and scan a printed sign on the base of the statue. After a quick read of the entire historical content on the placard, I disagree. "I'm sure Mr. and Mrs. Bunyan were married."

"It says Lucette was Paul Bunyan's sweetheart and the mother of Paul Bunyan, Jr. It doesn't say they were married."

"I'm sure it's an innocent omission by the park board. It would be nice, however, if you would be equally concerned about our situation and help bring this mess to some kind of satisfactory conclusion."

"I'm trying to do that, Samuel."

Not hiding my displeasure with his non-answer answer, I put the car back into gear and swing a quick, tight U-turn. "Not hard enough, my friend."

We duck to the left at First Street to avoid 371 until we merge at the County Road 4 intersection. Back on 371 now, the speed limit immediately increases to fifty-five and the Crown Vic rises to the occasion easily. When we come out of a shallow curve, I see distant headlights appear in the rearview mirror. Now well past dusk, the vehicle is difficult to make out, but appears to be a large SUV. It's not in a big hurry and stays several hundred yards behind us.

In his side mirror, Toors now sees the headlights, too.

"We have company."

"Not necessarily." Just as I deflect Toors' concern too easily, another pair of headlights joins the first set in the rearview mirror. From the shape, it looks like another SUV. *No big deal. Four-wheel-drive vehicles abound in northern Minnesota.*

I see Toors eyeing his side mirror. He asks calmly, "Who do you think they are?"

"Probably locals." My insides tell me different. "The guy in front has a smaller vehicle; a larger one is behind his. There are a lot of SUV-type drivers up here. No big deal."

Toors turns to me with a placid expression I find annoying.

"Probably locals," I reiterate more firmly, checking my speed to take it up a notch, quickly glancing up to the reflection of two pairs of headlights in the rearview mirror. Both SUVs are keeping pace.

Then, the first SUV is suddenly gaining on us. I resist the urge to speed up. The distance between us closes quickly. For a moment, the SUV in the rearview is large enough to block my view of the other vehicle, but I sense the second SUV is accelerating, too. The yellow-orange flashing from the first SUV signals a lane change moments before the Hyundai pulls into my side mirror and passes us in a blink. The windows are tinted dark and the driver is easily hitting more than 80 and still accelerating. My eyes return to the rearview to see the second SUV, a Suburban by the looks of it, also with tinted windows, closer but lagging farther behind. It doesn't lag for long. Two miles outside of town, we approach the Ten Mile Lake Road intersection. As I ease up on the accelerator for the turn to come, the Suburban behind me moves slightly to my left and then speeds up and passes us, quickly disappearing over a slight rise. For the first time in several minutes, I breathe easy.

Just locals. But then my breathing tightens up again. *Was that driver wearing a plaid shirt?*

At the intersection, Ten Mile Lake Road is on the left and Forty-fourth Street is on the right. Daniel Patterson had told me to take the right and follow that to Robin Lane. At the fork in the road I was to keep left. There's a right turn lane at the intersection and I turn off Route 371 and onto the narrow, irregularly paved eastbound Forty-fourth Street. I slow, moving carefully into a no-shoulder patch of weeds, stopping the car just short of a yellow diamond no outlet street sign. The black night sky smothered over us. Keeping a firm foot on the brake, I turn on the overhead reading light and from my jacket pocket pull the folded napkin on which Patterson had drawn the map. The split at Robin Lane was obvious with the north end leading to a stubby peninsula jutting out into Stony Lake. Patterson had marked his cabin's location with an X at the base of a shallow turn in the road deep on the peninsula.

I check the rear for oncoming traffic. There is none so I pull back onto the pavement. *Easy enough to find.*

THE LEPER

On either side of the too narrow road the irregular mix of coniferous and deciduous trees is thick: a patch of leafy elms backlit by a smattering of willowy birch with their characteristic peeling bark curling away from the long trunks like so much dried parchment, and masses of silver maple all of which are framed by towering pines. The air is a confusion of musty nature odors oddly curious and yet mildly offensive to my well-entrenched urban sensitivities.

So this is God's country, then.

The headlights burrow an illuminated tunnel of misty gray glow into the gathering darkness. A slight rise ahead dips away at a small turn. As we drive, every few moments a mailbox comes within the glow of the headlights, each mailbox marks a dirt drive disappearing back into the trees. A much wider curved dirt drive comes up on the left, framed by heavy pines, there's a carved wood sign with a cross that reads: Camp Emmaus. As we passed the sign, the road takes an immediate dip to the right and the relatively smooth pavement is replaced by compacted dirt.

"Very secluded, wouldn't you say?" Toors comments, his eyes scanning the depths of the surrounding trees as if he could actually see something beyond the darkness of it all.

"Good place to hide out for a while," I agree. In the rearview mirror the warm glow of my taillights illuminate the fresh billowing clouds of road dust kicking up from the tires.

I feel the caution in Toors' next observation. "Or a good place for something else, Samuel. Lots of cover everywhere. Someone could be on us before we'd be able to see them coming."

"I've come prepared." My reply is clipped, colored with impatience. I don't care. Toors may know a lot of stuff but he isn't a cop and he doesn't know police work. Right now, the important thing is to get to the lake cabin and get ready for what was coming.

"I'm sure you're prepared," Simon continues. "As prepared as you can be under the circumstances, but Samuel, if they come they be many or only one. Remember what happened to Dr. Tribby."

"I remember." My voice is hollow, as if coming from a distance, and I hardly recognize it. It reflects the real pain from the profound loss of a good friend. The memory of how it happened is still raw. "That's why I came prepared."

Toors nods silently and then looks away into the darkness.

"It's not like there has to be a big shoot-out, Simon. You trust me, don't you?"

Another silent nod comes from Toors.

"Well, there's a state attorney general. He's a pretty good guy. I don't like his politics but I trust him to do what's right. You turn state's evidence on this, and I can get him on board. You'll be a heck of a lot safer than staying on the lam with me."

Once more the narrow road curves easily to the left only to immediately dart to the right and straighten out. There's an undeniable sensation of claustrophobia as the headlights draw from the trees long stripes of dark shadows that eerily stretch across the road ahead of us.

Simon's reflection in the windshield looks sad. "You're perceptive, Samuel, but I won't tell you what you think you want to hear only to disappoint you in the end. Only the truth will help us now."

There he goes again! I already knew this would lead to nothing. After everything that has happened, if anyone in this car had the patience of a saint, it wasn't Toors!

"Truth is right, Simon. So how about some truth now? At last and finally, the truth. You gotta know why these people are after you. What is this thing, some kind of weird religious cult? Who do they work for? How is all this tied into the weird killings – killings following the same patterns, over and over in different parts of the country for the last ten years? You know a whole lot more than you're telling."

Simon doesn't answer – again – as he pushes a slender finger ahead and points. "The fork in the road. Take a left."

"Right, Simon," I grumble. "I can read a road sign."

A lone city-style street sign with a luminous Robin Lane printed on a green background seems out of place in the overgrown weeds hugging both sides of the gravel road. I take the left fork at 15 miles per hour and the tires slip on the loose dirt just enough to make it feel like I'm going too fast.

The mailbox numbered 4400 should be on my right and, I assume, a dirt path similar to all the other dirt paths we have already passed will be there. My claustrophobia achieves a heightened level of apprehension as the road becomes narrower.

The mailbox is where it should be. A hand-carved sign reading Onawim marks the narrow drive path.

"Onawim." I chuckle. "Clever."

I ease the Crown Vic into a shallow right turn, slowing to follow tire-worn tracings between tall jack pines, and come to an abrupt stop. The headlights illuminate redwood siding stained a deep brown as if to hide the tall A-frame structure in the surroundings. The lake cabin is dark with only the out-of-place glow of the septic tank's lone red status light indicating the place is wired for electricity. I douse the headlights and turn off the engine.

"Stay close," I caution Toors. "I lead, you follow. When I get into the cabin, you're on my ass like you're my long, lost gay lover, got it?"

"I appreciate your concern," Simon acknowledges with a disturbing calmness that continues to irritate. "But, Samuel, again, none of this is necessary."

"It's only my job!" I bark back, immediately regretting it. *Stay cool. Be tranquil. Be like Simon.* I take a breath. "Look, you gotta understand this: people have been killed because of you. The people who killed those people are still out there looking for you. Chances are, they're barely within three hundred miles of the great Minnesota North Lake Country, but we can't let the peaceful setting lull us into thinking we're home free. We need to stay sharp, stay alert, stay ready for anything at any time from anybody, right?"

"Of course, Samuel," Simon nods seriously and I can only hope he believes me.

"So follow my lead. Remember, like you're on my ass, okay?"

Toors nods once more, adding with a smile, "So colorful."

I do a quick double take before I exit the car. Walking around the back, Simon joins me. I pop the trunk with the remote and hand him a leather satchel and my old Navy canvas sea bag. I take the suitcase, slide the sleeved rifle under my arm and then ease the trunk lid down softly until it closes with a click. I motion toward the corner of the cabin where a raised wooden walkway leads around the side. The red glow from the septic tank status light aids our way. At the side door, from my pants pocket I fish the key Daniel Patterson gave me and work it into the keyhole. A twist and the deadbolt slides from the hasp with a loud snapping sound that echoes into the surrounding darkness. The doorknob turns easily.

Inside, the light switch is on the left. I flick it up to the on position and the lower level is bathed in incandescent warmth. The place is larger than I expect. We're standing in the back corner of an expansive front great room that includes a kitchen and dining area in the farther half. A stairway on the left leads to a loft facing the lake and a short hallway leading to the rear. Every square inch of wall and ceiling space is clad in unfinished knotty pine. A window wall two stories high fronts the room. Through it we can see the sentinels of towering jack pines populating a sloping grade of at least a hundred feet to the now starlit black ripples of Stony Lake.

"Nice place," I take a few steps into the living room. At the sofa, I offload the suitcase and sleeved rifle. "Rustic, to say the least. Mr. Patterson has good taste."

Toors steps from the entry into the center of the great room, lowers the satchel and sea bag to the floor and stands motionless for several seconds staring out the large window wall toward the lake.

I walk toward the opposite side. There's a short turn that leads to a modern and nicely equipped bathroom and two separate bedrooms on either side. When I return to the main room, I take the staircase up to a loft. With a waist-high unfinished wood railing, the loft overlooks the great room below. To the rear hallway I see another bathroom and two more bedrooms matching the two downstairs. Procedure dictates my checking each room to make sure they're empty. They are and I rejoin Toors on the main level. He's still looking out across the lake.

"Four bedrooms. Not exactly the cabin I was expecting," I chuckle. "Nice – very nice. I wonder if Patterson wants to sell?"

Toors looks at me with an annoying expression of his assured awareness. He points to the lake outside. "When they come, they'll come from the water."

God, this guy's such a downer sometimes. I shake my head to disagree and just as I open my mouth to tell him so, my cell phone warbles and I almost jump out of my skin. I hurriedly pull the phone from my jacket pocket. It's Carter.

"Hey, Big Guy, how we doing?"

The cellular reception was okay but not as clear as in the Cities. "You up there yet?"

"Just pulled in. Nice place. You'd like it."

"I'm happy for you."

I was about to come back with a snappy retort, but I wasn't quick enough and Carter cuts me off.

"Watch your back, Sam. All hell's broken loose down here."

Toors senses something wrong. I sit on the arm of the overstuffed sofa. Toors takes a seat in a matching chair across from me.

"What's going on, Carter?"

"Just keep your head down, that's all. Things have taken a turn to hell down here."

"Details?"

There's a long pause on Carter's end, and for a moment I wonder if he's dropped off. I pull the phone from my ear to check the reception bars on the display screen. We were still connected. "Tell me what's going on, Carter."

I hear a sigh and when he speaks my flesh turns to ice.

"Sam, it's a slaughterhouse down here. We found the two brothers and their wives in Daniel Patterson's basement. They're all dead."

It took all my strength to keep the phone at my ear as I asked the only question I could. "How?"

"Massive injuries delivered in key places to inflict maximum pain before death, Sam. Then, they were each shot. They used significant caliber rounds, two to the head for all of them. A professional hit, but messy. It's obvious they were tortured first, probably to find out about you and Toors."

The nausea rises and I swallow hard to keep it down. I look at Simon and I know he somehow already knows about the Pattersons. I return to the phone.

"You got that right, Carter – they wanted to know where we are. Somehow, they tracked us to the Pattersons. Somehow they knew Steeg and Daniel were helping us."

Carter responds. "I don't know how, Sam. The Fed prick doesn't know about the Pattersons. Even Tomlinson only suspects you have Toors and he sure didn't know about this mess when he sent me down here on a straight call from the Eagan PD. Hell, Sam, I don't even know where you are. Who are these guys and how would they know who is helping you? It doesn't make sense."

"Well, somebody told them!" My curse fills the room. "Someone blabbed something to someone and people died because of it!"

"Okay, okay, just breathe in and try to let it settle," Carter's voice falls to a whisper. "Hang on for a second."

Hearing some voices in the background on Carter's end, I lower the phone for a moment only to raise it again. "Carter?"

"Yeah?"

"Connect the dots, my friend. We find Toors near the scene of a murder; there are two bodies, one matching two other earlier deaths; we take Toors into custody for questioning; we lose him; the Feds show up and claim Toors is involved with similar murders in several locales over several years; the Cities are locked down in a manhunt; out of nowhere, a fire-fight supposedly involving Toors takes down three of our guys and now we know a third actor is seriously after the same guy we are. It's this third person who took out the Pattersons."

"Probably," Carter says.

"But how did they find the Pattersons?"

"I don't know."

I look at Toors looking at me and I can't help it. I wonder if he could have tipped the bad guys about the family that had done so much to help him.

On the phone, I again hear some indistinct voices in the background. After another moment, Carter comes back.

"Sam, any chance Steeg Patterson's in-laws were with you while you and Toors were at his place?"

The pressure gathers behind my eyes and I brace myself. "Why is that important?"

"We just got a report. Sam, they're missing."

The Glenwood Avenue Murders

CHAPTER 2

THE GLENWOOD AVENUE MURDERS

I first met Simon Toors three weeks earlier on the night I arrested him for murder.

He wasn't a murderer and I knew it. But it was past three o'clock in the morning, too late or too early depending on your point of view, and definitely too chilly for late April even in Minneapolis to put up with attitude. Toors was one of those guys with an irritating condescension I didn't much care for. Besides, he was found near the scene and after more than eighteen hours straight, I was already beyond tired.

The north side of Glenwood Avenue was already buttressed by an ample number of squad cars, their rooftop Magna emergency light bars rhythmically pulsated a colorful display of red and blue bursts guaranteed to draw more attention from the nearby residents. Many were already gathered at the yellow-taped periphery straining for a closer look. Near the middle of this dazzling display a single Hennepin County Medical Center van was wedged against the curb, its rear doors open to expose an empty lighted interior.

I took a left. In the small Thomas Avenue parking lot immediately south of Glenwood Avenue, I nosed the Crown Vic neatly between the painted lines of a parking stall providing a more direct view across Glenwood. Silhouetted by the pulsating glow of multi-colored glare, the six-foot-three-inch frame of

Carter Wolpren offered a weak wave as I opened my door and exited into a cold cloud of my own breath.

"Thought you went home." I grumbled as I pulled the lapels of my wool sport coat closer in an ineffective attempt to snug away what outside air movement there was. It was bearable.

Carter shrugged and returned ungloved hands to the warm-pocketed refuge of his camel-haired topcoat. "Yeah, well, when the dispatcher said the body was off Glenwood, I turned around."

"Commendable, you dedicated fool, you."

"You might want to get your coat," Carter's suggestion carried an implied "You idiot!" with it. "It's a little nippy out tonight."

I shoved my hands into the pockets of my sport coat and exhaled a cloud of breath. "Yeah, well, I left it at the station. It was warmer than it is now."

"Short people." Carter criticized with a shake of his head as we turned to leave the parking lot for the walk across Glenwood.

"Everyone's short standing next to you," I grumbled back.

"True enough," he acknowledged. "All the smart ones are tall. You should have learned that by now."

"The last thing I learned from you was back in sixth grade. You taught me how to swear like a sailor."

"And you joined the Navy – it worked, didn't it, Swabbie?"

"SEALs," I corrected. "I joined the Navy SEALs."

"Yeah, at the height of the Vietnam War," Carter shook his head again. "Brilliant move."

"Thank you."

"It just proves my point: you're short."

"Maybe," I sighed through a cloud of frozen breath. "But then I got medals for it, too."

"Congratulations. The question is, have you had Meredith, yet?"

Meredith Mathison, an attractive divorcee with natural auburn hair that required only modest chemical support, was two years older than I was and, thankfully, the same height. Meredith was also the third best friend Caroline Wolpren, Carter's wife who he always called Linnie, had tried to set me up with since my divorce.

"Meredith is fine," I confessed.

"Yes, she is," Carter agreed.

"I doubt we'll see each other again."

"You got to be kidding me."

"I don't think she's comfortable with what I do for a living."

"Neither was Shelly."

"That's why we're divorced."

"That was more than two years ago, Sam. Time to move on."

We stepped from the boulevard grass onto the pavement to cross Glenwood Avenue.

"I'm too old to start dating again, Carter."

"Age isn't your problem. Your problem is you're short."

I changed the subject. "Educate me: what do we got?"

Carter produced a small notepad from his inside coat pocket and quickly read a few handwritten notes. "Woman; mid-thirties I'd say; it ain't pretty."

My surprise slowed me by a half-step and Carter's longer stride took him past me. "A woman this time? On Glenwood?"

"Yeah." Our paces again matched and Carter allowed me to draw even with him. Together we reached the north side curb, left the pavement behind to weave between the parked vehicles and follow the grass-covered incline that led gently down to a narrow bike path. Beyond the path, darkness stretched across a flat grassy knoll toward a darker line of trees where a puddle of muted illumination backlit a gathered mix of patrol officers and topcoats. One of the topcoats had a bald head, heavy rimmed glasses and knelt close to a motionless lump covered by a sheet of moisture-resistant glare-white synthetic material.

I took a quick look around as the two of us crossed the matted sod wet-soaked from a late spring thaw and still dormant from a too-cold winter. Each step made a squishing sound.

Something wasn't right. "There used to be tennis courts here, wasn't there?"

Carter didn't know and didn't care. He motioned toward the nearing tree line and kept walking.

"Why did they take the tennis courts out?"

"Budget cutbacks," Carter offered half-seriously. "Why should we be the only ones?"

The soggy grass turned to low lying brush and matted leaves and we were soon there, standing over the lump on the ground with the covering sheet lowered to the victim's shoulders. Two of the topcoats acknowledged our arrival with shallow nods. We watched in silence as the M.E. went through his examination routine. The reddened slit lay open, running across the woman's throat, a wound so deep it was almost a decapitation. Carter had been right. It wasn't pretty.

The bald head and glasses belonged to Dr. Phillip Tribby. Tribby was well over 60 years old and on a regular basis complained he was getting too old for this kind of work. He was also the best medical examiner employed by the city of Minneapolis in at least the last 50 years. A highly decorated Vietnam veteran, he had come to the practice of medicine relatively late in life after being wounded in combat, and he rode the GI Bill educational benefits all the way through medical school. His military training combined with a profound respect for justice cemented his devotion to the forensic sciences. Tribby interned at the Hennepin County morgue and worked his way up to the county's chief medical examiner position before he was forty under the tutelage of the second-best medical examiner in the last 50 years, Dr. Elaine Grovesberg. When Grovesberg died from cancer, the search for her replacement was a short one.

As Tribby examined the body, he avoided knee contact with the ground. He repeatedly surveyed the surrounding area careful not to disturb anything. He made sure the other topcoats and patrol officers did the same. They all gave the doctor plenty of space. When he looked up from the body again, his eyes caught mine and he offered a respectful nod. After pulling the sheet back over the victim's head, Dr. Tribby stood up, retrieved a pair of insulated leather gloves from his coat's side pockets and slipped them on over his latex-gloved hands as he stepped lightly toward Carter and me.

"Good evening, Samuel." The doctor's pleasantry was betrayed by a noticeable frown. "I'm sorry to see you out so late. Aren't you a little cold? Where's your coat?"

"He forgot to bring it," Carter explained with disgust.

"True enough. It's bearable." I nodded toward the direction of the sheet-covered lump. "Any blistering or rot on this one?"

"I'm afraid not, Detective," Tribby's directed gaze followed my own back to the body. "Not this time. It looks like whatever happened here isn't going to fatten the file for your Glenwood Killer task force."

I shrugged. "Suits me. I might actually get home tonight."

The three of us stood in a tight circle, our collective clouds of breath rising into night air growing colder by the minute. The covered remains of someone who didn't fit the pattern held our attention and wouldn't let go.

Tribby added, "I can't say for sure until I get the body back to the lab, but unofficially I'd estimate she's been dead at least two hours. It was violent but quick. Oddly, the slashed throat appears to be an afterthought."

Carter and I both waited for him to explain.

"Post mortem?" Carter asked.

"Definitely," Tribby dabbed his nose with a handkerchief. "Too little blood to be otherwise."

Nothing was fitting right and I didn't care if my impatience showed. "So, how'd she die?"

"Broken neck; actually, it was more crushed than broken, so was her larynx. A powerful single blow possibly inflicted with a bare hand. Whoever did it was very strong, most likely right handed and knew what he was doing."

Carter asked what we were both thinking. "If she was already dead why would the killer go to the trouble of almost cutting her head off?"

Tribby shrugged. "Maybe to hide the real injury – make it look like something it wasn't."

The numbness of wet cold had successfully penetrated my shoe leather, and the discomfort accentuated my growing sour mood. "So, what was it, exactly?"

"Her clothing was removed to suggest rape but there's no sign of sexual molestation; no ID and no easy way to determine who she is or who knew her – we can do prints, dental records and DNA matching but it will take time and that's what the killer wanted; she has a fatal injury inflicted by someone who knew how to do it right the first time. It looks like a professional hit."

The grounds around the scene were well trampled. I could feel a familiar pressure gather behind my eyes. This wasn't making the kind of sense I needed it to make.

"Doc, could she have been killed somewhere else and the body dumped here?"

"I don't think so, Samuel." With his fingers spread, the doctor described his interpretation of the scene. "There's a lot of activity here, too much for a simple dumping. A struggle of some duration took place but it didn't last long. She fought back. She was very brave, I think. The compressed area looks like the body was rolled back and forth just in this immediate area, possibly when whoever did this removed her clothes."

"This doesn't match the earlier murders," I complained. "It isn't even close. First, she's a 'she' not a 'he' and that sucks. Second, she doesn't have any of the signs, right, Doc?"

Tribby nodded.

"No blisters, or diseased skin at all?" Carter was confused, too.

"No, she's clean. No leprous lesions."

"Then, why here?" I scanned the surrounding area looking for any sign that could point the way. "Why so close to Glenwood Avenue?"

Carter toed the ground. "The area is wet. Were there any tracks leading to or from the scene?"

An eavesdropping patrolman with a nametag on his vest that read "Swanson" stepped forward and responded. "Yes, Sir… That is, we think so. On the west side of the tree line, there appears to be something that looks like foot traffic from the trees moving off in that direction."

Too enthusiastically, I grabbed the policeman's arm and pulled him toward his pointed direction. "Show us, now."

Doc Tribby stayed behind to supervise the removal of the body as Carter, Swanson and I hurriedly squished our way along the edge of the tree line to where it fell away to a matted slope that led down to the twin pair of railroad tracks. We waited at the top of the slope as below two more uniformed police officers crossed

The Leper

the tracks and made their way to where we stood. Swanson introduced us.

"Officers Magan and Holtzman."

Magan was a tall slender young black woman who wore her hair short and tucked tightly under her cover. She was obviously attractive, even in the dim light. I shook her hand first and introduced myself.

"Samuel Culhane, Detective." I gestured toward Carter. "This is Detective Wolpren."

I moved from Magan to Holtzman who took my offered hand and held it a moment in recognition.

"Detective Culhane – Homicide?" He nodded with awareness. "The Glenwood Avenue killer murders, right?"

I nodded back. "Yeah, but not this one. It doesn't seem to fit the pattern."

Swanson pointed down the slope toward the railroad tracks. "Trail lead anywhere?"

Officer Magan shook her head. "It did for a bit, but it's odd – the trail disappeared on the other side of the first set of rails."

"Disappeared?" Carter threw me a knowing look.

"Yeah, it was two people," Holtzman offered, adjusting the shoulder strap of a leather kit bag as he turned and pointed back to the tree line. "You can see the trail leading from the trees right to this point where we're standing…"

I looked back and saw, with the illumination from Glenwood reflecting just right, remains of wet impressions left by two sets of footprints. One seemed to be behind the other, not side by side.

"Must not have been pals," I surmised with a squint. "One follows the other."

Holtzman continued, sweeping his arm around back down the slope and a grassy area between the two sets of railroad tracks. "They pretty much follow a straight path across the track, but then right in the middle of the grass near the bridge overpass, the two sets suddenly become one."

Magan jumped in. "And then, the last set disappears before the second set of rails."

"Yeah," Holtzman concurred. "Like they just flew away."

"Flew away?" I repeated. I waved down the slope toward the tracks. "Show me."

The slope was shallow with little chance of slipping. We easily followed the trail, stopping on the weedy patch between the two pairs of railroad tracks at the point where only a single set of impressions remained. I looked around the area. The single set of impressions followed through the stubby weeds of the narrow median under the Glenwood Avenue bridge. I threw a pointed finger in the direction of the bridge and took a half step when Carter stopped me.

"What's that?" Carter moved toward the far set of tracks, looked down and squatted. He remained motionless studying something near the edge of the gravel bed. "We have a weapon."

All of us hurried over to Carter. From his kit bag, Holtzman produced a yellow plastic tag with a "7" printed on it and placed it by the open sport knife. Magan next laid a six-inch ruler next to the knife for perspective, took her digital SLR in hand, snapped two close-in shots first, and then disturbed the stillness of the surroundings with a series of multiple electronic shutter snaps covering the immediate area from several different angles.

"Anyone got a baggie?" Carter asked.

Swanson pulled one bag from the small roll he carried in his vest. Careful to not smudge anything, Carter pinched the narrow edges of the knife and slid it into the baggie Swanson held open for him.

"Eagle-eye," I said admiringly.

"Just caught a glint of light off the blade, that's all," Carter explained, taking the bag from Swanson and cautiously putting it into his coat pocket. "The lab should tell us something."

We turned to make our way toward the bridge overpass. We were halfway there when the low ground off to the right revealed a small area darker than the darkness surrounding it. We stopped and I pulled out a pocket flashlight to direct a tight LED beam at the lump.

"My, my, my, look at that." I led the way to the body and stopped, the others forming a semi-circle behind me. The mottling and blistering on the exposed flesh of the face, neck and hands were unmistakable. I responded with our department's recently adopted code phrase for a Glenwood Avenue murder victim. "He's crispy."

From behind, Carter stated flatly, "Number three."

"Number three," I agreed. I turned to Swanson. "Get on your radio, tell Tribby we have another one."

Swanson nodded, pulled his radio from his belt and triggered it to relay the news. I stepped back to survey the area from the top of the slope we had just left all the way to the bridge overpass and continued with Swanson just as he ended the transmission.

"Secure this entire area. I want tape from the first body all the way to the bridge."

Swanson responded with a "Yes, Sir," and I turned to Holtzman and Magan.

"You two help Swanson lock down this whole stretch. Once things are secure, join Carter and me on the other side of the overpass, got it?"

Both officers nodded and Carter and I turned back toward the bridge overpass.

As we walked down the tracks, Carter tossed a quick glance back from where we had come. "The trail ended well before where we found the body."

"Yeah. Maybe the guy flew the distance before he died."

"What I mean is…"

I interrupted him. "Yeah, I know. Nothing disturbed around the body; no footprints; nothing pressed down…"

Carter interrupted me. "Just like the other two 'crispies.'"

"Yeah, I know."

We passed under the overpass to emerge on the other side and the well-lit conglomeration of buildings that made up the Glenwood water plant. To our immediate left a small rise led to the parking lot where I had left the Crown Vic. To my right, one set of railroad tracks snaked around the rear of a two-story brick building with another group of utility buildings farther to the right of those rails. Straight ahead, the two-story brick building had a small single-row parking lot in front and additional water plant buildings farther down. The first set of railroad tracks ran the length of the water plant property to disappear through the trees farther south. High-mounted exterior lighting on several building fronts illuminated the whole area from the Thomas Avenue crossing at the first set of tracks all along the entire length of the complex.

We both saw the figure at the same moment. It was as if the person had simply materialized outside the main door leading into the two-story building. It was so sudden, both of us instinctively reached for our shoulder-holstered 9-millimeter Glocks at the same time.

"Where'd he come from?"

"Probably there the whole time," I surmised. "Or, just came out of the building when we weren't looking."

The man was looking straight at us and didn't move. I stepped forward first and Carter trailed behind and to my right as we approached the man. He was tall, rather thin with dark hair, dressed in a simple pair of gray work pants, matching shirt, belt and boots, no jacket. The diffused outside lighting revealed a different complexion – not white; certainly not black, but perhaps Middle Eastern, maybe Arab. I wasn't sure. When I withdrew my hand from inside my sport coat, I held my badge up for the man to see.

"Detective Culhane, Minneapolis Police," I motioned to Carter. "This is Detective Wolpren."

The man smiled thinly and nodded. His eyes carried the heaviness of impatience, or sadness, or something else.

"Who are you?"

The same thin smile, unchanging, but no response.

"Do you work here, at the water plant?"

The smile remained, but noticeably hardened as the man's eyes locked onto Carter stepping around from my right side.

I raised my hand and the man's eyes returned to me. "Something happened tonight and we need to ask you some questions about what you might have seen or heard, okay?"

Carter threw a terse question at him. "Do you speak English?"

The man ignored Carter, keeping his eyes on me. There was a calmness about him that made me feel uncomfortable for no reason at all I suspected he was aware of everything that had happened on the other side of Glenwood Avenue.

Carter moved haltingly toward the man to get a closer look. The examination took only a moment and then he turned to me. "He doesn't understand a word you're saying."

"Yes, I think you do, don't you? Do you have identification? Identificación, comprenda?"

"If he's a Spic, I'm Japanese."

The man's relaxed composure and thin smile remained unchanged. His eyes didn't leave mine, not even to blink. Each passing moment he said nothing and just looked at me. My irritation grew.

Patience has never been my strong suit and the lateness of the hour had trimmed my fuse shorter than usual. I ended the staring contest.

"Look, pal, you're going to have to answer some questions, you know that, don't you? Either here now, or downtown; you tell me what it's going to be."

His placidity, combined with his now completely annoying smile, remained and he said nothing.

"Fine, be difficult," I groused, pulling the handcuffs from my coat pocket with one hand while I grabbed him by the opposite wrist with the other to turn him around.

Surprisingly, he didn't offer even a hint of resistance. It was like spinning an empty barstool. As he faced the building, he even brought his hands behind him without encouragement from me. I put the cuffs on, turned him back around and moved him over to Carter.

That was when a loud creaking came from the front door and light spilled out over the entry stoop where we all stood. A stubby, somewhat rotund silhouette appeared in the doorway accompanied by a gruff, "Hey, what's going on?"

I flashed my badge at the silhouette. "Police. Who are you?"

"I'm the night supervisor here," The man stepped from the door and I immediately appreciated the guy: he was a full head shorter than me. "Where you taking Simon?"

I exchanged quick glances with Carter and our suspect.

"You know this guy?" Carter asked.

"Yeah," the man shorter than me responded. "That's Simon. He's our janitor. What're you doin' with him?"

I shot a stern glare at our suspect before I answered. "Simon, the janitor, doesn't like to talk much, so we're taking him downtown for a little questioning."

The night supervisor threw a thumb in the direction of the janitor. "Simon doesn't talk much? He talks all the time."

I glared harder at our handcuffed friend. "Now I'm pissed."

I saw a subtle up-curl come to the janitor's steady smile and everything in me wanted to hit him.

"What do you want to question him for?"

"Murder," Carter said. "We have two bodies on the other side of the overpass. Any chance you saw or heard anything earlier tonight – disturbances; strangers in the area; anything?"

The supervisor shook his head. "Nah, nothing. We got cameras all over this place – I've been watching you guys on them – if anyone came through here we'da seen 'em."

I nodded. "You have surveillance recorded?"

The supervisor shot back an enthusiastic, "Yep, sure do. You wanna look?"

"Yep, sure do," I echoed.

The supervisor's whole demeanor suddenly changed enthusiastically as he turned on his heel and, with a noticeable spring in his step, bounded back to the doorway. "Follow me!"

I motioned to Carter to bring the janitor along and our little group quickly followed the supervisor into the building. A poorly lit interior hallway quickly led to a "T," and we followed our short chaperon to the right where a steel framed stairway led to the next level where another poorly lit hallway evidently traversed the entire length of the building. We kept following, this time past four closed doors to one on the left marked "Security." Our leader opened the door without a key and we entered a small, unoccupied office blindingly lit by too many overhead fluorescent lights flush mounted into a low suspended ceiling. To the right was an office area enclosed with clear glass.

THE LEPER

There was a single desk, computer and a bank of flat screen security monitors, each with a different image.

"You get HBO on those things?" Carter joked as he wedged the janitor into the tight space behind us. The janitor obliged willingly enough but remained as silent as he had been.

"Closed circuit, only," the supervisor answered, taking a seat at the computer and keying in a sequence that caused the center flat screen to go blank. There was a flicker followed by an audible blip sound. "How far back do you want to see?"

I leaned in close over the man's shoulder. "Can you pull up from three hours ago?"

The supervisor typed another couple of lines of coded command and then hit the return key. The center screen flickered again and then up popped a still image of the building's front parking area, the set of railroad tracks and the Thomas Avenue entry to the facility.

"We have twenty-three security cameras and I can key in just about any area you want."

I told him to start with the scene he had up and then added we might want copies of everything from the other cameras later. He nodded, made two keystrokes and hit return again. The screen image began to move. A couple of cars pulled from their parking spaces and drove away. There were no observable pedestrians. Several minutes went by. It was not captivating television.

"I can speed it up," the supervisor offered, running the cursor over the screen to a row of interactive icons. He clicked on a double-arrow icon and the video's digital date/time readout kicked into overdrive. I watched the images flicker as the time steadily rolled through the minutes, and then the hours. And then, I saw Carter and me enter the scene from the upper left corner of the screen.

"Slow it down."

The supervisor mouse-clicked the single play arrow and the counter slowed to a crawl. On the screen, Carter and I stop, talk and then look somewhere forward of our position.

"I can't see the front of the building," I pointed toward the bottom of the screen. "Can you switch cameras so I can see the front entry?"

"That's on that camera there," The supervisor directed me to the adjacent flat screen showing the now abandoned front entry steps and closed door. "I'll have to switch to key in the different camera. Are you done with this file?"

I hesitated and darted a quick questioning glance at Carter who shrugged back in reply. "Yeah, I guess so."

More keyboard work, followed by another blank screen on the center flat panel, followed by more keyboard work. It was getting monotonous. Suddenly, I was beyond tired.

"How far back?"

I rubbed my eyes to clear my head. "A little before we appeared on the scene."

"Oh, I closed that file; let me 'ballpark' it here…"

More keyboard work.

An image of the front entry area finally appeared on the center screen. The stoop was empty and the digital readout showed a time of '0309.54 CDT.' The supervisor pressed the return key once more and the time counter began to move at normal speed. For several minutes, only the front steps and the entry door were on the screen.

"Does this camera have us walking up to the entry?" I asked.

A slow nod came from the supervisor. "Well, yeah, eventually. It's a tighter shot than that first camera, and from a different angle, so you two will walk in from…"

The sudden bark came from Carter. "What the hell?!"

On the screen, in a blink the image of the janitor standing on the steps was suddenly there.

"Stop the tape!" I ordered too loudly. "Back it up and run that in slow motion."

More curious than stunned, the supervisor moved the cursor and said, "Yeah… let's look at that again."

The empty steps and door returned, the time readout crawled by slowly, and then, again, the janitor was just there. More quietly than the first, I ordered another replay. The same thing happened.

"I don't get it," the supervisor shook his head as he clicked back a few frames to the moment in time just before the janitor appeared. "It must be some kind of digital glitch or something."

"The clock is consistent," I pointed out.

The supervisor wasn't sure. "Yeah, but there must be something wrong with it..."

"People don't just tele-transport themselves," Carter said. He reached behind the janitor and grabbed hold of the binding handcuffs.

I looked back over my shoulder at our suspect. His face was completely at ease, unconcerned. The annoying, thin smile remained. I turned back to the supervisor and said, "You can punch this guy's timecard out for the night. He's coming with us."

The supervisor squeezed himself from the chair. "Simon's been off since midnight."

"Midnight?" Carter came back. "Then, what the hell is he still doing here three hours later?"

The man shrugged. "I don't know."

CHAPTER 3
SOMETHING UNSAID

No matter how much I rubbed them, my eyes still hurt. I didn't know if it was the gathering of another migraine or the harsh reality of early morning sun slicing through the office window to burn across the middle of my desk and right into the back of my eyeballs.

"Thanks," I said. Carter placed the refilled coffee mug in front of me. I took a sip and almost appreciated it. At least it was hot. "It's been a long night."

Carter leaned against the desk. "It's gonna be a longer day."

"Go home. Get some sleep. I can cover for you. You haven't seen your wife in two days. She's going to think you got a girlfriend or something."

"I wish," Carter chuckled. "What I have is an Arab mute and another crispy on a slab downstairs."

"Yeah. I know," I looked around the empty cubicles that comprised our office and then checked my watch. "It's six-thirty. The day shift oughta be showing up any time now."

"I hope someone brings doughnuts." Carter opened the folder lying on the side of my desk and paged through the personnel file we had taken from the water plant three hours earlier. "Simon Toors; forty-two; single; employed as a maintenance worker by the water plant for the last eight months. Before then, resided in Chicago, same kind of work, different kind of company all together – it was some kind of metalwork shop on the South Side. Before that, nothing's noted."

Carter shut the thin file and let it fall back to the desk.

I picked it up and moved it to my desk blotter. "And he hasn't said a single word the whole time. I'm going to backtrack his work history later today. I figure I'll get more that way than staring at him from across the interrogation room table."

"Tribby say anything about the crispy or the woman?"

My hands went to my eyes, trying again to relieve the pressure. "Tribby's sleeping on the cot in his office. He said the crispy looks identical to the others. He'll know more about the woman when the DNA match is in. Until then, let him sleep."

Through my fingers drawn down my face, I saw Carter's exasperated look.

"I just want to know how he did it," he said. "How he just materialized right on the front step of that place outta nowhere."

I wanted to know that, too. But first I wanted to know what Toors had going on to make him so smug about it all. He was too cool going through a process that is designed to rattle anyone, that was for sure and for certain.

"I wouldn't worry about it, Carter. Like the man said, probably some kind of digital hiccup."

"My ass."

"Well, maybe, but look at it this way: Toors is the first real lead we've had since the first Glenwood Avenue crispy. I admit it isn't much, but it's all we got. I'm going to ride it as far as it will take me."

A slow nod preceded Carter's incongruous response. "You're right. Linnie probably does think I have a girlfriend. It's time for me to head on home."

"Good idea," I acknowledged. "I'm staying to talk to the chief when he gets in"

Carter stood away from the desk. "Better you than me. Of course, Tomlinson likes you better. Call if you have to."

And with that, my oldest friend in the world, perhaps the only friend I had left, turned and made his way easily toward the twin doors leading to the outside hallway.

THE LEPER

From the top right drawer, I grabbed the less than half full bottle of migraine tablets, popped three into my mouth and tried to wash them down with a too-hot swallow of coffee. I almost screamed from the burning and nearly drowned from the gagging reflex that followed.

Clearing my throat by spitting into my wastebasket, I was startled when the desk phone rang. I wiped my mouth with the back of my hand and picked up the receiver.

"This is Culhane."

"Detective, this is Hemmelfinger in Holding. Could you come down here for a minute? Something weird's going on."

Toors was in Holding.

"I'm on my way, Sarge."

The new general population area, or Holding as referred to by the hired help, was a whole new world compared to the old dungeon deep in the bowels of the red granite edifice of Minneapolis City Hall. A temperature-controlled marvel of advanced incarceration engineering, Holding now positively gleamed with bulletproof safety glass and multiple layered safety zones in subtle shadings of designer wall color schemes determined by the shrinks to placate the hot-blooded emotions of all but the most volatile customers. It didn't look like a jail. It didn't smell like a jail, either. It was so frickin' pleasant there was little wonder why it was full almost every night.

I peeked through the skinny, steel-meshed-reinforced side-view window of the entry door to the place. I had just swiped my security card through the reader but nothing happened. From the first room on the left, the mostly menacing uniformed frame of Sergeant Hemmelfinger emerged and covered the distance between his room and my door within three steps.

"My card didn't work," I explained as he opened the door.

"We're having some kind of trouble with the security locks," the big Swede explained ushering me toward the room he had just left. "We got a call out to the company that installed them, but they haven't shown up yet – probably still too early."

"Cells work?"

"Oh, yeah. Locks solid there. That ain't the problem."

"I hope not. The paint hasn't dried yet on this place and already my security card doesn't work."

The sergeant opened the office door and I walked in as he followed. It was a large, well-lit room. A battery of video screens covered the lower half of three walls fronted by a horseshoe shaped desk amply equipped with computer keyboards, microphones on articulated stands, embedded three-button switch boxes at each station and ergonomically adjustable chairs around the curved length. Hemmelfinger moved around me and took the center chair. I grabbed the chair to his right, moved it closer and sat down.

The sergeant pointed to his center monitor. "Central Holding. Six cells, two-by-three configuration, individual entry for each around the periphery, steel reinforced framing with wire reinforced shatterproof safety glass. You couldn't drive a truck through that stuff. Take a close look and tell me what do you see?"

I leaned in. At least two, no more than four customers occupied all but one cell of the six. The remaining cell, the one on the far upper right corner on the screen, had one person in it – Toors sat on the furthermost bench, hands together resting in his lap, eyes closed and looking as peaceful as he had looked at anytime since I first saw him at the water plant.

"He's either sleeping or praying, I can't tell which."

"That's not what's weird," Hemmelfinger spread his fingers across the screen to point out what I hadn't noticed. "Look at everyone else."

All the other inmates were clustered against the farthest walls of their cells, some sitting on the floor, some squeezed into corners, all of them were huddling as if cowering or trying to hide from something.

"I tell you, Detective, things haven't been right since you brought your man down here."

"What do you mean, inside the last hour?"

"The first thing that happened after I locked the cell door, the two other people in with him started screaming."

"Screaming?"

"Yeah. I mean screaming. Here, look," Hemmelfinger shifted slightly to the next monitor on his left. With his computer's mouse, he clicked on first one icon followed by a second click on another. The central screen changed with a fifty-minute step back in time showing Toors on the bench and two others pounding at the cell door. "You see? I don't mean yelling, cursing, throwing a fit. I mean screaming. Like they were terrified. When those two guys started clawing at the door trying to get out, the other prisoners started yelling for help."

I could see the proof on the video. The other cells' occupants were panicked, stumbling about and waving their arms wildly.

Hemmelfinger clicked back to real-time and leaned back in his chair. "We had to split up your man's cellmates and move them to two other cells."

I looked at the now much quieter scene on the monitor. Toors still sat on his bench with his eyes closed. "What did Toors do during all that?"

"Exactly what he's doing now."

A fresh surge of pressure pushed from behind my eyes. The migraine tablets weren't working.

"And now, everyone else is subdued, cringing in the corners of their cells and afraid to even look over in that direction."

Hemmelfinger nodded. "Weird, ain't it?"

"Sarge, do you think you could put Toors in a more secure cell – a private cell down the hall?"

"Regular lock-up? Sure. Nice and quiet back there."

"Do it. Isolate him from anyone else. Keep his location quiet, too. I'll be down later to talk with him."

"You mean 'try to talk' with him, don't you? He hasn't uttered a sound since he's been here."

"That's okay. I have it on good authority he talks all the time – when he wants to."

***

I needed something to eat, so after leaving Holding I went straight to the reliable respite of vending machine delights the cafeteria was noted for. From the shiny rotating cylinder machine, I selected a six-ounce cup of fat-free yogurt; then I compensated with an egg-sausage biscuit from the multi-compartmented dispenser, slapped it into the microwave for 45 seconds and thanked God for the air pot full of freshly brewed real coffee. Okay, it wasn't Starbucks, but it wasn't instant, either.

It was still early and I had my pick of plastic chairs and Formica-covered tables.

"May I join you?" Dr. Phillip Tribby's request came from behind and startled me, but I hid it well.

"Why, yes, you may," I smiled as pleasantly as the hour allowed and the county medical examiner walked around to take a seat across from me. I added, "I'm surprised you're not sleeping."

"I was, you know."

"I know."

He added, "But you weren't, were you? You haven't slept at all, have you?"

I offered a disinterested shrug in response.

"Even divorced ex-Navy SEALs need their rest, Samuel."

"So do ex-Navy Corpsmen who volunteer for Marine Corps assignments."

"How is Shelly doing?"

"Thank you," I scowled at him over the rim of my coffee cup.

"Sorry."

I took a bite from the sandwich, which was comfortingly warmed in one spot but ice-cold in another all in the same chew. Through the partially masticated morsel I replied, "No reason to be sorry. At least you're not Carter's wife trying to set me up with Meredith Mathison."

It was Tribby's turn to shrug. "Remind me, please. Do I know Meredith Mathison?"

"No, I don't think so," I took another quick sip. "In fact, I don't think Meredith knows Meredith Mathison, if that makes any sense at all."

"Not really, but it sounds like more of the same vocational conflict nonsense with Shelly, if you ask me."

"It's not nonsense."

"Of course not," the Doc raised his own coffee cup in a salute. "It's always easier to blame the job than yourself."

The pressure behind my eyes throbbed once more. "Geez, Phil, thanks. What happened, you get up on the wrong side of the cot this morning?"

"It's surprising you didn't 'washout'," Tribby continued, ignoring my question. "I thought SEALs were tough?"

I wolfed down the remains of the sandwich and removed the foiled top from the yogurt container. "I'm getting older and I feel a lecture coming on. Spare me, please."

"Request granted." I could see he wanted to salute, but didn't. "I suppose you want to know about the bodies?"

"Ah, talking business at last!" Humorously, I bounced a quick upturned grin that just as quickly bounced back into repose. "Yes, that would be nice."

"Well, as you know, no IDs on either yet. I do know one thing, though. The DNA on the knife blade you found matches the female victim's DNA."

"Ah. We have a murder weapon, then?"

"Not really. Remember, she was dead before her throat was cut. You have a weapon used in the crime but not used to kill her."

"You sound like my mother. Picky, picky, picky." A spoonful of yogurt slid into my mouth. "Yum, peach flavor – no fruit, just flavor. What about prints on the knife?"

"No prints; clean as a whistle."

"Clean except for the blade."

"It was a sports knife with a folding serrated blade and locking hasp. The perp probably tried to wipe it off in a hurry but left some tissue behind. Serrated blades cut through stuff great but they're meat-catchers, too."

"Lucky us."

"Indeed," Tribby agreed. "How was that breakfast sandwich?"

"Hot and cold."

"I might try one."

"It's your stomach."

"Another thing you should know, Samuel. The man had latex gloves on just like the other two."

I nodded. "Makes sense. In fact, it's a relief."

"But there was something new this time. When you were in the field doing covert surveillance as a SEAL, what type of clothing did you usually wear?"

"Depended on the mission," I shrugged. "For night ops, it differs between military battle conditions or civilian urban environment."

"Civilian."

"Sea, air or land?"

"Land, urban."

"Two choices: if it's a big city, night or day, the best BDU would be 'Homeless' – worn-out dungarees, beaten-up shoes with no laces, rags in a burlap sack to hide the gear and three days' growth of beard. If it's covert and you need to be invisible, it's black all the way: lightweight synthetics; non-reflective; with a hood, face-black and/or a mask."

"And you'd carry your gear in a sack?"

"No. Electronics in a black waist belt; other stuff inside the Kevlar vest."

"Our guest on the slab downstairs was similarly dressed, even wore two vests."

That perked my curiosity. "Not like the others at all. Dressed in surveillance BDUs and wearing two vests?"

"A Kevlar vest under a lightweight equipment vest with all kinds of nifty pockets and loops to hold just about everything from a radio, notepad, pens, pepper spray, handcuffs, extra pistol magazines, you name it. Nice rig."

"Sounds like it. New stuff after my time, I'm afraid. Anything in the vests we could use to identify him?"

"No. The vests and every pocket he had were picked clean."

The pressure behind my eyes returned with another painful surge. "Oh, crap. That can mean only one thing."

"He had help."

My head bobbed but my shoulders sagged. "Either he emptied his pockets and vests of everything he carried before he died, or someone did it for him after he died. In either case, you don't go for a stroll through Wirth Park without some kind of ID and the fact that there's nothing on him we can use tells us other people are involved."

"Samuel, that means the Glenwood Avenue killings didn't involve a single serial psychopath. They're a group project!"

I massaged my brow to relieve the pressure and help my sluggish thinking processes. "Yeah, so it would appear. The BCA working on the guy's prints?"

"It's priority and fast-tracked. Should know something before noon today, maybe sooner."

"Get hold of our lab guy and have him dust the vests, both of them. It's slim, but there might be a print that doesn't belong to the perp we can use."

Tribby agreed and then excused himself to retrieve a breakfast biscuit from the big multi-compartmented vending machine. After the stop at the microwave, he returned to his seat.

"We're spending too much time together," he complained. "I'm beginning to eat like you, now."

"Oh, no, Phil. You can't get away with blaming me for your self-destructive behavior."

***

Later, the lack of sleep got to me. Sitting at my desk, the eyes closed and I slipped easily into a deep stupor. A moment later, the phone pulled me back to consciousness. On its own my hand moved to lift the receiver.

"Culhane?" It was Tomlinson.

"Yes, Chief?"

"You got a moment?"

"For you, anytime."

"Smart ass."

"Thanks, Chief."

"Now would be good."

"Yes, Chief. On my way."

I pulled my sport coat from the back of my chair and checked my wristwatch. It was 9:35. My moment of stupor had been more than two hours long.

Mark Tomlinson, fifty-four years old, amply graying on the sides and noticeably thinning on top, was an exercise fanatic. Good thing, too, because Tomlinson readily used his enthusiasm for physical fitness to help control his poorly concealed professional resentments. He was only our Division Chief. What he wasn't was MPD's Chief of Police, a title he completely believed he deserved after more than three decades of service, and he was convinced well-entrenched political forces conspired against him getting the job. He wasn't exactly sure who the well-entrenched political forces were, so he blamed just about everyone all the time. It was easier that way.

I always felt strangely comforted being in his office – a formal testament of chronic conservatism: wood paneling, plush carpeting, heavy oak office desk, overstuffed sofa and matching twin chairs and three flags – the Stars & Stripes in the middle, framed by a state and city flag on opposite sides, each on poles in shiny brass pedestals and standing at attention behind his desk. It almost made me want to sing. In Tomlinson's office, "God bless America!" would be a good tune.

"Another crispy," Tomlinson grumbled, his scowl directed only to the leather-trimmed desk blotter under his intertwined fingers. "The press is going to get hold of this and make me look like a complete ass."

I adjusted my backside into the leather armchair too comfortable not to fall asleep in and offered what solace I could. "I don't know about that, Mark. I haven't talked to any reporters at all about this latest one. It's not like we're issuing press releases – at least not until we have some solid leads to brag about – and they don't have any reporters energetic enough to build their own stories anymore."

"They will. People, you know who, will see to it this hits the local news stations as soon as they can. Probably something on the six o'clock news tonight, you wait and see."

"It won't come from me. You know that."

He nodded. His eyes momentarily locked onto mine and then quickly looked away. "I know. You're a good man, Sam. Besides, you're not high enough up and you don't go to the right

THE LEPER 53

parties. That doesn't mean you can slack off on this. I need you to nail this guy."

"It may be more than just one guy."

Tomlinson's face fell. "What do you mean? I thought you brought him in last night?"

I tossed a discarding gesture off to the side. "Toors? Whoever is killing these people this way, it isn't Toors."

"That isn't what Holding told me this morning," he shot back with noticeable displeasure. "Toors is a troublemaker; caused a big disturbance down there; had to move him for the safety of the other inmates. Why couldn't he be our guy?"

I tried to calm him before he heated up any more. "Don't get me wrong, Mark, Toors knows something about all this. He's just not the killer. We're keeping him for questioning as long as we legally can. Then, we'll let him out and follow him everywhere he goes. One way or another, he's going to help us get the people responsible."

"How do you know there's more than one?"

"Too many empty pockets on the new crispy."

Tomlinson didn't get the pocket reference, so I related to him everything Tribby and I had discussed earlier that morning.

He shook his head. "Pretty thin, Sam. Maybe he left everything in a car somewhere..."

"Just brought the knife, you think?"

"Could be. The knife and the girl's body; kind of a heavy load, even if you're in shape. He dumped everything he didn't need before he went into the park."

I thought about it, tried to picture the guy going about his business dumping the body, then slicing her neck open and calmly walking away... *Two sets of footprints!*

"Sweet Jesus, I forgot the footprints!"

Tomlinson shot me his "You'd better explain" glare.

"There were two sets of footprints leading from the scene, one behind the other. We followed them down the western slope to the railroad tracks where one set of prints just disappeared. The other trail went farther down a little bit and then it disappeared, too.

There were two people there, Mark: two people involved with the girl's murder."

The Chief's brow furrowed as he digested what I had just told him. "A dead woman, two more people; another body – crispy this time – and a suspect in custody. How far away from where the trail of footprints ended did you find the crispy?"

"It wasn't far, just north of the Glenwood overpass between forty to sixty feet."

"And you found this Toors guy in front of the main building at the water plant, right?"

For a moment I thought it was a good time to tell him about the water plant surveillance recordings and what they showed. Only Carter and I knew about Toors' little magic act. With reflection, I thought it best to keep it that way for the time being. "Right. He wouldn't answer any questions, so we took him in. I'm going to give it another try when we're done here."

Tomlinson looked worried. "The first two crispies were dressed in normal clothes and had wallets, IDs, cash, normal stuff anyone would carry. Easy to find out who they were and how they were connected – and they weren't. This new one is in black polyester from head to foot and wearing a bulletproof vest. No papers of any kind and apparently he did not act alone. The only thing that links all three is the way they died."

Running his hand through his thinning pate, Tomlinson took a moment to give the whole thing more thought. "Toors is the accomplice, Sam. He has to be."

I disagreed. "Sorry, Mark, I don't think so. He's a janitor at the plant. He was dressed like a janitor."

"Check your timeline, Sam. He could've changed clothes easily. Besides, you said he knows something about all this he's not telling."

"Yes, I did, but he's not the killer type."

"No? What if he's a 'cold-psychotic-capable-of-taking-a-person's-life-as-easily-and-conscience-free-as-most-of-us-are-when-we-buy-groceries' type?"

"He's not. He's the "Don't-talk-to-anyone-until-you-talk-to-your-lawyer" type. I'll tell you one thing, though: one way or another, whatever Toors knows and isn't telling, I'll find it out."

From across the desk, Tomlinson leveled a threatening index finger at me. "You better. Once this latest bit of news hits the media, I'm going to need something solid from you if I'm going to avoid my next lecture from the mayor and police commissioner."

***

At 10:30 the sterile interior of Interrogation Room #2 hadn't changed all that much since Carter and I left it five hours earlier: same metal-legged table bolted to the floor; same two stiff chairs on either side; same drab walls with gray/black slabs of soundproofing foam providing what little visual diversity the room had to offer, save the two-way observation mirror that spanned the wall behind me.

Toors, shackled to the chair and facing me, sat with the same posture and annoying placid demeanor he had held during our entire earlier session.

I leaned forward with elbows on the table and fingers interlaced. "They tell me you didn't eat your breakfast."

Other than a slight tilt of his head, there was no response.

I sighed. "You should eat, Simon. It's not the finest cuisine, I know, but it doesn't help you to starve yourself."

His head tilt relaxed a bit and his eyes moved slightly as if to look behind me. Within a second, his eyes returned to mine. He repeated the movement, looked behind me again only to quickly return back to me.

He's communicating.

I turned to look back over my shoulder and saw our reflection in the wall mirror. I turned back.

"There's no one in the observation room, Toors. We're alone. I promise."

The smallest nod came from him. He then looked upward and quickly returned to me. He did this twice. I leaned back in the chair and crossed my arms to study my prisoner. After a long moment, I made my decision.

"Yes, Simon, we're being recorded: video and audio."

Toors thinly smiled and barely moved his head back and forth.

"So you're willing to talk but not to be recorded?"

His thin smile widened just a bit as he answered with a slight positive head bob.

Fingers pinched at my mouth as I became cautiously encouraged and more than curious about where this was going. The problem was a familiar one: I knew I was going to get into trouble over what I was going to do next.

The ceiling wasn't bugged, but the table was. Hidden behind the table leg on my right, a hardwired cable came up through the false floor to a powerful state-of-the-art omni-directional condenser mini-microphone mounted by a Velcro strip to the table's underside. I reached underneath. My fingers quickly found the cable. I followed it to the microphone, tugged sharply and the Velcro pulled free. I held the device above the table for Toors to see.

"Audio is gone," I said, disconnecting the mic from the cable. "But the video recorder stays on. Agreed?"

An affirmative nod came from Toors.

I then held up a cautioning finger and pressed it to my lips. Toors' eyes followed me as I rose from my chair and walked over to the wall-mounted double-gang light switch next to the door. The switches were modern rocker types with a flush-mounted, friction fit cover that released with a simple pry of your fingernails and an easy yank. I pulled another microphone – same type as the first – from the circuit box, disconnected it from its cable and returned to my chair.

"Now, all audio recording is gone," I said placing both microphones on the table between us.. "I trust that is acceptable?"

His thin smile twitched a little broader and he leaned closer. "Acceptable, indeed, Samuel. I thank you for your cooperation. Now, if we could discuss these shackles?"

His British accent was noticeably muddled but with a clarity of tone and volume that caught me completely off guard. After a short stumble, I recovered quickly.

"Er, no, for now the shackles stay on. So, you're not from here, but England?"

A slight shrug preceded his answer. "Among other places."

"What other places?"

"South Africa for a few years; England for a few years; India for a few years. For the most part, you could say I'm from Israel. I move around quite a bit."

"How long you been in this country?"

The thin smile turned broad again. "A few years."

"Ah, my kind of suspect – a smart ass."

"Not intentionally, I assure you."

I wondered if I could trust his assurances in any of this. It was time to cut to the chase.

"Mr. Toors, you're what we call a person of interest in a series of murders that have taken place in our fair town over the last several weeks. To say these deaths have been unusual is an understatement. They all involve severe bacterial infestation complicated by massive blistering of the flesh and sudden, almost total degeneration of the body's nerve tissues. I need to ask you what you know about these killings."

The thin smile faded as, almost serenely, his eyes closed for two or three seconds. When his eyes opened, his expression could only be describe as extreme sadness.

"Things are accelerating very quickly now, Samuel. You will have your answers soon."

I was unmoved. "I need my answers now, not soon; not later. Last night we found you near a murder scene. I know you know something about what happened. Speak to me. Now."

"Change is coming," he said calmly. "You have yet to know the role you will play in all of it."

I pressed him. "I only need to know one thing: who's responsible for these deaths."

"And so you shall know."

I pressed harder. "Not if you don't first tell me what you know."

Real regret fell across his features.

"I'm not able to tell you," he said. "But perhaps I'll be able to show you if we could leave this place."

That cut it – flat out, he was lying to me.

My eyes narrowed to a purposeful squint. "Toors, I will stick you back in that cell and let you rot there if you don't start talking, and I mean right now."

The thin smile returned. "You look tired. You haven't had much sleep lately, have you?"

My irritation with this guy kicked up two whole notches. "Look, pal, start talking or we end this."

"You should go home to your wife."

"I'm not married!" I shot back firmly and came to my feet.

Toors looked up and his broadest smile yet turned into a beyond irritating toothy grin. "Yes, you are."

With a glare that could melt lead, I picked up the two disconnected microphones from the table and left the room.

Chapter 4

Un-arrested

My head was so far into the Wolpren's refrigerator my concluding statement echoed.

"And when he said, 'Yes, you are' married, I got up and left the room."

From his kitchen table, Carter laughed. I successfully retrieved three Grain Belt Premium long necks from the open case on the refrigerator's bottom shelf and joined him and his wife, Caroline, at the table. I twisted the cap from one bottle and placed it in front of her, hoping my smile hid my concern. She took the bottle and smiled a "thank you" back. She had lost more weight since I last saw her and that hadn't been all that long ago.

Slender as long as I had known her, Caroline Wolpren was one of those women who possessed a natural lithe athleticism complemented by a ready smile always framed with close-cropped blond-brown hair now subtly streaked with gray that comfortably proclaimed she wasn't a little girl anymore. It fit her. But months of radiation treatments and anti-cancer drugs had taken their toll.

I handed Carter a beer, took the last one for myself and sat down across from them.

"Too bad I wasn't there," Carter took a quick swig of his beer. "What that guys needs is a little good cop-bad cop to loosen him up. Or, turn off the cameras and work him over. He'd talk plenty then."

Caroline gave her husband a critical, albeit silent, glare. I just shook my head.

"Don't think so, Carter. He'd just sit there, let you beat him bloody and take it."

Carter raised an eyebrow. "A masochist, eh?"

"No, it's not that." Not having had dinner yet, the beer tasted positively luxurious. "I'm pretty sure he's not the psycho we're looking for, but he's a nut-job, alright. Nothing seems to get to this guy. He's taking it all in like he's on a tour bus seeing the sites. I don't think he even eats. I know he didn't eat breakfast this morning."

A cautioned response from Carter: "You surprised? Have you eaten any jail food lately?"

A small chuckle: "I've had worse. Remember, I eat from the cafeteria vending machines."

"Point taken," Carter nodded.

"Would you like to have dinner here with us, tonight?" Caroline asked with her characteristic matronly concern.

With another sip of beer and a wave of my hand I declined the offer. "Thanks, but no. I don't want to put you guys out."

She disputed the point, as I knew she would. "You aren't putting us out, Sam. We're going to eat dinner whether you stay for it or not."

"Yeah," Carter agreed. "So don't be the usual ass you are. Stay for dinner, okay?"

I raised my hands in surrender. "Two against one. You win."

Caroline smiled in victory. Too late I realized she had a hidden agenda in keeping me there.

A homemade dinner of beef pot roast with vegetables was a double-sided marvel: first, it was a feast compared to my normal fare lately. Thick, juicy and tender, the beef literally fell onto my fork. The boiled carrots, potatoes and slabs of celery and quartered onions were cooked firm and perfectly seasoned. My mother couldn't have made it that good.

Second, Caroline's unmatched epicurean skills painfully reminded me that lately I had spent too many meals eating out of a bag.

"We will retire to the living room," she said rising to her feet and reaching across the table to add my empty plate to her own.

"You take it easy," I protested. "I'll clean up in here."

"You will not!" Caroline shot back, offended. "Carter, take your friend to the other room."

Carter laughed. "Come my good 'friend,' let us 'retire' to the other room."

I shrugged. Carter laughed again. For emphasis, Caroline added with a backhanded wave, "Scoot! Both of you! We'll have coffee and dessert in a little while."

As we left her for the front room, I leaned in and whispered, "She shouldn't work so hard."

"She needs to," Carter whispered back. "Especially now."

I took the plush side chair next to the table lamp. Carter sat in the end seat of the adjacent sofa. Outside the picture window, the sun had set and the sky was turning a darker gray-blue.

Softly so as to not be overheard, I said, "I had hoped she'd be doing better. She's lost so much weight. Her hair looks great, though, better than last Thanksgiving, I think."

Equally soft, Carter supplied the answer I didn't want to hear. "It's a wig."

I sighed and my face fell.

Carter continued. "Nice one, too. Damn thing cost over three 'Gs,' but it looks good; just like before the diagnosis."

I didn't know what to say. I heard running water in the kitchen; the rattle of flatware getting rinsed before going into the dishwasher; more sounds of plates being dealt with.

"God, Carter, what can you do?"

He looked at me, the light reflecting off the gathering wetness in his eyes. "You can breathe in every moment you have left with her, that's what. It's the most important thing left to do."

"I meant medically; a cure?"

"We caught it too late, Sam. It's only a matter of time, now."

The moment was abruptly disturbed and I almost jumped out of my shorts when the front doorbell rang.

Caroline's request urgently resonated from the kitchen. "Get that, will you, Honey?"

"Better not be someone selling something," Carter complained as he unfolded himself to a standing position, walked around where I sat and headed for the door. "Well, hell-o there! Fancy seeing you again! Come on in!"

I didn't have to look around to recognize Meredith's "Thank you, you handsome married man, you" as she walked through the open door.

Carter, taking her light jacket and leading her into the living room, announced, "Honey, Meredith is here! Sam, you remember Meredith, don't you?"

I felt my face flush as I rose clumsily with a smile. I had to admit she looked good in her sharp mauve business jacket with matching skirt and the perfection of her obvious recent hair treatment: professional and sexy at the same time. Somewhere I found the guts to take her hand and look her in the eye. "So nice to see you again, Meredith."

She shook my hand and smiled back with honest insincerity. "Really? That's a surprise."

I looked away as Carter cleared his throat, draped Meredith's jacket over his arm and said, "I think I'll hang this up, somewhere."

Weakly offering Meredith Carter's seat on the sofa, I returned to my chair as she sat down. As if on cue, Caroline came in from the kitchen carrying a large tray with four plated desserts – a lemon cake thing with fancy icing, a chrome insulated serving pitcher and four saucers each holding a dainty coffee cup with finger loops much too small to perform any practical function. Before she reached the halfway point in the room, she cast an almost panicked look toward Carter as he returned from the front closet. Quickly, he took the tray from her and Caroline breathed easier as she found a seat on the sofa one cushion removed from Meredith. Carter placed the tray on the coffee table and snugged the second matching side chair closer to start serving.

"Well," Carter began, his hand slightly trembling as he placed a dessert fork on each plate and passed out the lemon cake thing with fancy icing one serving at a time. "Here we are, all together."

"Yes," said Caroline, taking the first serving from Carter and passing it to Meredith.

"Yes," Meredith smiled, passing the offered dessert to me.

I sighed too loudly and placed the cake thing on the side table next to the lamp. I looked at each one of them with my mouth hanging open and said absolutely nothing.

They all looked back waiting for me to speak. I didn't.

Carter continued to pass out cake. Meredith, on the other hand, had something to say. "It's been more than three weeks, Sam."

That embarrassed me.

She continued. "Not even a phone call. You could've called. Okay? I'm not perfect, I know that. I try the best I can. Not everyone likes me. That's okay, too. You don't like me, that's fine. But, Sam, you shouldn't do what you did and then ignore me afterwards. It's… It's not nice."

More embarrassed, my mouth still silent and gaping, I desperately fired a pleading glare at Carter. His mouth was gaping, too. I was a mute completely on my own.

However, Caroline, clearly carrying the weight of shame for which she now held me responsible, could speak. "And to think, I was the one who introduced you to her…"

I collapsed back into the chair, drew my fingers down my face in frustration and audibly moaned. Thank God, the moan helped me get my voice back.

I turned to Meredith and punched the air between us with a pointed index finger. "First! Meredith, I didn't 'do' anything to you. We met. We went out for dinner. We had a nice time. It was pleasant. I didn't make any promises; neither did you. I wasn't expecting anything…"

"You didn't even call," Meredith reiterated through her clenched teeth.

I leveled my finger at her and continued. "… But apparently, you were expecting something. Sorry to be such a disappointment. I'm not in the mind reading business."

My emphasis finger next turned to Caroline. "And you, you're to blame for this!"

"Me?!" It was a puny yelp of protest.

"Yes, you! Stop trying to set me up with your friends!"

I could see the knuckles on Caroline's clenched fists turn white. "It's been two years, Sam: two years! It's time you found someone. You need someone. It's not good for you to be alone now. You're not getting any younger, you know."

I sprang from the chair. "I'm not ready for what you want me to do! I don't want to hurt anyone's feelings, but you have to please stop doing this!"

As if still in sixth grade, Carter raised a tentative hand. "You know, Sam, she's kinda right."

My emphasis finger swung in his direction. "You're supposed to be on my side!"

"I am," he vowed. "I just think you need to move on, you know? I know Shelly left and that's hard, but Linnie's right – you're a better person than what you seem to be becoming."

"What the hell does that mean?" I growled at him.

"It means," Meredith's quiet response turned me back toward her corner of the sofa. "You're a good man and they don't want to lose a good friend. It means something else, too."

I could feel the fight drain from my body. "Yeah, what's that?"

I shouldn't have asked. Through a broken smile, Meredith looked at me with the sadness only truth could bring.

"It means, even after all this time, you're still in love with your wife, Sam."

My emphasis finger dropped. I stared silently down at my hands and marveled at how wrinkled and old they looked. *How does that happen? Whose hands are these, anyway?*

Carter's whisper filled my ear. "Maybe Toors isn't the nut-job you think he is. He's got you pegged."

I turned my head and our eyes met. Before I could say anything, my cell phone rang.

"Thank God," I said, retrieving the phone from my pants pocket. "Saved by the bell."

It was Tomlinson.

"Yes, Chief?" I grimaced when his voice blasted into my ear. I knew the others could hear so I moved away from the group and stepped toward the dining room. "Say again… How can that… Holy crap! ... In the cellblock! … No, Chief, he's here with me… Damn!"

I turned and gave Carter a quick heads-up nod. I brought the phone back up and said to Tomlinson, "We're on our way!"

"What's up?" Carter asked as I shoved the phone back into my pocket and quick-stepped back into the room.

"You're not going to believe this." I said in a rush. "An armed assault in the city jail itself!"

Carter bolted for the dining room to retrieve the sport coat he had left on the back of his chair. "What? How? Who?"

"Apparently, it was two of our own officers."

"Holy shit!" was all he could say.

"And that's not the half of it." I turned to Caroline and quickly thanked her for diner. I then turned to Meredith. "I'm sorry, Meredith, for being such a jerk. I promise: I'll call you later."

When I turned to leave, Carter stood frozen with his sport coat half on as he asked, "Who got hit?"

"No one," I answered honestly as we both turned and made for the front door. "But we have two new crispies in blue uniforms lying on the cellblock floor."

"Sweet Jesus – Mother of God!" Carter gasped as we hit the outside step running.

"You got that right," I agreed as we scrambled for the Crown Vic. "And Toors has disappeared!"

***

It was thirty-seven road miles between Carter's Burnsville house and the new jail in downtown Minneapolis. Thanks to the interstate and the Crown Vic's lights and siren, it took us a few ticks more than twenty-two minutes to get there. On Second Avenue, we bypassed the circus being fueled by calamitous flashing lights, scrambling patrolmen, hoards of onlookers and all the backed-up traffic by turning off at the old county government center ramp to the underground parking facility two blocks from the jail. I drove down two levels and parked across from a closed steel door labeled "TO CITY HALL." In unison, both of us bailed out and sprinted toward the door and to the tunnel on the other side.

It was a doublewide echo chamber with bare, flat cream-colored walls and hard vinyl tiled flooring that stretched ahead to only disappear. Our every footfall bounced loudly all around us as we ran. The endless tunnel abruptly turned to the left for about thirty feet, and then took a hard corner back to the right. Far up ahead, a small, gray rectangle grew larger with every stride.

Carter pointed ahead. "Door!"

"City Hall," I yelled back. "We want the jail and that's one more block down!"

At the door leading to the basement level of City Hall, the tunnel led to the right for at least another sixty feet. It then turned left and we followed without breaking stride. It must have been another two hundred feet to where the tunnel ended at a locked security door with an eye-level wire-mesh-reinforced view panel above the handle.

I blew out a heavy breath to clear the lungs and pulled out my security card. "You're in better shape than I thought."

Hands on his knees to catch his own breath, Carter nodded. "No, I'm not."

I couldn't help but chuckle as I swiped my card through the reader. Nothing happened. I swiped the card through the reader once more. No click; no buzz; nothing.

Carter tried the handle. The door was still locked.

"Oh, crap!" He moaned. "Don't tell me we gotta go back and come in from the street."

"If so, you're the one going up. I'll wait down here for you to come and get me."

I peered through the view port and, as I did so, I almost tripped backward when the face of a young patrol officer tilted in front of me.

"What the...?" I started to say, but the muffled voice from behind the door interrupted me.

"Badges?" The young man asked.

Carter and I shared a questioning look, pulled our respective badges out and held them up to the small window. A brief nod from the officer was followed by the sound of the latch giving way. The door swung open and we walked into the bowels of the new city jail.

"Sorry about that," said the officer.

"What the heck is wrong with the security locks?" Carter grumbled, letting the door shut behind him.

"They're down. None of them work," he explained simply. "We have officers posted at all the doors now and all the doors are locked all the time."

I shoved my badge back into my coat pocket. "They didn't work this morning in Holding, either. I thought they had someone in to fix them?"

"They did," said the man. "They got them working for a while, but since the shooting, none of them work now. Must be some kind of digital glitch."

Carter and I shared a quick double take as I said, "Seems to be a lot of that going around lately."

The officer nodded.

I nodded back. "Okay. We need to get to Lock Up. How do we get there from here?"

The officer pointed down the hallway. "All the way down, turn left to the security elevators. Don't use them. They don't work without security cards, and all the readers are down. There's a stairway on the opposite side. Take it three floors up to Level B and knock on the door. The guard will check your IDs again and you'll be in."

I nodded my thanks and we turned to resume the trek.

Carter rolled his eyes in disbelief. "Three floors up? No elevators? Where the hell are we, Chicago?"

Even I could feel the burn growing now with each running stride. "Complain, complain, complain."

The jog to the elevators was easy. The overly lit stairwell was dank and smelled of still wet concrete.

"How long's the jail been open?" I complained making the turn at the top of the first flight. "A year? Two years?"

"Year and a half, I think," Carter wheezed his answer from behind me.

"And the concrete hasn't set yet?" Pant-pant.

"Well, you know," he wheezed again. "They say the only time concrete is really dry is just before it crumbles."

"Really?" My chest was starting to hurt now. "I never heard that before."

We passed Level A.

"We're almost there." I could barely get the words out now.

"Bullshit!"

More steps, more clop-clop, followed by another flat turn followed by more clop-clop up another flight of steps. The next flat turn was there and we arrived at a large painted graphic proclaiming Level B. This time, we both stooped over with our hands on our knees to keep from passing out.

"Good - Lord - Almighty," Carter exhaled each word separately. "I – am – so – out – of – shape!"

"Yes," It was my turn to wheeze. "You are."

Carter's humor left him as he glared at me. "I'd punch you right now, if I could lift my hands."

"Don't bother. I'm so dizzy if I stood up to fight you I'd fall over anyway."

That was when the door opened and another uniformed officer stuck his head into the stairwell.

"You two alright?"

I wanted to breathe some more so I stayed stooped over and just waved at the guy.

"Yeah, Culhane and Wolpren," said the officer. "I was wondering what was taking you so long. The kid downstairs radioed you were coming. Thought you got lost."

Carter and I took a moment to exchange disgusted grimaces.

"Radio, eh?" I wheezed again as we walked past the guard to enter Level B. "What a concept."

Inside, we collected ourselves and pulled out our badges. The officer waived them back into our pockets. "Come on, I know you guys. Hell, you solve this mess, you're going to be famous."

I cringed at the thought. Carter, on the other hand, seemed to perk up quite a bit.

"Really?" he asked.

"Forget it," I said, beginning to feel the return of normal. "Fame is the last thing we want on this job."

"I don't know about that, Sam. Fame pays pretty good nowadays. A little extra could come in handy."

I shook my head and turned to the officer. "Where do I find Chief Tomlinson?"

The officer pointed to his left. "Down to the main corridor, take a right and go down to Holding. You'll probably find him in the Security Office, that's where everyone is."

"Thanks," I said, grabbing Carter by the coat sleeve and tugging him after me. "I'm familiar with that area."

It was a zoo. Every uniform in the department had to have been in the corridor or inside the Lock-Up itself. We had to swim through the throng to get to the Security Office. A quick double knock on the door, a twist of the knob and we were in.

"About time you two got here! What took you?" The gruff and unwelcoming voice of Chief Tomlinson came from the crowd.

The Security Office was packed as thick as the hallway outside. Tomlinson elbowed his way through to where we stood, his poorly concealed rage pulling his face tight. It was easy to recognize a short fuse getting shorter.

"Sorry, Chief. We tried to get here faster, but the streets are a mess out there."

It didn't soften him much. I knew his instincts dictated he had to offload jurisdictional responsibilities as quickly as possible, so I wasn't surprised when he turned on me first.

"You're the smart ass who brought that Arab in here in the first place. And, because of that, we have two dead officers and a psycho raghead back on the streets."

The best way to handle Tomlinson when he was operating in the "Everyone but me" mode was to let him vent and then ignore him.

"I need to see the scene, Chief."

"You lost him," he continued, pointing a threatening finger in my face. "You get him back, pronto. You don't, I'll have your badge. You got that, Mister?"

I took a breath. "I'll do my best, Chief."

"You damn well will do better than that!"

Carter moved between us, grabbed my shoulder and steered me back to the door. "We'll be in the cellblock, okay, Chief?"

"Yeah," I contributed. From over my shoulder I said, "I'll ask some officers to try to clear the hallway, okay, Chief?"

We exited the Security Office and heard the Chief yell, "If I go down, so do you two!" just as the door closed behind us.

"One thing you can say about Tomlinson," Carter surmised as I scanned the crowd for a sleeve with sergeant strips on it. "You always know where you stand with him."

I found the stripes I was looking for, took two steps into the crowd, reached through a couple of standing uniforms to tug on the sleeve that held them. The brass nametag on her shirt read "Danielson." She turned and I held up my badge.

"Sergeant Danielson?" I asked. "Get a few of these other officers to help you clear this area, okay?"

She looked at the badge and then back at me, bobbed her head twice, picked two other lower grade officers within arm's reach, clinched her whistle firmly between her teeth and moved forward into the crowd. The shrill blast got everyone's attention. That was immediately followed by the strongest feminine voice I'd ever heard.

"Alright! Alright! Listen up, people! We gotta clear this hallway! All those who don't belong here move back to the corridor please! Quickly, orderly, move to the corridor now, please!" She waved with her hand above the crowd to show them the way. Her efficiency was breathtaking. In mass and with the help of her two recruits, everyone began to shuffle in her direction.

Carter and I worked our way against the traffic flow and toward the lock-up itself. We showed our badges at the security door and the guard let us in. The regular lock-up was behind Holding through another set of security doors where we showed our badges again to two more guards. Down the hall a number of uniforms were mulling about accompanied by two white-coats and one familiar baldheaded older guy in glasses.

"Geez, does he ever go home?" I mumbled to myself as our pace quickened.

"Sure," Carter said, keeping up along side me. "Unlike some of us, Tribby actually has a life."

We arrived at the gathering where two debris-covered bodies in patrolmen uniforms lay on the floor.

"Ah, Samuel, Carter, so nice to see you again," Tribby's voice was smiling but his face wasn't. Something wasn't right.

"Doc," Carter nodded. "What can you tell us so far?"

Tribby took a deep breath. "Well, besides the obvious fact these men are dead, you will note they both have the mottled and severely blistered flesh characteristic of the other earlier victims. Our mystery deaths now total five in number."

"Were they shot?" I asked. "Tomlinson said there was a shoot out up here."

"No, Samuel, they weren't shot," Tribby turned and pointed to two futuristic-looking weapons lying on the floor between the bodies. Both rifles were the same: short and stubby barreled, with molded black composite stocks and matching black nylon shoulder straps. Tribby continued: "These men did the shooting in that cell in front of you."

The blown cell door hung by a single bottom hinge and debris everywhere testified to the violence that had caused the damage. I stepped around the bodies and walked inside the cell. The far wall was pockmarked with bullet holes, as were the walls on either side. Casings and bits of concrete and plaster were everywhere – on the floor, on the bed, even in the stainless steel combination sink and toilet assembly against the opposite wall. There was no blood. I turned to see Carter standing behind me in the doorway taking it all in.

"I love what they've done to the place," he commented dryly.

"Yeah, me too." I took a last look around, and before returning to the outside hallway, said, "Too bad no one was at home for the party."

At the bodies again, I pointed to the two rifles on the floor. "What are they, Phil?"

Tribby's eyes actually seemed to twinkle. I knew he loved this part of the job. "Those are very special, Samuel. They are IMI Micro Tavor MTAR-21 assault rifles. You will note the unique rear-mounted clip in the shoulder butt. There are many different configurations possible with this weapon, and normally this model would have a STANAG-type magazine with a capacity no greater than 32 rounds of 5.56 millimeter NATO cartridges. However, the suppressors on the muzzles would indicate these MTARs have been converted to a 9 millimeter configuration and the magazines have been modified to carry twice the normal number of rounds."

Carter whistled. "Sixty round clips. Loaded for bear."

"Indeed," Tribby continued. "Very small, very powerful. They fire in single-shot, semi- and full-automatic modes, at between 750 to 900 rounds per minute full auto. These models also have integrated laser sights and infrared heat detection."

"For covert operations and urban warfare," I added.

"A lot of firepower for cops," Carter acknowledged.

"A lot of firepower for anyone," I surmised. "Phil, who in the world uses this type of rifle?"

"Well, Samuel, the easy answer would be, 'anyone who can get their hands on one.'"

"What's the hard answer?"

Tribby took a deep breath and blew it out in a rush. "The larger models are popular with Germany's KSK troops. Recently, this weapon, the MTAR-21, was selected as the standard infantry weapon of the IDF."

That stunned me. "The Israeli Defense Force?"

Carter moaned. "Ah, geez, this is getting better all the time. Now we have cops moonlighting for the Israeli military."

"The only problem is," Tribby replied as he stooped over and loosened the shirt of the nearest corpse. "They aren't cops."

When Tribby opened the shirt, he revealed a fabric-covered chest plate over the black nylon of a Kevlar vest. He rapped hard on the center of the chest plate. It was something very solid.

"Ceramic ballistic shielding?" I asked.

Tribby nodded and handed me the nametags he had taken from the shirts. "These guys stole those uniforms, probably from the precinct locker room. Check it out with the lockers assigned to these two names, I bet you'll find I'm right. They knew what they were doing and they came loaded for a real fight, Samuel. They got one, but it wasn't the fight they were expecting."

I turned about toward the open cell. "And that's the cell our man was in?"

"So they tell me," Tribby said, motioning to his two assistants. "Let's bag these two and get them down to the lab, okay?"

The two white coats hopped to it and I turned to Carter. "The security recordings should tell us what happened here."

"I hope so," Carter said. "This whole thing gives me the creeps. Our pal is nowhere to be seen, but those guys were sprayin' a lot of lead at something. Did you see the number of holes in the walls in there?"

"I saw. I also saw there was no blood spatter anywhere. Whatever they were shooting at they missed. And then it disappeared – every last bit of it."

I handed Carter the nametags Tribby had given me. "Get over to the precinct locker room and check out what Tribby said. I'm going back to Security to watch some TV."

We left the crime scene, with Carter continuing on to the main corridor as I peeled off and reentered the Security Office. There were still too many people inside. I found Tomlinson at the central monitor station with the Security duty officer and his staff huddled around him. I slipped behind the group and found a spot where I had a clear line of sight to the main monitor.

Tomlinson was complaining again.

"I'm telling you, Kelsey, you're running a horseshit operation down here and it's the reason why two cops are dead and a dangerous prisoner is loose in the city!"

"I can't explain it, Chief," Kelsey pleaded. "The cameras are working fine. There's no problem with them. It's the recording itself, it has to be."

"Brilliant! I already figured that one out! I've seen the damn tapes three times!"

From behind his entourage I asked, "Could you play them one more time, please?"

Tomlinson looked over his shoulder. Through the small crowd our eyes met and I could see he was still his same cheerful self, spreading overwhelming positivity for everyone working so hard to do the best they could.

"You got any answers for me, Culhane?" He scowled.

"Maybe one or two," I smiled back.

His response was best described as stoic. "Give me one good one and I'll replay the damn recording for you."

"Okay, how's this: they aren't cops."

The sudden silence was as thick as a Christmas fruitcake. Tomlinson's face froze in mid-scowl.

I elaborated. "Well, they aren't our cops, that's for sure. From what they wore and their weapons of choice, my guess is they could be Mossad agents, or maybe even German KSK."

With a look as if he'd just been slapped in the face, Tomlinson turned slightly in Kelsey's direction and mumbled, "Play the tape."

In a few seconds, the center monitor blinked back on with a full overhead view of the cellblock corridor I had just left. From below left, the two phony policemen walked into view with rifles raised.

Someone in the surrounding crowd said, "I still can't figure out how they got past security."

"They're cops," someone else answered. "They are security."

On the screen, the "cops" walked to within a few feet of Toors' cell door. With admirable agility and skillful legerdemain, the man on the right pulled a shaped charge from inside his shirt, calmly stuck it tightly above the door's handle and lock assembly and quickly pulled the pin. His physically economical movements testified to superior conditioning as he flattened himself against the door's wall well off to the right side. With an equal display of physical prowess, his partner assumed a similar protective position farther down on the opposite side from the cell door. The explosion was huge but directed. It blew the cell door wide open, swinging violently on its hinges and missing the first "cop" by mere inches as boiling gray-black plumes of dust and debris vomited from the cell, out into the hallway and clouded everything on the screen.

I leaned in closer and saw two dark shadows, weapons raised, rush through the smoke and dust into the cell, one man going low and covering the left, the second trailing close behind going in high and taking the right; both men firing full auto and sweeping the cell with back-and-forth sprays of lead.

Then, more suddenly, the interior of the cell blasted into brilliant radiating white light that beamed out through the door to explode into the hallway. The glare covered the screen and everyone in the room shielded their eyes only to have the screen image turn to static and then go blank.

Tomlinson turned to me. "End of tape. When the cameras came back on, those two guys were lying in the hallway outside the cell, dead and crispy. Got any ideas on what we just saw?"

I didn't have a clue. So I tap-danced. "Well, for sure our 'boys in blue' weren't cops. They were highly trained, highly conditioned tactical specialist with state-of-the-art weapons and technology. That means they were well financed – you don't get what they used at Army Surplus."

"We know that," Tomlinson was still not impressed. "What took them out?"

I shook my head. "I don't know: something they hadn't counted on; something better than they were."

The group parted to clear the way as Tomlinson came to his feet and glared at me. "You're not helping me, Culhane. It's your man, no one else. Somehow Toors had something, or did something, to make what happened, happen."

I didn't agree. "I don't think so, Chief…"

"That's your problem, Detective – you don't think!"

I resisted the very real urge to sock him in the nose. "Chief, it's possible whatever took those guys out also took care of Toors."

Tomlinson finally blew. "You idiot! Whadda ya think, that was some kinda death ray from a space gun? Some kinda little green alien beamed down and burned two guys but disintegrated your guy instead? Get your head out of your ass and start coming up with some answers on this! People are being killed and you're dreaming up fantasies instead of doing police work to stop all this!"

I could feel the eyes around the room watch all this in silence. If I did anything to assuage my own ego right then, like haul off and slug the guy, it would spread through the department like wildfire with a very good chance of adversely affecting the morale of the entire force. For sure, the resulting attention from the higher-ups would adversely affect me. Then, common sense prevailed. There was the singular fact that Tomlinson was in peak condition and could beat the crap out of me. After all, rank had its privileges, and what was true for me in 'Nam was still true now: mine was not to question why, mine was but to do or die.

More calmly, I suggested, "Maybe we should call in some State or Federal help on all this…"

Still steaming, Tomlinson cut me off. "We're not calling in the Feds or anyone else."

"I don't see how it could hurt."

He glared back at me. "Because, the bodies are crispies, remember? That's your territory. Now, get out there, find Toors and get him back here. Now!"

That pretty much ended the conversation. As I left the Security Office, from the way everyone else avoided direct eye contact with me, I knew chances were slim I could count on any support from the rank and file.

CHAPTER 5

D.C. VISITORS

Within minutes after the explosion in the cellblock, the order went out to lock down a ten-block radius around the city jail. It took quite a bit longer for the lock-down to take effect than training dictated. The APB for Toors that followed not only alerted the combined police departments of Minneapolis, St. Paul and surrounding suburbs, it also alerted every media outlet in the country to what had happened. The resulting hubbub clogged the streets beyond reason, as I witnessed when I exited the jail on the Fourth Street side. The place was a parking lot, sidewalks were choked with cops, civilians of all stripes and media people, many with microphones in hand and camera operators in tow grabbing whomever they could to get something on tape in time for the ten o'clock news.

The familiar voice of one of them came from behind my right side and suddenly I had trouble breathing.

"Sam, can we talk?"

My head turned toward the dark-eyed brunette holding a microphone in her hand and an uncertain, tentative smile. Behind her Jerry Switzer stood checking his camera settings.

I felt my knees weaken as I mustered all the nonchalance I could and said, "Hi, Shelly. What's new?"

She offered a nervous half-laugh. "Apparently, quite a bit. Just look at this place."

I did, quickly, and then returned immediately to her. "Yeah, it sure is something, isn't it?"

"Can I ask you about it?"

"Officially?" I asked a little too defensively.

"Of course." A twitch of another uncertain smile.

I hesitated for no reason. I knew I was going to do whatever she wanted me to do. I just wanted to look at her.

"Well, Shelly, I don't know what I'm allowed to tell you."

She shrugged. "It's painless. I'll ask the questions; you answer as best you can; if you can't say anything, say 'no comment.' It's as simple as that."

I looked at her again; my eyes followed the smooth curve of her neck, down her torso and back up again to those incredible brown eyes. I nodded.

Shelly turned to Switzer for some quick instructions, and then motioned toward the side of the building. "Over here?"

I nodded again and the three of us moved from the curb, skirting around several onlookers in the process.

She adjusted herself, checked over her shoulder and said to Switzer, "Get the jail's marquee in the background if you can."

Switzer nodded and made an adjustment in his angle as he lined me up in his viewfinder. He turned on the top-mounted camera lights and the glare almost blinded me.

Shelly prompted me some more. "We'll just jump right in, okay, Sam? I'll record the intro, wrap up and cut-aways after."

Squinting against the camera lights, I nodded once more.

She brought the microphone below her chin and went for the jugular straightaway. "Simon Toors is now an escaped prisoner and primary suspect in the Glenwood Avenue murders. How was his gang able to penetrate the jail, initiate a fire-fight and break him out of his cell to make good his escape?"

I felt my jaw drop and I blinked. "What?"

Her eyes bored into mine with an unspoken urge to answer the question and she pushed the microphone closer to my face. A half-laugh preceded my response.

"That's not what happened."

She rolled with it. "Would you explain that?"

THE LEPER

A nervous glance at the camera lens – *Don't look at the camera* – bounced back to Shelly. "Well, first, Mr. Toors is officially a person of interest in this case, not a primary suspect…"

The microphone jerked back to her face. "That's not what Division Chief Tomlinson has said."

The microphone jerked back to me. *Of course, Tomlinson's already spoken to the press.* I took a quick breath to collect myself and uneasily said, "Perhaps not, but it's the truth…"

The microphone jerked away. "Is it not also true that two police officers were killed in the firefight?"

The microphone came back, but I only shook my head as I waved at Switzer to switch off the camera. Shelly stepped back and nodded her approval to her cameraman. Switzer lowered the camera and doused the lights. I put my hand on her arm and she turned back to me.

"You've got this all wrong, Shel."

She firmly pulled her arm from my grasp. "Well, now's the chance to set the record straight."

"This isn't like you," I started to say. "You're rushing into this and you don't know the facts."

"Enlighten me," she snapped back. "But make it snappy, I have a deadline and it's late."

"I don't care about your deadline…"

"It's the biggest story of the year!" Her voice raised several levels, but she reined it back in. "I need something solid to run on and I need it now!"

I looked at her for a long moment, after which, in a lower voice I quietly said, "It's nice to be needed."

I couldn't tell if what I saw in her eyes was pity or spite, but something registered there. She leaned a shoulder against the wall of the building, took a long breath, and without breaking eye contact, handed her microphone to Switzer and pulled her digital audio recorder from her jacket pocket. She looked down at the settings, thumbed up a new file, pushed the record button and held the recorder up to me.

"Okay, Sam, tell me what you know."

My eyes never left hers as I gave her what I could.

"Simon Toors is a person of interest in the Glenwood Avenue killings. He was taken into custody last night for questioning only. There is no evidence of his direct involvement in the killings, but we proceeded on the basis that he was found in the immediate area of the latest deaths.

"While in custody, two armed men disguised as police officers compromised jail security and assaulted Toors' cell with automatic weapons and explosives. During the attack, the attackers themselves were killed, we don't know how. However, their physical condition resembles that of the Glenwood Avenue killings.

"Somehow, probably before the attack took place, Toors either escaped or was removed from his cell, at this time we aren't sure which."

She asked a double question. "Who were the attackers and what is being done to find Toors?"

"We're not sure who the two attackers were, but we're certain they were not cops. We also know the equipment they used was high-powdered and expensive. As for Toors, the department has a complete lock-down over the immediate area, and there's an all-points bulletin out to take him into custody. It's only a matter of time."

Shelly turned off the recorder and slid it back into her jacket pocket. "Thank you, Sam. I'll be able to use that."

"It's not much, but it is the truth, Shel."

She smiled reluctantly, stepped close and gently patted my chest. I wanted to believe her eyes held honest concern. "You look tired. You should get some sleep."

"Thanks."

With that, Shelly and her cameraman buttoned things up. She smiled when they left to make their way through the crowd and across a street full of barely moving vehicles toward the opposite curb where the blue and white Channel Six News van was parked. I waited, watching to see if she'd look back. She didn't. She walked around to the passenger side and climbed in without so much as a glance in the general direction of my side of the street.

Pulling the cell out, I speed-dialed Carter as I turned for the opposite corner. He answered after the first ring.

THE LEPER

"Got anything?"

"Tribby nailed it," he said. "Both lockers were jimmied. Both of the patrolmen, the real cops, came in for their nightshifts tonight and they say they're missing uniforms."

"Tell them they'll have to replace them." I reached the corner and crossed against the light. The traffic was gridlocked anyway, so it didn't matter. "Meet me at the car, okay?"

"You got it."

***

Carter was already sitting on the back bumper of the Crown Vic waiting for me by the time I got there. I used the remote fob to unlock the doors as I walked up. He got in on the passenger side and I climbed in behind the wheel, and then thought better of it.

"Maybe you should drive."

Carter asked why.

"Because I'm really tired. I don't trust myself. Besides, someone told me I should get some sleep."

"Yeah, you do look like shit," he said half-seriously. "I'll drive if you want, but I get to move the seat back."

"Forget it." I started the car. "You think I'm crazy enough to let you screw up my car? I'm not that tired."

"No," he said, fastening his seat belt. "But you are short."

Exiting up out of the underground parking ramp, I turned on Sixth Street and headed east. Sixth Street was a straight shot to the I94-35W spaghetti junction area and comparatively unencumbered with traffic. When I hung a right on Chicago Avenue at the Hubert Humphrey Metrodome, I was relieved to see the outgoing traffic was half that of the incoming flow, and the incoming flow was practically at a standstill.

"Where are we going, Sam?"

"If you were an Arab and wanted to blend in, where would you most likely go?"

"Lake and Chicago?"

I nodded. "Lake and Chicago. There're several places, but let's try the Holy Land Bakery first."

"Didn't you get enough at dinner?"

"I did, but I don't think Toors has eaten a thing since we took him in," I squeezed down on the accelerator modestly to slide through a yellow light at Eighth Street. "He admitted he's spent most of his time in Israel. Maybe he has a yen for some home cooking, who knows? In any case, he'll need a place where he won't stick out. As Tomlinson would say, 'There's a lot of ragheads on East Lake Street.'"

Carter slid back in his seat, rested his head against the backrest and closed his eyes. "How quaint. Wake me when we get there."

The Holy Land Bakery & Deli was located in the Midtown Global Market, formerly the old Sears Building located on East Lake Street on the near south side. Originally constructed in 1928, the Sears Building was a huge multi-story brick and concrete edifice. In 2006, fully twelve years after Sears, Roebuck and Company had left the neighborhood, the redevelopment of the building's 1.2 million square feet was completed and the Midtown Global Market opened for business. Housing retail food, produce and merchandise businesses, a hospital-clinic and a mix of housing, hotel and government services, the complex served as a hub for Middle Eastern and African/Somali based commerce.

On Lake Street just west of the main entrance of the place, I poked the nose of the Crown Vic tight behind a beat-up Chevy with a rear bumper that overlapped into a no parking/load zone effectively boxing the car in. Despite the civilian package, the Crown Vic still looked like the cop car it was, so we left it there confident any passing patrol car would leave both it and the Chevy alone.

Inside the market, we headed straight for the bakery and the dark-haired Somali, Hassani Ebadat, behind her cash register, counting up the receipts for the night. It was almost closing time.

"Hassani, got a minute?" I asked as Carter and I made the turn into her shop.

She looked up from her paperwork with a suspicious squint and replied, "I guess I do; for the police."

THE LEPER

I leaned across the counter with elbows on the glass and smiled. "Suppose I were an Arab in need of some food and a place to stay for the night. Where would I want to go?"

She flashed a brilliant full-teeth grin. "You're looking for your lost friend, I take it."

Carter and I shared a quick, knowing glance. Hassani laughed.

"Don't be surprised I know this," she said. "Word travels fast around here and everyone has been paying attention since you took him in yesterday."

"Comforting," Carter pulled the mug shot of Toors from his inside coat pocket and placed it on the counter in front of her. "This is what he looks like. Have you seen him?"

She leaned over for a closer look, but didn't touch the photo at all. After a moment, she stood erect and shook her head.

"Do you know how many African- and Middle Eastern-owned businesses there are on Lake Street between here and Uptown?" She asked seriously. "Over five hundred. What makes you think he would come here?"

"Great cuisine?" I asked. "I was hoping he was a regular here."

Hassani leaned over the photo once more. "He looks better on TV, but, no. Not here. Although, if he's a rich Arab, you might look at the Hilton."

"He's a janitor," I said.

Carter retrieved the mug shot and returned it to his coat pocket. "What if he's not rich? What if he's been injured, or maybe shot? Where would he go then?"

She shrugged and turned back to her paperwork. "You might want to look in at the clinic here. The hotel has rooms by the night or week, so you should check there, too."

"Anything out of the ordinary happen around here tonight?" I asked, fishing my card out of my wallet.

"No, not really," Hassani admitted. "Business quieted down after the first television news bulletin about the bombing at the jail. After that, everyone left to watch TV to see if it was some kind of Jewish/Christian terrorist group, or something. I should put flat screens in this place – I'd keep more customers that way."

She laughed again, and added, "That's a joke."

"Which, the 'Jewish/Christian' thing or the TVs?" I smiled, leaving my card on the counter. "If you notice anything you think could help, especially if you see him, call me, okay?"

"I guess I will," she said, taking the card from the counter and pocketing it. "For the police."

We left the way we had come. In the Commons, patron traffic had diminished considerably. At a large backlit directory with its monochromatic floor plan, I compared the indicated "You are here" red-circled dot with the designated locations for the clinic and hotel.

"Hotel at the middle on the east side; clinic way in the back." I checked my wristwatch. "It's twenty to ten, already."

"Time flies," Carter commented dryly. "You think she's going to help at all, even if Toors shows up?"

"Doubtful," I admitted reluctantly. "Let's save some time here and split up."

"Agreed. I'll take the hotel."

"Your legs are longer. You should take the clinic in the back of the place."

"You're too slow," Carter grinned broadly as he quickly stepped away in an easterly direction. "I already have dibs on the hotel."

I resigned myself to the trek toward the rear of the complex. When I got there the clinic's lights were off and the doors were locked. I cupped my hands and looked through the entry glass for any sign of life. The place was closed up for the night. I pulled out my cell phone and called Carter.

"You got anything at the hotel?" I asked when he answered.

"Besides the fact they're less than half-occupied, no – not much. The desk clerk just came on duty, and the other guy's split. No one here has seen our guy, or so they say."

"You think they're lying?"

"I think 'birds of a feather stick together.'"

"I hope you're wrong, cuz we've come up dry on this lame effort. Any ideas?"

I heard Carter's chuckle. "I could use a drink."

"Not around here." I started the trip back to the front of the market. "Muslim territory, you know. Let's head over to the Third Precinct. There's that old fashion lounge place across Minnehaha."

"Ah, Hooker-Haven. Makes me feel clean all over just thinking about it."

I scolded him. "Complain, complain, complain."

***

We settled on the bowling alley on Twenty-seventh Avenue, three blocks north of the Third Precinct. At least the bar offered padded chairs at low tables. I chose a spot where I could keep an eye on the walk-in traffic and check out anyone new. Business was good with the rhythmic roll of heavy bowling balls and the cacophonous punctuation of pins scattering muted by the glass wall dividing the bar from the recreational side of the establishment. We sat nursing our beers, both of us pleasantly surprised – they served Grain Belt Nordeast on tap!

"I hope you're connected in the Muslim community," Carter was grumbling again. "Cuz, I'm sure not. I have no clue how we find this guy."

"Sorry, Carter, I'm afraid I used up my quota of community informants with Hassani."

"Great," Carter took another slow sip. "Things are shaping up. We're in trouble. Again."

At that moment, the newscast running on the suspended flat screen to my right switched to an on-location report and a waist-high shot of Shelly filled the screen. I immediately left my chair, darted to the TV and shouted to the bartender to turn up the volume. Carter came up behind me as the audio level increased. Shelly was in mid-report.

"... and this man, Simon Toors..."

On the screen Shelly was replaced by the grainy mug shot of Simon Toors.

"... identified by Detective Samuel Culhane of the Homicide Division of the Minneapolis Police Department ..."

My photo appeared next to Toors'.

"… as a person of interest in the recent series of grizzly deaths known as the Glenwood Avenue Murders …"

"Old photo," Carter criticized. "No way you're that young looking anymore."

I ignored him as the photos disappeared and Shelly returned.

"… and as such, not a primary suspect as earlier reported by other news sources. Detective Culhane believes Mr. Toors either escaped or was removed from his jail cell before the actual attack took place…"

My photo again appeared on the screen.

"Detective Culhane also informed me that the attackers were well armed with automatic weapons and explosives, some of which may have exploded accidently possibly causing the deaths of both attackers…"

I shook my head. She had made up that last part on her own.

"Police have confirmed the attackers, disguised in police uniforms, were not Minneapolis police officers and efforts are underway to identify the bodies. A citywide manhunt is now underway to find Simon Toors and take him into custody.

"Reporting from downtown Minneapolis, Shelly Culhane, Channel Six News."

"Wonderful," Carter groused. "'SC' finks out on 'SC.' You're screwed, you know that don't you?"

"Yeah, but we saved a bundle on the monogrammed sheets and pillow cases, didn't we?" My cell phone warbled. I fished it from my pocket and answered, "This is Culhane."

"Your ex just made you a media star," Tomlinson stated flatly. I could hear the disgust in his voice, but at least he didn't scream it. Tomlinson continued. "I just got off a conference call with the mayor and the city attorney. We're scheduled for a meeting first thing in the morning in the mayor's office. Be there by eight."

The line went dead.

"Things just keep getting better," I stared at the open phone in my hand. "Wanna attend a scolding at the mayor's office tomorrow?"

Carter arched a questioning eyebrow. "Was I invited?"

"Not really."

"I respectfully decline. What's next?"

I had no idea, so the phone went back into my pocket and we walked back to our table to finish our beers.

***

From where I had parked the Crown Vic – in the ramp across from the County Government Center on Fifth Street and Fourth Avenue – it was a block and a half sprint to City Hall just as the skies opened up. The torrential downpour plastered and matted my hair to my skull and drenched the sport coat. When I finally squished my way into City Hall, I made straight for the nearest men's room to tidy up. What I saw in the mirror gave a whole new definition to "What the cat drug in." Using paper hand towels from the dispenser, I patted the water out of my hair and then tried to comb out the mess with just my fingers. The result was a Mafioso-like slicked-back look; all I was missing was the fedora. I took my jacket off and draped it over one arm, checking out the image in the mirror. The wet darkness of a V-shaped neck-to-belt triangle on my broadcloth shirt stood out worse without the jacket. I put the jacket back on and snugged the tie tighter. It didn't help much.

I was tardy by five minutes when Mayor Oslander greeted me with a smile and handshake.

"Detective Culhane." His grin was almost syrupy as he took my hand. "Got caught in the rain, I see."

Profound! I swiped away a bead of moisture sliding from my hairline and smiled back. "It's only water, Mr. Mayor. It'll dry."

The mayor's office wasn't big enough. Despite the old-style spaciousness the place offered with its third-floor overlook of Fourth Street, there was barely enough seating capacity to handle everyone. Mayor Harvey Oslander had apparently arrived early, as had the city attorney, Warren Jabs. Tomlinson had been on the dot at eight o'clock making the short trek from the downtown precinct and protecting himself from a now driving rainstorm with a sturdy, full-sized umbrella. Also in attendance were Police Commissioner Mason James and Hennepin County District

Attorney James Horstfelder, both of whom stayed dry by taking the tunnel from their respective offices to City Hall.

I felt the other eyes following me as the mayor showed me to the last remaining seat to be had in the room: the right hand corner of the mayor's desk next to Tomlinson. The two government attorneys and the police commissioner shared the sofa next to the window. Outside, a lightning flash preceded the sudden thunderclap by less than a second and everyone jerked in their seats.

"I guess that's our cue to start," the mayor chuckled, taking a seat behind his desk. "Thanks to everyone for coming this morning. The purpose of this meeting is to review the facts concerning yesterday's attack on the jail and to help all of us get on the same page insofar as to what has to be done from this point on to successfully apprehend the escaped fugitive."

Mayor Oslander turned to the sofa on his right. "Mason, perhaps you'd like to start?"

I understood in his younger years, Mason James played college football for the University of Minnesota. Now city police commissioner and well into middle age, excessive weight and a pair of arthritic knees scheduled for knee replacement surgery in June noticeably encumbered his large frame. Understandably, he remained seated as he kicked things off.

"Thank you, Mr. Mayor," he began, directing his smiling face in my general direction. "It goes without saying that last night's excitement has touched all our lives. I have personally fielded telephone calls from our mayor, the state lieutenant governor, the governor and more local media reporter-types than I can list, including those from the major wire services. I'm sure many of you have had the opportunity to experience similar demands on your time."

The two attorneys nodded silently, Tomlinson cleared his throat while the mayor chuckled again.

The commissioner directed his steady gaze and humorless smile at the chief. "Frankly, in this situation, insofar as specific information is concerned there's little I can offer all these folks. For that, I have to rely on Chief Tomlinson."

Never one to mince words, Tomlinson's defensive response was quick and deferring. "I answered every call, Mason. You knew what I knew as soon as I knew it."

"That's very reassuring," James responded pointedly. "Who gave the USA TODAY reporter that little tidbit about the attackers actually trying to break the suspect out of jail?"

That caught my attention. It was the same misinformation Shelly had approached me with last night.

"It wasn't me!" Tomlinson's head turned and I could feel his heated glare bore into the side of my head. "I'm not the one with family ties to the media in this town."

All eyes turned to me. I cleared my throat, crossed one leg over the other and looked out at the steady downpour outside the large window behind the sofa, hoping they'd think I was coolly looking at them instead.

The mayor opined, "You know, Samuel, the chief makes an interesting point. Judging from the channel six ten o'clock news last night, you evidently did spend a little camera time with your ex."

My tight grin confirmed what everyone already knew, but I said nothing.

"Maybe more than 'camera time,' eh, Culhane?" That came from Horstfelder, the county DA.

The tight grin loosened a tad as I directed a warning glance back to the DA. He decided to ignore it.

"If there is any evidence of police incompetence or malfeasance in this matter, I will prosecute to the fullest extent of the law," warned the DA. "The public deserves better from our law enforcement agencies and I'll make sure they get it."

I sighed and said nothing.

Apparently, it was Warren Jabs' turn next. The Minneapolis city attorney, a mousy little man with a receding hairline, leaned forward, clasped his hands together in heavy concern and earnestly stressed the importance of protecting the city.

"If evidence shows that any kind of police department error contributed to what happened last night, I'm afraid the city will be exposed to great risk of loss. This is especially true if the escapee damages private property, or worse, injures or even kills someone before being apprehended. Litigation against the city will be practically assured and police and city officials alike will be held corporately accountable. The financial cost to the city in legal fees alone would be substantial."

The mayor tapped his desk blotter with a ballpoint pen. "So what's important now is not recriminations but agreement on what is being done and what needs to be done to find this guy and get him back into his cell. Am I right in this?"

The three on the couch all nodded. Tomlinson squirmed in his chair. I just looked at the others and wished I wasn't there.

The mayor looked to Tomlinson. "So what's being done?"

Tomlinson stated the facts. "We have an APB out for Toors; we've alerted state and federal law enforcement agencies. We have sent units to the suspect's place of employment and his last known residence. We've talked to anyone who knows the guy or where he might be. So far, it seems he isn't too well known by very many people; apparently keeps to himself a lot. We also have taken blood and DNA samples to help match up Toors with the victims. As yet, results are inconclusive."

"He's probably long gone by now," I grumbled. "If he returns to anywhere it'll be Chicago. That was where he came from, at least most recently."

The mayor turned to me. "I understand from last night's news reports, you don't believe Toors is the killer."

I shook my head. "No. He's not the guy. But Toors may know who the guy is. He certainly knows more about the killings than he has said."

The mayor arched an eyebrow. "And why do you think that?"

I shrugged, quickly deciding not to reveal anything about Toors instantaneously appearing on the water plant steps. "A feeling, really. From the way he avoids answering questions; the way he doesn't say some things while saying others. Then, of course, there's the attention he draws."

That brought a repeat raised eyebrow from the mayor. "What sort of attention?"

I failed to contain a critical snicker. "You don't really think those guys were trying to bust him out of jail last night, do you?

They came after him. They knew exactly where he was supposed to be. Even I didn't know which cell he was in, but they knew. How? They walked past security carrying explosives and high-capacity automatic weapons. They were well-trained, hit the jail cell hard and fast, and they both got killed in the process."

From the sofa, James interrupted. "Killed by their own explosives, not by any of our people."

"Nice cover story," I shot back. "Keep using it. It's baloney, but it works for now. The fact is, we don't know how they were killed. We only know they were crispy."

"Like the others?" the mayor asked.

I answered in the affirmative.

The commissioner disputed it. "How do we know for sure their own explosives didn't do the job?"

I sighed in frustration, leaned back in my chair, threw up my hands and let Tomlinson take over.

"Lack of secondary explosion damage to the cell, Mason," Tomlinson answered more calmly.

With frustration growing, I kicked in a chip: "That, plus the fact the bodies were intact – no missing parts; oh, and then there's the other little thing: bombs don't cause massive bacterial infection, blistering or pervasive cellular breakdown of skin and nerve tissues!"

The commissioner didn't blink. "I guess I haven't seen the ME's report on that, yet."

"Cut Tribby some slack," I growled. "He's a little backed up right now."

The mayor felt the need to cool things down a notch. "Okay, let's calm it down a bit and consider what we need to do now. Suggestions, anyone?"

The commissioner was the first to jump in. "Perhaps a new lead investigator is in order."

I shot him a dirty look. "You wanna blame me for what happened, is that it? You think that will keep you safe?"

The mayor interceded before James could respond. "No one's blaming anyone, Sam. We just need to know what's best to do next and stay ahead of things."

"Keeping the press out of it would be wise," City Attorney Jabs offered, tossing another look in my direction.

"With so much of this already in the media," the Mayor responded, "putting a lid on the press now would be problematic at best."

"More like impossible if you ask me," Mason James said, his knees causing obvious discomfort. He adjusted his seated position on the sofa as he continued. "Too much has leaked out already and putting the cat back in the bag isn't going to be added to the list. It would be better to control the press. Limit their access."

Mayor Oslander raised a pointed finger of inspiration in response. "We designate a press ombudsman; one person acting as the city's authorized source for the press."

James added. "Someone close to the front lines on this, but in authority as well. We need someone who is already known and respected by the press."

Eyes turned toward Tomlinson. In turn, Mark met each with an unspoken assuredness.

"No problem," he said calmly. "They know me and I know what to say to keep them in line."

"That means," James swung his attention back toward me, "everyone else defers to the chief. Anyone from the press wants to talk to you about what's going on, you tell that person to talk to the chief. No special treatment for anyone, especially ex-wives."

Suddenly, we were back where we started.

"She asked me a question," I defended weakly. "I told her what I thought I could to help."

"Them," James returned sharply. "To help them, you mean."

"I meant 'us,' too, Commissioner."

"You didn't clear it with anyone!" He bellowed. "We don't need you using department procedures to smooth out your marital problems, Culhane. We need to steer the media in the proper directions!"

"The press doesn't need to be told what directions to take on anything," I sprang to my feet in protest, glad to know the commissioner's knees prevented him from doing the same.

"They'll figure that out themselves; probably a lot quicker than we will."

The commissioner fell back into the sofa. "We don't tell them, they won't know. It's that simple. Tomlinson will see to it. That way, we keep them in line and get the job done without them mucking things up. Right now, they're focused on Toors. On their own with no help, they won't deviate from that track."

"Think not?" My temper got the best of me as I blurted out too quickly, "Try this on for size: there's one thing all of us in this room know for absolute certainty about last night's assault on the jail – those guys had help. Despite what some might hope exists concerning police incompetence, there's no way armed assailants disguised as police officers just walk in without someone on the inside helping them. The next thing to do, and the press will be working this angle if they aren't already, is find out who the inside person is."

"What about Toors?" James bellowed back.

"Screw Toors!" I barked. "The attack on the jail is a separate crime! Follow where the trail leads and find the inside man!"

James leveled a pointed finger at me. "You said yourself, the attackers were crispy."

"They died in a similar way to the Glenwood Avenue killings," I admitted. "But what they did in the jail is in no way related to the earlier deaths."

"How do you figure that?" James roared back with his prima facie point. "They're crispy!"

My volume level matched his. "Because, the jail isn't on Glenwood Avenue! It's not anywhere near it! The MOs don't match up! The attack was unlike any of the previous deaths. There's only one common link between the jail and the latest crispy and I'm on it!"

The commissioner scoffed. "Which is what, exactly?"

"Simon Toors!"

That stopped the commissioner for about two beats. That was when he laid on me an obvious implied threat, "So find him. Get him back into custody."

I returned to my chair and sat back down. "I'm working on it."

"Not good enough," James added in conclusion.

Tomlinson leaned over and whispered to me: "Let it go."

"So," the mayor interjected with a smile. "Step one: we find our missing suspect and pursue the link with the Glenwood Avenue killings. Step two: we launch a quiet investigation to find the inside person or persons who aided the attackers in penetrating jail security and follow wherever that may lead, confident the two efforts will intersect soon in a satisfactory manner. Are we agreed?"

James wasn't happy. "Step two requires IA involvement. If we got a bad cop in this mess, we need Internal Affairs on top of things leading the way."

Tomlinson agreed. "No problem. I'll liaison directly with IA."

I looked across to the window and said nothing. Outside, rivulets of rainwater still streamed down the glass.

"Well, then, we're agreed!" The mayor announced with a smile. "Anyone have anything to add?"

Tomlinson spoke up. "I'll have Cathy announce a press conference for this afternoon in time to make the six o'clock news. That should give me plenty of time to draft out the text and get it to you, Mr. Mayor, and the commissioner here for review."

Another fifteen minutes was wasted with a back-and-forth gabfest about who should be copied on Tomlinson's notes for the press conference and whether or not others in the room should also be included in the press conference itself. The mousy city attorney wanted to be included to make sure the city was protected; the commissioner and his bad knees wanted to make sure the MPD chief of police was brought in from his Caribbean cruise vacation. The DA stated flatly he would not be part of the event because, as the chief prosecutor for the county, the potential for city or police department malfeasance in any of this could later present an embarrassing conflict of interest for his office. The mayor proposed Tomlinson lead the press conference with the commissioner and mayor standing behind him for support. If a reporter asked a question not addressed to Tomlinson, the person asked would defer to the division chief. The proposal delivered a note of agreement and finality to the meeting. I was just glad the meeting was finally over.

I tried to be the first one out the door, but Tomlinson's hand on my elbow stopped me.

"We need to talk," he said as people began to leave. "Let's share my umbrella back to the office, okay?"

The mayor walked up with a smile and an extended hand in my direction. "I have an umbrella you can use, Sam. Hang around for a moment, will you?"

I took his hand and shook it, grateful for the excuse to delay the confab with Tomlinson.

Tomlinson nodded with acceptance. "See you back at the precinct right away, okay?"

I agreed with a nod, stepped off to the side and watched him bring up the rear of the small migration shuffling from the office. Tomlinson looked back at me when his hand reached the door.

"I won't be long," I assured him. The division chief closed the door behind him.

"I wanted to apologize," the mayor began, returning to his desk to pick up the phone receiver and press a single button on the base. "Joan, would you bring in some coffee and a couple of cups, please? Thank you."

I returned to my chair, sat down and crossed my legs. "Apologize for what, Mr. Mayor?"

He smiled. A shadow of regret, or something like it, seemed to be there. "Harvey, please. My friends call me Harvey."

"I appreciate that." I patted the front of my shirt and pulled at the tie to smooth out the wrinkles the rain had brought. The shirt was almost dry. "Does this mean we're friends now?"

"I hope so," my new friend smiled again as his secretary walked in with a small tray holding a chrome thermal coffee server, two ceramic cups, separate containers for packets of dry creamer and sugar. The tray went to the low table in the middle of the room and Joan quickly poured two cups. "Thank you, Joan. We'll take it from here."

Alone again, the mayor came around the desk, grabbed one of the cups, a spoon and two packets of sweetener. He returned to the desk. "I thought they were pretty rough on you about your wife. I'm sorry for that. Family is out of bounds, or should be."

With a sideways grin, I offered, "Well, as one friend to another, people standing out of bounds make easy targets."

"You don't trust me, do you, Sam?" He tore open both packets in the same movement, unceremoniously dumped the contents into his cup and swirled the mixture with two quick turns of the spoon.

I leaned forward, retrieved the remaining cup and took a sip. Black coffee straight up: there're few things better. "Don't let it bother you, Harvey. I don't trust anyone."

A smile and a small laugh: "Ah, yes. I see. Wise policy. I'm concerned, though."

"Welcome to the club," I took another appreciative sip and nodded. "What concerns you so?"

The mayor returned to his chair and sampled his coffee. There was a small tilt of an approving nod. "I know you're very close to this whole mess…"

"Comes with the job."

"Yes, I can understand. Your observations about the attackers and inside help they obviously had were profound."

I disagreed. "Profoundly obvious, you mean."

"No one else brought it up."

"That's because everyone else is scared. The attack on the jail adds a whole new dimension to everything and ripples across everyone's jurisdictions. The Glenwood Avenue killings were one thing. Last night's assault on the jail was something else. The fact that the two are linked threatens everyone on the political food chain. You saw how quickly the commissioner brought in Internal Affairs. He's counting on IA to cover his ass. Tomlinson will support the mole hunt to the hilt for the same reason. Both of them know where this is going to lead and it scares them. Heads are going to roll on this."

"You scared, Sam?"

"Not really," I admitted. "I'm actually relieved, Mr. Mayor."

"Harvey," he corrected me again.

"Yes, Harvey. Well, just between us friends, the investigation of the Glenwood Avenue killings was stalling out too quickly. With every new crispy we found, we had fewer answers. The deaths are almost sanitary in everything except the gruesome physical consequences. There are no real clues and fewer leads to follow. All of it was going nowhere. The first two victims were easy – both of them carried IDs and getting background info on them was a snap. They were bad characters, no question. But the third one, the crispy found near the water plant, was different. He was picked clean – no ID and nothing to point us in a specific direction for us to follow. But instead of normal civilian dress like the first two, the third was in a BDU…"

"B-D-U?"

"Sorry: it's a military acronym for battle dress uniform. He wore a Kevlar vest with a bulletproof ceramic shield insert. State-of-the-art stuff and that's significant."

"Why?"

"Because our visitors to the jail last night wore the same type of gear. All three of them were dressed for survival success in a firefight situation and it didn't do any of them any good. Whoever their tailor is, I bet he's pissed."

The mayor pinched the corner of an eyebrow between thumb and forefinger as he considered what I had just shared.

"Sounds like a conspiracy," he said.

I frowned as I said, "Yes, kinda does, doesn't it?"

"You're not happy about that?"

I shrugged. "Yes and no. It's true our little drama now has a third actor no one knows and that complicates things. One thing is certain though."

"What's that?"

"Whoever the third actor is, he's from a fairly exclusive club. Not too many people have access to the kind of money needed to equip a small army of covert operatives with the type of gear we've seen over that last forty-eight hours."

"I see," the mayor acknowledged. "But there's something else that's certain, too, Sam."

"What's that?"

"Every other person who left this room this morning is figuring ways to make sure a big target is pinned to your backside. If you're right about them covering their own asses, they'll do it by making sure you take the fall on this. If or when everything hits the fan, like it or not, Sam, the first head that's going to roll will be yours."

***

"Nice umbrella," Cathy Werness commented as I walked through the division's doorway. A twenty-year veteran of city administrative services, for as long as I had been with the department Cathy Werness had been Tomlinson's right-hand person. Widowed with no children, she was the 'job' in every way you could define it. If she was older than I was, she sure didn't look it. "Too bad you didn't wear a trench coat, too. It looks like you could've used it."

I slid the locking clasp up and down to shake out as much remaining moisture as I could before clicking the umbrella all the way down and shutting it.

"It's the mayor's. He let me borrow it," I explained, following with, "and I don't have a trench coat."

Cathy shook her head. "Too bad. You'd look just like Humphrey Bogart in one."

"You mean, sexy and mysterious?"

"No," Carter said, emerging from our cubicles hiding behind the corner. "She means all wet and short. Have a nice time at the mayor's office this morning?"

"Next time, you go and I stay away." I handed the folded umbrella to Cathy. "Please hold onto this for me so I don't forget to get it back to the mayor."

She took the thing with her customary pleasantry: "It's so nice to feel needed."

I replied with my customary, "I'd be lost without you."

With customary modesty, she agreed. "Yes, you would."

I turned back to Carter. "I have to check in with Tomlinson before anything else."

Cathy raised a finger. "He has visitors in with him now."

"What kind of visitors?"

"The official-looking kind," Carter answered.

"FBI," Cathy added more specifically.

I raised a sincere eyebrow of appreciation. "Ah, the chief's moving up in the world. It must have to do with what happened last night."

"You're so perceptive," Cathy agreed with a sarcastic nod.

I pumped my shoulders with a James Cagney shrug and snugged my tie up tight. "They can't stick their Fed noses into my case without me in there. I'm going in. How do I look?"

"Damp," Cathy observed honestly.

I ignored her and turned to Carter. "Wanna come along?"

"Why, just to hear him berate you again, only this time with the Feds sitting in on it? Wait a minute; let me think about that for a moment. Okay, you talked me into it."

The heavy overcast and the steady rain still falling outside muted the majesty of all that woodwork and the three flags in Tomlinson's office. The overhead fluorescent lighting colored everything with a pale bluish tint, including the two suits sitting in the two stuffed chairs facing Tomlinson's desk.

The visitors turned in our direction as Carter and I walked in. Tomlinson looked up. "Ah, good, you're done with your little chat with the mayor. What did he have to say?"

With the visitors already sitting in our customary seats, Carter took the far corner of the sofa. I choose to stand behind and to the right of the farthest Fed, forcing him to turn the opposite way to see me.

"Hi," I said extending my hand. "I'm Sam Culhane"

He was hair follicle-y challenged and even from his seated position I could tell he was tall, so I felt justified in contributing to his uncomfortable contortion as he wrenched sideways to shake my hand. "Wayne Stephens, FBI, Washington. We were just talking about you."

"Nothing good, I hope," I replied with a smile and turned to his somewhat younger and more hirsute partner coming to his feet to shake my extended hand. Thankfully, like me this guy was average height.

"Rupert F. Anderson," he said with a genuine smile. "Minneapolis FBI office."

"It's a pleasure," I gestured over to Carter on the sofa. "The tall drink of water over there is my partner, Carter Wolpren."

Carter tipped two fingers to his right eyebrow in a silent, disinterested salute.

I turned back to Tomlinson. "So you're talking about me, Chief? Words of praise, maybe a raise in the works?"

Under his breath Carter said to no one, "If he gets a raise, so do I."

Tomlinson displayed his usual humor. "Whatever you and the mayor covered after the meeting, from your cheery disposition I have to assume it wasn't the ass-chewing I was hoping for. What'd you guys talk about?"

"The long and short of it was," I turned a wary and more sober eye to our Federal friends, "the mayor told me to watch my back."

"Maybe these guys can help," Tomlinson pointed to the Feds. "Stephens, here, says the FBI is making their services available to us."

From his corner of the sofa, Carter offered, "How generous of them. Why would they do that?"

Anderson almost said something but stopped himself as Stephens answered instead. "It's part of the Homeland Security provisions. You know: cross-agency cooperation, information exchange, that kind of stuff. We're here to open the door, in a manner of speaking; help you out with your investigation and collar your escaped suspect before he does any real harm."

I walked around the left side of Tomlinson's desk and looked out the window. It was still raining heavily. The night before in the jail, Tomlinson had told me he didn't want outside agencies involved in this. Now, two FBI pukes were sitting in his office. I wondered if a higher-up was encouraging Tomlinson to shake things up a bit.

"The investigation of the Glenwood Avenue killings has been going on for some time," I said, turning from the rain outside the window to Stephens directly. "Why all the interest now?"

Stephens didn't blink. "Well, frankly, until last night, we didn't know all that much about your investigation."

"And now you do?" That came from Carter.

Anderson stayed quiet as Stephens shrugged. "You guys made the news. What can I say?"

I turned to Tomlinson. "Shoot straight with me, Chief: someone been leaning on you about our investigation, what we've done or haven't done?"

Tomlinson's eyes locked onto mine, but at the critical moment, he looked away as he said, "If that were true, I would have told you."

I knew the chief to be three things: loud, suspicious and, when it came to his career, conspiratorially paranoid. At that moment, I learned something new: he was a terrible liar.

"Good enough for me," I lied. To Stephens I asked, "So how do we unwrap this gift from Big Brother?"

I didn't much care for Stephens' cold half-smile as he said, "That's why we're here. I wanted to meet with your team and introduce Rupert. He'll be your main contact."

I nodded to the FBI's Minneapolis section head. "Welcome to the minors, Rupert."

Rupert's objection was almost apologetic. "It's not like that, Detective. We just want to help any way we can."

A mild, throat-clearing cough came from Carter's corner of the sofa. It was a welcomed opportunity to direct the FBI's help.

"That's good," I acknowledged a little too enthusiastically. "Lord knows we could use some help on this, especially now. Maybe you guys could do some bird-dogging on the attackers for us. They're a new wrinkle in all of this and we haven't a clue where they came from."

Stephens showed one too many cards with his next statement.

"I don't know about that, Detective. Word has it they were part of Toors' gang…"

Carter shoehorned in a pointed comment. "Toors has a gang?"

Noticing what Carter said, but not missing a beat, Stephens continued. "They provided a diversion for Toors to make good his escape. Too bad they blew themselves up in the process. We could've got something from them."

"You might want to talk with our ME about that," I suggested seriously. "I can call down and tell him your coming."

Stephens looked as Rupert nodded and said, "Yeah, good idea."

"As for Toors," I offered. "My hunch is he's making his way back to Chicago, if he's not already there."

That caught Stephens' attention. "Chicago? Why Chicago?"

"Last known place of residence," I answered. "Apparently lived there for some time. May have family or some other kind of support there that he doesn't have here."

"That's a little thin," Stephens commented dryly. "Of course, psychos are known to return to their former haunts for other reasons. Don't know if that applies to Muslim extremists, though. Wouldn't hurt to run a check on Chicago area murders with the same MO. I'll see what I can turn up."

I almost said, "You do that" but I caught myself. "That could be very helpful, Agent Stephens."

The cold smile said, "Please, call me Wayne."

"Well, then," Tomlinson spoke up. "Sounds like a good place to start. Carter, why not take these gentlemen down to meet with Tribby, cover the facts on the crispies and get them up to speed on things?"

Carter and I exchanged wary glances as he said, "Sure, Chief, happy to do it."

The chief turned to me. "Sam, hang loose here for a moment, will you? I'll be right back."

The matched pair of Mutt and Jeff's left the office together. I almost chuckled as I returned to the window to contemplate the rain along with what was coming next. It didn't take long.

Tomlinson shut the door none too gently and returned to his side of the desk but didn't sit down. Instead, his fist hit the desktop more than firmly. "Damn it, Culhane, you're purposely trying to make me look bad in all of this!"

"Absolutely not," I denied calmly, avoiding his glare as I flapped my still damp sport coat to hasten the drying process. I took a whiff from a sleeve. A polyester/wool blend weave, the jacket now had a faint, unpleasant musty odor. "Really high humidity today. Nothing's drying out."

"Whadda ya think that little circle-jerk in the mayor's office this morning was all about, anyway?" Tomlinson's anger-meter moved up a few clicks as his fist hit the desktop once more. "They're using this whole crappy mess to get rid of me!"

"Interesting. I thought they were all after me and my ex-wife."

"Smokescreen! What are you, blind?!"

I leaned against the window frame and smiled back at him. "Ah, there he is…"

"There's who?!" Tomlinson barked.

"The same old Chief I've grown to appreciate so well, that's who. You had me going there for a while, what with all that 'Minnesota-nice' BS with those FBI pukes."

Tomlinson sank into his chair, drew both hands down his face in frustration and moaned in resignation, "Yeah, you're right. I almost puked a couple of times myself."

"What were they doing here?"

"They were waiting for me when I got back from the mayor's meeting," the chief explained. "Out of nowhere. I thought you called them in."

"I wouldn't do that, Mark." I leaned toward him and made sure he looked at me. "I know you don't believe it, but there's no reason for you to think I would do that."

"Then how'd they know? Someone had to tell them." Tomlinson looked like a defeated prizefighter still on his feet, but fully aware the fight was lost. "You don't believe that stuff about seeing us on the news do you?"

"Not even a little bit," I answered plainly. "No, someone told Stephens. Wayne-Baby is honchoing this gig, but someone else is in charge, no doubt about it."

Tomlinson chuckled. "It ain't Rupert."

I laughed, too. "No, is certainly isn't Rupert."

"What kind of parent names their kid 'Rupert' anyway?"

"I don't think I want to know."

Grim seriousness shadowed Tomlinson's features. "We have to find Toors, Sam."

Outside the window the rain fell harder.

"I know."

CHAPTER 6

BEER AND CRISPIES

The rain continued throughout the first day and well into the second, causing extensive flooding across the metro area. Most of the city's low-lying intersections became impassible; and where major thoroughfares dipped under overpasses, runoff formed lakes so deep no vehicle could pass and many abandoned cars were visible only at their rooftops. Roadside gutters became rushing rivers with currents strong enough to lift parked cars and deposit them on boulevards, against trees, or even on top of other vehicles. Culverts and drains became submerged depositories for maelstrom debris so voluminous city maintenance gave up trying to keep them clear. This succeeded in making conditions worse, and a local weather forecaster's clever turn of a phrase to describe the metro area's plight became a banner headline for both the Minneapolis and St. Paul newspapers the next day: "Lake Minnesota!"

During the two days of torrential rain flooding the city streets, emergency calls flooded the 911 switchboards. Fire and EMT vehicles plowed through axle-deep water only to stall out when the depths became too great and waves engulfed engine compartments. More than one health emergency was rescued with the aid of a neighbor's duck boat or canoe.

I was late getting into the office the second day, not because of the rain – my condo was walking distance from the downtown precinct – but because of a prolonged telephone argument with my landlord over next month's scheduled rent increase. As far as landlords go, Bliss was a nice enough guy. Older and retired, he lived off Social Security and the net proceeds from the rents on three condos he owned in the same downtown high rise off Washington and Nicollet. He needed neither. His wife still held her high-powered executive position with a major Minnesota manufacturing concern and she pulled down an embarrassingly large salary all on her own. When he insisted my second rent increase inside the last twelve months was absolutely necessary to cover property tax increases, I finally had to remind him of what I did for a living, along with a veiled threat:

"…Bliss, you know it's never a good idea to have a cop as anything other than a friend."

Through the pregnant silence on the other end of the line, I could almost hear the wheels turning. After a long moment, Bliss said, "You know, now that I think about it, Sam, I did already increase your rent just this last year. I think we're fine."

I agreed and hung up.

***

"You're late," Cathy Werness said as I walked in.

"You're right," I acknowledged, hurrying past her desk. Making the turn at the corner, from over my shoulder I said, "Don't tell anyone, okay?"

"No need," I heard her reply. "Old news."

At my desk I tucked the mayor's folded but still dripping umbrella between my desk and wastebasket. I then peeled off my newly re-dampened sport coat, shook it and draped it over the back of my chair.

Looking down, the blinking red message light on the phone demanded attention. I dialed into my voicemail.

The computer said, "You have 17 messages. Press 1 to listen."

I pressed 1 and the oldest message came first with a computerized preamble of "Message received this morning at one-thirty-seven."

It was from the 911 dispatch office. "This is a duplicate of the message I just left you on your cell phone. We have a hit on your APB guy. Contact Sergeant Horbath as soon as you get this."

Message on my cell phone? I retrieved the phone from my pants pocket and checked it only to curse the fact that the battery was dead.

The computer said, "Next message – received this morning at two-o-nine."

The voice of the same person followed. "We got another hit on Toors. Contact 911 dispatch ASAP."

I triggered the next message, also from 911 dispatch. It was a third sighting of Toors. So was the next message, and then the remaining messages all coming in at different times, all individual sightings of Simon Toors.

Stunned, I looked over to Carter's undisturbed desk and empty chair, retrieved my still damp sport coat and slipped it back on as I returned to Cathy's desk.

"Where's Carter?"

"He was here, but he didn't stay long," she explained, "He said he was going over to dispatch for something."

I took my phone out, popped the back, pulled out the drained battery and handed it to her. "Any chance your recharge racks have a fresh one of these?"

She left her desk, stepped over to the double-door metal cabinet that concealed her stash of electronic gear. On an eye-level shelf she had a battery of battery rechargers. She matched up the appropriate type and swapped my bad one for a freshly charged one.

"Here you go," she said.

I slipped the power cell into my phone. As I turned to leave, I said, "I'm going over to dispatch for a while. Call Horbath and tell him I'm on my way."

***

Horbath's cubicle overlooked a modest array of three computer terminals arranged on an equally modest wedge-shaped table that was 911 emergency dispatch. To avoid disturbing the morning crew, Carter and I squeezed into the tight space to review the sergeant's printouts.

Paging through the individual reports, Carter shook his head. "Seventeen different sightings, seventeen different places, all of them from people after emergency responders arrived. None of them from cops."

"That's right," Horbath pointed at the top sheet in Carter's hand. "Each person said they recognized our guy after he had helped them out of whatever fix they had been in."

"And he did it before our responders arrived at the scene," I reiterated, making sure I was clear on it all. "Toors disappeared before they got there?"

Horbath nodded as Carter thumbed to another report and began to read. "Pregnant woman in labor, trapped in her own car as garage floods, called for help. When we arrived, she was sitting on the front porch, high and dry. She identified the man in the APB flyer photo as the person who helped her. Baby and mother doing fine at the hospital."

Carter turned to the next report. "According to this, two minutes earlier a panic call from a wife said her husband had a heart attack when he tried to stop a sewer backup from flooding their house. When our guys got to the residence, victim was resting comfortably on the living room sofa. Wife said she recognized the man who helped from a TV newscast earlier that evening."

"That's not possible," I said. "It's some kind of media-induced mass hallucination."

Horbath was amenable to the idea. "That's the best explanation I've heard all night. Look at the addresses – they're miles apart. No one can travel that fast across the city even under perfect conditions. And, in this weather, hallucination makes more sense than anything else anyone has suggested so far."

I scratched my head. "And every one of these emergency reporting people ID'd Toors?"

"Yeah," Horbath acknowledged. "Every EMT, cop and service responder in the city has the APB. After the first couple calls like this, we alerted everyone from that point on to make sure to confirm things every time."

I pushed harder. "And, in each case, after responders arrived, there was no sign Toors had been or was still in the area?"

"That's right," the sergeant concurred.

Carter moaned. "Geez, Sam, this whole train ride has just taken a weird turn into Crazy Town."

I had to agree. "Tomlinson's gonna blow when he hears this. One thing we have to do is keep this out of the media."

Carter turned to Horbath. "Tell no one about this. Keep a lid on it. Make sure your dispatchers talk to no one, okay?"

Horbath nodded and we left with Carter tightly holding onto the stack of printed reports.

***

Simon Toors was all over the noontime news.

Responding to a bellowed summons heard by everyone on the entire floor, Carter and I reluctantly stepped into Tomlinson's office and the comforting warmth of the man's magical aura.

"What the hell is this crap?!" Tomlinson pointed to Shelly's frozen open-mouthed visage on the chief's TV screen, the DVR playback in pause mode.

Cautiously I stepped to my favorite armchair and took a seat. Carter found his familiar corner of the sofa.

"I'd appreciate it, Mark, if you'd resist the urge to refer to my ex-wife as crap. For a woman her age, she's actually quite nicely put together."

The chief glared back. "No jokes, Culhane, I'm pissed! Toors is the top story by lunchtime!"

Carter softly reminded the chief we had told him about the sightings earlier.

"That's right, Wolpren, you did! You also told me you were keeping it quiet, too – you two know quiet, don't you? 'Quiet' means out of the press." The chief pointed the remote control at the screen, pressed play and growled, "This isn't 'out of the press!'"

Shelly's image jumped to life in mid-sentence. "... a total of seventeen different sightings across the metropolitan area of escaped murder suspect Simon Toors last night during the most severe periods of the thunderstorms that rocked the Twin Cities and caused so much localized flooding. People contacting 911 emergency services for help with storm-related problems verified each sighting. Apparently, Toors, or someone who was very similar in appearance, arrived at each location after 911 was called to aid the people who were in distress. In each case, when emergency responders arrived, the mysterious Mr. Toors was nowhere to be seen. Police are baffled as to how a single person was in so many places across the metropolitan area almost simultaneously during a torrential rainstorm."

Shelly turned to the camera on her left and continued. "In other news, the governor announced a new tax initiative to close loop holes for the rich. More on that after the break."

Tomlinson clicked the set off and slammed the remote down on his desk blotter. "What the hell do you call that, Culhane?"

I shrugged. "Well, I think I'd call it sloppy reporting."

"What!?!"

I shrugged again. "Her basic facts are good, but she called Toors a 'murder suspect.' He's not a murder suspect, he's a person of interest."

Tomlinson buried his face in his hands. "Holy crap, always the jokes with you."

"Hey, it stopped raining," Carter said pointing to the window. "Maybe we won't need to build that ark, after all."

Tomlinson ignored him and swung a purposeful finger at me. "I know where she got her information."

I shook my head. "I didn't say anything to her. She didn't call and if she had, I would have sent her to you, just like we agreed."

Tomlinson replied with a muted "Bullshit."

"Mark, her report isn't an exclusive. The same information is on the other stations' noontime shows, too. Whoever got them their information knew how to do it."

The chief almost got a word out in rebuttal, but Cathy's intercom call stopped him.

"Wayne Stephens of the FBI on line one, Chief."

Tomlinson's face fell. "Great. That's all I need."

He took a breath, plastered a false smile on his kisser and picked up the receiver. "Yes, Wayne, how are you doing? ... Why, yes, I did see the report... Yes, it is accurate... Of course we would have talked to you or Rupert before going public with the information, but Wayne, we didn't go public... I'm not sure, but we're checking on that right now..."

Tomlinson looked up and across at me as he added, "... no, I don't believe Culhane would do that; they're divorced, you know... Yes, I agree someone did, but I don't believe it was Culhane... Actually, I have him and Wolpren bird-dogging the sighting reports right now. They're the best leads we have had since the attack on the jail and I think they're going to help us a lot. Like it or not, Wayne, the media coverage on this latest development could be a big help, too. More eyes out there looking for the killer, that kind of thing... As a tag-along? I don't know, offhand I don't think it would do any harm... Sure, I'll talk to them about it as soon as they get back in... You, too. Bye."

Gently he replaced the receiver in its cradle. "When you two get back in later this afternoon, we'll need to talk about improving your investigation by adding Rupert Anderson of the Minneapolis FBI office to your team as a tag-along. Of course, you both will be adamantly against the idea. I, on the other hand, will be for it. Our discussion will be enthusiastic, but your stubbornness will mean we won't reach final agreement on the issue and I'll be forced to tell Wayne-Baby we've tabled the idea until next week. On a related note, I'll be out of the office for the rest of the day attending to matters at my Masonic Lodge. Any questions?"

Carter and I exchanged looks but neither of us said anything.

"Good." Tomlinson rose from behind his desk and headed for the door. "You two have until next week to find Toors. After that, the Feds are in your faces mucking up things for you big time."

***

A four-person crew of yellow-jacketed city maintenance workers dislodged the body from the submerged drainage grate. It wasn't an easy thing to do, but when they finally succeeded, a loud sucking sound filled the air and the high water flooding the

Meadow Lane and Glenwood Avenue intersection immediately began to lower. It took all four workers to pull the corpse from the renewed rushing current and onto the higher ground of the road shoulder.

Tribby, his two assistants, Carter and I stood a good ten yards away on Meadow Lane, watching. Two squad cars with lights flashing blocked traffic flow, one on our right another on the eastbound lane of Glenwood. Officers were on Glenwood directing traffic around the scene.

I looked down at my soggy slip-ons. "I should have worn boots. It's hip-deep out there."

"Waders are more like it." Carter concurred and scanned the afternoon overcast. "Things are lightening up, though; might get some sun yet."

I looked over at Tribby and his two-man crew. Each of them wore black rubber-zippered overshoes. "I didn't think they still made those things, Phil."

"Dress for success, Samuel," Tribby smiled. He summoned his two guys to follow as he stepped ahead into the settling murky water. "We're up, gentlemen."

They skirted the deeper stuff in favor of the ebbing edges and sloshed their way through the shallow ripples, then up out of the water to where the body lay. Carter and I took the driest possible route the long way around on the highest ground available. My feet still got wetter. The city workers returned to the low-lying gutter with rakes in hand to keep debris from clogging things up again as the waters continued to drain. Tribby's two assistants made way for Carter and I to join the ME squatting over the body conducting his preliminary examination. The body itself was a disturbing mess.

"Body temperature of a submerged corpse isn't going to help us much," Tribby commented, his latex-gloved hands exploring the exposed mottled flesh of the face and neck, and then removed a latex glove from the victim's right hand to check the discoloration under the corpse's fingernails.

"Even with the water," I surmised, "and assuming he drowned last night in a flash flood, that looks like a lot of decomp for a twelve-hour old body."

Tribby looked up at me for a moment and then returned to his work, pulling at the resistant zipper of the victim's windbreaker jacket as he said, "As soggy as he is, Samuel, that isn't decomposed flesh. And I doubt he drowned."

The zipper released and the jacket opened to reveal the same type of Kevlar vest with utility harness we had seen before. The harness held several canisters, what appeared to be a type of cell phone with a cord extending upward toward the man's shoulder and clipped to his collar. At the end of the cord dangled an earpiece with an articulated stem microphone. There was also a zippered kit or some kind, a 9mm Glock in a side holster and four clips of ammunition in the harness on the opposite side.

"Oh, crap," Carter winced when he saw it all. "He's a crispy."

"That he is, Detective," Tribby concurred, carefully removing the Glock from the holster. He released the magazine and it fell into his hand. He slid back the slide to check the chamber. Out popped a cartridge. "Full magazine with one in the chamber. No shots fired. Whatever hit him, hit him fast."

I scanned the immediate area for traffic cameras. There were none. "Chances are, whatever hit him was accompanied by a blinding white light. We have some of that on video from the jail, remember?"

"People in the area might have seen something," Carter offered.

"If it occurred in the area," Tribby responded, stretching out the kinks as he rose from his squat. "The body was most likely carried here by the flooding. Follow the path of the flood and you may find where it happened."

"Good idea," I agreed, looking west on Glenwood where the slope of the road dictated the direction from which the runoff would have flowed. "Wherever it happened chances are good Toors was there at the same time. If someone saw something, or if we find something at the scene that could offer a clue to his current whereabouts, a trip up the road could help."

"It's worth the stroll," Carter pointed in the direction I was looking. "That-a-way."

We left Tribby and his crew to their work and headed for Glenwood. The boulevard low spot at the corner disguised what appeared to be relatively dry ground. In fact, it was ankle-deep black muck covered with sod. Both of us stepped in it at the same time, cursed as we leapt from the depressed area, and in vain, tried to shake off without much success, the consequences now soaking our socks and covering our shoes.

"These are new Florsheims," Carter grumbled as we continued west along the road shoulder. "The department owes me a new pair."

Shaking muck from each foot with each step, I offered my standard sympathetic response. "Complain, complain, complain."

Evidence of overrun from the night's flooding was everywhere. The grass and low shrubbery was matted down even at the higher elevations west of the intersection. The smeared multiple lines of debris deposits left behind when the water receded made it clear the rain had come very fast and very heavy. At this point, our groomed boulevard of soggy grass became a relatively short stretch of unkempt, scraggly weeds, leafy bushes and quack grass that fell away from the shoulder into a shallow depression bordered by a thick line of long-standing oaks. The trees had performed barricade duty during the flood. The confined area was situated between two private residences in this upper-middle-class neighborhood with neither property owner apparently taking care of it. In the depression, the flood had deposited substantial amounts of trash, rubble and storm-torn remnants from trees and bushes.

I waved a cautious finger in the direction of the ditch. "You wanna go down in there to comb through that stuff?"

Carter almost choked. "No, not really. How about you?"

I shrugged. "Well, one of us is going to have to."

"Why?"

"Because, old buddy, old pal," I pointed more directly to the middle of the collected mess below. "If I'm not mistaken, that's someone's foot sticking out."

***

In short order, our two traffic controlling squad cars at the Glenwood Avenue-Meadow Lane intersection increased by a factor of eight, including numerous squad cars, two emergency response vehicles from the fire department, two ambulances, and several gray sedans with modest Bureau of Criminal Apprehension seals on the side doors. Glenwood was completely sealed off for a half-mile in all directions. Aided by quickly strung yellow crime scene tape spanning the thoroughfare and every adjoining side street, uniformed officers controlled security. Two-person teams of plain-clothed Homicide detectives and uniformed officers went door-to-door interviewing local residents about the events of last night and whether they may have witnessed anything out of the ordinary.

Carter and I stood outside the open rear door of the ambulance as Tribby conducted his initial examination inside the vehicle, the second body still strapped to the backboard used to haul it from the ditch.

"The first one's partner, no doubt about it," he stated plainly. "All the same gear and getup, fully loaded utility vest; same leprous lesions."

"Makes sense," I said.

Dressed in an ill-fitting raincoat and charcoal gray fedora, Tomlinson came from around the street side of the ambulance and said, "Explain to me how two more crispies make sense."

Carter and I turned toward the surprisingly calm and collected voice of our normally fearful leader. Patrolwoman Magan dressed in department-issued raingear stood behind him and nodded at me in recognition.

"Officer," I nodded back and turned to Tomlinson. "Sorry to have interrupted your Masonic Lodge endeavors, Chief."

"I'm touched by your concern," he lied and continued. "Please, tell me what makes sense about this. Interested people want to know."

I think I knew to whom he was referring. "Well, Chief, it wouldn't have made sense if there wasn't a second crispy."

"Why's that?" He was doubtful.

"Since the first two civilian victims, each of the crispies we've found worked in pairs."

Tomlinson disputed the point. "Not the one found near the park. He was alone."

I nodded again. "You're right: his body was alone. But he had help. Remember, his utility vest was completely cleaned of everything. Someone removed his weapon, ammo, communication, and any other gear before we found him. He had help."

Silently, the chief digested that fact for a moment, and then asked, "How do the first two civilians, as you call them, fit into this? Two different locations; two different days."

Carter added, "Two different approaches, too, Chief. Those first two carried personal IDs, cash, no special gear to speak of other than the knife found on the first and that 357 revolver on the second one."

"Both weapons equally lethal in their own right," Tribby offered from inside the ambulance.

"True enough," I concurred. "A 357 magnum handgun isn't a Saturday night special, and that knife wasn't the pocket variety – it was a Rambo-style survival tool, fourteen inches of serrated, high-carbon steel from tip to hasp. Either one in the right hands would get the job done."

Tomlinson was still reluctant. "Still, they're two separate guys at two different places at two different times. What's the connection?"

Moving from his examination, Tribby leaned out the ambulance door. "Perhaps the lack of similarity is the connection."

All of us turned toward the ME and waited for more. Tribby took a breath and gave it.

"First, let us assume all the victims are someone's hired guns out to work his or her questionable whims on some predetermined target. Planning on a quick kill, the employer, whomever that may be, initially underestimated the prey. After the first two failed attempts using local, less qualified muscle, the employer decided to kick it up a notch and contracted with a resource capable of providing highly trained experts to conduct a prolonged search-and-destroy operation. The operation continues, and will continue until the objective is achieved."

Tomlinson, Carter and I exchanged aware glances. Tomlinson offered a one-word summation.

"Mercenaries."

"Of a type, yes," Tribby agreed.

"You mean, something like Blackwater?" Carter ominously commented. "That's hairy."

"Blackwater-esque, maybe," I acknowledged with a nod. "Or perhaps former Blackwater personnel running some kind of independent contracting gig. For sure, it complicates our inside man question. Whoever the inside man is, he isn't financing the operation; he's another hired gun of whoever is driving the thing."

Carter injected, "More than that, the driver is connected big-time to our communication networks. How else do the hired guns follow 911 calls during severe storms and flooding to nail the target?"

"The same 911 calls where people claim they were helped by Simon Toors," I added. "Where're the printouts from dispatch?"

"Back in the car," Carter answered, mildly irritated he didn't have the documents in hand.

Tomlinson relieved Carter's irritation a bit. "Don't bother checking that, for now just assume there was a 911/Toors call around here. All of this tells us Toors isn't what he appeared to be. Our growing crispy collection proves Toors certainly has lethal defense capabilities beyond anything we've considered. He's also something else: he's the target."

"Of course he's the target!" I snapped back at Tomlinson's obliviousness to the obvious, my irritation with the man almost imploding right then and there. "You didn't believe all that BS about Toors' gang attacking the jail to cover his escape, did you?"

He bit back. "It was a plausible theory, Culhane."

Another thread of restraint popped in my head and the pressure behind my eyes swelled with a surge. I could take his temper tantrums; I couldn't handle his incompetence. "Your plausible theory was nothing more than FBI sloth based wholly on media conjecture and lazy journalism. Shelly hit me with that dribble the first night. Your plausible theory was on the street within minutes of the attack; the Feds just picked it up and ran with it. It was total crap from the beginning, and the fact you gave it any serious weight at all is pathetic!"

"Alright," Carter tried to interject, stepping between the two of us. "This isn't helping. Let's calm down."

Tomlinson wouldn't have it. He shook a white-knuckled fist in my face "What's pathetic, Culhane, is your investigation! We've got two more bodies and Toors is still out there killing people!"

I moved to the left away from Carter's outstretched hands. "Toors is the target, Chief! You said so yourself!"

Tomlinson took an intimidating step forward. "That's right, I did, but he sure as hell ain't the innocent victim in all of this, that's for damn sure!"

At that moment, Tribby's relatively quiet voice from the ambulance backdoor was oddly effective in rising above our elevated volume levels. "What's needed right now is a firm reminder that we are all on the same team. We aren't adversaries; the only agenda is a common one: put an end to these deaths. Can we agree on that?"

The pause and a purposeful step backward was enough to help me. It seemed to do the same for Tomlinson who shook his head and looked away.

"That's being good little boys," Carter chided just as his cell phone rang. He answered it. His easy smile quickly disappeared. For several sober seconds he listened to the caller and said nothing. There was a silent nod followed by, "I'm on my way."

Carter returned the phone to his pocket and looked at me, worry pulling at his face. "That was Meredith. Linnie's in emergency. I have to leave."

"What happened?" Tomlinson asked with sincere concern. He was fully aware of Caroline's health situation.

"Internal bleeding," he muttered, suddenly disoriented as he searched his pockets for something. "Coughing up blood. Where are my keys? No, wait, I didn't drive, you did, Sam..."

I pulled my car keys from my pants pocket. "Here, take the Crown Vic. Just go."

Tomlinson intercepted the exchange. "No, I don't want you driving, Wolpren. Sam, take him down there. Make sure things are all right. Check in with me when you know more."

Tomlinson grabbed my arm as Carter turned to go. "Stay with him. Watch that he doesn't go into shock or something, okay?"

"No problem," I nodded. "And about all this... It's not like I'm not on top of it, you know?"

"I know." Regret shadowed his face. "And I'm out of line blowin' up like I do. It's just that you don't know the pressure I'm getting on this. Sam, you gotta find this creep. Get him back into custody and these killings will stop."

"I will, Mark. It may not look it, but we're getting close. I'm sorry for flying off like I did."

He looked down and away, everywhere but at me. "Me too."

I nodded, turned and quick-stepped it to catch up with Carter already halfway to where I had parked the car.

Chapter 7

Closing In

The Ridges Hospital complex faced Nicollet Boulevard with the emergency entrance tucked around to the rear. I dropped Carter off at the curb and he rushed in while I followed the drive back to the southwest parking area to find a spot. It took me only a few minutes, but when I entered the ER lobby through the automatic sliding door with its smoky brown-tinted glass, Carter was nowhere to be seen. I followed the curved golden oak woodwork of a clutter-free reception counter to the lone attendee in a starched white uniform. Her red-on-white plastic nametag read, "Deloris Whelm."

I cleared my throat and bounced an uncertain smile in her direction. "Hi, Deloris, I just brought my friend in to see his wife – Caroline Wolpren – could you tell me what room she is in?"

Completely unimpressed with me, Deloris turned to her computer screen for a quick check and asked, "Are you family?"

I cleared my throat once more. "Well, not actually 'family,' no. Just a friend."

With a hint of self-satisfied pleasure, she almost smiled as she said, "I'm sorry, but Mrs. Wolpren is in Intensive Care. Family only."

"Oh," I verbally stumbled, looking for something to say. "Yes. Of course. Rules are rules, after all. Well, then, that makes sense. Maybe I'll just wait somewhere."

Without sympathy, she squinted in the direction of the seating lounge with its barely populated buttresses of back-to-back stiff wooden armchairs. I nodded my thanks to Deloris and proceeded in the indicated direction.

I arrived at a suitable corner seat as the undeniable attractiveness of Meredith Mathison emerged from the adjoining hallway. Unlike the attendant at the counter, Meredith's smile was genuine. When she approached, I could see through her perfect makeup and her neat pageboy hairstyle that she was worried and very tired.

"Ah, Sam, it's so good you are here." She leaned in and took my hands in hers with a firm grasp that surprised me. My surprise grew when she gave me a welcoming peck on the cheek that actually made substantive contact.

My uncertainty showed as I looked at her and saw something in her eyes more desperate than just worry for a sick friend.

I collected myself and motioned her to the chair facing mine. "Well, it's not under the best circumstances, but I'm glad you're here, too. Have you seen Carter?"

With her perfectly straight posture she sat down and bobbed her head toward the hallway from which she had appeared. "He's with Caroline now. I thought it best to come out here."

"You got to go into the ICU?" I threw a quick glare at the attendant still sitting behind the counter typing something on her keyboard. "You family?"

Meredith smiled. "I told them I was Caroline's legal counsel."

"Ah, which of course, you are, aren't you?"

"I don't lie, Samuel."

"Of course not. So how's she doing?"

Her shoulders sagged noticeably. "The internal bleeding is another complication of the disease and the CHOP."

"CHOP?"

"I'm sorry – it's an acronym for the drug regimen they have her on. She's on a combination chemotherapy they call CHOP – prednisone with a couple of other things thrown in. She doesn't produce blood platelets, so she bleeds. The lymphoma has spread to so many internal organs, radiation treatments would kill her, and so they're going to re-juggle the drug mix to try to better manage the symptoms."

"You mean come up with something other than CHOP?"

"Maybe CHOP added to another combination altogether – a real alphabet soup." She re-braced her shoulders, and then carefully so not to smear the mascara, she cleared something from each tear duct with her little finger. "They'll keep her here overnight for observation, maybe longer depending on the new drugs. Then they'll send her home."

I leaned forward, resting my elbows on my knees. "Don't take this the wrong way, okay, but you look like you could use a drink."

She responded with a smile and a suggestive bounce of one eyebrow. "I'm waiting for someone who promised me he would call."

"Oh, I see. Poor guy must be overburdened with work or something. I'm sure he's not ignoring you."

"I'm sure." Behind a smile now suddenly turned shy, Meredith almost blushed.

I could work with what she gave me. "Well, if he doesn't call you, he's a clod hung up on things you'd be better off avoiding."

I was surprised when she didn't agree. "We all have our little quirks, Samuel. Life will do that to you, sometimes."

"I suppose you're right," I surrendered. "No one's perfect."

"Even when we want to be," she added with a small laugh that wrapped around me so comfortably, I almost leaned forward and kissed her. She might have sensed my intent as she hastily added, "Of course, you and Carter are near perfection – from what I've seen on the news lately, you are all over this Glenwood murders case."

"Umm, yes." I eased back into my chair, increasing the buffer zone between us to ease too many sudden warm yearnings. "You've been watching channel six."

"Not just TV. Newspapers, too."

"Take my word for it, being a media celebrity isn't all that it's cracked up to be."

Meredith shrugged. "You shouldn't knock it. It could mean greater job security in uncertain times."

It was my turn to laugh. Actually, it was more of a chortle. "You think? You should have heard my chief's latest threat to fire me – just before we got your call. I think that's the third time in the last week he's told me I was toast."

Meredith shook her head. "He's bluffing."

"You don't know him."

"Don't have to know him. Who does he trust?"

"No one. He's hyper-paranoid everyone's out to get him."

"Wrong again, Detective." She made sure I was looking at her. "He trusts you. He may not trust anyone else, but he trusts you."

It was a comforting thought. I wanted to believe she was right. "And how do you know that?"

Meredith didn't hesitate with a simple answer. "Because he knows you're the one person in the department capable of solving this case and bringing the killer in."

I didn't want to accept that. "You might be a little bias on that. The department has a lot of good people, Meredith."

"And, yet, you're the one in charge of the investigation. Do you really think that would be the case if your chief didn't believe in you?"

Now it was my turn to almost blush. "Nice thought. But there's another little complication."

"And what would that be?"

I leaned forward, elbows resting on my knees and hands clasped together. "The killer the chief wants me to bring in isn't the killer. Whoever the killer is, it isn't Simon Toors."

Meredith's scrunched expression spoke volumes. "Well, if he isn't the person, who is?"

"Beats me," I reluctantly admitted. "See, I'm not all that perfect after all, am I?"

Another warm yearning as she softly offered, "Perfection is in the eye of the beholder, Sam."

A self-conscious rush of air followed a very real mental image of Meredith with her hair hanging loose and without her perfectly applied makeup. She'd be lovely, so much more so.

From the hallway, Carter entered the lobby and walked up to us.

"I'm sorry to be such a bother for you two," he said. He stepped between our seated positions but remained standing.

"No bother, Carter," I said honestly. "How's she doing?"

"Linnie's resting," he answered. "I'm going to spend the night here with her. I think I should."

"Of course," Meredith concurred.

Carter added, "I'll take a bus in tomorrow morning…"

"You're not going in tomorrow," I objected. "Your wife is more important. You do what you have to do until they send her home. Then take what time you need after that to make sure she's okay. When you're ready, call me and I'll pick you up."

"What, you coming all the way from downtown to Burnsville to save me cab fare?"

"Your car is downtown. Give me the keys and I'll bring it down for you."

Carter objected. "I can take care of my own car. You don't have to do that."

"I'm just trying to help out," I grumbled. "Give me the keys. I'll take care of it for you."

"Don't worry about it."

"Don't be a stubborn SOB like you usually are! Give me your gawdam keys!"

Meredith chuckled. "You boys always get along this well, or do you two just naturally dislike each other?"

Carter and I both turned to her.

With a motherly pat on my chest, she directed her comment to Carter. "He just wants to be useful."

"He's been useful enough already," Carter admitted gruffly. "I can take it from here."

She turned to me. "He just wants to take care of his wife as best he can. Let him do it."

My eyes bounced between the two of them. "Fine. No problem. It's almost dinnertime. Wanna grab something to eat?"

Carter hesitated. "Actually, I'm not very hungry. I probably should be, but I don't think I could eat anything right now. Kinda funny. Probably should get back to Linnie's room, anyway."

I didn't understand it, but evidently Meredith did. She slung her purse strap over her shoulder and came to her feet.

"Well, I'm going to let Carter do what he needs to do," she said, adjusting herself with a solid leave-taking cue and turning toward me. "And you, Sir, should walk me out to my car."

She was handing me my own leave-taking cue. I came to my feet, crossed over to her side and pointed to Carter as I instructed him straight-out, "Just call when you're ready, okay?"

"Okay," Carter nodded. "Thanks, you two, for everything."

I walked Meredith across the lobby and out the sliding glass doors. On the walkway leading to the parking lot, I leaned in closer as I said, "You know, you do smell really good to me."

That brought a broad smile. "Thank you. You do, too."

"Oh, that's a bad sign," I objected seriously. "It must be from the vending machine lunch I had at the precinct!"

Her giggle was cut short. She pressed against my side and warmly whispered, "I mean it, you know. From the first night, I felt something. I hoped you felt it, too."

I couldn't make promises I couldn't keep. There was still too much of Shelly inside. But that didn't stop my arm from finding its way around Meredith's waist. I gave her a little hug as we walked. "It's not that I haven't felt something. It's more that you deserve better than some lonely guy and a lot of muddled thinking."

She rested her head on my shoulder. "You're not the only one who's lonely. You can still make that call you promised me."

We continued to the second row of parked cars. Meredith directed me to her white Toyota sedan where, when she reached the door, she offered an intriguing suggestion.

"You know, it is close to dinnertime. How about I cook you a dinner tonight?"

Through a toothy grin I said, "I didn't know you could cook."

She almost laughed. "Among other things, yes, I can cook. I'm no Julia Child, but I'm pretty good. What do you say?"

"How can I pass it up?"

At that moment, the familiar muffled tones of my cell phone came from my pocket. I cursed as I retrieved it and brought it to my ear. "This is Culhane."

Meredith noticed my surprise. The call was from Hassani Ebadat at the Holy Land Bakery and Deli on Lake Street.

"You asked me to call you if I saw anything?" Hassani asked.

"Yes, I did. Thank you for calling. What is it?"

"You know the Arab gentleman you showed me the picture of? You would be surprised to see who is sitting here in our restaurant tonight. He just ordered our top-of-the-line Holy Land Vegetarian Combo with a side of hummus."

My eyes caught Meredith's as I asked, "Are you sure it's him?"

"He looks better on TV, I think," Hassani answered. "But it's him. What do you want me to do?"

Looking at Meredith, I couldn't hide my regret as I shook my head and said, "Take your time in filling the order, Hassani. I'm on my way. It will take about a half-hour."

I returned the phone to my pocket as the real pain of an unspoken apology pulled at my face. I briefly turned toward the hospital and thought about Carter. I immediately dismissed the idea of summoning him. I turned back to Meredith.

"I'm sorry," I began all too familiarly. Somehow it felt as if I had done this to her before. "I... I have to go."

She replied with a thin acknowledging smile and a slight head bob. "I know."

"I don't want to..."

Suddenly, she reached up and pulled me close, her mouth clamped on to mine with the urgent passion of an unmistakable message. I returned the kiss, and for the first time in a long time, I stopped thinking of Shelly.

***

Minutes later the Crown Vic flew down the entrance ramp to the interstate. Meredith's soft fragrance lingered, as did the pleasure of her lips on mine. I had to admit, she not only smelled good, she didn't taste half-bad, either. I pulled my cell phone up and speed-dialed Tomlinson's private number; in the process I silently cursed both my job and my lack of a social life.

He knew it was me. "How's Carter and Caroline doing?"

"She's spending the night enjoying the hospitality of Fairview Ridges. Carter's staying with her. It looks like she'll be going home tomorrow after they check on her new drug regimen. I told Carter to take whatever time he needs."

"Solid," Tomlinson concurred. "Tribby says he's received lab results on the last three crispies and he wants to cover them with us tomorrow morning first thing."

"Sounds like a plan. However, I've got a plan of my own I need your help on right now."

"What's up?"

"I'm en route to the Midtown Global Market…"

"Yeah, the old Sears building."

"Right. My contact tells me Toors is at the Holy Land Deli having dinner right now…"

Tomlinson's "Holy crap!" interrupted me. I continued.

"I need to confirm, Mark. But on the quiet, I want you to get backup to the place. Station outside the building; cover all the exits. Seal it up tight. I'll go in, check things out. If it's Toors, I'll call you on the walkie-talkie…"

"Good, use secure channel twelve."

"Channel twelve, got it. Get things set up but don't go in until I give the signal. Agreed?"

"It's your show, Sam. I'll take care of the backup at Sears."

The line went dead. I slid the cell phone back into my pocket.

Late rush hour traffic on the interstate still pressed hard in the opposite direction. The oncoming southbound side was multiple rivers of bumper-to-bumper headlights. The northbound flow was a comparative trickle of intermittent red taillights with plenty of easy gaps for the Crown Vic to weave in and out of. The weaving was made easier by the rhythmic alternate pulsing of my own headlights and the flashing red and blue beams normally concealed inside the car's front grill. Nevertheless, the thirteen minutes of the drive seemed interminable.

I doused the flashing lights when the Thirty-first Street exit came up. I took it and slid east to Elliot, then north one block to Lake Street. On the south side of Lake Street I slid into a curbside parking spot directly across from the main entrance to the

Midtown Global Market. I checked the vicinity for signs of my backup. There weren't any. Grabbing the walkie-talkie from the center console, I clicked over to the channel twelve setting and triggered the talk key.

"Check-check-check. Culhane to Tomlinson: are you there?"

A brief click was followed by Tomlinson's voice. "We're here, Sam, all set."

I triggered back. "I can't see you guys. I said quietly not invisible."

"Trust me, we're in position. Do your thing and let me know when we can go in and have some baklava."

I triggered the switch twice, turned the volume control all the way down and slid the thing into my coat pocket. Outside the car, I waited for a break in the slow two-way Lake Street traffic flow, got one large enough and darted across to the main doors of the market.

Inside, the clientele milling about the main floor concourse was a diverse accumulation of disinterested shoppers and loiterers who paid me little mind as I made straight for the Holy Land Deli and the front counter behind which Hassani Ebadat stood waiting. She looked worried as she saw me emerge from the shuffling crowd.

"He's in the far booth in the back," she hurriedly whispered in her thick Somali accent as I walked up to her. Her eyes nervously scanned around and behind me as if she was expecting trouble from someone other than our person of interest.

"Are you alright?" I earnestly asked. "You've done the right thing by calling me, Hassani. You're not in trouble."

She leaned forward and in an even softer whisper said, "He is a dangerous man. There is much danger for you. He knows you are coming."

I looked past the cash register and into the dining area. I couldn't see the rear tables of the place. I returned to Hassani. "Did you tell him I was coming?"

She shook her head. "You don't understand. Just now, when I served him his food, he told me you were coming. He said to me, 'When the detective arrives, bring him to me directly.'"

Instinctively, I reached inside my coat to the holstered Glock. "How long ago?"

"Only a minute, maybe two minutes," she said, still nervous.

I considered calling Tomlinson right then, but thought better of it. If it was Toors, and if he knew I was coming, why didn't he leave? Why would he hang around to wait for me?

"Hassani, bring me an order of baklava to go, will you? I'll be at our friend's table."

The dining area was veiled in subdued incandescent wall lamping positioned above each table along the outside wall. Fewer than half of the tables were occupied and the far rear table along the inside wall was the only table in that corner. A simple lit candle in a glass vase provided the only illumination for the singular customer the table held. With his back to the corner, he had a perfect view of the entire room. The man looked up from his platter of food and smiled at me as I made the turn.

It was Toors. Still smiling, he waved me over.

"So nice to see you again," Toors' British accent irritated me.

I sat down across from him. "Wish I could say the same."

He took a quick bite from his pocket bread stuffed with a roasted vegetables concoction and between chews suggested I should try some for myself. "It's actually very good. Not as spicy as I usually like, a little Americanized, I think, but good."

I was hungry. I eyed him cautiously as I took the offered loaf of pocket bread and the spoon he had used to load his sandwich. Toors slid his platter toward me and gestured for me to take what I'd like. I tore the loaf in half and carefully spooned in some of the mixture.

Toors was right. The food was very good, indeed.

I talked with my mouth full. "You almost scared poor Hassani to death, you know."

Toors shrugged it off. "Not intentionally, I assure you. She's Muslim. I'm afraid she doesn't like me."

I swallowed, reached across for Toors' water glass and took a quick swig. The vegetable combo was spicier than I anticipated.

"She's scared of you," I said returning the water glass to Toors' side of the table. "She's a Muslim; you're a Muslim.

You're also a big celebrity since you broke out of jail the other night. Your face is on the television news shows and she recognized you as soon as you came in."

Toors took a sip from his water glass. "I'm not a Muslim, Samuel. I'm Jewish; always have been."

"Oh, my apologies, I just assumed…"

"Yes, I know. You're sharp, observant; you have superior intuitive abilities, Samuel. You know the simple answer is usually the correct one. To your credit, you also know the obvious answer is almost always a diversion."

I lowered the half-eaten sandwich. "You give me too much credit, Simon. I just go with my gut on things. That's all I have."

A half-nod preceded his reply. "You have your gut and you also have the truth."

That made me sit up a bit. "I have the Truth? What is truth in all of this, Simon?"

A really annoying smile spread across his face. "That's ironic. Long ago, that same question was asked of someone who could have answered it fully, but chose not to."

"Answer it now, Simon. Answer it for me before I take you back into custody."

He was absolutely calm and completely unperturbed about what was going to happen to him. His face conveyed such peace, a real sense of guilt flooded over me.

"Simon, I have to take you in. There's no escape from this place. All the exits are covered and if you try to run, they will shoot you down."

His continence didn't waiver with so much as a blink. He moved the platter of food toward the outside edge of the table, leaned in closer and clasped his hands together.

"Samuel, what if truth was a real thing…"

I tried to make him understand the game was over. "You need to take this seriously, Simon. You need to be straight with me. Time is not on your side. They'll come in here, on their own if they have to, and you will die."

He continued as if I hadn't said a thing. "… and not a vague moral or ethical concept, or a philosophical theory subject to all kinds of situational manipulations? What if truth was as solid as this table; what if it was something you could hold in your hand, feel the weight of, wield like a sword or use as a shield? What if truth – real truth – was always right, never wrong, and continually performed its purpose? What if truth was everlasting and absolute? What do you think would happen to this world if truth was all of that?"

His words made their way through my mental clutter and disjointed thinking. I looked at him as they slowly registered in my brain and a picture took shape in my mind. After a long moment, I shook my head in a poor attempt to clear away what he had put there.

"You're very good," I complained. "What is that, some form of hypnotism? You use those soft, melodic tones of yours and that irritating British accent to put me under some kind of spell, or something? That kind of crap doesn't work on me."

He leaned in even closer. "I'm not trying to trick you, Samuel. Answer my question: what do you think would happen to this world if truth was all that I just said it was?"

I mentally replayed everything he had said, word for word, and the truth revealed itself to my mind. All I could do was look at him in stunned silence.

"And so, now you know," Toors acknowledged. "You, too, are a defender. This will not be comfortable for you. The forces working to destroy me will now try to destroy you, as well. They may succeed, but not in destroying truth. My protector is greater than they and I am not afraid; nor should you be."

Hassani walked up from behind me and placed on the table a paper sack holding a Styrofoam container filled with my order of baklava. I found my voice and thanked her. Hassani offered a suspicious look at Toors, and then she retreated.

Toors watched her leave, smiled and shrugged as he said, "She does not like me."

"I don't like you much, either."

Toors chuckled. "Truth hurts, sometimes."

"Yes," I agreed, leaning back and observing the man for perhaps the first time. "There is much I still don't understand. You and I, we need to talk through all of this. You have to come in with me. I can keep you safe."

That irritating, peaceful expression restated itself. "As in the jail earlier this week?"

He had a point. "No, I suppose not. But you can't just walk out of here. I'm serious, Simon, you take one step outside and they will shoot you down."

A shallow nod: "Yes, they would. They would believe they were doing the right thing, fully justified given all that has happened over the last few days. You see, Samuel, your police department is now subject to forces that use people, institutions of law enforcement and government to undermine what is true. Those who would destroy truth believe they are right and that truth is evil. They will try to snuff it out at every opportunity. You and I are that opportunity. What you need to remember, to know completely without doubt, is that truth is real, solid and wieldable. Truth cannot be defeated."

I laughed softly. "Yes, Master Obi-Wan, I believe I am beginning to understand. May the Force be with us."

Surprisingly, Toors' face went blank. "I don't understand."

Momentarily befuddled, I explained it to him. "You know: Obi-Wan Kenobi, the Jedi Knight? Darth Vader? 'Star Wars?'"

Toors shook his head and continued. "Well, then, what would you suggest our next move be then?"

"Evade," I answered, trying to figure out how it was he knew nothing of 'Star Wars.' "Evade and go dark to buy time to figure things out."

"It's already been figured out, Samuel."

"Not to my liking, it hasn't."

"You don't understand my meaning."

"I understand enough," I rapped a pointed finger on the tabletop. "I understand you're a target. I understand someone wants to make sure you're put out of commission, for what reason I'm not sure but that's not the important thing right now. The important thing right now is to make sure the good guys don't accidently do the job for the bad guys and blow you away! What we need is a diversionary tactic and get you to a safe house somewhere."

"I appreciate your valiant concern, but Samuel there's really no reason..."

"Every reason in the world," I interrupted, pulling the radio from my coat pocket, turning up the volume and triggering the talk key. "Tomlinson, Culhane – come in."

"Yeah, Sam. Go."

"False alarm, Mark. I'll be out with your order of baklava in a couple of minutes."

"Ten-four."

I switched off and returned the radio to my coat pocket. "What's going to happen is this: I'm going out to meet with the chief and give him a completely false story about mistaken identity and a near-hysterical Somali woman convinced she saw Simon Toors. While I'm doing that, you're going to hide out in the market some place until closing time. Don't screw that up. At closing you will exit the building on the east side, that's Tenth Avenue. You will see me in my brown Ford Crown Victoria parked across the street. I'll be waiting for you. I'm taking a helluva risk here, Toors. You don't do exactly what I just said, if you take off on me I'll hunt you down and shoot you myself. Any questions?"

"Very thorough," Toors nodded, and then added, "But, again, Samuel there is really no need to go to so much trouble. I assure you, I am able to meet you wherever you wish..."

"I wish you to meet me at my car at closing time. I'll be on Tenth Avenue. If you don't show, I'll consider you officially gone over to the Dark Side, and that changes everything, got it?"

Again, he had that curious blank expression, unaware of what I was referring to. Nevertheless, he nodded his agreement.

At the counter, I paid for the baklava and conferred with Hassani one last time.

"Thank you, Hassani, for calling me. You're right, he does look an awful lot like our man, but he isn't the guy we're after. A lot of similarity, for sure, but definitely not the person I want. But I do very much appreciate your call. Very helpful. You have a good night, now."

She almost apologized for making such a monumental mistake, but I reassured her again by asking her to call me anytime she saw something she thought might help.

I exited the building on the Elliot Avenue side and walked across to the parking lot where the chief stood with two patrolmen leaning against a squad car. I handed him the bag with the baklava in it.

"It's fresh – still warm," I said, turning to the two uniformed officers with a nod. "Couple of extra pieces for you guys if the chief shares."

"Don't bet on it," Tomlinson commented, peeking into the bag. "So who was the guy?"

"At first, I thought it was Toors, but when I got close, it was easy to see how you'd think it was him. Mistaken identity, simple as that."

The chief persisted. "So who was he?"

"Hasan Tadabe," I lied. "An engineering student at the U. Too young. A lot of similar features, but our guy is much older. Where's the rest of our group?"

Tomlinson had the lid off the Styrofoam box and had taken his first bite. Through the beginning mastication process he said, "Called them off. They're still around but onto their regular work. Where you headed for now?"

I explained my plans to return to the hospital and check on Carter and Caroline yet tonight and Tomlinson seemed to accept it as he finished off the first piece of baklava, closed the box and returned it to the paper sack.

"Sorry, gentlemen, but the rest goes home with me," he said to the other two officers. He turned back to me. "Do you have any other leads on Toors you can follow up on?"

I nodded. "I think so. I'll know more later tonight. It may not look it, but the pace of things is picking up on this deal. I should have something more solid by tomorrow morning."

"I'm counting on it," Tomlinson waved a warning finger in front of me. "Don't forget about Tribby and the meeting tomorrow morning, okay?"

"I'll be there, Chief."

He then turned for his car parked a few spaces away.

I apologized to the two uniformed officers for not buying enough baklava for them, and then returned to my own car. In the car, I pulled out my cell phone and placed a quick call.

"Hi, it's me... Yeah, so soon... No, it's not exactly the call I promised, but it's close. I was wondering if you'd do me a favor tonight..."

I felt the warmth rise in my cheeks at Meredith's guess of the favor she supposed I needed.

"I'm sorry, as pleasant as that might be, that isn't it. I need a quiet place to babysit someone tonight. Given our earlier discussion at the hospital, I thought you'd be interested in helping out... I'd rather not take him to my place, what with so many people knowing who I am and where I live... Who am I babysitting? Well, you have to promise not to tell... Why? Because your life might depend on it... It's the person everyone is looking for – Simon Toors."

Chapter 8

Flight

More than an hour before closing time, most signs of life in and around the Midtown Global Market had diminished to the point of near nonexistence. The night sky was a thick black moonless shroud hiding behind a thin low overcast. The lights of the city reflected off the low haze washing everything in a brownish sepia coloring. At ten minutes to ten, I parked the Crown Vic where I had told Toors I would and waited. Twenty minutes later, the gentle rap on the passenger side window startled me.

"I didn't see you come out," I said as Toors climbed into the front passenger seat.

"Obviously," he pulled the seat belt across his lap and fastened it with a click. "What is your plan for this evening, Samuel?"

I started the car, lowered the shifter into drive and pulled away from the curb with my signal flashing. "We're taking a little ride south of the river and we're going to talk a bit more. I'm putting you up with a friend for the next few days to keep you safe while I track down some leads on the people who tried to take you out. Hopefully, after tomorrow morning's meeting with the medical examiner, I'll have enough on those guys to bird dog where they came from, and if I'm really lucky, who hired them."

"Commendable," Toors commented seriously. "However, you may not like what you find."

At Twenty-sixth Street I turned left and headed west. "If you know something, you need to tell me, Simon. I don't like chasing my tail."

"I understand your desire to find the source of what you think has been happening, Samuel. However, you are going against forces you do not understand. Powerful people usually try very hard to keep their power. Regardless of how successful you might be with your investigation, you alone will not bring the matter to a satisfactory conclusion. You need special help."

I hung a hard left on Blaisdell and headed for the bridge over the railroad tracks. "You'd be surprised what I can do when I put my mind to it, Simon."

"You have a well-earned reputation, Samuel, and it is true there is good reason for why you are feared by a certain local social strata. However, it is important for you to keep a proper perspective on a conflict that will continue, at least for a short while longer, as it always has regardless of what you do. You will need something unique to temper your frustrations."

"Unique?" A block beyond the overpass, I stopped at the red light on Lake Street and eyed his reflection in the windshield. "Unique in what way?"

His eyes met mine in the mirror and there it was again – that serene placidity that really annoyed me.

"A type of internal peace deep in your soul," he answered plainly. "A peaceful soul is a powerful thing. No weapon, no person, no evil intent can destroy it. At times, you have known this peace. You have felt it when you pray…"

The light turned green and I moved through the intersection eyeing the waiting traffic on either side. "When I pray? You think I pray? When have you ever seen me pray?"

I caught his smile in the corner of my eye.

"Samuel, you pray all the time."

I almost laughed. "I don't have to take that kind of crap from anyone, Simon. I'm no holy roller. I don't belong to any church and I sure as you-know-what don't pray all the time."

"You're a good man, Samuel," he replied plainly. "And you do pray: you pray for your friend; you pray for the health of his wife; you pray for the safety and return of your wife; sometimes you even pray for yourself."

"Myself? When did I ever pray for myself?"

"This evening," he answered in the mirror. "When you asked to keep from hurting Meredith."

I slammed on the brakes and squealed to a quick stop just short of Thirty-first Street. I turned and faced him squarely.

"That cuts it, Toors! You're out of line! You're messin' with me and I don't let anyone mess with me. Stop acting like you're Gandhi all overflowing with peace and love for your fellow man and start shooting straight with me. How do you know these things and who else is working with you?"

His serenity was absolutely unruffled. He took a calming breath. "Actually, Gandhi was a pacifist and a profoundly effective revolutionary. The whole Peace and Love thing came much later, corrupted by social excesses of illicit drug use and indiscriminate sexual behaviors, the consequences of which society suffers yet today. Later, the Peace and Love movement was commandeered by anarchist opportunists and neo-Marxists intent on destroying established Western culture."

I jerked a double take at him as my mouth fell open. From behind us, a car swerved and passed on our right; the driver leaned on his horn to let us know how he felt. I let up on the brake pedal and allowed the car to roll to the left side curbing.

I slapped the gear shifter into park and turned back to Simon.

"I don't care about Gandhi, okay?"

"Well, you did bring him up."

"You don't have to be so literal about it! How do you know what I pray about, anyway? How do you know about Meredith?"

Amazingly, he actually seemed to become even more at ease than he already was.

"Oh, that. Well, I guess I'd have to say that I simply... know."

Another double take and all I could do was squint at him in response. So he continued.

"I guess it's because I've been around as long as I have. You live long enough, you learn things."

I squinted harder. "You're no older than I am. In fact, I'm pretty sure I have several years on you. I don't know if you're stupid, or just being evasive, but you gotta start shooting straight with me, Simon, or I'm going to beat you to death! How do you know about Meredith?"

He took a deeper, more cleansing breath this time. "Well, you see, it's like this: you're right to be concerned about hurting her. She likes you an awful lot. It would be upsetting to her if you decided she wasn't right for you. And of course we both know, she's not. And then, there's the other thing."

"What 'other thing'?"

"You realize you're unnecessarily putting her in danger with this plan of yours, don't you?"

"What do you mean?"

"What I mean is, the people searching for me do not stop searching. You risk that they will find me at Meredith's house, and if that were to happen, she could be injured or worse. It is not necessary for you to hide me."

"I need to keep you on a short leash, pal. I lose you, I lose this case and probably my job. I lost you once already. That can't happen again."

He leaned toward me. "You didn't lose me. You'll never lose me. You had me in a locked jail cell and these people came for me anyway. You were powerless to stop them. You will be powerless at Meredith's house, as well."

I knew he was right. It didn't matter. It was more important he was out of sight and in a place no one would suspect. I pulled the gearshift back into drive and pulled away from the curb.

"You're spending the next few days at Meredith's place," I reiterated grittily at his mirrored reflection. "No one will know."

***

Meredith's place was a spacious rambler on two rolling acres outside the little town of New Market west of I-35 off County Road Two in southern Scott County. When I was a half-mile out, I called her.

"We'll be there in a few minutes," I told her.

"I'll open the garage door when I see you pull into the driveway," she explained. "Drive straight in. The stall closest to the house is open for you."

"Thanks, Honey."

"Umm, that sounds nice."

The warmth in her reply bothered me. I hadn't intended a promise in the simple statement of gratitude and for a moment I thought it would be wise to say as much. I glanced at Toors looking at me with an "I-told-you-so" expression on his face. Annoyed, I pressed the end button on the phone and disconnected from the call.

I looked straight ahead but I could still feel the press of his stare as he said, "You're not being fair with her, you know."

"Just shut up, okay?" Ahead on my right, the entry monuments of the housing development emerged from the darkness. "I'm a grown man and I know what I'm doing, alright?"

He chuckled. "That's called an oxymoron."

"Shut up!" I repeated more firmly as I turned onto the street framed by two tall brick obelisks spanned by a high arch of faux wrought iron with an sculpted inset proclaiming "Countryside Hills Estates."

There couldn't have been more than forty homes situated along a small web of curving interconnected streets. Meredith's house was deeper into the development on a cul-de-sac where the landscaped lots backed up to a line of mixed thick oak, elm and ash trees. I slowed and guided the car onto her long, narrow concrete driveway and the right-hand door of the matched set of three opened to reveal the well-lit interior of her garage. I eased the car over the apron and into the stall, with the garage door immediately lowering back down when I turned the ignition off.

Meredith emerged from the opening corner door joining the house. She was smartly dressed for business in a skirt and still crisp white blouse, her hair still perfect, as was her makeup. She seemed genuinely happy to see me as I walked around the front of the Crown Vic, but her affectionate smile disappeared when she saw Simon exit the car. In quick succession, her expression went from doubt, to fear, to surprise.

Simon, of course, picked up on her insecurity straight away and approached her with impressive empathy and honest humility.

"I am Simon Toors and I so appreciate your help in this matter," he said, stepping forward and extending his hand.

She took his hand in hers with more surprise. "You're British!"

He glanced at me and immediately returned to her. "Actually, I'm from Israel, but I lived in England for a time. Please excuse the accent, it is difficult to overcome."

"That's okay, Simon," I interjected and motioned toward the doorway. "Us Minna-sotans gotta fig're ven somebody don't sound Norwegian or say 'Uf-dah' a lot, vel-den, theys has to be from England, doncha know?"

Meredith's relaxed giggle was a relief for me. Simon, on the other hand, looked confused. He didn't get the joke.

Inside, everything was as neat as a house could be. I wondered if she had maid service. She was in her element as she gave Simon a quick tour of the place: the dining area we walked through from the garage, the adjoining modern kitchen looking out across the great room with its scattered seating areas (two) and a home office nook partially walled by a partition fronting the entry alcove.

"Very nice," Toors commented honestly.

"This was my father's place." She commented lovingly, taking it all in with a melancholy quality laced with sad regret. "When he died, he left it for me."

"It's been awhile, though," he added. "I see a lot of you in the details here."

She nodded. "Yes, I suppose you're right; ten years already. Time flies."

Toors' eyes took on an almost humorous glint. "Yes, it does, doesn't it?"

"I hate to break this up," I purposefully interrupted, "but it's getting late."

"Oh, excuse me," Meredith apologized for no reason and hurriedly waved Simon to follow her toward the hallway and the rear of the rambler. "I have a room for you, Mr. Toors. I hope you will be comfortable."

He eyed me with open criticism as the two of them passed by and disappeared down the hall into the first room on the left. I stayed standing in the middle of the great room appreciating the space and the fact that it wasn't a downtown one-bedroom condo. Down the hall, I could hear Meredith talking. A few moments later, they both returned. Meredith sat on the near corner of the sofa; Simon remained standing, as did I.

"Okay, then," I began without really knowing where to start. "First, Meredith, this is really great of you…"

Toors interrupted. "Ms. Mathison, your hospitality is beyond measure. Given the circumstances and what you must obviously think of me with all that has been in the press, I can only say I am eternally grateful for your Christ-centered charity in this matter."

Christ-centered charity?

Meredith turned toward me. I couldn't have deflected her intimidating vibes with a Captain America bulletproof shield.

I didn't recover very well as I cleared my throat and said, "Yes, well, me too."

"You won't have to put up with me for long," Toors continued. "Samuel has an important meeting tomorrow morning and it appears he is close to uncovering the truth behind these killings."

Her dour expression turned to a smile. "That's my Sam."

"And, Samuel, I can free Ms. Mathison from the burden of my unfortunate intrusion. There is someone who is willing to assist us. He lives not far from here and he is very discrete, I assure you."

I was suspicious. "A member of your social circle, no doubt."

"In a manner of speaking, yes," he admitted. "A former Navy man, I understand; not much unlike yourself. The two of you should get along quite well, I would think."

Toors' offer did not overwhelm me. "Too bad you didn't think of mentioning this guy earlier. It would have saved us a trip."

"Perhaps," he nodded. "But then, I wouldn't have had the opportunity to meet Ms. Mathison. After everything you've told me about her, I couldn't very well pass that up."

Suddenly wide eyed, Meredith was genuinely impressed. "Why, Sam, words of praise from you to an escaped felon about me. That's the nicest thing you've never said to me."

"He's not a felon." It was as good a time as any to set the record straight on the current status of Simon Toors. "He hasn't even been charged with anything. He's officially a person of interest and beyond that I only know two things: first, he's not a killer; second, he knows who is. He may be a con man, or a target: most probably, he's both. But he's too damn gentle to have killed anyone."

Meredith was confused. "Well, then why did he run?"

Toors' wide-eyed countenance matched Meredith's as they waited for my answer.

"I'm not sure," I admitted, eyeing Toors suspiciously. "But if I had two guys with machine guns shooting at me, I don't think I'd hang around to see if they hit anything. Besides, the fact that he didn't have large parts of himself splattered all over a jail cell wall tells me he knows how to take care of himself."

Toors silently nodded. With the beckoning of a curled index finger, I motioned for him to follow me to the bedroom Meredith had prepared. He did so and when the two of us entered the room, I softly shut the door behind us for a private chat.

It was a simple, well-furnished room with a low dresser and mirror on the inside wall fronting a single bed covered with a down comforter, a double closet to the right and a double-hung window straight ahead. I walked over to the window, pulled the roller shade all the way down and drew the short drapes closed.

"She's very nice, Samuel," he said quietly.

"Shut up."

"As you wish."

He followed the suggestion when I pointed to the bed and motioned for him to take a seat.

"I have no doubt that I'll regret for the rest of my professional career not cuffing you to the bed frame, but you listen tight: I'll be outside this room all night and if you even scratch yourself in a way I don't like, I'll beat you to death."

A mild objection from the edge of the bed: "But you told Ms. Mathison I wasn't the person you were after."

"Shut up," I ordered again. "You've had your fun; you've put on your little act for Meredith's benefit. She seemed duly impressed, but you didn't impress me. All that talk about what's truth and what's not; your phony clairvoyance routine knowing what I pray for; how you're so concerned about my safety and how I might not like what I find if I continue this investigation. I know what you're doing, Toors. You're trying to throw me off the trail. I'm getting close and you know it, and you also know you need to protect the people behind all of this. Your whole shtick is just one big diversionary Jedi mind trick…"

"Jedi-what?"

"Mind trick!" I quelled the bark too late, but proceeded at a lowered volume. "Jedi mind trick, for the love of God! That's another thing: anyone who doesn't know crap about 'Star Wars' is at least a Commie if not a Jihadist! Maybe you're both, I don't know, but you're staying under wraps until I know where to put you. And, Toors, you do anything to hurt Meredith, I swear to God, I'll…"

He held up a hand. "I know: you'll beat me to death."

I squinted back at him hard. "We understand each other. Get some sleep. We leave early in the morning."

I left Toors and returned to the sofa in the great room. Meredith slid in close to my side. My arm automatically wrapped around her and pulled her close.

"He surprised me," she said. "He's nothing like what they say in the news, is he?"

"Journalists need stories that sell," I pinched the bridge between my eyes. I was too tired. "Toors needs to be scary if their stories are going to do the job."

"I suppose you're right about that. Should I stay home tomorrow? I can work here and keep an eye on him easily enough."

I shook my head, "Not necessary. I'm taking him to Carter's tomorrow first thing. I'm sorry, but it was a mistake to involve you in this. Toors is right. It puts you in danger. I shouldn't have done it."

"He's not dangerous, Sam. I can handle things."

I turned to her and firmly grasped her shoulder. "He might not be the Glenwood Avenue Killer, Meredith, but at least seven people have died horrible deaths and at least two of those people were trying to kill Toors when it happened to them. We have that on tape. This guy attracts death like nothing I've ever seen."

"But it doesn't make sense, does it? What about those sightings of him helping all those people during the storms? Was that made up?"

None of that was made up. It was easier for people to assume one person couldn't be responsible for so many instances across so short a span of time. The human brain couldn't register it, so the human brain simply ignored it.

"No, Sweetie, seventeen different people can't all be lying about the same thing. Toors did all of that stuff that night. I don't know how, but that was him, alright."

***

Some time around two o'clock in the morning, with a barely audible "Good night" Meredith stirred, left the hard discomfort of my boney shoulder and shuffled down the hallway for the soft coziness of her own bedroom. I stayed seated in the corner of the sofa. The room was dimly lit from the far corner by the lone floor lamp switched to the lowest setting. Crickets creaked outside and I appreciated their company.

About an hour later, I found a resealed bag of Kona Special Blend in Meredith's pantry and made a large pot of coffee. As the coffee maker dripped away, I stepped down the hall for another check on Toors. Through a barely cracked door, I looked into the darkened room. On the floor at the foot of the bed his shadow sat erect with legs crossed. The shadow didn't move, nor had it moved from that position since I last checked on him almost three hours earlier. He was an odd duck, but what did it matter to me how he slept? I softly closed the door and returned to the kitchen to pour my first mug of the day.

The clock read 5:30 when I poured my third mug full. The sheer volume of what I had brewed had helped keep the coffee fresh, but now it had a noticeable bitterness to it – good enough for my insensitive tastes but I wouldn't serve it to anyone. I washed the remains of the pot down the kitchen sink and returned to my corner of Meredith's comfortable sofa. The crickets were still cricketing and through the center slit of the window draping the sky was turning a pre-dawn black and blue. It would be daylight within an hour.

At six o'clock on the nose, I dialed Carter's cell phone. It rang several times before it clicked over to his voicemail greeting.

"It's me. Call me when you get this."

I disconnected the call and moved back to the kitchen to prepare a fresh pot of coffee. My phone warbled as I dumped the old coffee grounds from earlier into the garbage.

"Don't you ever sleep?" Carter growled drowsily.

"When I can," I put a fresh filter in the basket and measured in three rounded scoops. "How's Caroline?"

"Unlike you and me, she's asleep. But the new drugs work great. She's doing much better now. So what's up?"

"How'd you like to drive over this morning?"

Carter grumbled something intelligible and then he said, "Not particularly. Consider me still on spousal leave, will ya? It's Friday, I'm at the hospital and I don't want to go all the way downtown to get the 'Vette.' It's too close to the precinct and Tomlinson might see me and I don't need him to think I'm back on duty, or something."

"I'm not downtown."

"Well, where the hell are you?"

"I'm in New Market."

Several seconds of dead silence preceded Carter's assumptive chuckle. "You spent the night with Meredith?"

"Well, in a manner of speaking," I switched ears with the phone, checked the water level on the pot, added a bit from the tap to hit the "10 Cups" mark and dumped it into the coffee maker reservoir. The pot went under the basket and I hit the brew switch. "I guess you could say that yes, I spent the night with Meredith…"

"Halleluiah! It's about frickin' time!"

"It's not what you think."

"It better damn well be, or I'm getting a new partner!"

"Remember, you're still on spousal leave', alright?"

Carter agreed and quieted down.

"Keep it on the down-low and get over here. I need your help with our guest."

"Okay, but you owe me the cab fare to get the 'Vette.'"

***

Carter shook his head in disbelief. "Christ Almighty, Sam, why didn't you just take him in?"

Meredith was in her private bathroom taking a shower. Toors hadn't left his room. Carter arrived as the third pot since of the day stopped dripping. He could see I was buzzed by a major caffeine overdose when I nodded in agreement as he said I owed him fifty-three dollars in cab fare. I poured him a fresh mugful, sat him down at the dining room table and gave him the full story.

"I thought about turning him in," I admitted from across the table, "but that wouldn't do any good at all."

He wasn't happy. "So a sleepover at Meredith's is better? You can't be serious!"

"Look, Carter, think about it: they're still cleaning up the jail from the attack and I'm not about to waltz him back into a cell there. Everyone, especially the people who we don't want to know anything, would know where he is. They walked right in last time and they can do it again. This way, we have Toors, they don't know we have him, and we aren't welcoming another attack."

For a quiet moment, Carter mulled over what I said. "Okay. Where does that leave us?"

"I need you to stay here with him until I get back from this morning's meeting. Tomlinson will assume you're staying with Caroline, so no one is going to suspect anything different. When I get back, you go home and take care of Caroline, and I'll take care of Toors."

Carter nodded. "I can do that. What's he shackled to?"

"He isn't shackled. He isn't even cuffed. He's in the first bedroom down the hall."

Carter glared at me in disbelief. "You're shittin' me!"

I tried to calm him down. "Think about it for a moment, Carter. This guy while locked in a jail cell evaded a coordinated attack by two trained professionals armed with high-capacity automatic weapons. Do you really think a pair of handcuffs would do any good?"

"He's not frickin' Houdini, Sam!"

"You're right, my friend. He's much better than that."

***

Friday morning traffic on the northbound interstate was comparatively light, and I was able to comfortably walk into Tomlinson's office at the stroke of eight o'clock. Nevertheless, I was the last to arrive.

A larger crowd than I anticipated was in attendance. Tomlinson was seated behind his stately oak desk with his backdrop of three flags behind him, as usual. Phillip Tribby was seated on the sofa corner closest to the chief's desk. Our two new friends from the FBI, Rupert Anderson and Wayne Stephens joined him there. The two leather seating chairs fronting the chief's desk, including the one I liked so much, were occupied by Mayor Oslander and Police Commissioner Mason James. It was James who sat in my chair.

With a thin, self-conscious smile but without a word, I moved behind the chairs to take up a standing position next to the credenza to the left of the commissioner. As I did so, the chief began the meeting.

"Now that we're all here," he said with a disapproving squint in my direction. "We can start with a recap of last night's events. Detective Culhane, would you summarize for our guests what transpired at last night's stakeout of the Midtown Market?"

I grimaced. He had sprung his little surprise on me without warning, and a sleepless night with a caffeine hangover was poor preparation for any substantive response.

"I'm sorry, Chief, but I thought we were going to cover Dr. Tribby's report this morning."

"Oh, we will, for sure," Tomlinson nodded in Tribby's direction and immediately turned back to me with a self-satisfied smile. "Right after your report on last night. I'm sure everyone would be interested and it could shed some light on developments in this case, don't you agree?"

I felt everyone's eyes on me. I cleared my throat. "Of course, Chief, I'd be happy to."

"Make it brief, Sam," he said leaning back in his chair. His smile told me he was enjoying himself too much. "Just the high points will do."

I took a breath. "Well, let's see. I regret there's not much to report, really. Yesterday evening I received a phone call from one of my informants that Toors had been sighted at a deli in the Midtown Global Market building on Lake Street. I considered the source reliable and immediately responded. En route to the scene, I contacted Chief Tomlinson to arrange for backup and to discretely seal the building. He did so. When I arrived, I met with my informant who directed me to the suspect. It turned out not to be Toors. I bought an order of baklava to go and gave it to the chief before leaving the area. End of the report."

Wayne Stephens shot a quick question at me. "Why did you call Tomlinson? Isn't dispatch standard operating procedure?"

"Normally, yes," I answered calmly. "But I felt it important to first confirm the sighting. I needed the chief to coordinate backup quietly so as not to spook our guy. I wasn't confident standard procedure would produce the desired results."

Stephens followed up. "But with it not being 'our guy' you didn't have to go to the extra trouble, anyway, did you? You could've followed normal procedure, gone in and taken him into custody just like any other apprehension, couldn't you?"

I didn't know where Stephens wanted to take the discussion, but I wasn't much interested in following along with the FBI's direction on this, either. "Discretion seemed to be in order. With the way things worked out, it proved to be the proper thing to do."

Tomlinson jumped in before the FBI could make another contribution. "Okay, then. Let's proceed with Dr. Tribby's report."

"Thank you, Chief," Phil said, coming to his feet and standing at the corner of the chief's desk with an open notepad in hand. "Autopsy results for the body found at the park and the two bodies from the attack on the jail have confirmed all three died from the same type of massive infection and nerve degeneration disorder of the earlier first two victims. In other words, they died from what we all assumed – a hyper-leprous condition of unknown origin…"

"No blast damage from the explosion in the jail?" It was Stephens again.

Tribby shook his head. "None. However, we've received information from the BCA on the identities of these three people."

Tribby turned to the next page of his notebook. "One of the men killed at the jail was a local boy: Richard Jonathan Corks; twenty-eight; formerly employed by a security contractor out of Oklahoma called 'BlueCore Intelligence' – one of several security contractors the government has used in Afghanistan. Apparently, he left them more than two years ago. His immediate employment situation is, as of yet, unknown, as is his place of residence. His mother lives in St. Louis Park. She told us she has not seen or heard from her son since his discharge from U.S. Army Special Operations Command about five years ago. At that time, he was honorably discharged with a 'Weapons Sergeant' rating."

"A Green Beret sergeant at twenty-three," I summarized from my side of the room. "Well trained and tough. How did he end up dead in our city jail?"

"I haven't figured that one out, yet, Samuel," Tribby admitted and turned another notebook page. "Enois Peteka, Greece national; thirty-two years of age; has the prestige of being on Interpol's Top-25 list; known gun for hire who has been linked to more than one political assassination in Eastern Europe over the last decade. He was the other man from the attack on the jail.

"But our body from the park is the most interesting: Frank Tubbs, thirty-eight years old; former special security consultant to the Secretary General of the United Nations; also former Green Beret proficient in weapons, tactics and communications. About eight years ago, Mr. Tubbs, while on a deep-sea fishing junket in the Caribbean, just disappeared. There is no record of him being seen anywhere since that time; at least until he decided to take a stroll in Theodore Wirth Park this last week."

I glanced over to Stephens to see if he was going to jump in with a query. He looked at Rupert, who looked at him, and said nothing. It was my turn.

"Phil, do you have anything on the two crispies reccoverd from the flood?"

Tribby shook his head. "Not yet, Samuel, but give the BCA until next week. This last go-round greased their skids a bit, so things might come a little faster with the newbies."

The commissioner was next. "These are interesting profiles. One thing seems to be certain: those guys on the slabs at the morgue aren't your run-of-the-mill gang-bangers. Someone hired them to do the job."

"Someone with a good-sized checkbook balance," Tribby added. "Those men didn't come cheap. Neither did their gear."

"Someone, too, with more than a little pull," I threw in. "Don't forget the way they walked into the jail, or the fact they so easily compromised our secure communications network, especially during the storm."

Tomlinson fingered his upper lip. "Maybe not so easily now that one of their communications experts is dead."

"I don't know, Chief," I said, unconvinced. "Tubbs was killed in the park, but the storms were just the other night. The 9-1-1 calls during the storms were hacked into somehow. We find the hacker, we find who's steering this thing."

"It's gotta be Toors," Stephens piped up. "That's it, isn't it? Toors is our man. Everything points to him. I think if you guys put out a fresh APB and we get our guys to cover your flanks, we can zero in on our man pretty damn quick."

"You're thinking of a coordinated interdepartmental operation of some sort?" Tomlinson asked.

"Sure, why not?" Stephens quickly replied. "I've had our guys in Chicago do a little digging on Toors and his former hangouts there. Also, we're working on what appears to be similar deaths a few years back in the Chicago area, New Jersey, maybe other places. Who knows where this will lead? But we're going to keep digging. All of us work together, corner this guy, and he has no way out. Batta-bing-bang-boom: case closed."

I was leery. "Sounds like an armed incursion to me."

"Whatever works," Stephens said firmly.

Tomlinson turned to Oslander. "Mr. Mayor, I know you've been taking more than a little heat from the press. Have you anything to add?"

The Mayor smiled. "Well, Chief, I have heard it said that there's no such thing as bad publicity. That being said, the growing attention our city is experiencing from the press isn't as beneficial to the city as we might like to think. You all are evidently on top of things. That's good. I also understand Agent Stephens' desire for all of us to work together as a team. However, talk about armed incursions and cornering people concerns me. You know, Tombstone never really recovered after the gunfight at the OK Corral. Minneapolis won't benefit from a gun battle in the streets, either. I encourage everyone to be professional about what needs to be done respecting the law, individual rights and presumed innocence until proven guilty."

Stephens offered a clipped, "I assure you, Your Honor, no one implied otherwise."

Oslander acknowledged the comment with a silent nod.

Stephens directed his attention at me as he continued. "So we find Toors and take him in. If memory serves, I believe you, Detective Culhane, said you were on top of the Toors situation."

The corners of my mouth curled upward. "Yes, Agent Stephens, I did say that."

"Perhaps you could enlighten all of us," Stephens smiled.

Again, all eyes were on me. I hated it.

"My latest information," I started carefully. "Leads me to believe Simon Toors may have a personal acquaintance he relies on for support."

Stephens raised a questioning eyebrow. "And where exactly is this acquaintance located?"

"Somewhere south of the river, or so I understand. I'm narrowing it down and should know more later today."

The FBI agent smiled. "You must have quite the support staff yourself. Who is this acquaintance?"

"All I have is my partner and that's about it," I answered firmly. "As for Toors' friend, I'm working on that, too."

"And you'll know more sometime later today?"

Tomlinson interposed himself in our little discussion. "That's what he said, Agent Stephens. Sam's a good cop and he gets results when he isn't crowded."

With his hands raised and a grin best described as part disgust and part sinister, Stephens acceded to the chief's wishes. "Well, then, we certainly wouldn't want to crowd the man. Let's give him as much rope as he needs."

Chapter 9

"You Do Not Know Who This Man Is."

"I trust Stephens just about as far as I can throw him," I complained as soon as the elevator door slid shut. Tribby and I had the elevator car all to ourselves.

"Buy you a coffee?" Tribby offered, pushing the button for the third floor. "You look like you could use it."

The car began its descent, the slow change of the luminous green digital readout atop the button panel holding our attention.

"I didn't get much sleep last night."

Tribby tsk'd me as he shook his head. "You young people – so much to learn, so little time."

"Gee, thanks, 'Dad' – I think I have at least a two maybe three years on you."

"You say that about everyone."

"The meeting went too long," I complained looking at my wristwatch. "It's after ten o'clock already – gawdawful punishment if you ask me. Your info was good, but any meeting that takes more than an hour isn't worth having."

I reconsidered how far I could throw the FBI guy from Washington if I had to. "Actually, Phil, I could toss Stephens around pretty good. He doesn't look all that tough."

"He's taller, though," Tribby reminded me. "However, I must say he did seem to have an axe to grind this morning. The word 'complementary' does not adequately describe the working relationship between the two of you."

"Working relationship, my ass," The readout clicked down another number. "He's after something, Phil. He wants this whole thing in his lap, and as far as I'm concerned, he can have it."

"You don't mean that."

"Oh, yes I do."

"I find that hard to believe, Samuel. I sense you are close to solving this case. Why else would you reveal so much about your progress in tracking down the leads, and so reassuring about having even more solid information yet today?"

Another number change as the car moved past the next floor.

"I wasn't prepared for the flash quiz routine. Half of everything I said was tap-dancing and blowing smoke, my friend."

Tribby shook his head. "You're telling me you put yourself in a box and then closed and locked the door? I don't believe you. You're hiding something. You already know what you need to nail this thing, and you know where to get it, don't you?"

I turned my head back toward the digital readout, suddenly worried I may have revealed too much to the others during the meeting. If Tribby had picked up on any of my unintentional verbal or nonverbal lapses, others in that room may have as well.

A knowing grin spread across his face. "I thought so. Can you let me in on it?"

The digital readout clicked to 3 as I said, "I don't know what you're talking about."

Tribby shrugged. "I guess that answers my question."

The doors opened and we exited toward the left, following the large arrow wall graphic that read Cafeteria.

In the cafeteria, we stopped at the counter with its line of four air pots – two for regular, one each for decaffeinated and hazelnut. Grabbing sixteen-ounce-size Styrofoam cups from their neatly stacked towers, Tribby and I pumped them full of the high-test stuff and found an empty four-top close to the window side of the nearly half-occupied room.

"So if you won't tell me what you've got," Tribby began anew, "may I share with you a theory I have?"

I took a sip of the hot stuff and nodded my permission.

"Well, it struck me as odd that so many people were so quick to accept the idea the attack on the jail was an escape attempt to free Mr. Toors, while at the same time, absolutely ignoring the oddities staring them in their collective faces."

A small snicker as I commented, "It's odd you noticed the oddity of their oddly ignoring the oddities of the case."

Tribby bounced back a brief grin in response. "So very redundant of you, Samuel. Still, just the same, there are many oddities that have yet to be explained."

"And your theory explains them?"

"Possibly."

"I'm intrigued. Please, continue."

"It's not that profound: Simon Toors is the target of the attacks, not the instigator."

"That's a supposition Tomlinson already made at the flood site. I agree with him on the point, but it isn't proof."

Tribby added a provision for my consideration. "Remember what I suggested at the Glenwood scene – the idea that the bodies weren't targets but actually hired muscle that had failed in taking out the real target?"

I nodded. "I remember you stopped an argument and that was when Tomlinson had his brainwave of inspiration."

"And that was also when you blew up at him," Tribby added.

"Among other occasions," I perused the immediate area in an automatic security check. "The guy drives me crazy sometimes."

"Don't you think it odd the FBI hasn't accepted the truth of this? Even now, at this morning's meeting, Stephens talked about cornering Toors – 'Bing, bang, boom – case closed' remember? He thinks Toors is orchestrating all this. And yet, it is obvious Toors is not the instigator. Toors is, in fact, the target. Why would the FBI be looking at all this through the wrong end of the telescope?"

I took another sip pleasantly surprised to find the coffee holding its temperature. "It wouldn't be the first time law enforcement ignored the obvious in favor of some preconceived, completely wrong notion they were driven to just make things look completely right."

"But would the FBI do that?" It was an interesting question. "Wouldn't that kind of influence be local and not come from the Feds? If you're right and we have people driven to steer this case in the wrong direction, who's driving: our friendly neighborhood mob boss, or someone from out of town?"

"I'm not sure, Phil, but whoever it is, it would be helpful to get a peek at their agenda. It must be pretty substantial to intimidate frontline personnel enough to sway what gets done on the ground."

Tribby's befuddlement overflowed with an exasperated sigh. "The only thing that doesn't fit in any of this is the woman. Why kill a woman, make it look like a rape and dump the body in the park? The woman wasn't the target, was she?"

"Not likely," I commented, the sleep-deprived wheels of my mind slowly kicking back into gear as I experienced a brainwave of my own. "On the other hand, if you're a hunter, what's the best way to attract your prey?"

I could see the lights come on in Tribby's eyes. "You use bait."

"The most evil kind of bait possible," I added, my wheels shifting into the next gear now. "To draw the attention of a poor, deluded sap convinced he's some kind of invincible do-gooder who is destined to save the world."

"Toors?" Tribby asked.

"Toors," I nodded. "How could anyone consider that milk-toast a threat worthy of stalking and killing? It doesn't make sense. Someone's after more than just taking Toors out."

"So you agree – there is someone pulling the strings. Someone we don't know."

I nodded over the rim of my cup and took in a full swallow this time. "A puppet master good enough at what he's doing to make all of us go in the direction he wants us to go."

Tribby had his doubts. "I don't see Stephens as that guy."

"He's not," I concurred. "But Stephens might know who is. The real things are the whys behind Stephens' act. Why go after Toors if he's not really our guy? If we collar the shmuck, we end up with the wrong guy and the right guy gets away. Who gains from that? Whoever the puppet master is, he has to be the guy who gains the most when we bring Toors down. If he doesn't benefit directly, who does? Does the puppet master have a puppet master of his own? I tell you, Phil, just thinking about all this gives me a headache."

"Take two aspirin and call me in the morning," Tribby leaned closer. "You and I are on the same page, Sam; so is the chief, at least I think he is. Stephens isn't helping and I believe it's because he's getting orders to take this case away from us. But he has to do it smart. If he succeeds and solves the case in the right way, it'll be a big feather in his cap."

"And you think his plan is to make me look incompetent?"

"You and, by association, the whole department, yes. What other reason would he have pulling the crap he did at the meeting this morning?"

"Maybe it's his idea of a cross-agency cooperation thing again," I rubbed my temples with the hope of relief. It didn't come. "Man, I'm tired."

"Take two NoDoz and call me in the morning. But before you do, do me a favor."

"What would that be?"

"Let me tag along with you this afternoon," he almost pleaded. "You're onto something, Samuel. Let me be a part of it."

I could trust Tribby with my life. However, I didn't trust myself with risking either his life or his career.

"That might be a bad idea, Phil."

"You don't need to worry, I can take care of myself."

"I know that," I agreed. "But things have happened you might not want any part of. I can take some risks, but it isn't fair to put you in the middle of my consequences."

Tribby pulled back into his chair. "I think I see. You know, you have two major faults, Samuel: you have no respect for people in authority and you have even lower respect for yourself and your own career. In the end, you're good at what you do because you don't give a shit whose toes are stepped on as long as the job gets done. That's okay. Given what you do and what you see all the time, the job is more important than any one person, including you. I understand.

"That being said, today is a critical day for you and you could use someone to watch your back. I can be that person."

"Carter's my partner," I mildly objected.

"Carter's taking care of his wife. Consider me a pitch-hitter."

I had to admit, having Tribby along wasn't a bad idea. If I got shot, he'd be there to patch me up. I doubted I could count on the same thing from either Carter or Toors. One last time I tried to put off the former Navy medic who was obviously itching for some frontline action.

"You're letting yourself into more crap than you can possibly imagine. When this little surprise hits the fan, and trust me, Phil, it will hit the fan, don't say I didn't warn you."

A satisfied smile spread wide across the man's face. "Deal!"

***

Tribby followed me through Meredith's front door. Carter's face immediately fell when he rose from the sofa and saw Tribby.

"Oh, Jesus, Sam, not Phil."

"Don't blame me," I waved him off. "He forced me to bring him along."

Tribby smiled and extended his hand to Carter. "My fault entirely, I assure you. How's your wife doing, Carter?"

Carter took the man's hand in greeting and nodded without hiding the solemn shroud of embarrassed guilt he carried. "Thanks, Doc. She's doing much better now. I hope to get back to her pretty soon."

"Hence Dr. Tribby's presence, my friend," I interjected and then asked, "Where's Toors?"

"He's in the bedroom," Carter mumbled. "After Meredith left for work, I handcuffed him to the bed frame."

I didn't hide my displeasure. "That's not necessary."

Carter disagreed. "You have to restrain your prisoner, Sam. You don't do that, you're breaking with procedure."

"He's not a prisoner," I stated flatly. "And don't you think handcuffs are a little inadequate to restrain someone who has so effortlessly managed to compromise the more rigorous confinements the police department has to offer?"

Tribby nodded with newfound awareness. "So this is the surprise, Sam. You have Toors in custody and he's here. Funny, but oddly I'm hardly surprised at all."

"You should be, Doc," Carter cursed. "My partner's turned his back on procedure and we're all in jeopardy because of it."

I turned to the hallway and walked quickly to the bedroom. Inside the day-lit room, Toors sat cross-legged on the floor, hands folded in his lap, as he had been the night before. This time, he looked up when I walked in and smiled.

"Good to see you again, Samuel."

I knelt down and began with an apology. "I'm sorry. Carter told me he cuffed you and that's not necessary…"

"Oh, yes," he reached behind him, pulled out the handcuffs and handed them to me. "Here you go."

I examined the hardware he handed me. The cuffs were pristine as if never worn, folded and ready for use. I looked down at his wrists for marks, scratches, or any evidence of struggle. There were none. His expression wasn't boastful, or conceited in any way. At that moment I knew: Simon Toors had a reason to be there with me. What I didn't know was what that reason was.

I helped him up to his feet. "Time to go see your friend."

***

While Tribby and Toors acquainted themselves with each other in the Crown Vic, Toors in the backseat, Tribby in the front, Carter and I held a brief confab standing in the driveway. He was clearly disturbed by the recent turn of events and not all that supportive of what I was doing with Toors. I chalked it up to the stress of dealing with Caroline's mounting health problems. It was easier to excuse the more disagreeable side of his nature that way.

Carter was not convinced Toors held the key to solving this case. He was more convinced Toors was the cause of the mysterious killings and someone who deserved less courteous treatment to help encourage more substantive answers.

"You may be right," I admitted. "And if this friend of his doesn't pan out, I'll be taking him in once more for booking. But I have to check out the lead first, okay?"

Carter's eyes nervously darted from me to the car and back again. "You're taking too many risks in this thing. It's not like you to be this reckless. This guy could be the coldest killer in history and you're letting him lead you around like you're on a bus tour of the park system. For all you know, he could slit your throat in a blink and smile while he's doing it."

I glanced toward the car and watched Toors and Tribby exchange pleasantries giving the two of us squabbling in the driveway very little mind at all. "He's not like that, Carter. He's different, all right; I'll give you that. But he's not the killer."

Urgently, Carter grabbed my wrist and forced me to face him. "He's a sociopathic homicidal madman not worth the risk you're taking. Turn him in now. I don't want to be responsible for what could happen from here on out."

My opposite hand gently covered his and I gave it a reassuring squeeze. "Don't worry. Nothing will happen; if anything does, you won't be responsible, and if the friend is a dead end, Toors is back in a cell by dinnertime. I promise. Now go home and take care of Caroline. I got you covered."

With a solemn, almost regretful nod, Carter stood away as I walked to the driver's side of the car and got inside. Backing slowly, through the windshield I caught a glimpse of him watching us, still standing where I had left him. I cleared the driveway, slipped the gearshift into drive and drove away.

"Carter seems upset," Tribby noted a moment later.

I didn't soft-soap things. "He thinks I'm making a big mistake. He's probably right."

From the backseat Toors added, "There are other things bothering him, Samuel. He is under more than a little stress, I'm afraid."

Toors' comment irritated me. Carter Wolpren had enough on his plate already, and he wasn't any concern of Simon Toors.

"Simon, this person you know who can help: who is it and where can I find him?"

He sat back in his seat, hands folded in his lap. The less than pleased expression on his face told me he had picked up on my growing impatience.

"His name is Steeg Patterson. I don't know where he lives but I do know he lives on the south side of the river somewhere."

My impatience grew by at least a third. "Well that's terrific. Steeg Patterson. Certainly narrows things down a bit knowing the territory covers everything from St. Paul to the Iowa border! For cryin' out loud, Simon, you gotta help me out here! Your continued free breathing depends on this!"

Tribby pulled his smartphone from his jacket pocket and punched in an app. As he did so, Toors calmly supplied something helpful.

"Go back to the interstate and head north. Take the 35-E exit and head east. Follow that route until I tell you where to exit. I don't know the house number, but I'll recognize the landmarks in the area when I see them."

"How very reassuring," I sneered at his reflection in the review mirror. Tribby leaned over and with a lowered voice supplied a useful bit of information from his smartphone app.

"Marvelous invention, this new phone. A GPS navigation capability, a white pages directory web page coupled with Google Maps – truly remarkable technology. Did you know there's a Steeg and Carol Patterson residing in Eagan – on Coachman Road just south of Yankee Doodle?"

I nodded and looked up at Toors' reflection in the rearview mirror. He was smiling again and my irritation grew another two clicks worth on the meter.

***

The Leper

It was ten minutes past two on a clear and bright Friday afternoon when we pulled into the driveway of the Patterson residence. For a community known for larger, more opulent homes, it was a modest house. The lawn was nicely greening for the first week in May, the planting beds nudging against the house and stretching along the driveway had been recently raked and cleaned, primed for the planting of potted flowers soon to come. The sun was bright; the air carried just a hint of spring coolness. The doublewide garage door was shut, but the upper and lower front windows of the house were opened, the window dressings moving slightly with the gentle breeze.

I unfastened my seat belt and turned to Tribby. "You stay here with Toors. I'll see who's home first and do the talking."

Toors raised a pointed finger. "Perhaps I should accompany you, Samuel. I might be of some help."

"No, you stay here with Phil. I don't want your face outside this car until I know the coast is clear."

Tribby nodded his understanding and Toors yielded. I left the car, walked up the two steps of the front stoop and rang the doorbell. From the far side of the door and behind a rounded evergreen bush, I heard a muted "Yes, can I help you?"

I walked down the stoop and around the bush to see a middle-aged man with thinning hair holding a telephone receiver against his ear. His hand covered the mouthpiece as he looked back at me through the lower level window screen.

"I apologize for disturbing you," I began with a slight stoop and a self-conscious smile. "Are you Steeg Patterson?"

The older man smiled back. It was a nice smile. "Guilty as charged. And I know who you are. You're that Glenwood murders police detective, aren't you?"

"Guilty as charged," I echoed.

"Well, you're a long way from Glenwood Avenue, but if I can help you in any way, I will."

"I appreciate that," I excused myself. "I'll wait out here until you're done with your phone call."

The man laughed. "What phone call? I've been on hold for more than twenty minutes. Have you ever had to call the Social Security Administration?"

"I can't say that I have."

"Well, take my word for it: don't. The government's got a computer answering the phone now and the thing talks to you, asking you to talk to it. You go back and forth with this twenty-questions thing getting nowhere. It's insufferable. The computer finally gave up and told me I was being connected to the next available service representative. That was so long ago I forgot what I was calling them about. I'll be right up."

The man was good to his word. Inside a few seconds the front door opened and I watched him eyeball me, the Crown Vic in his driveway and the two passengers inside. He offered his hand as I stepped forward.

"Come on in," he said sincerely and nodded in the direction of the car. "Bring your friends, too. No sense in wasting the tea water."

I was reluctant to take the offer. I threw a cautious look back at the car, wishing I had thought things through a bit more. "I don't want us to be a bother, Mr. Patterson…"

Patterson's laugh was pleasant, even comforting. "I've reached an age when I'm not bothered enough. Come on in, all of you."

He stepped from the door and held it open wide. I waved Tribby and Toors out from the car to join us, which they quickly did. I introduced Tribby first.

"This is Dr. Phillip Tribby, our medical examiner."

The two shook hands as Tribby stepped over the threshold. Next came Toors.

I verbally stumbled over myself. "I understand you, er, may know this gentleman…"

Patterson smiled and took Toors' hand firmly. "Hell-o, Simon. It's an honor."

"Thank you, Steeg. How are Carol and the children?"

"Carol's shopping and the kids are all grown up," Patterson motioned Toors through the doorway and urged me to follow. "So tell me, Detective, how might I help your investigation?"

Patterson's familiarity with Toors shouldn't have surprised me, but it made me feel slightly ill at ease. Inside, he led us to the upper-level living room that overlooked the backyard. The mid-afternoon sun shown through large opened windows and the low humidity breeze floated refreshingly across the room. Patterson offered Toors the most comfortably upholstered chair the room had while Tribby and I shared an adjacent sofa fronting a low coffee table. Our host turned toward the small kitchen and motioned for me to follow. I returned to my feet and did so.

The teakettle was on low and the water was steaming. Patterson efficiently marshaled the necessary tea ball, measuring spoon, serving pot, cups, saucers and tray. He pulled a dark wooden box with a small top lid hinged on one side from the cupboard.

"I hope you like freshly brewed tea, Detective."

I shrugged self-consciously. "Actually, if it doesn't come in a bottle with a screw-off cap, it's a little foreign to me. You really don't have to go to any trouble, Mr. Patterson."

"No trouble at all, and I mean it." Patterson loaded the dry tea into the tea ball, placed it in the serving pot, retrieved the kettle from the stovetop and poured the hot water in. "This is my own special blend. Actually, Simon started me on this stuff years ago, so I know he'll like it."

Leaving the now full pot to steep, Patterson retrieved a small carton of heavy cream and a fresh lemon from the refrigerator. This was followed with a beautiful crystal serving schooner and matching sugar bowl from a cabinet shelf. He proceeded to slice the lemon into small wedges, placing them in a separate serving dish made of fine china. Next, he pulled a French baguette from a lower drawer, a serrated bread knife from the countertop butcher-block holder and swiftly sliced off ten uniformly thin slices. These he placed in a silver basket he first lined with a cloth napkin. Two matching cruets, one of olive oil, the other vinegar, and a wooden pepper mill were placed next to the basket. He then appropriately filled the creamer and sugar bowl, quickly assembled four more cloth napkins bound by silver napkin rings, grouped four china teacups with matching saucers and neatly organized all of it on a black onyx serving platter almost as large as the coffee table in the living room.

Patterson beamed with satisfaction. "There, it's ready. Would you be so kind as to take the tray into the next room, Detective?"

He had done all the work, it was the least I could do. When I placed the tray on the coffee table, Patterson immediately set about serving everyone, starting with Simon Toors.

"It's not much," he apologized sincerely. "I wasn't sure I'd see you, but I tried to have something ready just in case."

Toors graciously accepted the ringed napkin from Patterson, pulled it free and laid it smoothly across his lap. Patterson followed with a saucer carrying a full cup of steaming tea already with cream and sugar added.

"I believe this is how you like it," Patterson said confidently.

After a brief sip, Toors nodded. "So nice of you to remember, my friend."

Tribby and I exchanged curious glances, neither of us certain about what was transpiring between the two men.

After Patterson had served each of us our tea, he prepared a saucer with oil, vinegar and some freshly ground pepper, and then placed it next to the silver breadbasket. He then took his own tea and sat in the facing chair across from us. Behind a careful sip he said, "Please, help yourself."

I watched Toors retrieve a single baguette slice from the basket, dip it lightly in the oil-vinegar mixture, take a bite and smile at Patterson in appreciation. Embarrassed slightly, I felt my face suddenly warm with a blush. It bothered me that Toors might not have had anything to eat yet that day.

Toors' eyes caught mine. It was as if he could read my thoughts. "Don't be concerned, Samuel. It's quite all right."

A weak smile of acknowledgement preceded my hesitating turn toward our host. "Mr. Patterson, the reason why we are here today is Simon suggested you may be of some help in our investigation..."

Patterson nodded with a small, tight smile and an acknowledging glance in Toors' direction.

I continued. "I have only a few questions for you, but I need to first ask how is it you know Simon? You seemed genuinely excited, even pleased to see him; you certainly made an extra effort in welcoming us – remarkable considering we didn't announce our visit in advance. I guess I find it curious."

Patterson's smile widened into a grin. "You and I are about the same age, I think."

He may have had a few years on me, but not more than that.

"You have a bearing about you, Detective," Patterson continued. "Your posture, the way you carry yourself. Ex-military; Marine, perhaps?"

"I'm the Marine," Tribby offered with a small laugh. "Well, Navy Corpsman, actually. Culhane's the swabbie."

Patterson raised an eyebrow. "Ah, I see, Navy men; me, too. I pushed airplanes around the hanger deck on the USS *Hornet* for more than three years."

I knew the ship and I admitted it easily enough. "I was on her for a short time. Early '69, Gulf of Tonkin."

Patterson's other eyebrow went up. "Now that is interesting. How did you happen to do that?"

It was none of his business, but the war was over decades ago and we had lost. I decided to leave out most of the details.

"My team was pulled out of scrape north of the DMZ. Our chopper got hit by ground fire and the *Hornet* was the only safe landing spot in the neighborhood."

Patterson's face lit up. "That was a Marine gunship. You guys spent a lot of time in CIC, as I recall. I was on the hanger deck crew that dollied your chopper into Hanger Bay Two so the Brown Shirts could patch things up."

It was my turn to smile. "Small world, isn't it?"

"Very," Patterson agreed. "1969 was a very eventful year."

"Yes, it was," I wasn't much for reminiscing about the good old days. "I don't want to be rude, Mr. Patterson, but I am curious about your relationship with Simon Toors."

Patterson took another sip of tea and placed his cup and saucer on the coffee table. "Ah, well, I first met Simon many years later, 2006 actually, at a rest stop in Wisconsin. We were introduced to each other by a mutual friend."

I was confused. "You mean you were introduced at a rest stop?"

Tribby could not contain himself. "This isn't going to be something kinky, is it?"

Toors laughed as Patterson explained things. "Back then I was going through a rough time. Our mutual friend helped me understand what was going on, and then he introduced me to Simon who helped train me on the basics. Simon proved to be a very good friend. My only regret is that I can't spend more time with him."

I looked at Toors. His face was calmed by that irritating self-satisfied smile of his. Time to get back to the investigation.

"Mr. Patterson, Simon has told me you could help us. What do you know about the Glenwood killings and Simon's connection with them?"

Patterson smiled with a sideways shrug. "I know what everyone else knows: they are horrible deaths; they happen quickly; there have been several of them. In addition, I also know Simon did not kill those people."

"Okay," I said, returning my half-finished cup and saucer to the tray. "Do you know who did?"

"I have my suspicions, but I would have to confirm them first."

"With whom?"

"With Simon."

That irritated me and I turned immediately to Toors. "So help me, God, if you're tying knots in my tail Simon, I'm going to beat you to death!"

Toors' irksome placid smile was followed with an equally irksome calm rebuttal. "You're so physical, Samuel. It's not healthy for you. Steeg only wants to make sure his suppositions are correctly attributed to the proper person."

Toors turned to Patterson and nodded.

"I see," Patterson said as he turned back to me. "I'm not sure you will accept this, Detective Culhane. It requires a certain level of understanding."

Through gritted teeth I said, "Try me."

"Very well." He took a deep breath and let it out in a rush. "Simon is a special person. Unfortunately, what makes him special also makes him a great threat to certain people. This has been true for a great length of time. These people are relentless in their pursuit of him. Because he is a special person who is also a great threat Simon is protected. It is the Protector who is responsible for the deaths you are investigating."

I pushed down my now rising fog of confusion and noticeably struggled to focus on what Patterson was saying. "I need you to speak plainly now. Are you saying Simon has a bodyguard out there capable of killing people with some kind of chemical or bacterial weapon?"

Patterson's answer skirted the question. "I think Simon's concern at this moment is the consequences of closed-thinking. You may hear the Truth, but you may not recognize it."

I replied sternly. "You tell me the truth, I'll recognize it."

A disturbed sadness fell over Patterson's face. "That's good. So there you have it: Truth is Simon's protector."

I rejected that straight away, opting for more clarity from the man. "I told you to speak plainly."

Patterson leaned forward. "Your problem is, Detective, you do not know who this man is."

Chapter 10

Hammer Down

I didn't beat to death either Patterson or Toors, but it wasn't because I didn't feel like dong it.

After I blew up and vomited a stream of obscenities at both of them, Tribby forcibly removed me from the room, in the process literally pushing me outside the French doors leading to the deck overlooking the backyard.

The comfortable breeze outside was pleasant enough, but I ignored it, pulling angrily away from Phil's grasp and moving to the deck railing. From there I could see through the large window back into the room where Toors and Patterson remained where we had left them, calmly talking as if nothing was wrong.

"Toors' going back to jail!" I punctuated the statement with an abbreviated string of descriptive adjectives. "And as far as I'm concerned, this Patterson guy is going to share a cell with him. He's in with Toors on this and I'm taking both of them in!"

Tribby disagreed. "You don't really believe that, Samuel."

I glared at him. "You wanna know what I believe? I'll tell you what I believe, Phil: I believe Toors is exactly what Carter said he is – a homicidal sociopath!"

Tribby shook his head once more. "I don't see that, Samuel, and you don't either."

"Well, I sure as hell can believe that a helluva lot easier than the fairy tale Patterson is feeding me! He says I don't know who this man is?! What the mother-f... "

Tribby quickly raised a warning finger to my face and interrupted me sternly before I completed the statement. "All right, Sam, it's time to calm down."

I glared back at the window, swallowed hard and struggled to adjust my language.

"What I mean is, Phil, I don't know what Patterson says is supposed to mean. And then he adds this dribble about how Toors is spiritually protected by God; how he's on some kind of mission and satanic forces are trying to destroy him before it's completed! For the love of Mike, what the hell is going on here?! I got a growing pile of bodies in your morgue, two goodie-two-shoes in on the other side of that window living in a fairy tale world, and the only thing we're missing, Phil, is a guy in a purple dinosaur suit singing 'I Love You, You Love Me'!"

Phil's placid demeanor remained intact through my tirade. "Sam, I know it all sounds too fantastic. But look at these guys. They're not hysterical. They're not zealots. They're not thumping their Bibles over your head telling you to repent. You asked them questions. They're giving you answers to those questions; fantastic answers, to be sure, answers you may not like because they don't conveniently plug into your paradigm, but Sam, these men believe what they're saying to you is absolutely true."

I didn't want to hear it anymore. "I haven't got time for this, Phil. I promised Tomlinson I'd have solid information this evening. One way or the other, Mark's going to get it."

Phil understood, nodded as I joined him in a repeated glance back through the window. Toors and Patterson remained seated where we had left them.

"They're still in there, waiting for you."

"Toors isn't stupid," I replied sourly. "He knows if he bolts, I'll shoot him down."

"I believe you would," Phil admitted. "But that would be a mistake. I'd hate to have to perform an autopsy on you after you're turned into a crispy."

Our eyes met. "You don't really believe that crap about the Protector and mission from God stuff, do you, Phil?"

Tribby let out a slow breath. "Suppose you're dealing with a particularly skillful suspect – say a con man who was an absolutely flawless liar; or someone mentally impaired and thoroughly delusional – in a world completely of their own making. They weave a tale of woe with nuggets of truth stitched together by lies and distortions. But because they could be the guy, or at least capable of leading you to the guy, you need to uncover every bit of truth you can from them. How would you use their play-acting or delusion to get what you need?"

I cringed as Phil's common sense put me in my place. It was painful when the words left my mouth. "I'd gain their trust; let them talk and uncover everything I could. I'd play along as long as it took."

Phil nodded with a smile. "You'd play along."

Through the window, my prisoner and his fellow zealot remained seated in quiet conversation.

I shook my head. "I blew it. Can't play along and gain their trust now. I've shown all my cards and there's not much left to play."

"Use your leverage."

"What leverage?"

"Both of these men appear to want to help you, Samuel," Phil explained patiently. "Use that to your advantage."

"So why aren't you the detective?" I joked, my stress relieved a little by a small chuckle.

"Because I'm taller," Tribby returned as he turned toward the French doors.

"No, you're not," I protested mildly, following from behind. "Your average height like me."

"I'm still taller."

Both men looked up as Phil and I walked back through the French doors and returned to the living room. My apology was a simple one.

"I'm sorry," I said plainly, looking at each man in turn. "You didn't deserve that. I was out of line and I behaved poorly."

Toors' placid nature remained constant and reliable as he said, "You're under a lot of pressure, Samuel. We understand. Events are accelerating and we only want to help you be prepared."

Patterson nodded in agreement as Phil and I returned to our seats on the sofa.

"I know it is all so bizarre for you, Detective," Patterson added. "At the same time, however, you must appreciate the position you have been placed in at this precise moment in time."

Although I was prepared to play along with all this, I couldn't deny the sense of real regret growing in my gut. I was in completely new territory, and the only thing I could anticipate for certain was that I couldn't anticipate much.

"If everything you say is true, Mr. Patterson, the only thing I can appreciate at the moment is the simple fact that I'm in way over my head. Early on, we theorized Simon was the target and not the instigator of the killings. I mean, look at him: he's so gentle it's absurd to think he's a murderer. But when you say his Protector is the cause of these deaths, and not someone's hired goon or Jihadist with some kind of bacterial weapon we don't understand, that puts a whole new spin on everything. At the very least, it means Toors is responsible, and where does that leave me?"

Toors leaned forward. "You, more than most other people, must know there is true evil in this world. You battle against it every day. You have immersed yourself in continual combat against this evil for years. Certainly, you have relied on your love of Christ to manage all the consequences this struggle has brought to you."

"I'm not a religious man, Simon."

"And yet, you talk with the Father all the time. So much so, it's become automatic and you don't even realize when you're doing it."

My sense of regret stumbled into a clumsy embarrassment. "Those are quiet, private little conversations, Simon. I don't talk about them."

"Christ knows your heart, Samuel," Toors returned sincerely. "He has chosen you."

Playing along stepped up to a more difficult level as I felt the moisture gather in the corners of my eyes. I fought back the emotion and said quietly, "I'm not worthy to be chosen for anything. You don't know me, Simon. You don't know what I have done."

Toors leaned still closer, placing a hand on my shoulder. "He knows you, completely and better than you know yourself. That's all that matters. A great battle is coming, Samuel. He has chosen you for a great purpose, just as He chose me."

That brought my eyes up to Simon. I was dealing with a man who was absolutely convinced he was chosen by God for a specific purpose; a man equally convinced that God had also chosen me for some mission – the objective of which I had no clue. And the only thing I had to work with were the sheet-covered crispies in the morgue.

I pulled my gaze away from Simon and looked across to Patterson, who silently agreed with a simple nod. When I looked at Tribby, he nodded too. I turned back to Toors.

"Okay, Simon, let's say you're right. How did you know, really know, God had chosen you?"

Toors leaned back into his chair, his face at rest with that annoying, completely peaceful smile of his. "It is not convenient that you have so little time, Samuel. The Lord gave me much more time to learn. Your time is short, I'm afraid. But then, you are much quicker and brighter than I am."

"Flattery does not become you," I warned him, perhaps with too stern a tone. "I need an answer: how did you know God had chosen you for this mission?"

With serene simplicity, Toors said, "He told me, Samuel."

"You have a direct line to God?"

"Through my Savior and Redeemer, yes."

"Okay. Then tell me specifically: what is your mission?"

"To evade capture, divert attention of satanic surrogates while the way for the two prophesied witnesses is prepared."

"Two witnesses? What two witnesses?"

Toors' reply was a mild rebuke. "Read your prophecies, Samuel."

"Maybe later," I fell out of playing along just long enough to rub my brow and marshal my thinking. I looked at Tribby sitting next to me and shook my head. Tribby offered a slight shrug of his shoulders and an encouraging nod. I turned back to Toors. "Simon, I'm going to take you at your word on all this. I accept what you say about your mission. However, my lines of communication with God have mostly been one-way in nature. Unlike you, He hasn't told me my mission. Would you be able to help me out on that; maybe provide some insight into what you think God wants me to do?"

"Of course, Samuel," Toors readily agreed. "I can tell you what He wants me to tell you for now. Perhaps you and I could step outside onto the deck for a moment and get some air?"

I came to my feet, turned and bent low toward Tribby. "Keep Mr. Patterson company, okay?"

Tribby glanced at Patterson and nodded. Toors and I departed through the French doors for the outside deck.

The afternoon was already approaching early evening. The sun was noticeably lower in the sky, drawing advancing shadows from behind the surrounding trees and stretching them across the lawn toward the house. I leaned my forearms onto the railing as Toors joined me on my left and began his explanation in a quiet voice.

"Samuel, the Lord prepares each of us differently in His own way for His own purposes. We are equally His instruments as well as His brothers or sisters. Because we believe, we are connected directly to Him through the blessings of the Holy Spirit who resides in each of us. This is a great power, the full measure for which He prepares us over time. At this time, for you, you need to know the most important aspect of your mission is to rely on His wisdom and allow Him to do what must be done. He will protect you. Everything that is happening is doing so because He wills it. Regardless of what happens, you must believe He is greater than the trials you are about to face."

"Trials? I just want to know what I'm supposed to do. What does He want me to do?"

Toors reached over and covered my clasped hands with both of his own. "Don't be concerned with how this will be done. Rely on Him to do it. For now, know you will destroy the satanic surrogates closing in on my mission. Understand this will pit you against great evil and powers in high places. You will be hunted. You will be betrayed. Do not lose heart. Do not be afraid. You are greatly blessed, my brother. Christ is with you and you are His chosen warrior."

I almost laughed in his face, but his open and simple sincerity stopped me cold. I shook my head. The one fact I could accept was that Simon Toors was completely insane.

"His chosen warrior, you say? If that's true, He has chosen poorly, Simon. I'm old and getting older. I haven't been a warrior in any sense for more than thirty years."

Simon squeezed my hands. "He will strengthen you, Samuel. You will not fail. He has faith in you. Strengthen your own faith in Him. Spend more time in His Word. Allow yourself more quiet time with Him over the coming days. He will breathe new life into you and you will be young again."

A small laugh accompanied my response. "Young again? Well, that could be refreshing."

Toors chuckled. "Yes, refreshing when you let it show."

I nodded, accepting the role Toors had laid before me. Insane or not, the man was the only lead I had to bringing this case to an end. "Okay, Simon, you have yourself a warrior. What's next?"

"Don't be concerned," Toors coached me patiently. "All that must happen is already in motion."

From my pants pocket, my cell phone chimed its familiar melody. I pulled it open. "This is Culhane."

"Tomlinson," came the one word reply. "Where are you?"

"In Eagan, working the case. What's up?"

"The case, that's what!" Tomlinson barked excitedly. "You got anything for me, yet?"

"Working on it."

"Well, we have a lead! I just got off the phone with Rupert. He says their people have received a solid tip Toors is in Hutchinson and he wants a combined forces operation with full tactical support ASAP."

I was mildly impressed and threw an arched eyebrow at Toors standing next to me. "Rupert's either been eating his Wheaties again, or he's getting direction from his boss, Stephens. Did he mention when and where the tipster saw Toors in Hutchinson?"

"Actually, he did. Toors was spotted having a cheeseburger in the local Hardee's burger joint around lunchtime today."

I smiled at Toors and continued with the Chief. "Interesting, Mark. So you think this tip is viable?"

"Could be. What do you think?"

"I have my doubts, but then, what do I know? I'm just the chief detective on the case. How do you want to play it?"

"I got Cathy contacting the Hutchinson police chief and the McLeod County sheriff's office. I'll have more in a few minutes on SWAT support. We're buttoning things up now and moving out within the next five minutes. If you're in Eagan, start heading for Hutchinson. We'll coordinate en route. Got it?"

"Roger, wilco," I hung up and slid the phone back into my pocket. I turned to Toors. "It seems someone has tipped the FBI that you were spotted eating cheeseburgers in Hutchinson."

Toors shook his head. "I don't eat meat and I don't believe I've ever been in Hutchinson. What does 'Roger, wilco' mean?"

"Geez, Simon, sometimes you're as dumb as a stick." I waited for his reaction but it was evident my complaint fell on deaf ears. I gave up and explained as I stepped toward the French doors. "Roger means 'I understand'; wilco is short for 'will comply.' It's not new, Simon. It goes back to World War Two. If you're going into a battle, the least you can do is learn the lingo."

"I appreciate that," he said with exasperating sincerity. "You know, Samuel, you are very colorful in your way."

***

Outside in the driveway, we said our good-byes to Steeg Patterson. After Toors and our host embraced in parting, I directed Toors to the backseat of the Crown Vic and shut the door behind him. I turned to Tribby. We moved to the front of the car for a short near-whispered confab out of earshot of either man.

"How do you want to play it?" Tribby asked.

"I want you in the backseat with Toors," I explained without looking back at the car. "Make nice with him – you're better at it than I am. Keep him talking if you can – it can be a challenge, so don't get frustrated. I'm calling Carter before we leave."

Tribby nodded, turned and stepped to the rear passenger door on the far side of the car. I pulled my cell phone from my pocket and speed-dialed Carter.

Carter answered my call as if we were already in mid-conversation. "You can't live without me, can you?"

"Always stating the obvious." I shot back. Over my shoulder I saw Patterson wave at me with a smile and walk back into his house. "I might need your help."

"And I'm the one stating the obvious? I just got off the phone with Tomlinson. Guess who the FBI thinks is in Hutchinson?"

"I already know, Carter. Curious, isn't it?"

"Curious, my ass," Carter disputed bluntly. "Someone's setting someone up. Unless your Crown Victoria has been turned into some kind of time machine, there ain't no way Toors made it to Hutchinson in time for lunch."

"At last, we agree on something."

"Yeah, well, maybe. He's still a frickin' murderer as far as I'm concerned and you can take that to the bank."

"I'll give you this: he's a wacko all right; maybe a member of some kind of fringe religious cult or something. He's got friends. He's convinced he's on a mission from God and that I'm part of it. Tribby told me to play along and it seems to be working. Toors has opened up quite a bit, and with this latest thing from the FBI, the trail is heating up. What did you tell the chief?"

"I told him I can be there if he needs me."

"Nothing about Toors?"

"Of course not," Carter sounded a little miffed by my question. "You're in the lead on this. I'm not going to screw it up for you. Of course, it'll be your ass when Tomlinson gets wise to what you're doing. Speaking of which, what are you doing?"

"I'm going to Hutchinson to help collar Simon Toors, just like the chief wants."

"The same Simon Toors you and Tribby are driving around town with?"

"So it would seem," I glanced back at the car and the two men waiting in the backseat. "The FBI tip is obviously bogus, although whoever gave it to them is someone we need to have a heart-to-heart discussion with as soon as possible. The chief is going along with it in the spirit of inter-departmental cooperation and for general CYA principles. I need to find the person pulling all the strings and that means I need somebody I can trust to watch my flank. That's you, Carter."

"I'm your guy," Carter accepted without hesitation. "How are you going to be able to go to Hutchinson to collar the same guy you already have riding shotgun with you? Isn't that going to cramp your style a little?"

I hadn't figured that one out yet, so I changed the subject. "How's Caroline doing?"

Carter laughed. "You're not going to believe it. She just left with Meredith to do some shopping!"

"Whoa. That's a little amazing, isn't it?"

"Yes, I'd say it is. That's why I'm taking the 'Vette to Hutchinson. Maybe I'll see you there, help you out with keeping Toors in your trunk or something, whadda ya think?"

"I'd appreciate the company."

***

The most direct route to Hutchinson from Eagan was across the river on the Cedar Avenue Bridge, west on Interstate 494, then west again after the Highway 7 exit. It would normally take about an hour and one-half from where we started, but westbound 494 was slammed with evening rush hour traffic. Until Tomlinson called with updated instructions, I elected to not use the lights and siren, content to crawl along bumper-to-bumper until things loosened up past the US Highway 169 interchange.

Before the freeway turned north, Tomlinson called.

"We're doing this on the quiet," he said. "We're assembling at the airport. Turn off Highway 7 at the County Road 22 exit; go south to Airport Road, then west to the airport. When you cross County 15, the road curves and there's a maintenance building with a parking lot on the left. We'll be there. You can't miss it cuz we're coming in two SWAT vans."

"Subtle," I chuckled. "Couldn't you guys carpool?"

"No time to work out anything different for the squad we're bringing," Tomlinson explained. "But we're not the problem. The FBI is the problem. They're coming in helicopters."

"Like that won't draw attention?" Ahead, the first advisory sign for the Highway 7 exit came up on my right. "Mark, at normal speed we're still about an hour out. What's the situation out there, do we have a location on Toors?"

"So Rupert tells me, but he hasn't said exactly where. He's saving it for the briefing on-site, I guess."

"Or, he's being careful and trying to keep communications as secure as he can," I added.

"I'm not real comfortable going to this much trouble without having more specifics, but they're FBI and they want to play."

Tomlinson sounded uncertain. With the real Simon Toors sitting in my backseat, I had my doubts, too, not the least of which was keeping this simple truth from the chief. "You think something else is going on, Mark?"

"Maybe. Things don't feel right. I can't really go into it right now, especially on a cell phone. We'll talk at the airport maintenance garage, okay?"

"Roger and wilco."

Both Tribby and Toors leaned forward to contribute to my sluggish thinking. Toors was the first of the two to offer his input on the situation.

"Samuel, this is a somewhat precarious situation for all concerned, don't you agree?"

"Yep," I stated flatly as I speed-dialed Carter.

"I have faith, Sam," Tribby's eyes caught mine in the rearview mirror. "And I admit I'm the amateur here, but it seems to me you're unnecessarily putting yourself in jeopardy."

I smiled back as Carter answered after the third ring. "That's what makes it fun, Phil."

I brought the phone back up to my ear. "How far out are you?"

"Not very." Carter sounded grumpy. "I made the mistake of coming up 35-W. Came to a screeching halt a mile south of the 494 exit. I'm just passing France Avenue now and I'm seriously thinking of turning around and going to Perkins for dinner."

"You'll miss the fun if you do," I advised. "Keep coming. We're a few miles ahead of you, just now turning onto Highway 7. Does Mark know for sure you're coming?"

"No. I thought I'd surprise him."

"Don't bother. I need you to babysit for me again."

"Oh, no. You just told me I'd miss the fun if I stopped for something to eat. I think I've already done enough babysitting gig on this case and I'm not all that good at it, anyway. Stick him in the trunk like I suggested."

I wasn't confident Toors hadn't heard every word Carter had just said. "Actually, that's the fun I was thinking of. We need to do a switch on this, and with you bringing the Corvette, you'll blend in nicely. Besides, I don't think Simon has ever ridden in a real Corvette before."

I looked at the rearview mirror and saw Toors shrug slightly and shake his head. I continued with Carter. "I'll be waiting for you at the Hardee's parking lot in town."

"I'm doing this under protest."

"So noted. See you at Hardee's. Cheeseburgers on me."

"That's small consolation, Culhane."

"That's what I can afford. Later."

I hung up and Toors leaned in close once more.

"I don't like cheeseburgers," he reminded me seriously.

I dismissed his concern with a wave of a hand. "So order a side salad. I'm sure they have those, too. Besides, you get to sit in Carter's bodacious Corvette – you'll love it. This little excursion shouldn't last for long."

I leaned slightly to the right and caught Tribby's reflection in the mirror. "Phil, you stay with me. We're going to follow this as far as it will take us."

Tribby nodded. "You're the detective, Samuel. I assume you believe, in some way, this will lead to the real 'Man Behind the Curtain' in all this?"

I shook my head. "You give me too much credit for a plan that doesn't exist, my friend. I'll be happy if we find the guard at the Emerald City gates. I can work with that."

In the mirror, Tribby smiled and leaned back into the seat. "You know, of course, in the movie 'The Man Behind the Curtain,' the guard at the city gates and the Wizard of Oz were all played by the same actor."

I digested that bit of cinema trivia for a moment and said, "Let's hope life imitates art."

***

Acronyms appeared to be the order of the day. In the approaching dusk, my headlights illuminated the driveway sign that read "HASAM" in large reflective lettering with "Hutchinson Airport Service and Maintenance" printed underneath. The pavement immediately led to an elongated parking area, the far side of which held two local Hutchinson police cruisers and two large, solid black utility vans with boldly displayed "SWAT" painted in white on the back side panels.

Tribby, sitting in the front passenger seat since we switched Toors to Carter's Corvette at the Hardee's Restaurant, observed the gathering of law enforcement vehicles and chuckled. "Do you think we'll succeed in sneaking up on poor Simon Toors without him noticing?"

"Not likely," I answered, slowing the Crown Vic and rolling to a smooth stop on the street side of the parking area well clear of the rear SWAT van. I slapped the gearshift into park and doused the headlights. "No one seems to be out here, so they must be inside the building. Let's go find them."

When we reached the halfway point in the parking lot, Tomlinson emerged from the front door of the building and waved us over. As we walked up, I smiled and reached to shake his hand.

"Nice to see you could make it," Tomlinson sounded grumpy again. He released his grip and turned to Tribby. "Hi, Doc. Whadda ya doing here?"

"Samuel invited me, Chief."

I expanded on the point. "He's my temporary partner, Chief, until Carter gets back on board. Besides, Phil wanted to be in on the kill."

Tribby nodded in agreement, but Tomlinson's brow furrowed with unmasked concern. "I'm not crazy about that idea, Doc. Things could get a little messy if this turns bad on us. I want you to stay well behind the lines, okay?"

Hesitantly, Tribby nodded again. I stepped closer to Tomlinson and suggested a quick confab before going into the building. The three of us moved a few paces west of the doorway.

"Is everyone here?" I asked.

"Everyone but the Feds," Tomlinson replied.

I grimaced. "They're flying in on helicopters and they're late to their own party? That's not good."

Tomlinson's nervous glance bounced between Tribby and me. "I agree. There are several things not good about all this, not the least of which is their keeping you out of the loop."

"I'm still the detective in charge, then? You haven't replaced me? You haven't offloaded the whole mess to the Feds?"

"Of course not."

"You did threaten to get someone else to handle the investigation, Mark. And this little sojourn into Central Minnesota springing on us like it did, I just wanted to make sure of what was really going on."

Tomlinson shook his head, his face carrying sincere regret. "For cryin' out loud, Culhane, you gotta know when I'm serious and when I'm not."

"For survival, I default to serious almost every time. I figure it's safer that way."

"Yeah, well, you gotta know by now most of what I say isn't exactly said the way I want to say it."

"Good enough," I acknowledged. "Tell me again why we're letting the Feds run this op."

The chief expelled a heavy sigh. "Inter-agency cooperation, pure and simple. I don't like it either, but Rupert called me…"

"Instead of me," I interjected.

"Yes, true enough. He called, said the magic words…"

I interrupted again. "Which were what, exactly?"

"Actually, he said, 'You promised.' He brought up all the stuff we had verbally acquiesced to before, claimed the tip on Toors was from solid source and, presto-chango, here we are, armed to the teeth 60 miles outside of Minneapolis, and if everyone and his brother doesn't already know we're here, they soon will."

I shook my head. "Rupert's been listening to his boss. Stephens has the kid convinced he's some kind of Eliot Ness and we're his own little team of 'Untouchables.'"

Tomlinson agreed. "You may have a point. Still, the profile of this case, all the interested parties, the people muscling us to get things done – all of it suggests a little go-along-to-get-along might be in order, if only to cover our asses a little."

"I've never been much good at CYA, Mark."

"Don't worry," he smiled. "I'm an expert at it."

"Glad to hear it." I glanced at Tribby and quickly turned back to Tomlinson. "As our resident CYA expert, could you advise us on how we're going to cover ourselves from the consequences when this bogus operation blows up in our faces?"

The chief's expression was rock solid and he was not surprised. "Bogus in what way, Sam?"

"What if I told you there is absolutely no way the Fed's tip on Toors being in Hutchinson was legitimate?"

"I'd want to know how you know that to be true."

I turned to Tribby. "Phil, do you believe Toors was in Hutchinson for lunch earlier today?"

Tribby smiled and shook his head. "Sorry, Samuel, but no, I know for a fact Toors was not in Hutchinson for lunch."

"How do you know?" Tomlinson repeated solemnly. He turned between the two of us expecting a straight answer. He didn't get one.

"For now, let's just say we know he wasn't here earlier today," I stated flatly. "How would that fact change your position on interagency cooperation?"

Tomlinson's face darkened noticeably. "That would piss me off. It would mean we're being played. It would mean there's another actor we haven't accounted for, maybe someone higher up in the FBI, or somewhere else on the Federal food chain – a politician, entrenched government asshole of one sort or another. Hell, I don't know. I only know someone is trying to make us look bad and I wouldn't like it."

Both Tribby and I nodded in agreement.

"Chief, I'm thinking someone else is pulling the strings now; God knows we're not – this circle-jerk in Hutchinson is proof of it. This whole setup stinks and the one thing I know for sure is, when it's all over, Simon Toors won't be in custody and the Feds will take over this case. Whoever's pulling the strings, he doesn't give a crap about making the department look good or bad – he's got bigger plans and he'll crush anyone to reach them. We'll end up taking the blame for botching things up and only the string-puller will win."

Tomlinson fingered his furrowed brow. "Wins what? What would anyone gain by any of this?"

I didn't know where the word came from, but somehow it tumbled from my lips.

"Victory."

***

The assembled task force patiently bided its time in the open expanse of a large and way-too-clean garage adjacent to the building's four-room front office area. It was a colorful gathering made up of twenty helmeted SWAT officers in black BDUs covering concealed Kevlar vests, four Hutchinson police officers in blue duotone khaki duty uniforms and four more McLeod County sheriff deputies similarly dressed in brown khakis with each wearing their characteristic flat-brimmed hats. The SWAT guys pretty much kept to themselves, checking and rechecking their gear and weapons. The city and county cops more comfortably mingled – they knew each other; they didn't know the SWAT guys. Tomlinson, Tribby and I did our waiting in the front office proper, along with a Hutchinson Police Department liaison officer doing his best to hit on the familiar and attractive Officer Magan whose ready smile beamed in my direction when the three of us entered the room.

"Nice of you to join the party, Officer." I said to her as I walked in.

"Wouldn't miss it for the world, Detective," Again she smiled that marvelous smile of hers. She followed with more of a serious statement than an actual question. "It looks like we're going to finally get the Glenwood Killer?"

I purposely tried not to wince at that, but my failure reflected in the flash of concerned doubt crossing her face. With a half shrug I sighed, "Well, we'll see."

Twenty minutes later, it was past dark when the county sheriff's SUV pulled up to the maintenance building. From inside the office I watched through the window to see the sheriff emerge from the driver's side as Rupert Anderson and his taller, still bald boss from Washington, Wayne Stephens, exited from the two passenger side doors. Rupert studiously keyed in something on his cell phone as the three hurriedly made their way toward the front door.

There was a flurry of hurried handshakes all around as Tomlinson did the honors introducing our side to the county sheriff. The cordialities were barely completed when Rupert looked up from his cell phone. Interestingly, perhaps because of the chief's higher intimidation factor, Rupert directed his attention to me.

"We have to move!" Rupert announced in a rush. "The source says Toors is in town but not for long."

Tribby and I shared a troubled look and I quickly turned back to Rupert with a blunt question. "How do you know?"

He held up his smartphone for me to read his latest text message displayed on the screen.

"Impressive," I observed, unimpressed. "Who's GK636?"

THE LEPER

Rupert almost smirked with assuredness. "That's how I know the info is legit. It's encrypted and completely secure."

"Most impressive," I repeated, still unimpressed. "So, tell us, who is your source?"

"Well, if I told you that," Rupert's smirk returned. "It wouldn't be completely secure anymore, would it?"

Tribby stepped back as a grim-looking Mark Tomlinson moved in closer to contribute to the conversation. "We've got a whole lot of firepower in the next room, Agent Anderson, and a whole lot more on the line if something goes wrong on this. How did you find this guy?"

"He found me," Rupert declared. "I got a tweet from him two days ago. He told me what he knew. I checked him and his info out. It's solid, I can assure you."

I was incredulous. "You were tweet from him? He and you follow each other on Twitter.com?!"

"Initially, yes." The agent cast a quick, almost plaintive look toward his boss, got nothing in return and assumed a more aggressive defense as best he could. "We set up things for direct texting after I was convinced he was legit. It's called social media, Detective. Twitter, Facebook, YouTube have all become valuable tools for us."

It was time for my direct question. "Who is your source?"

"I can't tell you that."

Tomlinson jumped back in. "What does your source say about where Toors is at this moment and how do we know we aren't walking into something that's going to blow up in our faces?"

Anderson answered back without hesitation. "Because I trust him, that's how and he tells me Toors is back at the Hardee's Restaurant at Fourth and Main."

***

In the scramble that followed our immediate exiting of the building, the multi-colored uniformed task force quickly loaded into their appropriate vehicles as Tomlinson responded with a firm rejection of Wayne Stephens' order for him to ride in the county sheriff's SUV so they could talk.

"I ride with my men, Agent," Tomlinson's jaw testified to his determination. "You want to talk, talk now or stow it until later."

In the parking lot, Tribby and I fell in behind Tomlinson to offer our support. Tomlinson didn't need it.

"Okay, as you wish," Stephens acceded, firmly planting his feet to make sure the three of us respected his space. His eyes fell on me for only a moment and then returned to Tomlinson. "There's a leak in your department, Chief. We know who it is."

Tomlinson wasn't impressed. "A leak in my department? Really? And you know who it is? Fascinating. Do you need me to issue an arrest warrant, or what?"

"We're serious, Chief, you've been compromised in this investigation and you need to take action."

Tomlinson placed a soft hand on Stephens' chest. Irritated, Stephens pushed it away.

"Agent Stephens, I appreciate your concern. However, right now, let's take care of Toors. If your source is as solid as your boy says, I can deal with my department leak later."

Tomlinson stepped around the two FBI men and headed for the first SWAT van. Tribby and I went to the Crown Vic. The engine roared to life, but I stayed parked and let the other vehicles exit from the lot.

I put the cell phone in hands-free speaker mode and gave the command: "Call Carter."

As I waited for the call to go through, Tribby said, "It's an odd coincidence, Samuel, that the source who claimed Toors was in Hutchinson when he wasn't now claims Toors is in Hutchinson when he is."

The ringing of Carter's phone came over the speaker.

"I don't believe in coincidences, Doc."

Carter's voice answered the call. "About time, I was beginning to think you went home and forgot about us."

I saw both Rupert and Wayne look at me as their sheriff's SUV passed by and exited the lot. I slipped into drive and followed in behind them.

"Carter, where are you right now?"

"Staying low at the local Amoco station. Simon needed a restroom break and I needed an orange soda to wash out the French fry residue."

"You're not at Hardee's, then?"

"Not for a while, no."

"In about five minutes, there will be about three dozen heavily armed law enforcement people converging on the Hardee's to take Toors down."

"That's interesting. Funny how they figured out Toors was at the local Hardee's, isn't it?"

Before I could answer, Tomlinson's obviously irritated voice gruffly crackled from my portable radio. To the cell phone I said, "Carter, eavesdrop on this if you can, but stay quiet, okay?"

"Okay."

I placed the portable unit in my usual console cup holder and triggered the mic. "Go ahead, Chief."

"Go to secure channel four now."

"Going to secure channel four." I thumbed the channel selector knob over two clicks. In seconds, the chief came back.

"All force personnel, this is Tomlinson. Recap of instructions: at the Mall, county and city squads turn on Grade Road, west to School Road. Go north where the city squads turn east on Third Avenue and the County squads on Highway 7. You approach Hardee's, seal off the streets and hold positions at the corners of Glen, Main Street, and Third Avenue. Both SWAT vans stay on Main, with Command turning on Third Avenue and van 2 covering all egress points on the Highway 7 side. Secure the area and wait for instructions. Any questions?"

We heard a mic click followed by Stephens' voice. "If the suspect resists, lethal force is authorized."

I heard the anger spit from Tomlinson's reply. "Belie that! No one fires without my order. Agent Stephens, you're with me at Command van."

Stephens returned a double-triggered mic click in reply and nothing more.

I muted the portable mic while continuing to monitor the channel. "You get all that, Carter?"

"Pretty much," Carter cleared his throat. "You guys are going to pass our position. Amoco's right across from the mall."

"Is your 'Vette visible from the street?"

"We're sitting in the north side parking area of the store, but you'll see us if you look. I can see your group's string of headlights coming now, Sam. If I move, it could be messy. I'm sitting tight parked where I am."

"Roger. I'm bringing up the rear. When you see us pass, take 15 back the way we came, jump on Airport Road and nonchalantly make your way back to the cities."

"Okay, where do you want to meet later?"

"Your place, if that's okay?"

"Maybe. Give me a call when you're clear."

"Will do."

I disconnected from the call as our caravan slowed for the speed zone near the southeast corner of the mall. From the corner of my eye, I caught Tribby's tightlipped expression of concern.

"Don't worry, Doc. Nothing's going to happen. This little party gives a whole new definition to wild goose chase."

Tribby shook his head. "I don't know how you do it, Sam. You're cool as can be while my guts are tied in knots. This entire operation flies in the face of everything you and I know to be true, and yet we have a small army ready to shoot down a person who isn't even where they believe he is."

He took a breath, with effort quelled his apprehension well enough, and then added, "Someone could get hurt, Sam."

I couldn't argue with that. "True enough, Doc. You and I will keep our heads down, but remember the guy they're going after isn't really there. Nothing's going to happen."

At Grade Road, the city and county squad cars turned left as instructed. Less than a half-block later, Highway 15 veered to the right and we passed the Amoco station. Sure enough, I could see Carter's Corvette in the shadows of the rear parking area, the vague outline of two people sitting inside the car. The two SWAT vans and the county sheriff's SUV kept pace and continued through the curve that would take them to Main Street. There was no indication of anyone noticing anything at the Amoco station.

In my rearview mirror, I saw the 'Vette exit from the station parking area, move easily onto Highway 15 and drive away in the opposite direction. I allowed myself to feel a little more relief.

***

The local cops were flawless in their timing, executing their move in and shutting down the streets in perfect coordination with the Command SWAT van's turn onto Third Avenue. The van parked against the curb blocking the Hardee's parking lot entrance. Task force personnel quick-stepped from their vehicles and immediately took up positions even before the county sheriff's SUV pulled up behind the Command van. I brought up the rear and parked behind the sheriff's SUV. The sheriff and the two FBI pukes exited their vehicle and quickly trotted to the rear of the van.

Almost reluctantly, I unfastened my seat belt. "It's show time, Doc. Let's go see Stephens take control."

I grabbed the portable and we left the Crown Vic to cautiously move toward the van. Around us the night scene was colored by the rhythmic pulsing of red and blue flashes coming from the mix of mounted digital LED light bars on top of the squads.

"I guess everyone in the neighborhood knows we're here." Tribby's chuckle helped relieve his tension.

I looked around. "Yep. They're already starting to gather."

And they were. Cars diverted from the sealed-off streets contributed to the cacophony of sights and sounds that drew immediate attention from passersby and local residents alike. With each passing second, more faces of curious onlookers emerged from neighborhood doorways and sidewalk shadows to see what was going on. Within the few moments it took us to reach the van, a nearly unbroken line of hundreds of people materialized along the opposite boulevards surrounding the area. It was impressive and I said so to Tribby as I opened the van's rear door and stepped inside.

"It's your intel, alright!" Tomlinson bellowed, ignoring our entrance as he continued with Stephens and Anderson, his finger forcefully directed at the senior FBI official. "But it's my men and my ass on the line out here!"

I let Tribby pass me and I closed the rear door behind us.

Stephens' reply was blunt. "We know what we're doing, Chief. This guy is a killer. He deserves to be handled accordingly."

Tomlinson exploded. "You don't give God damn kill orders to my men on my watch! We don't know how solid your intel is. We don't know who your so-called vetted source is. There are innocent people sitting in that restaurant staring out the window at their worst nightmare, and I don't need Eliot Ness here to turn trigger-happy with my guys!"

The junior G-man glanced over at me and I smiled with pride. The chief was using my line to describe Rupert and it felt good to hear it.

"Culhane," Tomlinson barked, "I want you to go into the restaurant and put any patrons and staff at ease. While you're in there, confirm Toors' status if he's in attendance. If he's there, do not, I repeat, do not approach or take any direct action. Is that clear?"

"Clear as day, Chief," I smiled back, turned and directed Tribby to follow me out of the van. As I stepped down to the pavement, my portable barked out in unison what every other radio unit within earshot carried.

"Officer down! Officer down! We're taking fire!"

I froze for only a moment, and then spun around the corner of the van to see two city cops dragging an obviously wounded third officer behind their squad car for cover. My portable squawked again with a second alert.

"Man down!"

I heard no shots. I didn't know where to look, but several people from the gathering crowd near the Highway 7 corner began running toward our position. Following me on my heels, Tomlinson, Stephens and Anderson unintentionally blocked my retreat when I turned for the back of the van. I elbowed my way through to the corner of the van and saw Tribby standing where I had left him.

"Phil! Get behind the Vic – the doors are ballistic equipped!"

Almost as soon as I said it, the right side of Tribby's head disappeared in a pink cloud of blood and brain. A second later, with eyes wide open and completely void of life, his knees folded, his body collapsed to the pavement and the whole world slowed to a crawl.

I tried to run for him, but my legs, heavy as lead, resisted every stride. I could feel the strength drain from me even as I strained to reach him before he fell. Too late, I slid to my knees and cradled Phil's lifeless body close to my chest.

"God, no," I could only repeat it. "God, no. No, God, no. Please, no. Please. Please."

There were no shots, yet my ears rang with a high-pitched squeal drowning out almost every sound as frightened people ran in all directions, screaming, trying to find cover anywhere. I could see them crossing in front of me, moving through the darkness, the slices of multi-colored flashes cutting through the dark wedges of surrounding night; everyone in slow motion and the constant squealing in my head.

How much time had passed? It couldn't have been long. It felt like an eternity.

Tomlinson was kneeling in front of me now, holding his portable to his mouth barking orders I partially heard but could not understand. The noise in my head muddled everything else. He looked concerned as he reached for my shoulder and said something, my name, I think. I didn't hear him. He shook my shoulder again; his lips moved again. I still didn't hear him. I watched as he reached over to me, gathered Tribby's body and lowered it carefully to the pavement. I could only watch. I felt so cold. Why was I cold?

The two FBI pukes were there, their guns drawn. Tomlinson stood up and said something to them. Suddenly, Officer Magan's face was close to mine. Her lips moved saying something, my name, I think. From far away, a faint sound quickly gathered into a forceful vortex of jarring proportions and my hearing returned with painful effectiveness.

"Don't move," Officer Magan said once more. "You're in shock. Medics are en route."

Shock, my ass. "I didn't hear any shots, did you?"

She shook her head. "No one did. They're securing the area, but no one can tell where the shots came from."

"Suppressors," I mumbled to myself. I looked over at Tribby's body and his dead eyes stared back at me. "I betcha Phil called it – Micro Tavor MTAR-21 assault rifles, suppressor equipped and modified for 9mm rounds. The shot exited on his right side. It entered on the left. The shots were fired from behind and to the west of us."

Quickly, she looked in the direction I indicated, and then back behind her toward the restaurant. She grabbed her portable and triggered the mic.

"Chief! Hold! The shots came from behind us, not from the restaurant! Our backs are to the real threat!"

From over the radio she held, I could hear Tomlinson's voice. "All personnel hold your positions! Every other man pivot 180 to guard your rear and flank positions! Stand by!"

Chapter 11

BAIT

With news helicopters circling overhead, a flood of people filling the streets and an overly enthusiastic EMT finally giving up in his well-meaning but pointless efforts to get me into his ambulance, the only place I knew that wasn't in turmoil was inside the command van. There Tomlinson, Officer Magan and the FBI's version of the Frick and Frack boys were conferring with the Hutchinson police chief and the county sheriff over the unexpected proceedings of the evening.

The far end of the bench was not the most comfortable seat, but it was far enough removed from the others to help me recover from the current events. From chest to groin, Tribby's still damp blood covered the better parts of my shirt, jacket and slacks. Anger over all that had happened was waging a successful battle against the waning nausea in my gut. The same anger was also filling me with a growing resolve, a resolve I chastised myself for not having possessed much earlier. With eyes closed and head resting back against the bulkhead, I listened to the resident brain trusts bitch at each other.

To his credit, Tomlinson kept his head. He was on the portable with the CSI and BCA teams that had arrived by chopper an hour earlier to survey the locked-down area outside and analyze the crime scene. In addition to Tribby, two other cops, one Hutchinson PD, the other a country sheriff deputy, had been killed. The analysts were sorting it out with tripod-mounted lasers and handheld LED flashlights while the local police talked to anyone who might have seen something. Between frequent reports across the portable radio, Tomlinson kept up the pressure on Frick and Frack to produce their inside source for questioning.

"What do you mean you're trying to get hold of him?" Tomlinson leaned against the small arms cabinet and glared first at Anderson and then his boss, Stephens. "I thought you were in constant contact with him? You guys tweet each other, right? What's the problem?"

I heard Stephens mumble something I couldn't make out, but Tomlinson had no trouble understanding. His response in a low and ominous tone scared even me.

"You mean the only way you know this guy is through his cell phone number and code name? A code name you gave him? You don't know who he is, where he lives, anyone else who might know him, or where he might be?"

I kept my eyes closed during the prolonged silence that hung on the chief's open question. After a protracted moment, the chief's portable radio clicked with another report from outside.

"Chief, it looks like one shooter."

Tomlinson raised his portable and snarled back impatiently, "Stanski, that's not possible."

"Sorry, Chief, that's the way it shakes out. The trajectories of each hit converge at a single point elevated twelve feet off the ground behind a line of shrubs about 40 yards from your position."

The chief resisted more strongly. "I'm telling you the shots came too fast for only one person – within seconds – and three men went down, head shots all of them. Too fast and accurate to be one shooter."

"Sorry, Chief, I call it like I see it."

"Any other evidence?"

"Matted grass; a bent twig on a bush; a pair of gouges on an oak tree. The shooter may have used some kind of telescoping tree stand for elevation and bracing."

"Shell casings?"

"None found. We'll keep at it, Chief, but things are pretty clean out here. Whoever it was, they were tidy and they knew what they were doing."

That sounded too much like something Phil would have said. I opened my eyes to see Officer Magan's look of concern. I smiled at her. A slight upward twitch at the corners of her mouth preceded her step closer to me.

"How are you doing, Detective?"

"Really shitty," I complained unsympathetically. "It's late. I'm a mess. We've been played by pros and good people are dead. How's your day been, Officer?"

Magan stepped back, lowered her head with no reply and everyone turned as I came to my feet. I straightened my tie and tugged my shirt cuffs out from under the sleeves of a now ruined jacket. The left cuff was blotted with more of Tribby's blood. I ran my finger across the dried blotch and said more to myself than to the others, "I need to change."

Tomlinson looked sad. "I wish you would have gone with the EMTs, Sam."

"I'm not the one who got half his head blown off!" I snapped back too imprudently. Too late, I poorly tried to squelch the anger, and then more poorly recovered with a simple, "Sorry."

"I'm just saying that," Tomlinson countered carefully. "It would have been a terrible shock for anyone, Sam."

My glare began with Tomlinson and grew darker as it proceeded to each man in turn, ending with Stephens. "From what I'm hearing, some of us are more concerned about covering their asses than getting the assholes who did this."

Stephens bounced a sideways smile mixed with a nervous distain. "The chief is right, Culhane – it was terrible. You should get yourself checked out. We can handle things from here."

I offered a professional summary of my opinion on the G-man's observation. "Bullshit!"

As much as the limited space in the van allowed, the county sheriff and Hutchinson police chief stepped clear as Tomlinson and Anderson both moved in closer to intercede.

Tomlinson placed a calming hand on my arm. "You need to get some rest, Sam."

Anderson was more direct. "Everything that can be done is being done, Detective."

I turned, already mad enough to kill the junior G-man and I was in no mood to hide my feelings. "Why don't you tweet the son of a bitch who set this trap and tell him to get his ass in here?"

Surprisingly, Junior G-man didn't back down.

"We're tracking him, but our source is not responsible for what happened. He's a solid source!"

I wasn't in a mood to back down, either. "You're an idiot! This was an ambush and your man set us up! Hell, he probably was the triggerman on the whole thing!"

Stephens pressed in between us, bumping his chest against mine. "Back off, Culhane!"

It was Tomlinson's turn to hurriedly wedge in, elbowing Stephens aside as he wrapped an arm around my shoulders and turned me toward the door.

"Take it easy, Sam," he said quietly. "Now's not the time."

I glared over my shoulder at Stephens. A menacing voice I didn't recognize as my own answered. "Phil Tribby was my friend. He's dead. I'm going to find the person who killed him and return the favor."

The chief nodded his understanding. "Phil was my friend, too, Sam. I know what you're feeling. I want you to go home, take a hot bath and get some sleep."

"I'm not tired."

Tomlinson looked behind me and beckoned with a wave. "Officer Magan is going to make sure you get home, isn't that true, Officer Magan?"

"Yes, Sir," She replied, quickly stepping up from behind.

I objected again. "I drove here. I can drive back."

"Magan will make sure you do," Tomlinson reiterated and opened the rear door.

I stepped down from the van with Magan following. I turned back to Tomlinson's backlit silhouette standing in the doorway.

"Let's meet tomorrow," his shadow said. "Lunch is on me."

The door shut behind him and I turned and pointed a stern finger into Officer Magan's face. "I do the driving, got it?"

"Got it."

Even in the dark, I could see the shadings of Tribby's dried blood on the pavement where I had held him. The two of us stepped past the stain and headed to where I had parked the Crown Vic. Twenty yards away, perhaps several hundred people crowded behind a yellow-taped boundary that stretched completely around the two-block area now illuminated by multiple stanchion-mounted high-powered halogen lamps. Here and there shadowy figures of law enforcement personnel were busy doing what they had been trained to do.

I pulled my key fob from my pants pocket, pressed the button and unlocked the car doors. At that moment a prolonged distant scream filled the night air.

"Sam!!!"

The panicked yell came from the crowd behind the tape. I looked up to see Shelly frantically running toward us. On the other side of the car, Officer Magan pulled her Glock and held it up in a vertical ready position. I held out my hand to put her at ease.

"She's my wife, Officer," I said calmly. "As much as I might appreciate you shooting her, please don't."

Officer Magan smiled then nodded and holstered her weapon.

Shelly's frantic sprint from the tapeline downshifted to a lower gear as she ran around to my side of the car. Her expression quickly changed from terror to confusion.

"Sam, Sam," she stammered, coming up quickly, stopping to reach for me, and then just as quickly pulling back a step to keep her distance. "You're hurt! You are hurt, aren't you?"

I looked down at my blood-covered clothing. "No, Shel, it's not my blood. It's Phil's."

It took a second for the full import of the truth to register, but then her eyes welled with tears and she trembled noticeably. "Phil Tribby? Phil was one of the victims of this?"

A hollow "Yeah" followed my shallow nod. Shelly stepped back once more and caught herself against the side of the car. I reached to steady her, but she visibly shrank away from my touch.

"They wouldn't tell us who was killed," she muttered more to herself than to me.

"What are you doing here?"

From behind the tears, she leveled her "You-Dumbass" look at me. "My job. I'm a reporter. I'm reporting. I finished my stand-up and we were packing to get back to the station when I saw you come out of the SWAT van. I thought you were shot. You're not. They said they'd release the names of the victims after their families had been notified. I didn't know who... I thought you were hurt, that's all."

If it weren't for her "You-Dumbass" look, I would have been flattered. As it was, I couldn't be sure she really cared, or she had just really wanted to use an overly dramatic gesture to jump past the police tape and grab an "exclusive" with the lead detective.

I looked away as I said, "Well, I'm okay, just the same."

A heartfelt sob escaped deep from her throat. "But Phil?"

I shook my head and seriously wondered if she would be feeling better if it had been me whose brains got splattered across the street.

"It was quick," I avoided the details. "He never felt a thing."

"Oh, Sam," she sobbed again, folding her arms tightly across the front of her.

I stood there and looked. Her tears were real and I hated myself for wanting to hold her. I offered the only thing I had.

"I'm sorry, Shel. Can I give you a lift home, or do you have to go back to the station?"

To my surprise, she accepted my offer of the ride home. With an understanding nod, I walked her around the car to the passenger side. Officer Magan stepped aside as I opened the front door and helped Shelly step inside.

"Everything's fine, Officer," I said as I shut the door. "I'll be okay. I'm taking my... I'm taking Ms. Culhane back to her place and then going home as the chief ordered. I'll tell him tomorrow you did your job, understood?"

Officer Magan looked at me, then at Shelly sitting in the car, and then again to me. "I can follow in a squad."

"You can," I nodded. "But you won't, will you?"

"No, Sir. I guess not."

***

It was almost 1:30 in the morning when Carter's 'Vette' pulled into the near empty parking area of Mickey's Diner on Seventh Street west of downtown St. Paul. I watched him slide the 'Vette' easily next to my parked and abandoned Crown Vic. Observing through the diner window, I took another sip of coffee as Carter climbed from his magnificent machine, walked around the front to the other side and opened the passenger door. He bent down toward the shadowed outline of his seated passenger and whispered into Simon's ear while reaching down and below the seat. A moment later, Carter stood erect, shoved the handcuffs in the right-hand front pocket of his leather flight jacket as Simon exited the car. The two made for the diner and joined me in the booth. Toors sat inboard across from me, his unassuming expression mildly compromised by irritation when Carter took the outside seat.

"You actually cuffed him?" I groused at Carter.

He shrugged. "I don't take chances with crazy people."

I didn't argue. Carter's description of Toors was succinct and quite possibly accurate. I turned to Simon and offered an apology of sorts.

"You could have shown him your little escape trick," I said. "He'd see firsthand how silly he was being."

Toors full imperturbability returned with a half smile and a small shake of his head. "I didn't want to make him any more nervous than he already was."

"I wasn't nervous, I was prepared." Carter leveled a purposeful finger at me. "As you should be, pal, based on what I saw on the news tonight."

"You guys hungry?" I took another sip of coffee. It had cooled, so I signaled the guy in the paper hat and soiled apron behind the counter for a warm-up and two more cups.

With his characteristic docile smile, Toors said, "I could go for some soup. Do they have vegetable soup?"

I looked back at Carter. "You fed him, didn't you? At Hardee's or the gas station?"

Carter shook his head. "We didn't actually go to Hardee's. I preferred keeping to the shadows. The parking lot behind the gas station was perfect – secluded with a full view of the highway."

"Twinkies," Toors added. "He bought me a package of Twinkies and a bottle of water. Delicious – a banquet in a bag."

"He doesn't eat meat," Carter offered with a shrug. "I got a hoagie and a soda for myself. That only left Twinkies or Zingers for him, what can I say?"

I apologized to Toors again. "I can get you a cheeseburger..."

"I don't eat meat," Toors reminded me once more. "The soup will be sufficient."

The guy in the paper hat and apron stepped up to the table, a well-used coffeepot in hand with two more cups hooked by the index finger of his really large right hand. He plopped the cups down in front of my tablemates and proceeded to fill the cups all around as he answered Toors' question without looking at him.

"Beer cheese is the soup," he said humorlessly. "I can open a can of vegetable if you really want it, but I'd have to charge you double. It's a big can."

I leaned forward. "Stick with the beer cheese. Wisconsin cheddar – you'll love it."

Toors' smile disappeared, falling into a disappointed frown as he half-nodded his reluctant acceptance.

Paper hat man left for the kitchen and I turned to Carter. "I missed the news, but Shelly filled me in the main points of her report on the way back to her place."

Carter raised an eyebrow. "Ah, you two met, then? And you're still friendly after what she said on the news?"

"Sure, why not?"

"She pretty much said our prisoner here orchestrated the whole thing just to get some cops in his crosshairs."

I shook it off. "They had her on a live feed with no real facts to run with. She reported on what she knew at the time, which wasn't much, and filled the rest of her airtime with supposition, that's all. Not exactly the highest journalistic standards, I know, but she's so insecure in her job sometimes she shoots from the hip when she really shouldn't. It's irritating but she's often more concerned about her hair and makeup than getting her facts straight. What a job, eh? We talked about it on the way back, and I set her straight on what had actually happened. She was pissed I didn't give her a heads up before everything hit the fan, but she understands I was a little busy at the time."

"What does she know about our friend, here?"

I looked at Toors looking back at me. "Nothing. As far as anyone is concerned, Simon Toors is still on the loose. That's okay. It'll keep people on their toes."

Over the rim of his raised coffee cup, Carter observed, "You look like you're dressed for travel. Going somewhere?"

"You betcha," I admitted, pulling my foot out from under the table to show off my outfit. "I dumped the suit and tie for my hunting clothes and deer stalker boots. I got some extra stuff I need to add to the trunk, yet. Simon and I are going huntin' for some bad guys."

Carter cast a wary glance at Toors. "You might be better off with me. Taking this guy along with you leaves your flank exposed and you won't have anyone there to cover it for you."

"My flank faces the general direction of downtown, and that's where I need you to be."

"Please explain."

"Until now, we've been played for saps. That's gonna change. All I need is to find a place to set up. The people pulling the strings will come to me, and when they do, I'll be waiting for them."

Carter shook his head. "What're ya gonna do, tell them where you're at?"

"Look, Carter, whoever these guys are, they've been plugged into this operation from the get-go and that's for sure and for certain. They've known our every move even before we made it – Hutchinson proved that. Now we have two dead cops and one dead ME who, next to you, was my best friend. These guys are playing for keeps. It's time to take the gloves off."

Carter agreed but only to a point. "Whoever they are, they have backing and a lot of money. And they're well entrenched.

Who knows how far they can reach? If they can sway the FBI into taking action, they can squash you like a cockroach without even thinking about it. If you want me to stay on the inside and cover your flank, I need to know how you think this is going to work."

"First, I find the place to set up. Then they'll find me."

"Why? What's gonna lead them to you?"

I eyed Toors and quickly went back to Carter. "Because I have the one thing they want."

Carter followed my meaning. "Bait? You're using Toors as bait in this? What makes you think that'll work now, especially after Hutchinson? My guess is things are way too hot, especially now. My guess is whoever is behind what happened in Hutchinson will pull back and cool it for a while."

I looked out the window into the darkness to think about that for a moment. A big part of me wanted to go along with Carter's theory – it would be easier. A small voice in the back of my head cautioned against it.

I looked at the two of them and shook my head. "The ambush in Hutchinson was meant to embarrass us – specifically our department. It sets the stage for a major power grab by the Feds, or the governor, or somebody else. Like it or not, where Simon Toors is concerned, someone wants our department out."

With a near scowl at Toors, Carter disagreed. "He's a janitor, Sam: a homicidal sicko, for sure, but essentially he's a nobody. There's no political collateral to be had with him. What politician in his right mind would even bother with this guy?"

His placidity undisturbed, Toors' eyes locked onto mine. Slowly, an answer crystallized in my mind. "No politician would, Carter. This whole mess transcends politics. The political manipulations are means to an end and nothing more, used by someone who can make life really good or really uncomfortable for our collective bosses."

"So let them have him," Carter shrugged effortlessly. "They want him, give him up. He's a janitor, for Christ's sake. He's a fugitive. He's wanted. Turn him in and get on with your life."

Toors kept his eyes on me. I turned to Carter.

"That wouldn't be doing our job, Carter."

"Our job is to enforce the law. The law wants this guy. You have him. It's your job to turn him in."

"Our job is to protect and to serve," I countered seriously. "Right now, there are really bad people after this guy and it's our job to find them. We need to flush them out into the open."

"Noble, but dangerous. As everyone knows, you're short, but you're letting your height-deprived condition cloud your thinking. You can't trust this guy," Carter almost sneered at Toors before he continued. "I don't care how Pollyanna he seems to be, he's playing you and you're going to get hurt. Not that I care, of course. My professional ass is on the line, too, Sam. It's not just you, you know. There's a lot riding on your plan and if you lose control, you'll end up dead and I'm in the shitter. For a short guy, you're asking a lot."

He was right. I was asking a lot. But Tribby was dead and this was the one way to draw out the people who had killed him.

"I'm sorry, Carter. If you want out, I'll understand."

Carter cursed under his breath and took another swig from his coffee cup. "Hell, I'm already screwed so what difference does it make? Besides, I'm your partner. So what's your time frame to produce the results?"

"Not long; we're close." I turned my half-empty coffee cup in place as my mind raced to calculate the consequences. There were too many of them, but all of them led to just two possible conclusions: these people get pulled into the light, exposing them for who they are and what they are trying to do; or my own people find me out and they put an end to me. In fact, my own people could already be in the pocket of whoever the real bad guy was in all this. If that was true, with either outcome, Simon or I could both be killed. What was it about Simon Toors that made him a target for this kind of attention? Carter had said it: he was a janitor – a nobody. It didn't make sense. Why would anyone care? Why shouldn't I just turn him in and be done with the whole thing? Let the DA prove he's the Glenwood Killer, if he can.

"You need the answers," Toors calmly offered from across the table. "Together, we can find them."

Carter scoffed. "Don't listen to him, Sam. He's a psycho."

I leaned back, crossed my arms and eyed both of them as I considered things once more. "You may be right, Carter. Before this is over Simon Toors may prove to be the death of me; or not. But the one thing I do know is he didn't kill Phil Tribby this evening. Toors was with you. We find the people behind the Hutchinson ambush and we find all the answers we need: the Glenwood murders, the attack on the jail, the whole nine yards. The ambushers are our targets now. Simon Toors is our bait."

Carter sighed and shook his head. "Okay, Sam. We play it your way for now. Where is your bait going to be to draw these guys out?"

"Don't know yet," I admitted. "But we need to let them know he's out there. Like it or not, they consider this guy a threat. Let's make sure they know he's more of a threat now because of the attack."

Carter nodded but said nothing.

I continued. "If these guys are plugged into our operation as completely as they seem to be, let's make sure we let them know what we want them to know. Call Tomlinson and tell him you saw me with Toors at this diner. He's predictable. His standard operating procedure will draw enough attention from those who listen in on everything we do so well, they know what's going to happen almost before we do. I've already planted a story with Shelly that she's promised to release as an exclusive on this morning's Channel Six News broadcast."

"What kind of story?"

My small chuckle was accompanied by a sly smirk. "It's just to make sure the word gets out, but if she does it right, the chief will become an instant media star with the press as Minnesota's number one crime buster."

"Tomlinson is gonna be pissed. He'll say you're aiding and abetting a fugitive, Sam." Carter shook his head. "You're putting your own neck into a noose."

"The department is already compromised by the same people who pulled off the attack in Hutchinson – the same people responsible for all the crispies we have in the morgue. The chief will do what he has to do, and in the process, he'll help draw the people we want out of the shadows and into the light."

"What about the Feds?"

I shook my head. "The FBI is more compromised than our own department. That whole mess in Hutchinson followed a bouncing ball that started with them. Rupert and Wayne-baby were set up. Hell, Carter, their own bosses may be the very people we find at the end of the string we're following now. It's time to find out for sure."

"Yeah, Sam, but you'll be as much a target as Toors. That isn't going to end well."

Across from me, Toors was as passively unassuming as ever.

"It's necessary, Carter."

The guy in the paper hat and apron returned with a steaming bowl of beer cheese soup for Simon. As he placed it in front of him, the guy turned toward me.

"Just so you know, every night around this time, the same two St. Paul Police squad cars pull in. They take their lunch break here."

"Thanks," I said. My tablemates had heard every word.

Toors tried his soup and offered an approving nod.

I turned to the paper hat guy. "Could you put it in a to-go container for him?"

Unceremoniously, paper hat guy retrieved the bowl from in front of Toors and quickly returned to the kitchen. Toors held his empty spoon in his hand and looked disappointed.

"Sorry, Simon," I grinned. "You'll have to finish it in the car."

CHAPTER 12

SETTING THE TRAP

The dashboard clock read 2:45. The half-full moon hung low in the almost black western night sky. Sunrise was a good three hours away, yet. The storage facility was nestled in the southwest quadrant of Highway 13 and Cedar Avenue south of the Minnesota River just inside Burnsville's eastern border with Eagan. Access was anytime. The well-lit establishment with its many rows of identical, single-level storage garages was secure with a wrought iron fence that surrounded the place, a single gate opened by an assigned ID code punched in on a pole-mounted touch pad, and just to let you know you were being watched, an ample number of overhead video cameras peppered across the rows of padlocked roller-curtained doors. It was in locker number 233 where I kept most of my worldly positions since the divorce. Number 233 was two rows in and halfway down after a tight turn to the left.

I pulled the Crown Vic to a stop, doused the headlights and unbuckled my seat belt. "Simon, stay in the car."

Toors wasn't entirely in agreement. "Samuel, before we continue, perhaps it would be appropriate to discuss the specifics of your plan and what you have in mind."

"I already told you: we're going hunting and you're the bait. What more do you need to know?"

He wasn't fearful. He wasn't complaining. His expression held so much annoying patience I had to resist the real urge to punch him in the nose.

"Samuel, hunting is not necessary."

"You're telling me I don't know how to do my job?"

"Of course not, nothing of the kind," Toors took a breath, smiled with more nose-punching patience and continued. "Your motives are noble. However, your actions put yourself and others in severe jeopardy. This is not necessary."

"I see," my eyes narrowed. "So the long and short of it is you *are* telling me how to do my job."

It was difficult for me to believe he could become even more placid, patient and pliable, but somehow he did exactly that.

"You have been chosen, Samuel, for a daunting task. Your commitment to triumph over a terrible evil you have only begun to witness is admirable. In order to succeed and achieve true victory, our God who controls all things must be allowed to control what you do, too. You must give yourself completely to Him so you are an instrument of His will, and not of your own. I know you understand this to be true."

I almost laughed, but something in his look stopped me. I collected myself, shelved my resentment for his suppositions, his preaching and, most of all, this annoying aura of peace and patience he projected like the Pope. I knew exactly what his problem was.

"You're right, I understand: you're scared. Who wouldn't be? Hell, Simon, I'm scared, too. We're wading into this deal and I have no idea how deep the water is going to get. But I'll tell you one thing: I know how to do what we need to do. We're going to flush these people out into the open. I'm not saying we won't get dinged up in the process, but if I go down, I'm taking as many of those bastards with me as I can. I owe Phil that much."

He stopped himself from slapping on a little more moralizing. Instead, he paused and asked, "What about me?"

I couldn't help my little laugh as I reached under the dashboard and pulled the heavy-duty 10-inch LED flashlight from its Velcro mount. "Now there's a surprise: you concerned about you. I'll tell you what – you stay behind me all the way, you'll be fine. I'll see to that. In fact, don't stay in the car – come with me, instead."

At the locker, the combination padlock released on the first try. I pulled up on the roller door and swept the flashlight's bright white beam across the locker interior and the well-stacked collection of boxes, bags and crates. Things were undisturbed and where they should have been. The two of us stepped into the locker.

I pointed to the right side of the small enclosure. "I need three things outta here, Simon: a leather satchel, an old gray and brown suitcase and a sea bag. I think they're stacked somewhere behind these boxes."

He accepted the first box I took down from the top and guided it across the floor to the opposite side of the tiny room. I handed him three more boxes in turn and Simon neatly stacked each on top of the first. The last container on the bottom of the stack was a wooden crate, bulkier than the cardboard boxes and a great deal heavier. He helped me drag the crate free and together we slid it across the floor and against the newly relocated stack. We returned to the opposite corner and I directed the light into the new alcove we had just made: more boxes stacked on top of other boxes.

From behind, Simon looked over my shoulder. "Maybe on the other side of the storage area?"

"God, I hope not." I stepped forward, nudged an opening between two stubborn eye-level boxes and shoved the flashlight into the opening to see what I could see. "I think what we want is just on the other side of these boxes."

I wedged the flashlight under the eye-level corner of a box stacked to my left, positioning the beam to direct a little light on the situation. I then proceeded to dismantle the wall of cardboard cartons in front of me. When I had whittled the wall down to waist-high, I saw the leather satchel on top of the suitcase.

"Whallah!" I cleared the remaining obstruction, grabbed the satchel and handed it to Simon. Next came the suitcase. It was weighty. I wiggled it free by the handle, and with a strenuous grunt, guided it over to Simon.

"Heavy," he said as he took the faded and dusty piece of luggage and moved it next to the satchel on the outside pavement. "More than underwear and socks."

"You got that right," I acknowledged, grabbed the flashlight again and looked back into the small tunnel where the suitcase used to be. The sea bag was on the floor and tucked deep in the recess. I squeezed myself into the tight opening, almost falling into the hole as I reached in and got a firm grip on the bag's thick canvas strap. It took several back-and-forth tugs to work it free, but the sea bag finally released and I pulled it from the hole. I breathed heavy and a thin film of perspiration now covered my face.

"Okay," I huffed from the burst of sudden exertion, slung the sea bag by the strap over my shoulder, picked up the satchel and pointed Simon to the suitcase. "Let's put these into the trunk."

We loaded the three things into the rear of the Crown Vic, returned to the locker to move everything back to where they had been, lowered the roller-curtain door, and locked everything up nice and tight. We then got back into the car and moved out from the facility.

The service road led back to Highway 13. I pulled to a solid stop at the corner. The road was quiet with no oncoming traffic.

"Okay, then: I need a place to set things up. A place where I control the ground and see them coming – a place where it will be just them and us and no one else to get into the line of fire. Any place like that come to mind, Simon?"

"Not really, Samuel," he replied with an almost sad disappointment. "Perhaps if we prayed for it, asked God to direct us, He would show us the way."

I groaned with growing exasperation. "God bless America, Simon, I'm serious."

"As am I, Samuel. Like it or not, you are His instrument. You must rely on Him and not on your own abilities to control what will happen. Without Him, you will fail. Let Him take control. Your success and His glory depend on this."

I wasn't even half-listening to the guy. "I need a Wal-Mart or Best Buy that's open right now. I gotta dump my phone and get a pre-pay to use from now on."

Simon responded with an off-putting bit of mild humor. "It's not necessary. God doesn't use cell phones."

"Very funny. I get it," I pulled away from the corner and headed east. "What you have to understand, Simon, is that our target has probably been tracking my cell phone for weeks, and whoever is after you may have us on GPS surveillance of one sort or another even now. We need to disappear. We switch phones. It'll slow them down a bit. It'll also buy us a little more time to get ready. And we need to find a place before the Channel Six Morning News if I'm going to return the favor to these guys."

"Favor? Return what favor, Samuel?"

"They ambushed us in Hutchinson, Simon. They had the advantage then. What's fair is fair, you know?"

With his own audible sigh of exasperation, almost impatiently Simon replied, "You know, fairness is a concept found nowhere in nature. It's purely a human convention and has no basis in reality. Remember, Samuel, 'Avenge not yourselves, but rather give place unto wrath: for it is written, Vengeance is mine; I will repay.' Paul's Letter to the Romans, chapter 12, verse 19."

That really irritated me. "Yeah, well, an eye for an eye, pal. I haven't a clue what chapter and verse it is, but it's there."

"Actually, our Lord was quite specific concerning Moses' edict on retribution. In Matthew, chapter 5, verses 38 and 39, He says: 'Ye have heard that it hath been said, An eye for an eye, and a tooth for a tooth. But I say unto you, that ye resist not evil; but whosoever shall smite thee on thy right cheek, turn to him the other also.' Christ is your Lord, Samuel."

My irritation pumped up another couple of notches. There was no way I was going to beat this guy at Scripture quoting without sooner or later using my fists.

"Our side's already turned enough cheeks. We're drawing these guys out and ending their crusade against whatever you're all about. They want you bad enough; they'll walk right into it. If a few of them happen to lose an eye or a tooth in the process, let's consider it collateral damage. One way or another, they're going down."

***

The Wal-Mart at Eagan's Town Center was open 24 hours. I found a pre-pay cell phone in their understaffed electronics department, and walked it to the self-checkout area where I swiped the card and grabbed the receipt without bagging the phone. Back in the car with Simon, I used my flashlight to review the ultra fine print of the instructions. It was easy, although I could have used my cheaters to make out the small print faster. In less than five minutes, the phone was activated and plugged into the car's hands-free cell phone adapter.

We remained parked in the car; the rest of the lot around us was pretty much empty. The dashboard clock read 4:10 and the eastern night sky hinted at an approaching dawn.

The Channel Six Morning News would air at 5:00 am. If Shelly were successful in getting her news director onboard, the lead story would be her exclusive update on the Glenwood Murders and the Hutchinson shootout. If she tailored the story the way I had suggested, Tomlinson would become the media darling of every Twin Cities journalism outlet before noon and our target would be hot on my trail shortly thereafter, if they weren't already. Lord knew I had left enough breadcrumbs to follow: Carter's call to the chief about seeing Toors and me at the diner; private code to enter a secured storage facility in Eagan; video surveillance at the storage facility and at Wal-Mart; using my credit card to pay for the pre-pay phone. Another crumb or two wouldn't hurt.

I punched in Carter's cell phone number. He answered on the second ring. I said nothing in response and hung up, knowing he'd capture the new number and save it. I felt Simon's questioning glance as I surveyed the vacant parking lot. Every other light stanchion had a mounted security video camera.

"It's show time again, Simon," I pressed the trunk release button and pulled up on the door handle. "Join me outside, please."

I raised the trunk lid all the way up, the interior bulb illuminating things well enough to see the suitcase, satchel and the sea bag inside. I reached in and removed the sea bag, handing it to Simon. He placed it on the pavement as I maneuvered the suitcase to the center of the trunk compartment and flipped the latches open. Inside, the case was lined with molded foam compartments, each compartment filled with oilcloth-covered items of various shapes. I removed the largest item from a center compartment.

"In the sea bag, Simon, there's a folded leather rifle sleeve. Take it out, would you?"

The sea bag was secured by the single metal clasp on the strap – no padlock. Simon opened the bag as I removed the cloth from around the rifle stock. Next, I retrieved the barrel assembly from the case, unwrapped the protective cloth and easily slid the two components together. They snapped into place perfectly.

"Is this it?" Simon asked, holding up a rolled bundle of suede light brown leather bound by a matching leather strap.

"That's it," I said, taking it from him and placing it in the trunk next to the suitcase.

"What sort of weapon is that?"

I removed the bi-pod assembly from the case. "It's an M14; forerunner of the M16 and the original platform for the M21 sniper rifle, which in turn was further modified to the M25, standard issue for Navy SEALs. This one has a few modifications I made myself."

"Such as?"

I tightened the setscrews of the bi-pod onto the barrel, folded and locked the two legs into the retracted position. I then retrieved the scope from its compartment in the suitcase.

"This is an American Technologies Network ThOR Thermal Imaging scope. It is perfect for night ops; sees through dust, smoke, fog, haze, just about everything except maybe lead. It emits no visible light or RF energy so it's virtually invisible."

I fastened the scope onto the rifle's top mount.

"Why do you need it?" Simon asked seriously.

"To see them before they see us."

"Wouldn't they have something similar?"

"In fact, yes, they do. Tribby spotted it early on. Their MTAR-21s have laser sights with thermal detection. Only lousy shots use laser sights. We didn't catch the Hutchinson shooter, but he was good and I doubt he used a laser site. Doesn't matter. The ThOR is a whole lot better. They're also at a disadvantage with the limited range and accuracy of their 9mm loads. The M14 uses a .308 Winchester center fire cartridge: much better accuracy and range. I'll be able to reach out and touch them, so even if they see me, I'll be too far away and they'll miss."

I removed another item from the case, unwrapped it and attached it to the muzzle. "This is a variant of the old Heckler and Koch MP5SD suppressor. It's an Omega 300 made by SWR Manufacturing in South Carolina. I had it modified for the M14. Super quiet. Very helpful if I have to get in close and stay invisible."

"Impressive," Simon leaned against the lip of the trunk and watched me complete the assembly. "Without question, lethal and very impressive. You know your weapons, Samuel. What other surprises are in your case?"

I smiled and handed Simon the fully assembled rifle. He took it in both hands with an audible grunt. I removed the top layer of molded foam from the suitcase to reveal another layer underneath and covered the highlights for him. On the right side of this second level, I pointed to the thirty 20-round magazines neatly stacked side-by-side. I directed him to the left and a canvas shooting bag that not only performed as a terrifically stable gun rest from which to shoot, its numerous padded pouches contained a number of useful items: a coil of thin, ultra-high tensile strength wire, a roll of duct tape, a small cow bell, a box of matches, a can of lighter fluid, a small first-aid kit, signaling mirror, whistle, a bundle of 24-inch plastic zip ties and several other things; behind the bag lay a coiled reinforced two-inch duty web belt. Attached to the belt was a double magazine pouch, a cuff case, a flashlight case, universal radio case, one sheathed Bowie knife on the left side with 7-inch stainless steel saw-back blade, and a quick-release tactical holster with a Smith & Wesson M&P Compact .40 S&W automatic, complete with another dual magazine pouch fully stocked with loaded clips. Behind the belt and filling the rest of the lower level was a thick folded mass of what appeared to be a pile of dirty, hairy weeds.

"And, that's my ghillie suit," I concluded. "It's made to look kinda grassy, weedy, dark and wooly all at the same time. It's a blanket wrap that not only helps hide you in a natural setting, it's insulated to help hide you from infrared heat detection. Someone could be standing right next to me, and even with their heat detection scope, not even see me – assuming I don't give myself away with a sneeze or something."

"And the leather satchel? What do you have in that?"

I let the satchel lay. "Oh, just a few odds and ends; mostly electronic communication aids. With any luck, I'll be able to hear them coming long before they get to us."

Toors nodded his understanding, but I could see he was concerned nonetheless.

"Do you believe all this will be necessary, Samuel?"

"Maybe," I retrieved the leather rifle sheath, untied the lace strap and let it unroll and fall open. Simon handed me the rifle and I slid the weapon muzzle first into the cover.

"Let me put it this way: I'd rather have it and not need it, than need it and not have it."

Toors nodded again, but his face darkened with more concern. As he stepped away to return to the front of the car I heard him say, "I pray You protect Samuel; for Your glory let him be Your instrument of peace; as You will what is to come, give him Your strength and grant him victory over the evil confronting us."

My sheathed rifle joined the closed suitcase, satchel and sea bag in the trunk. I lowered the lid and pushed it down until the latch caught with a loud click.

Toors' simple prayer had left a bothersome mark, not because of what it implied lay ahead, but because whatever it was that did lay ahead simply didn't bother me at all. Preparing for the worse was part of the dark appeal of this; part of the perfunctory exercises you do to help you concentrate so you get a messy job done as efficiently as possible. But by itself, preparation wasn't even close to the meat of it.

Wimps deal poorly with messy, yet necessary, realities. A dirty job, even your first one, will quickly show you what kind of person you are. The hellish tortures of what it took to become a Navy SEAL were moments of utter physical collapse; times when the fear of death made one man freeze rock-solid while another man screamed and ran away. More than a few couldn't rise above it. Strangely, for me, no matter how desperate the situation, I always had something in reserve to draw on. In actual combat, those reserves were always there and I drew from them with ease, calculating what had to be done and doing it efficiently. The fear was always there, but always under control. I never lost sight of the job. I grew accustomed to the high that came with it. The increased adrenalin levels acted almost like a sedative. If the adrenalin didn't kick in, then I'd be concerned. It always kicked in. It was what kept me alive.

I slid in behind the steering wheel with an ill-defined need to explain some of this to Toors.

"I've been well trained to do certain things, Simon. I used to be very good at doing them. A lot of time has gone by, but even though I'm too old, too out of shape, and I probably carry some emotional baggage from it all, I'm foolish enough to believe I can still do what has to be done. Shelly, my wife, excuse me, my ex-wife, got fed up with my pig-headedness always standing in the way of what she needed her life to be, no doubt because of some of the old things I still let get in the way; all of it my fault, I'm sure.

"That's all history. The point is if I've been, as you say, chosen to protect you and end the threat against your mission from God, I want you to know there are no doubts in my mind about doing exactly that."

Annoyingly, Toors felt it necessary to temper my commitment to the mission. "Not to avenge your friend's death, Samuel. That would be wrong."

I started the engine and dropped the shifter into gear.

"No, Simon," I corrected him as the car jerked from its parking space, "that'll be dessert."

***

A couple of slow moments passed after I pushed the doorbell button and heard the muted tones chiming from inside the Patterson house. The deadbolt was thrown, the door wedged open slightly and through the narrow opening came a curious look from an attractive middle-aged woman already dressed for the office, her brunette hair subtly streaked with gray.

"May I help you?" Mrs. Patterson asked.

"Yes, Mrs. Patterson," Self-consciously I checked my wristwatch for the time. It was almost 7:30. A gathering of thin clouds had muted the sunrise. I glanced back at my car parked in the driveway. Toors watched from the front seat. "My name is Samuel Culhane, I'm with the Minneapolis Police Department. Your husband has helped us with an investigation we are presently conducting, and if he's available, I'd like to speak with him, please."

She widened the door opening slightly, peered beyond me to the Crown Vic in her driveway, and then opened the door fully. "Yes, of course. Steeg told me all about it. Please, both of you come in."

I turned and waved Toors to join me, which he quickly did. We followed Mrs. Patterson through the entry.

"We're just having breakfast," she informed us as she led the way into the main living area and toward the kitchen. "You're welcome to join us if you'd like."

"That's very kind," I replied from behind. "But we were just enjoying a sumptuous feast from the McDonald's drive-thru. We were sitting in the car discussing the options on our situation munching on Egg McMuffins and hash browns when Simon suggested we pay you a visit and see if Steeg could help us out."

She made the turn into the kitchen. "Coffee, then? I know Simon likes his coffee."

Steeg Patterson sat at the table. He was dressed in a tired brown tweed sports coat over a black cotton turtleneck sweater, jeans and sneakers. He lowered his newspaper and left the table to greet us with a welcoming smile.

"I was hoping to see you again, Detective." He took my hand with a firm grip and immediately turned to Simon, welcoming him with a sincere embrace. "My friends. Please, sit."

We took our seats around the small table as Mrs. Patterson brought additional cups and saucers over. Next came the coffeepot. I declined her kind offer of cream or sugar and Toors did the same.

"I saw the Channel Six Morning News program," Patterson continued. "There was a very disturbing report about what happened last night and it put you, Detective, in a less than complimentary light."

That was reassuring.

"We missed it," I admitted, returning the cup to the saucer after a brief, appreciative sampling. "We've been a little busy. What did the reporter say?"

Mrs. Patterson joined us at the table. "Did you know their reporter has the same last name as you?"

I nodded.

"She's his wife," Simon contributed from behind the rim of his raised cup.

"Ex-wife," I clarified.

"Ah," Mrs. Patterson nodded. "Maybe that explains it, then. She as much as called you a crooked cop."

"It's comforting to be appreciated by the press," I smiled, feeling the penetrating once-over from our hostess. "What else did she say?"

"I wish I had recorded it, but I didn't," Steeg Patterson's regret was obvious. "She amended her earlier report from last night when she had said Simon was behind the shoot-out in the town – we both knew that wasn't true – and instead, said an anonymous source within the police department had informed her that you have had Simon in protective custody all along and that corrupt elements within the law enforcement community had targeted both of you for elimination!"

"That's interesting," I admitted lightly. "It doesn't make me sound like a crooked cop, though."

Mrs. Patterson jumped in. "The denial from your police chief does, though. She had an audio interview with him from last night commenting on the allegations, and he denied it all – which you'd expect – but then he also said, 'If Detective Culhane is harboring a known fugitive, he will be prosecuted to the fullest extent of the law.' And, that's a direct quote."

Simon offered an ironic grin. "He supports you with a firm denial, and then immediately denies the denial with a conditional threat. Nice employer you have there."

"Mark's my boss; I work for the city. Besides, Mark's a union guy from way back. He's used to having things both ways." Another sip of coffee gave me a moment to reflect. "On the other hand, he may be communicating something to us through his denied denial."

"Like what?" Patterson asked.

I rubbed my tired eyes and echoed Mark's words. "'…is harboring a known fugitive, …prosecuted to the fullest extent…' The chief may be telling us I'm right – there are people after us now because they know we're together. He may be saying he knows, or at least suspects, who they are and there'll be no room for negotiation with those people when the time comes."

Worried, Mrs. Patterson asked, "What are you going to do?"

I half-smiled. "First, I'm gonna keep my head down. We need a place to help draw these people out into the open. Simon said your husband might be able to help."

Mr. Patterson's brow furrowed. "I can't imagine. What kind of place do you mean?"

"Something in the open and away from people. We need a place where we can see them coming with no mistake."

The husband shared a contemplative glance with his wife. "A place where you can prepare for what might happen; maybe catch them unaware. It's almost as if you're looking to set them up like they did to you in Hutchinson."

"You're very perceptive," I acknowledged. "And, basically, you're right. Anything come to mind?"

"Maybe," Patterson admitted with a thoughtful nod. "I need to make a phone call and check it out first, but it might work."

"You look tired," Mrs. Patterson noted with concerned.

Simon concurred with a quick confirmation. "He's a stubborn man, Carol. He has not slept for some time, now. He thinks he can just keep going until the job is done."

"Well, it's been a busy couple of days," I admitted and rubbed my eyes once more.

"Carol, why don't we let these gentlemen get a little rest in the guest room downstairs?"

"That's a good idea." She came to her feet. "Please, Detective and Simon, follow me."

"I don't think that…" I began to object, but she shut me off.

"Precisely. Not getting your rest will do that to you, Detective," she interjected forcefully as she made for the hallway.

"Do as she says, now," Steeg smiled and waved the two of us on to follow his wife. And so we did.

Downstairs, the spacious room was warm, comfortable and had twin beds once used by children now grown and moved on.

"The linen is clean," Mrs. Patterson informed us as she pointed out the additional blankets on the shelf of the double closet. "The bathroom is down the hall to the left."

"Does the TV work?" I asked.

"Of course," she said and then waved a warning finger at me. "But keep it off. Get some rest. You're going to need it."

She left, closing the door behind her. I took a seat on the edge of the nearest bed.

"Comfy," I admitted and began to untie my hunting boots. "Not that I can sleep, though. Just too much whirling around in my head right now."

Simon lowered himself to a cross-legged position on the floor at the foot of the next bed. "Stress will do that to you, sometimes."

I pulled up the pillow, sitting back onto it in a semi-reclined posture and watched Simon adjust his sitting position on the floor, clasp his hands in his lap and close his eyes.

"The bed is softer, you know?"

His eyes remained closed as he said, "I know, Samuel. Nevertheless, I prefer the floor."

"I'm not the only one who needs his rest."

"No need for concern. You see, Samuel, I have recuperative sources you do not know."

My sarcasm was intentional. "I bet."

"Close your eyes, Samuel, and focus on God's Spirit within you. You'll be surprised how remarkable it is."

I echoed again, "I bet."

The room fell into silence. Simon sitting on the floor and I lounging in the bed, sock-covered feet extended out in front of me, one across the other at the ankle. I gave a quick thought to getting up and turning on the TV to see if there was anything about us on the local channels, but then I just as quickly dismissed it. It was time to give it a rest. Lord knew things would be getting busy enough soon enough.

I closed me eyes for just a moment of quiet thought.

***

Almost six hours later, I opened my eyes.

It was two o'clock by time Simon and I made our way back to the Patterson kitchen table. Curiously two elderly people who were, I quickly learned, Carol Patterson's mother and father, joined us. Introductions were made and I lied skillfully as I expressed how nice it was to meet the two of them. Well into their eighties, Carol Patterson's parents had simply dropped in for a visit over lunch. The mother, Eloise James, was short, with drawn features lined by the weariness of age, thinning gray hair and obviously almost blind. The father, Herbert, apparently suffered from Alzheimer's and kept repeating things.

Although Simon and I had slept-in, Carol Patterson had prepared a welcome lunch for both of us consisting of a thick roast beef sandwich and hearty vegetable soup. Simon graciously accepted the soup while declining the sandwich. I, on the other hand, too greedily scarfed up both.

"So where's our lunch?" Herbert complained gruffly.

"Dad, you already ate," Carol Patterson patiently explained.

"He doesn't remember," Eloise chimed in with a disgusted tone directed at her husband.

From my right, Steeg Patterson leaned over toward me as I shoved another spoonful of soup into my mouth. "Family. Whadda ya gonna do, you know?"

On my left, Simon had a suggestion. "Perhaps Mr. James would appreciate some tea."

"I like tea," Herbert agreed. "With sugar."

"No sugar," Eloise scolded him and then turned to Simon and me. "Diabetic. You got to watch him like a hawk. He's always hiding candy and sweet stuff from me."

I could see Carol Patterson move to the stove and light the gas flame under the teakettle.

"Is it time to leave, Lou?" Herbert asked.

"Not yet," Eloise answered more irritated with him. She turned to me, again. "He's always wanting to leave and go someplace else. Even if we just walked through the door, he wants to leave."

I half-laughed. "He must keep you on your toes."

She rolled her barely functioning eyes and chuckled. "You don't know the half of it."

Cnfused, Herbert pointed at me. "Who are you again?"

"Sam Culhane, Mr. James. I'm a detective with the Minneapolis Police Department."

"Oh, yes." He seemed to remember. "Gregory do something wrong? If he has, you can arrest him."

Steeg Patterson and I shared a quick confused look. Behind us Carol's hand slapped down hard on the countertop.

"I'm not married to Gregory, Dad!"

Herbert leaned toward me and lowered his voice as he explained, "Gregory's not the right guy for her. She needs to find someone better. You know how it is with daughters."

Now I'm the confused one. "I can imagine."

Steeg touched my arm and I turned to him.

"I think I have a place for you and Simon to use. It's a bit of a drive, but it could work. We will have to go see my brother, though. It's his place up on Stony Lake."

"Where's Stony Lake?"

"It's up North," Steeg pointed in the general direction on the other side of the patio doors. "Outside Hackensack."

I shook my head. "Never been there."

Steeg explained, "Nice town. Beautiful country. Plenty of space to hide out in."

Simon's severe look of concern troubled me. He was observing Eloise as she comforted her confused husband. Herbert mumbled something about Gregory again; Eloise patiently tried to fill in the blanks for him. A few moments went by and Herbert's continued discontented muttering made it clear she was not succeeding. She sighed as another defeated moment with her husband weighed down on her.

"Steeg says his brother has a place for us," I said quietly.

Simon nodded but kept his eyes on the elderly couple on the other side of the table. "Go with him. Let me stay here. When all is ready, come back for me."

I shoved the last of my sandwich into my mouth, buying a few seconds before explaining what he already should have known. "That would not be wise."

Herbert, noticing me coming to my feet, asked again, "Is it time to go, now, Lou?"

I heard the sadness catch in her throat as her eyes moved toward the indistinct shadow of her husband. "Not yet, Herb."

There was nothing I could do to help them, and it was time to go. "You're still in my custody, Simon. You stay with me."

"I promise you can trust me. I won't go anywhere, Samuel."

"I can't take that chance."

Simon hesitated as the James' continued their confused conversation. "Then, before we leave, may I have a few moments alone with these people?"

"For what? We need to go."

Simon rose from his chair and leveled a surprisingly purposeful stare at me. "Samuel, it is not an accident that we are in this place at this moment. I need time alone with Eloise and Herbert. All I ask is that you give it to me."

I was put off by his insistence. "Time for what? There's nothing you can do. Let's get going."

Simon's placating demeanor remained firmly in place even as he amplified his request to an order. "This will only take a few moments, Samuel. Please, leave the room."

"Carol and I will stay, Detective Culhane," Steeg Patterson calmly injected. "Nothing will happen with Simon, I assure you."

My growing irritation percolated to the surface. "Why do I have to leave if you don't? What's going on here?"

Simon placed a reassuring hand over my own. "No offense is intended, Samuel, but what has to be done now must be done among those who are fully faithful. The presence of any doubtful spirit would certainly injure our work."

"Your work?" I took a step back, confused. "Doubtful spirit? You mean my doubtful spirit?"

I looked at each of them in turn.

Herbert, still seated next to his wife, asked once more, "Is it time to go now, Lou?"

With tears in her eyes and her hand patting blindly along the table, Eloise found his hand and quietly answered, "No, Herb, it's not time yet."

"It will only be for a few minutes," Simon's sympathetic glance returned to the elderly couple. "If you'd wait in the next room, Samuel, I'd very much appreciate it."

I didn't want to go, but something deep in my gut pulled at me. As if on their own, my feet stepped away from the table and I moved silently around the corner into the adjoining living room. Briefly, I paced in front of the sofa, hands shoved into my pants pockets, and wondered what it was that bothered me so. And I was bothered – hell, I was pissed – and I didn't know why. I crossed the front of the sofa once more only to lower myself into the corner seat, all the while wanting to take just one peek at what was going on in the kitchen.

From the kitchen, I could not quite make out what Simon was saying. A moment of absolute silence followed, and then, Simon's quiet, soft voice returned. I leaned forward but remained seated as I strained to hear. Simon was praying, speaking to Christ as calmly as if he was talking with a close friend over a backyard fence about the weather. They were simple words. No religious underpinnings, no grandiose liturgical hyperbole, just straightforward honest expression of love, concern and, oddly, confidence in accepting His will for Eloise and Herbert. And then, again, there was absolute silence.

The shrill and mournful wail from Eloise jolted me from my seat and I rushed back into the kitchen to see her crying as she held Herbert in a tight embrace.

She almost screamed in startled amazement. "I can see! I can see! Praise God, I can see you, Herb!"

Herbert held his wife tightly, their faces inches apart, he beamed with eyes completely cleared of any confusion or doubt.

"I know!" he said almost laughing yet crying at the same time. "Lou, I know! I know everything! I remember everything!"

Steeg and Carol held each other, tears streaming down both their faces. A few feet away near the sink counter, Simon stood off to one side quietly watching. Across the way, Herbert covered his wife's face with many small kisses. Haltingly, I walked over to where Simon stood.

At first, I could only look at him. None of this made any sense. "What did you do? How…?"

Simon's face held the peace-filled expression of complete understanding. His hand rests on mine. "Remember, Samuel, our Lord said, 'The thief cometh not, but for to steal, and to kill, and to destroy: I am come that they might have life, and that they might have it more abundantly.'"

The Lake Country Revisited

Chapter 13

Breathless Anticipation

Daniel Patterson's cabin on Stony Lake is tranquilly quiet at night. My wristwatch tells me it's barely nine o'clock. Outside, a black shroud falls around the place like a smothering blanket. Inside, the descending glow cone from the lone deer antler lamp above the butcher-block dining table warms us, but it fades away into the deep shadows of the surrounding great room.

My leather satchel lies open on the table. The scanner is older and heavier than the current model. I flick the power switch on and off a couple times. The indicator on the backlit display tells me the batteries are good. Across from me, Simon sits watching.

"It looks ominous," he says with a smile. "What is it?"

I turn the portable handheld scanner in my hands. "This, Simon, is the Uniden BC92XLT Bearcat Scanner. It's a peach."

"Odd, it doesn't look like a peach? What does your peach do?"

"It monitors radio signals – police, fire, ham radio operators, that sort of thing. This model scans 200 channels, has multiple preprogrammed searches and something I really like – a close call RF detection capability. It can locate the source of strong local transmissions such as mobile and handheld two-way radios, and locks onto them automatically."

"So if someone is in your immediate area using such a radio, you'll be able to detect them?"

"Hopefully, Simon. The other signals have to be within the detection range. Ultra-high, or ultra-low frequencies outside the scanner's VHF or UHF range will not be detected. Still, it's better to have it and not need it than to need it and not have it."

"Ah, it seems I've heard that before."

I smile in reply, setting the optimum ranges for frequency detection. I then adjust the detection alert signal to the Alt bp-Lt setting so the scanner's backlit display will flash and beep when a close signal is detected. Next, I connect the headset Y cable to the headset jack on the unit, and plug in the two headset leads into the cable. I slip the headset on over my ears and clip the scanner to my belt to make sure everything fits. I activate the close call program and give Toors an affirmative thumbs up.

"You need a headset?" Toors asks.

"Well, I don't need any unnecessary beeping coming from the thing as I wander through the woodland, that's for darn sure."

"So, you're going out tonight? Nature is a wonderful thing."

"I don't appreciate the sarcasm, Simon, especially when I'm working as hard as I am to keep you from getting killed."

He smiles. "I can come with."

"No, you ca…"

I stop as I hear a slow, rhythmic pulse come over the headset.

"Samuel?" Simon asks with sudden concern.

"Shush!" I press the headset tighter against my ears. The scanner has locked onto the frequency and the pulse comes again. I listen intently for several seconds. "It's not audible. It's electronic. It's a tracer of some kind. Shit!"

I tell Simon to stay where he is and I leave the cabin through the side door. To the rear clearing, the Crown Vic is where I left her. The septic tank status light annoyingly illuminates the immediate area with a halo of red glow, which turns everything beyond the lamp's radiance completely black. Slowly, with my eyes poorly struggling against the darkness that surrounds me, I move toward the car. The Bearcat scanner has no signal strength or directional readout capability, but if we had inadvertently brought a tracer with us, chances were more than good the tracer was somewhere on the car. My hand follows the fold of the front bumper, around to the passenger side front fender, and then to the wheel well. I follow the rocker panel to the rear wheel well, along the rear fender and around to the back bumper. Inside the top rim of the left rear wheel well my fingers find an obstruction. It is small, maybe two inches long, one inch wide, half an inch thick. My fingers tighten to pull the object free, but stop as another idea comes to mind. With key fob in hand, I unlock the driver's side door and slide in behind the wheel. It takes only a few moments to back the Crown Vic down the dirt drive, slap the car into drive and weave through the trees onto the lot next door.

Inside the cabin, Simon sits where I had left him.

"What did you find?" he asks as I return to my chair and unclip the Bearcat from my belt.

I go into program mode on the scanner and block the tracer frequency. Now that I know we're being tracked, there's no need to keep hearing the darn thing in my ear. I then return to normal mode and press the scan key to initiate a full band scan of the radio frequencies in the area. All I hear in the headset is the light hiss of dead air.

"Well, Simon, we now know we're being tracked," I announce calmly, adjusting the squelch settings on the unit to minimize the hissing in my ears. I remove the headset and place it with the unit on the table. "This is a good thing."

"How's that, again?"

"This is a good thing in that, with the tracer still in place and sending out a signal, our observers believe their tracer has not been detected and that we are vulnerable because of it. This gives them a false sense of security that can work to our advantage. I have relocated the tracer to a spot that is close enough to not let them know that we are on to them, while at the same time just far enough away to give us an advantage in close quarters."

"Meaning what, exactly?"

"Meaning that, when the shooting starts – if it starts – they'll be shooting in the wrong direction. We, on the other hand, will be shooting in the right direction."

Simon's face falls. "I prefer it if no shooting starts."

"Me, too. But, if it does, every little bit helps." I let that settle with Simon for a moment and then ask, "You hungry?"

His wide-eyed wonder is almost comical. "How can you think of eating at a time like this?"

"Well, a guy's gotta eat. Don't forget our little doggie bags from the restaurant. Besides, you're pretty cool with all this, aren't you? You're disappointed with me personally, that's obvious. But, all in all, you seem to be handling this pretty well."

"I'm not worried about me, Samuel. Neither should you be. And I'm not personally disappointed with you. I know you are God's chosen now. I don't question that. If I'm concerned at all, it is because you question God's choice."

A half laugh poorly hides my soiled conscience. Part of me resents Simon's awareness. It places a layer of obligation on me I don't appreciate. A larger part of me wants to rise above any concern he may have and just get to the bottom of what's behind this thing he so simply refers to as a great evil.

"Simon, I have a hard time understanding how God would chose me for anything important enough to concern Him. I'm not a saint and I'm certainly not you. God could do better."

Simon shrugs and smiles. "He's very good at working with what he has. This is true for both of us."

"I hope you're right," I offer back, pulling the AC power cord from the satchel and plugging it into the Bearcat scanner. I remove the headset adapter from the unit's jack port, adjust the volume knob slightly to monitor the unit's speaker. No longer receiving the tracer signal, things are quiet.

I wave Simon in the general direction of the back bedrooms. "You should get some sleep. I'll take the first watch."

"If it's all the same to you," Simon nods toward the main room sofa. "I'll take the divan."

***

It's almost one o'clock in the morning and I'm back at the butcher-block table with one ear tuned to the still silent scanner. There are more than a few moments of head-bobbing sleepiness. Minutes crawl by like hours when the only company you have is the sound of breezes off the lake stirring the high branches of jack pines surrounding the cabin. Sleep pulls at my eyelids like lead weighs, and a dog-eared paperback of Vince Flynn's "Term Limits" I find on an under shelf of a living room side table doesn't help. My body aches for sleep.

Growing old sucks. Physically, too many parts that should work simply won't, and other parts either demand too many bathroom visits, or simply express their complete indifference. Under my breath I mutter an appropriate colorful expletive, pick up the paperback, turn to the next page and continue reading.

The flashing scanner display is accompanied by two muted beeps. My pulse quickens as I adjust the volume control, quickly plug in the headset cable and slip the earpieces back on. There's a faint hiss of dead air. Then, over the unit's speaker comes a whispered voice.

"Roter Hund vier ist geht ein."

It sounds German to me. My German is more than a little rusty. "hund" is dog and "vier" is four. Something "Dog four" something, something.

Another whispered voice quickly follows the first.

"Roter Hund zwei an der richtigen stelle."

"Zwei" is two. That's dogs two and four in the neighborhood transmitting on radios way too early in the morning to be a coincidence. Keeping the headset in place, I clip the scanner back onto my belt and leave the table for the stairway leading to the second level. I grab the sheathed rifle leaning against the banister and Simon comes to a fully seated position on the sofa.

He asks a simple question. "Trouble?"

I take the steps two at a time and reply over my shoulder, "We've got company."

Simon is close on my heels all the way up to the west-side bedroom. I enter, removing the rifle from the leather sheath I let fall to the floor. I tell Simon to leave the lights off. He does so. At the lone window I can see the rear of the lot below and have a decent view of the road in both directions. It's very dark and the shadows surrounding us are deep and concealing. It doesn't matter. I check the scope settings, raise the window sash fully open and stand well off into the room, the rifle butt snug into my shoulder. I sweep the scope in sections across the scene below, starting low left, moving high left, then high center to low center. I shift slightly to my left to scope out the right side in the same manner. The scope shows humans in a flat yellow color. There were only two small, ground-level hot spots, probably raccoons, rummaging around a couple of garbage cans near a garage two or three lots down the road to my right. Other than that, the scope is a cool, dark mass of foliage and jack pines. I lower the rifle.

"The rear is clear. I didn't agree with your earlier idea about them coming from the waterside of things, but you may have been right. For sure, we have at least two people within 1,000 yards of here chit-chatting about dogs and stuff."

"Dogs and stuff?" Simon repeats confusedly.

I pass him, exit the room and head for the lake-facing loft. "Yeah, it sounded like that. They were speaking German, I think."

Simon follows me. "That's interesting. German tells us a lot about who they might be, then, is that right?"

I reach the loft and bring the rifle up in a single motion. "Yes and no. If it was German, it wasn't 'German' German, but Americanized. Both of them lacked a German accent."

The window wall offers a superior view. Through the scope I repeat the check of the entire area.

"No accents? Are you sure?"

"Pretty sure, yeah." I check the outside once more. "It's clear. Nothing. We may have time, yet."

"To do what?"

I think for a moment and it occurs to me the window wall's insulated glass may be blocking the scope's heat signatures. "Maybe take a proactive measure or two."

"Like what, exactly?"

I move past Simon and head for the stairs. "Like taking a walk outside, for instance."

We scramble to the bottom of the stairs where I point at the light above the butcher-block table. "Turn that thing out. I want this whole place blacked out."

"What should I bring?" Simon asks as he quickly moves to douse the light.

"Nothing," I answer, stealing a peek out the small window of the side door. "You're not coming."

The lower level falls into complete darkness. I pull the suitcase out from where I had stashed it next to the staircase, open it and pull out the web utility belt and ghillie suit. Through the pale reflected starlight from outside the window wall, I remove the scanner and slip it into the radio holster on the duty belt that I quickly put on, strapping the base of the tactical holster around my right thigh. I check the pistol's safety and move it to the off position. Next comes the ghillie suit. I pull it on over my hunting togs grateful the oversized design easily adapts to my added girth.

From the corner of my eye, I see Simon making his way through the darkness and toward me.

"Samuel, I need to be with you on this."

I pull the suit's hood forward over my brow, adjust the fit of the headset, take up the rifle again and quickly double check the scope and suppressor. In a lowered but no-nonsense voice, I explain things so even he can understand.

"What you need to do, Simon, is exactly what I tell you. This is no game and these people are serious. You stay here until I come back. You keep your head down and stay out of sight. If anyone comes in here while I'm gone, get real small. You gotta do this, Simon. You don't do what I tell you, God can't hold it against me if you get killed, and we can't have that, now can we?"

I feel his incredulity. "You're telling jokes, now? You tell me this is serious and you make a joke of it? How can you do that?"

I pat him on the shoulder. "It's a little stress relief exercise I use. Don't worry, I won't be gone long."

The darkness prevents me from seeing his concern but I still sense it. The headset interrupts with yet another transmission.

"Roter Hund zwei und vier, fahren sie fort. Roter Hund ein und drei beginnen fortschritt."

Again, there's no German accent. I repeat the transmission to myself, trying to translate it. "'Roter Hund zwei und vier, fahren sie fort. Roter Hund ein und drei beginnen fortschritt.' That's dog two and four, one and three, something…"

Simon fills in the blanks. "Red Dog Two and Four, proceed; Red Dog One and Three, begin your advance. German is a second language for me. Perhaps I could be useful monitoring the radio transmissions for you?"

"Not a chance," I snap back impatiently. "Crap! That means there're four of them. Look, Simon, just hide in here, okay? I gotta find these guys before they find us and it sounds like I may already be too late."

I leave him before he can object and exit the cabin through the side door.

The jack pines shelter me all the way down the hundred-foot slope to the rocky shore of the lake. Making too much noise to get there, I flatten myself against the largest grouping of boulder-sized beach stones and bring the rifle and scope up to examine the stretch of shoreline. The well-defined yellow tinted heat signatures reveal two groups of two men each to the east at least one hundred yards apart. They're crouching low as they make their way through the jack pines up the slope. Four men on this side mean four more men coming from an opposite direction. Eight men in a pincher movement with maybe one other guy in the neighborhood running the op and giving orders.

I quickly swing the rifle up toward the west side of our cabin. No heat signatures. I double-check the area once more and then return to the four known targets to the east. The clarity of the yellow-colored images on the scope show they are all well armed, probably with the same type of MTAR-21 assault rifles we had recovered from the jail attack. That gives me an advantage as long as they don't see me.

I take a moment to adjust the ghillie suit and make sure it covers me fully. I return to observing through the scope. These guys aren't on a track that takes them to the cabin. They're too far to the east and heading at an angle that would take them past the cabin on the far side.

Of course, the Crown Vic! They're following the tracer signal from the car, literally feeling their way in the dark. The other two teams would be doing the same, probably from the tree line to the north. Clever: half coming up from the lake, the other half from the opposite side of the peninsula. It's too bad they're going to the wrong cabin. I'll have to follow after them and every time I move I'll be exposed. This might take more time than I thought.

Keeping flat against the stones, I slither back to the weeds and grasses bordering the tree line. I'm far west of their position, and with the tall trees as cover, I'm confident I can skirt around the distant side of the next cabin and up to the road without being seen. I dart from tree to tree. The matted padding of fallen pine needles help silence each step. I pause behind every second tree, raise the rifle and observe through the scope the progress in turn of each heat signature moving up the slope. They are very careful and very slow. They are concentrating straight ahead and facing away from me. I soundlessly move from the last tree and make it to the west side of the neighboring cabin. I follow the faux log siding of the vacated building to the rear lot. From there I go low and scurry across a shallow clearing to the northwest corner of a detached two-car garage. Using the corner as cover, I raise the rifle and immediately see a heat signature in the scope making its way through the trees on the opposite side of the road. I pan to the left. Farther back through the trees and about fifty yards to the first man's right, I see the yellow portrait of his partner having trouble stepping through the bothersome undergrowth. Lagging well behind the first man, this guy's the perfect target. With the suppressor, I could drop him easy and no one would know.

Bracing myself against the corner of the garage, I bring the crosshairs of the scope to bear dead center on the man's head, only to have the sight slide off the mark. Irritated, I bring the crosshairs back on target, but they bounce again and ruin the shot. I reset and try again. Again, the sighting doesn't hold.

I pull away from the corner and lean back against the wall of the garage. My pulse explodes against my eardrums and I realize it's my own heavy heartbeat pulling my shot offline. I'm a mess. I'm so out of shape and my breathing is so labored, I'm almost hyperventilating. In this condition I'd miss a city bus at twenty paces using a bazooka!

A colorful expletive escapes from under my breath. There was an exercise they taught us to keep breathing under control, but I was in shape back then and a heck of a lot younger. Now, my body wasn't even close to recovering from the exertion and all the mind games I could play to help calm me down would work only a little. I need time to collect myself and time is the one thing I don't have.

I raise the scope and take a quick peek around the corner. My target on the right is less than thirty yards away and moving eastward from my position. Farther down, his partner makes similar progress. I pull the bipod legs out from their folded position and slide to the ground. Lying prone under the ghillie suit in the scrub growth surrounding the garage, the bipod helps steady the shot. But as I reacquire the nearer target, he moves farther down across the road and beyond the line of trees fronting the posted Onawim sign marking the drive path to the Patterson cabin.

Before I curse my slowness, the soft sound of a booted foot scraping against road gravel comes from my far left and I freeze in my prone position under the ghillie suit. Out of the corner of my eye, to my far left another man steps from the undergrowth on my side of the road. Slowly, I pull the rifle close, hiding the muzzle under the sleeve of my suit as I watch the approaching shadow. Seconds seem like an eternity and it takes all I've got not to obey the urge to bolt. The man is only yards away now and his line will take him straight across the front of my location. This guy looks straight ahead, doesn't check his flanks at all, and steps past no more than five feet from the front of my rifle's suppressor. He continues beyond my sight and only then do I allow myself a controlled, shallow breath.

The guy has to be the lead man of the fourth team. That means his partner is nearby. Oddly, my breathing and the pulse rate suddenly slows considerably. A familiar sensation takes over with the exact opposite affect anyone else would normally expect: not hyper, jazzed, or out of control, not at all. I'm completely normal and calm. Amazing. It's been such a long time since I last felt this way – so ready; so strong. It must pay to be an adrenalin junkie, after all.

Almost imperceptibly, the quiet is disturbed by the less than cautious shuffles of a too-confident soldier. From behind me I hear the soft swish of his boots against the low growth of grass and weeds. My ears tell me he is moving eastward between the cabin and garage, his unbroken pace tells me he doesn't know I'm lying no more than thirty feet away. Carefully, I steal a look under my hardly raised right elbow and see his shadow move behind the garage corner. Without a sound and in one motion, I'm on my feet with the Bowie knife in hand. I leave the rifle and silently move to the same garage corner behind which Mr. Shuffles had just disappeared. My back presses against the wall and with the knob of the knife's hilt I scratch twice against the wood siding just loud enough. The man's returning shuffles sound impatient to me, perhaps a little annoyed.

My left fist tight around the knife's hilt, the blunt end leads a backhand swing with my body's full weight behind it. I feel the man's Adam's apple crumble as the force of the blow lifts him off his feet. Hanging in the air for a brief moment, the man's assault rifle falls away and he almost flips before he hits the ground neck-first. In a blink I'm on top of him, fist pulled back to cold-cock the sucker, but I hold back. The guy isn't moving at all.

I pull my right glove off and check his left carotid artery. There's no pulse. I feel around the rear base of his skull and upper neck where I find the undeniable bulge of misplaced vertebrae. I slide off of him, cursing myself as my rump hits the ground. I didn't want to kill the guy, I just wanted to take him out of action, maybe get some information from him.

I look at the motionless lump lying next to me. The regret swells inside. It wasn't anything I haven't felt before. What could I expect from all this, anyway? Like I told Toors, this isn't a game. Well, what is it, then? They're coming to kill us. Drawing them out was part of the plan all along. Draw them out, and then what? Have a nice chat in the woods? I don't think so. Get your head on straight or you're going to get it shot off. I push down the gathering remorse. I just don't know my own strength, that's all. Why should I? At my age, I shouldn't have any strength. And the realization hits me that being an adrenalin junkie has a downside.

I come to my feet, sheath the knife and retrieve my rifle. In a clump of weeds against the garage, I find the other guy's weapon and take it with me, figuring it might come in handy. I leave the body where it lays. I know his pals are all heading toward the Crown Vic's signal. I'll stay behind them and observe. If they see me, hopefully they'll think I'm the dead guy.

Staying low covering the distance from the garage to the back of the Patterson lot, I find sufficiently concealed refuge behind another tall pine. A quick glance to the darkened windows tells me Simon, too, is staying low and keeping out of sight. In a weedy clump between two exposed tree roots, I find a place for the MTAR-21, and then raise my own rifle and scope out the area around the Crown Vic. I click the magnification knob to the widest angled setting, which at this close range isn't very wide at all. Able to get only one heat signature in the frame, I move from one to the next to see the three men are well spaced and moving cautiously in a loose semi-circle toward the rear of the cabin next door. I swing the rifle toward the lakeside slope. The two other two-man teams are just now settling into their positions. My headset alerts me with a pair of reports in Americanized German.

"Roter Hund zwei in position."

"Roter Hund vier in position."

A third voice replies. *"Verstandenen. Stehen sie durch."*

I don't understand the last bad guy at all and I can't help the annoying question from popping into my mind: why isn't there a Simon Toors around when you really need one?

I check the rear-side heat signatures once more. The two targets of the first team have settled behind jack pines beyond the Crown Vic. There's perhaps twenty yards between them and the same distance from the cabin. The third guy, my "Roter Hund team member," is following a parallel course. When he reaches an equidistant position ten yards this side of the car, he crouches low against another tree trunk, brings up his assault rifle and levels it in the direction of the cabin. I center my crosshairs on his temple, and this time, my aim is rock solid.

The seconds tick silently by with agonizing slowness. For the longest time, the only sound is that of the gentle breezes stirring the tops of the pines. The headset scratches a whispered request.

"Roter Hund drei. Zustandsberichte bitte."

"Bitte" means "Please." The leader is asking for Red Dog Three to report in. In my scope, my teammate moves his hand from his rifle stock and brings it to his ear.

"*Roter Hund drei Bäcker in Position. Ich kann Roter Hund alpha nicht sehen.*"

"Nicht sehen" is "no see." He can't see his partner, but I can see his head turn in my crosshairs and look directly at my position. I exhale slowly and squeeze the trigger. The suppressor's zwap is louder than I expect, but very quiet, nonetheless. In my scope, the yellowed image folds to the ground in a heap.

Through the treetops the sound of high breezes return and I swing the muzzle around to the farther heat signature on the other side from the car. He's where he should be. At this range, I can't miss. I bring the crosshairs to bear, exhale slowly and squeeze the trigger once more. Another whispered zwap from the suppressor and the man's head jerks violently back and to the left. His body sags and comes to a motionless rest against the tree he had hoped would serve as cover.

"*Wir sind unter feuer! Erhalten sie tiefpunkt! Bleiben sie tiefpunkt!*"

The warning almost screams from the headset. Too hurriedly, I scan across this side of the cabin for the other heat signature. I don't see him. I swing the rifle to the far right. Both men of the near team on the slope simultaneously flatten against the ground where they lay. I assume the other team on the unobservable slope behind the cabin is doing the same. I swing back to where I last saw the other guy. Everything's dark. I move the scope in framed sections right to left until I arrive at the body I had dropped. I then follow the same procedure left to right all the way back to the corner of the cabin. No heat signature, just a stack of firewood.

The white glare sweeps across my scope's display and almost too late I realize it's a red beam from a laser sight. I duck and roll to the left just as the bark of my pine tree cover explodes in a steady stream of fire from a suppressed MTAR-21. I turtle-crawl through the low growth as the tree I leave continues to erupt and the air fills with the thup-thup-thup of ongoing suppressed nine-millimeter fire. If he's like me, he'll empty the mag, reload and then move to attack. I have to move closer to where he should be. If he does what he should, we trade positions giving me the advantage.

I'm flat against the ground, crawling from one pine tree to another. The inundating fire stops. I freeze and strain to hear. There's a sound of metal against metal – he's reloading another clip. From behind the front of the Crown Vic I see his low shadow dart across the rear of the cabin and disappear behind another pine tree only a few feet from where I had been. I look back at the Crown Vic and know that is where I should be.

My headset crackles.

"Hund zwei, erscheinen sie die östliche seite des gebäudes. Hund vier, schließen sie mich zwischen auf der west side zwischen den gebäuden an."

Whatever he was saying, he was telling Dogs Two and Four to do something. Time to get to my car.

My stealth impresses me. Blending well with the low growth and the many trees, the fact I hear the overhead breezes more than the noise of my own movement testifies to how well I'm doing. It's like riding a bike, I guess. I slide close to the ground, reach the rear wheel on the driver's side, and then with the car as cover, come to a kneeling position. I raise the rifle and a sudden sharp pain stabs at my right side. I crouch back down behind the car, my left hand exploring the pain coming from my mid-right ribcage. My fingers almost fall into the wound and it's everything I can do to not cry out as I pull my hand away, blood dripping from my fingers. The prick actually hit me.

At first, I'm pissed. But through my anger, I hear Tribby's voice in my head reminding me what he said about their ammo load: nine-millimeter rounds, more than sixty rounds in a modified magazine. Hell, that's one lucky shot out of sixty and it's hardly more than a scratch! That's nothing!

"Hey, shithead!" The loud sentiment in perfect American English comes from the guy behind the tree near the rear of Patterson's cabin. He's a cocky S.O.B. with his microphone still on giving me the stereo treatment over my headset. "You still breathing over there?"

Silently, and with a little additional effort, I bring the rifle up over the front fender. Keeping as low a profile as I can, I find him in my scope. He's well hidden, but facing in the direction where I once was and not where I am now. He's exposed. I have a shot. I take it. He falls away from the tree. My regret quickly fades away with each painful throb from my right side.

The bright red dot of a laser sight lights up the chrome trim on the side mirror and I dive for the ground only to fall through a string of nine-millimeter slugs raking across the sheet metal of the front door. One bullet cuts into my upper left side but another round impacts my right-center back and knocks the wind out of me. The ground comes up and punches me in the face as I gasp for air that doesn't seem to be there. I roll onto my back and see the red dot sweep across the length of the car. A second red dot joins the first. Two more bursts of fire and too many holes pop into the car's bodywork and shower me with paint flakes and tiny slivers of ballistic window glass. I've lost my rifle, but there's no time to look for it. Still on my back, my heels dig in as I push myself along the ground to the rear of the car. Somehow, even as another burst of lead plows into the rear fender and the pain from the new hits quickly defeat any remaining tolerance I may have, I make it around the back bumper and to the far corner of the car.

My back feels like it's on fire and my lungs don't work as well as they should, but there's something remarkably exhilarating about still being alive. I pull the Smith & Wesson from the tactical holster, slide a round into the chamber and roll onto my knees.

There's the sound of overhead breezes again, now joined by my own arduous wheezes. The Bearcat is silent. Sweat stings my eyes. I wipe them clear with a wrist dripping with blood. I don't know what to do, but I do know I can't stay where I am. With more pain-racked maneuvering, I get low on the balls of my feet, keep my head low as I bring the pistol up and point it overhead toward the east corner and toward the general direction from where the shots had come. After three quick, excruciating breaths, I take off for Patterson's cabin, squeezing off four quick shots that explode as loud as canon fire through the night. I hear two more spurts of automatic fire coming from behind as I leap over the body of the cocky S.O.B. I nailed a moment before. I reach the corner just short of the wooden walkway when my left thigh is pulled violently across my body and launches me sideways through the air. The gaping wound on my left side hits the walkway first, but I roll with it and come to a stop on my back. The all-over pain glows white-hot and it's all I can do to take in each breath with a muted whimper.

"I got him!" I hear someone yell.

I feel the grip of hands under my shoulders lifting and dragging me toward the cabin entrance.

"I have you, Samuel," Simon says in a low voice.

I see only his silhouette against the moving treetops and the stars in the domed night sky beyond. The outside door opens and he drags me inside. My boots catch the door as it closes. Simon half-carries me to the sofa and lowers me onto the corner cushions.

I can barely make him out in the darkness but I see the reflected wetness of tears on his face as he looks over my wounds.

My words come in deep, painful gasps. "You get what ... you pay for ... I didn't do so good, Simon."

"You did what you could," he says quietly as he carefully begins to peel the ghillie suit from my body. "You tried to do what you know how to do."

"Not good enough ... I'm sorry."

I can't help much. Simon gets my arms free and pulls the hood back from off my head. He takes the headset off and holds up what's left of the Bearcat Scanner now in pieces. He disappears for a moment, quickly returns with a kitchen towel and begins carefully dabbing one bloody hole after another. He pauses at the ragged open tear across my upper thigh.

Simon is next to me on the sofa and I groan as he presses the towel firmly onto the thigh wound to stop the bleeding. The pressure hurts and I don't know if it's doing any good.

Almost comically, my cell phone rings.

"Talk about bad timing," I laugh, lifting the phone from my pocket with difficulty. I answer in short rasps. "This, ... this had, ... better not be a telemarketer."

"Sorry to disappoint," Carter responds quietly, his voice heavy with concern. "How you guys doing?"

"I've had better nights, and you're up awfully late."

"Or, awful early, depending on one's perspective."

"Look, I'd like to chat, but things haven't actually gone the way I planned..."

"I know." There's a long pause as I wait for him to explain how he knows. "They want me to talk you out of there."

Suddenly, I know Carter is in trouble. They must have him. How else could he know we've run out of options in here?

My rasping softens and slows. "No they don't, Carter. They want us dead. There's no mistake, old friend. They came loaded for bear. I'm living proof."

Carter's voice noticeably thickens. "I know that, too. I'm coming in, so don't shoot me, okay?"

That stuns me "You're what? What do you mean. . . ?"

The line goes dead. I look at Simon's shadow sitting next to me. "Carter says he's coming in. He says he wants to talk to us."

Simon drops his head down. He examines my leg wound again and says, "I'm sorry, Samuel."

"He's in the Cities. How can he be here? He doesn't even know where here is."

A soft rapping at the side door precedes a shallow squeak.

"It's me," Carter's voice comes from the shadows. "I'm coming in. Don't shoot."

The Smith & Wesson still hangs loose in my hand. I don't know if I have the strength to even lift it. Draped in his open topcoat, Carter's tall figure emerges from the shadows. In the darkness I see he's in his dapper best: topcoat, sports jacket and a turtleneck sweater. The darkness mutes the style of the ensemble. Only muted shades of gray and black are visible, no colors.

Carter points a finger toward Simon. "They want him, not you. Just hand this guy over and you walk out of here."

What starts as an uncertain, shallow titter rolls into a hearty laugh. "Not as easily as I might like."

"Just do it, will ya? Please, just hand him over."

I weakly wave the pistol past him. "And after I do that, everything goes back to the way it was? We'll all be buddies again, is that it?"

"You'll be alive, Sam. Let's get out of here. Forget this guy."

I struggle to sit more upright in the sofa, but every move racks me with pain and I settle back with a groan. "Tell me, Carter, what brings you to the neighborhood? How'd you know where we were? I didn't tell you. I wouldn't hang you out to dry like that."

He curses and his voice hardens with anger. "No, you wouldn't. That was done already."

"How's that? I'm curious, seeing how I'm probably going to bleed out right here in the next few minutes. Fill me in."

Carter steps back shaking his head. "Man, what a piece of work you are. What the hell do you want? You took out half their team, Sam. They're willing to patch you up and let you go on your way. All you gotta do is hand over Toors, but you won't do that, will you? You'd rather sit here and bleed to death?"

My teeth clench with pain as I rephrase the question. "How did you know?!"

His shoulders sag. "They always knew, Sam. There's a transmitter on your car."

"You put it there?"

He seems to shrink a bit more. "I had to. It was part of the deal. Each time we talked on the phone, I was to keep you on long enough so they could triangulate the cell towers. They just needed to be sure about where you were going."

The awareness of Carter's role in all this adds a turning stomach to my growing list of physical complaints. "And so they tortured the Pattersons and found out we were coming to their rustic abode on Stony Lake?"

Carter's voice sounds hollow and defeated. "They didn't learn a thing from any of them. They put those people through hell, Sam, and didn't get anything out of them."

"You help?"

His shadow shakes his head. "No, I didn't want any part of that. But I was there when they did it."

"So all that stuff about Tomlinson sending you down there to help out the Eagan PD was bullshit?"

"What I'm telling you, Sam, is these people mean business. You'll give them what they want, whether you want to or not, like it or not. There's no other way it's going to go. How you leave here, walking or carried out, is up to you."

"And, you've been in their pocket how long, then? Why?"

He shrugs. "Alright, Sam. They covered me, okay? You don't understand. Linnie's medical bills were killing me. The insurance was gone. We're broke. We were losing everything. They offered to cover me."

"You and Caroline needed money, all you had to do was ask."

He looked up. "You're coming off a divorce and I'm going to come to you for money? You made out that well, Sam? Not to the tune of half a million dollars, I'll bet."

"They covered that much for you?"

"More than that much. Getting you killed was not part of the deal. I'm sorry. It was the only thing I could do. Let's go now. You can shoot me later."

I shook my head. "I won't have to. They'll do it for me."

He extends an impatient hand motioning me to grab it. "No jokes, Sam. No more talk. Come on, let's go."

As Carter leans forward I level the pistol at his gut. He stops and uneasily reminds me, "I said you could shoot me later."

"Let me explain some things to you, old friend. No on who's not in their little club is going to walk away from this little episode in the North Woods Lake Country of Minnesota. Toors, me and now you aren't on their members list. We're dead already."

"I told you, they don't want you."

"Who are they, Carter? Who are the troops?"

"They're a private security company from Oklahoma, I think. It doesn't matter."

"Oklahoma? That's Red River Consultancy – the same contractor the military used in the Gulf Wars. Those guys don't come cheap. Who's the moneyman? Who gave you the money?"

"No one. It didn't happen that way. I was having lunch in the precinct lunchroom. Some guy sits down and says he could make the bills disappear. A week later, I start getting statements showing the balances are paid. There's an offshore account in my name with a whole lot more. I never met the moneyman. Except for the lunchroom guy, I never met anyone. Right after you and I talked on the phone last night, their people took me to Fly Cloud Airport and flew me up here by helicopter."

"And now it's time for them to collect. You're into them big time aren't you, Carter? What happens next is not going to end pretty. You know that, don't you?"

"You're wrong, Sam. It's not like that. All you have to do is give them what they want. I'll go out there right now and make it work. I promise, they'll keep their word."

Simon leaned over, pulled up the bloody towel to check the leg wound once more. I kept the Smith & Wesson on Carter.

"You can promise all you want, Carter, the only word they're going to keep is the one they took to finish the job they started. You go back out there, you're a dead man."

Carter hesitates, looks at the darkened side entrance door and then looks back at me. It's as if he already knows I'm right. There's a slight denying shake of his head.

"I have to go out there."

"No, you don't." I lower the pistol into my lap. "I admit, the alternative isn't all that pleasant, but you can make a stand right here with us. Between the two of us, we might be able to take out the other half of their team. Whadda ya say?"

He's almost despondent as he shakes his head again. "I gave them my weapon before I came in here."

I look down at the pistol in my lap. Now I'm the despondent one. "Well, that throws a kink into things. I don't suppose they'd be willing to give it back to you?"

Carter coughs out a small, nervous laugh before he turns for the door. Over his shoulder he says, "I hope you're wrong, Sam."

In two steps, he opens the door and shouts, "I'm coming out!"

The door explodes into a hail of wood splinters and disintegrating glass. I grab Toors to shield him from the shower of bullets and debris as Carter falls back into the room and lands face-up at my feet. It's over in a second and everything falls silent.

Against the pain of every movement, I slide from the sofa and cradle the head of my oldest friend in my arms as Toors tries to still Carter's body spasms. Carter's torso is a mass of riddled flesh, and each breath he takes is a tortured rasp.

He looks up at me and whispers, "I'm sorry. I'm sorry."

I see a heavy burden of something terrible etch across his face. A hard sob catches deep in my throat.

"Nothin' to be sorry for," I strain at the words. "All's forgiven. No harm; no foul."

A tortured smile is followed by an ironic chuckle. Blood begins to seep from the corner of his mouth. "Thanks, but you're still short."

"What?" My laugh chokes back another sob.

"Oh, crap, Sam," Carter's words struggle through his torment. "Linnie's going to be so pissed…"

The life leaves his eyes and he's gone.

Not even in the war had I felt such agony. A mournful wail pulls from somewhere deep inside. I embrace him and the moans flood from me as the cabin's window wall erupts into a spray of pockmarked splintered holes.

Window wall glass crashes into the cabin and darting thin red beams of laser light too numerous to count slice through the air. The crush of Toors' full body weight hits me as three successive slugs punch violently into his back and pound the breath out from his lungs.

"Simon!" It's my voice I hear screaming but I don't recognize it.

My arms wrap tightly around him as Simon's momentum rolls both of us to the foot of the stairs. The deafening machine gun fire continues unabated. Through the rain of lead Simon reaches up with one hand.

In torment, he says, "It's time for us to go."

Somehow his outstretched fingers tear open the very space before us and from the opening emerges an incredible flood of dazzling white light and the cabin is consumed.

CHAPTER 14

PRINCES AND PRINCIPALITIES

A kaleidoscope of brilliant light surrounds us. All around us a cocoon of the stuff allows only faint passing shadows to be visible. Sound is a rolling rumble buffered in a way I cannot understand. The sensation is that of effortless and very fast movement. It lasts for only a short while, and then we are lying on our backs in a clearing beneath a star-blanketed night sky. The rush of fresh air returns and I suck in a startling, wondrously brutal breath to fill my lungs.

I turn my head. Simon lies on the ground next to me. He appears to be unconscious. Only the pain of Carter's death surpasses the aching throbs from my own wounds. My body almost screams its complaint as I reach for Simon's arm and give it a small shake.

"Simon. Are you hit bad?"

His eyes remain closed, but from barely moving lips he breathes out a cautioning "Shsssssh."

I try to raise myself to one elbow, but I fall back to the ground.

"Wait," Simon says weakly, finding my hand with his.

My strength leaves me. I hold on tightly to his hand and resign myself to the death I know now must come. I turn again to him.

"I'm sorry, Simon. I screwed everything up."

He only returns another "Shsssh."

That's when I feel as if I'm weightless and lifting from the ground. There's a glow of some sort, as brilliant white as the light that carried us here, emanating from all around my body. Toors still tightly holds onto my hand. His body glows even brighter, light radiates from beneath both of us, warming and filling each of us completely.

I'm frightened. "What's happening?"

"Shssssh," Simon says once more, slivers of the white light showing from under his closed eyelids.

The glowing aura encompassing us begins to pulse in forceful waves, each shock flowing through our bodies. The thrusts of incredible sound surge through me, each pulse stronger than the preceding one, building in power while pulling the excruciating torment of my injuries from me in large, rhythmic yanks.

And then the glow is gone, the night returns and we lie in the sudden smothering quiet of it all.

Still on my back, all I see are the stars above. My breathing is normal and the agony of my wounds is no more. I move first my fingers, then my toes. Everything seems to work. Carefully, I roll away from Toors and rise up on all fours with surprising, almost effortless ease that is difficult to trust. Wobbly, I sit upright on my knees; my hands reach for the torn and bloody holes of my clothing. At every spot of injured flesh, my fingers trace the outlines of scars, but the wounds themselves are sealed. There is no pain.

I point a shaking finger at Toors as he rises to his feet.

"What are you?!" The trembling starts as I stab my finger at him. "How did you do this? We're supposed to be dead! I don't understand any of this! Who are you?!"

Toors offers a small laugh, bends down and picks up several small, misshapen objects from the ground where he had lain. Two steps over to where I had laid next to him, he picks up another similar object from the ground. He softly rattles what he holds in his hand, turns and offers the pieces to me. With increasing uncertainty, I reach up and he deposits four spent nine-millimeter slugs into my hand.

"Three from me," he says with disturbing mirth. "One from you. Your other wounds were through-and-through."

I look down at my torn thigh. The fabric is ragged and blood soaked but inside the torn cloth my fingers find only the sealed scar. I search his face for answers, and with even more uncertainty and confusion, I more quietly repeat my questions.

"Who are you? How did you do this?"

Simon lowers himself to sit cross-legged next to me, folds his hands in his lap and as calmly as if he's talking about the weather, says, "My name is Simon Toors, as you already know, and I do nothing. Our Lord does it all."

Somehow I find the strength to resist the very real urge to sock the guy in the jaw.

"I mean it, Simon. You gotta level with me, cuz if you don't, I'm going to complete this excursion into insanity and what happens to you isn't going to be pretty."

He giggles and his face holds so much love it embarrasses me.

"So very colorful," he says softly. "I understand why our Lord blesses you so."

I look away. "Blessed is not the word I would choose to describe me or anything about my life. I'm a mess."

"But, you're a beautiful mess."

I still can't look at him. "Everything I've touched is either dead or divorced, Simon. That's not beautiful, it's pathetic. It doesn't matter in the grand scheme of things, I'm sure, but what does matter to me right now is you and your honest, truthful, no B-S story. I want all of it, Simon, right now."

His face holds that irritating peaceful expression of his. "Yes, well, you might not like what you hear, Samuel."

"Try me." I wave an arm across our dark and empty surroundings. "It's not as if there's anywhere else we need to be."

Simon takes pause and carefully searches my face for a reason not to continue. He fines none.

"Very well, Samuel, you can't say I didn't warn you. You know my name, already – Simon Toors. I was born in Joppa in the country of Israel. My father was a merchant. When I was a child, he taught me to be a merchant, too. You could say I was born into wealth. In my memory I cannot recall ever being denied anything I ever wanted. To my father's credit, I became very skilled at bartering and accumulating a significant amount of personal treasure even before my marriage, which occurred when I turned sixteen…"

"You were married at sixteen? Why so young?"

Simon shrugs. "Young is relative. In my time such things were common and expected."

"Your time? What time was that?"

He shrugs again. "Awhile back. Anyway, my father died when I was yet in my early twenties. I had my wife, my two sons and two daughters and the combined wealth of my father's fortune as well as my own…"

I interrupt again. "Your mother didn't inherit the estate?"

"In my native country, that sort of thing was not allowed."

"Interesting."

"Not really," Simon continues. "What was interesting was what happened after my father died. I became ill. Today, you call it Hansen's Disease, a chronic infection caused by bacteria now called mycobacterium leprae and mycobacterium lepromatosis. Back then the affliction was considered to be a severe curse from God and there was no cure, no real treatment of any kind. It's a horrifying thing, really. Skin lesions spread all over your body, bleeding ulcers, severe nerve damage, dead tissue on your arms, legs and hands; even your eyes. Infection leads to other infections, and those infections eventually take your life. Leprosy is the definition of the phrase 'Living hell.'

"As horrible as all that is, it is the ostracism that is the most difficult. The fear of contagion with this disease is very real, and so I understood when my wife and children left me. Although my business suffered at first, it still prospered. Even though I was not acceptable company in normal social circles, my wealth still was highly valued. My money kept my business associations viable while my illness kept everyone at arm's length."

Simon reaches over and places his hand over mine. "You do not know how important human touch is until you are denied it, Samuel. This one simple sensation, a person's touch, is as vital to survival as air to breathe."

He removes his hand from mine and continues. "And so I became wealthier, and at the same time, very much alone. I had but one friend – a servant – who cared for my needs. He fed me, washed my clothes, kept my house and conducted business in my name. He comforted me when no one else could.

"One day, my servant asked me to go with him to see a traveling young rabbi who was preaching nearby. He said to me, 'His words are unlike anything you will ever hear, Master. He can heal you.' But I didn't deserve healing and no rabbi would want my presence to disturb his congregation or his preaching. So I dismissed my servant and returned him to his chores. But he persisted. 'Master, please come,' he said again. 'I have heard him speak and I tell you God is in him.' I became angry and told him I did not have time for holy men or false prophets, nor would they have time for me. My servant is steadfast and repeats his desperate plea. 'He is not false, my Master,' he insisted. 'He has healed others, many others. People come from all the land to hear him and be healed. He can heal you; I know he can. You have but to ask Him, Master, and you will be cleansed of this curse.'

"I raged in my anger against him. I struck him down with my staff. He lay at me feet, bloodied as he tried to shield himself from the next blow, and then the next. My staff was raised a final time to take his life but somehow my hand was stilled. His face showed so much love as he looked at me my knees weaken. I fell to the floor in tears. My servant took my hand and helped me to my feet.

"We traveled for more than half a day before we reached the valley where my servant told me the rabbi would be. But when we arrived, the preacher was nowhere to be seen. On one side of the valley a great crowd of people gathered at the base of a large hill. My servant guided me through the people. Many saw me and cleared a path as they pulled away. I told my servant the rabbi is gone, but he said to me, 'He will return, Master. We must wait.'"

"Down from the side of the hill, I saw Him coming with several of his disciples following. His eyes met mine and I quickly moved from the crowd and bowed low at his feet. 'Lord,' I say in sorrowful repentance, 'if You are willing, You can make me clean.'"

"And He reached out his hand, rested it on my head and says, 'I am willing. Be cleansed.'

"Immediately, Samuel, my leprosy leaves me. In a moment, I was cleansed of it and completely healed. The Rabbi took me by a hand once deformed and weeping with sores, but now young, full and whole, and I stood before Him. He said to me: 'Tell no one of this, but go your way, show yourself to the priest and offer the gift that Moses commanded, as a testimony to them.' And so, I went and did as He told me to do."

Simon's story pulls a distant memory from me. To the east, the night sky shows a sliver of pre-dawn bleeding up from the distant horizon. Everything in my being believes this man, but his story is too fantastic. For a long moment, neither of us say anything as we sit in the darkness looking at each other. My brain struggles with what he has just told me.

"Simon, I am familiar with this story. It is in the Bible, the book of Matthew, I believe."

"Yes, Samuel, you are correct: chapter 8, actually. It's a bit of personal ostentatious notoriety I normally choose not to claim, but in this case, you are a special exception."

His tranquil admission crushes me. Now I know for certain Simon is delusional and in need of professional help. No matter how much I may want to, I can't allow myself the luxury of believing anything he tells me.

"That's okay, Simon, that's, that's okay. I, ah, I don't know what to say, actually. Had I known you were doing the Mel Brooks' '2,000-year-old-man' routine, I'd be better able to roll with this…"

His light laughter surprises me. "Oh, Samuel, what must I do so you know I speak the truth?"

I deny my doubt. "It's not that…"

"I am the leper in Matthew, chapter 8. Christ healed me, and when He healed me, He healed me completely – perfectly, for his purposes. I have never died. I live according to His will." He points to me and enthusiastically asks, "You are your own proof! Where are your wounds? Are they not healed?"

Instinctively, I reach for my injured lower side. "Well, you're right about that. The pain is completely gone; there's no bleeding, only scars."

"What is in your hand, Samuel?"

I still hold the spent slugs – one from me, three from him.

"Your own scars and what you hold in your hand prove everything I have told you, Samuel," Simon explains patiently. "As for your scars, wear them with pride for all the days the Lord gives you. He still has His scars, too, you know."

"Yes, but Simon, what you are saying happened two thousand years ago. You know you aren't…"

He interrupts. "I live according to His will, Samuel. When He wills it, I will be with Him wholly. You see Samuel, time and space are like a curtain. When you pull the curtain back, you enter another room."

That stops me. "I don't understand how…"

"Well, it's simple physics, really. What is the circumference of the Earth at the equator?"

"What? How should I know?"

"Go ahead, take a guess."

I miserably fail trying to recall the mathematical formula for calculating the circumference of a circle. "I don't know, Simon, maybe twenty-five thousand miles."

"Very good! The Earth has a circumference of precisely 24,901.55 miles or 40,075.16 kilometers, take your pick. A complete rotation on its axis takes 24 hours. Do the math, Samuel. How fast is the earth turning?"

Through the fog of my aging gray matter, I figure it out. "Slightly more than 1,000 miles per hour, I guess."

"Close enough," he comfortably laughs again. "That's more than 1,466 feet per second. Now imagine you can wrap yourself in a space-time curtain where you are completely motionless while everything around you continues to move at 1,466 feet per second. What would happen?"

My brain stumbles through the imaginary picture and I haltingly answer. "I guess everything would pass by you, warping around you, speeding past as you remain motionlessness. It would seem as if you were traveling far away very fast."

I hear his satisfied sigh. "Ah, Samuel, I think you are beginning to understand."

"But, how is that even possible?"

"'All things are possible through Christ who strengthens me.'"

I lower my head into my hands, wrestling against the wonder of all of this. "This sounds like something Einstein would come up with. I'm not Einstein, Simon, and I'm having trouble keeping up."

"Ah, yes, Albert," He echoes with a disturbing tone of familiarity. "I enjoyed Albert. He was great fun! A remarkable mind, the most significant since Newton, really. He possessed a marvelous sense of humor, too. His personal life was somewhat challenging for him, however. I think he found human relationships too difficult to figure out. Ironic."

My mouth agape, I fall back on my haunches and stare at Simon. Against the growing blue-gray horizon of an approaching dawn he's becoming a well-defined silhouette.

"Are you telling me you knew Einstein?"

"Worked with him," he responds matter-of-factly and then chuckles. "He was constantly frustrated with his failed attempts to successfully postulate the mathematical equation that would prove the existence of God. Funny fellow, and our Lord got such a kick out of him, I can't tell you."

"You're kidding, right?"

"Of course not."

"Of course not," I repeat, my head returning to my hands. The stunning simplicity of everything he suggests overwhelms me. He uses space-time as a conveyance. This was how he had disappeared during the attack on the jail cell. It was how he was in so many different places across the Cities so quickly during the storms, helping all those people. He was using space-time to do what he was supposed to do.

Somehow, I found my voice. "The bodies at the scenes; the crispies. Did you kill them?"

His silhouette sags a little with regret. "I told you before, Samuel, I am protected."

"Yes, you did, by Truth you said."

"Evil has always opposed our Lord. And He promises his church that the gates of hell shall not prevail and those who accept his gift of eternal life shall never perish nor be plucked out of His hand. Remember, He says to us, 'I am the way, the truth and the life: no man comes unto the Father but by me.' He is as He says He is. Evil attacks against His people are dealt with severely, Samuel. It isn't a pretty thing. In the Book of Revelation, chapter 11, Christ's two witnesses are protected during their mission on Earth. In the fifth verse it says, 'And, if any man will hurt them, fire proceeds out of their mouths and devours their enemies; and if any man will hurt them, he must in this manner be killed.' It is harsh purification, unfortunate but necessary for those who are evil. Do not be concerned, Samuel. Evil's days are numbered."

"So you did kill them, then?"

"No. They destroyed themselves."

"You mean, this fire as you call it, is not controlled by you?"

"I control nothing, Samuel. All control rests with our Lord."

I draw both hands down my face, struggling to digest all this. "But at what price, Simon? Phil; the Pattersons; Carter."

"Yes, a terrible price. It is unfortunate your actions brought death to so many who shouldn't have died."

I jerk back up. "My actions?!"

His silhouette expels an audible sigh. "I do not mean to offend you, Samuel, but you need to realize it was you who tried to control what would happen instead of trusting Christ to make things happen. By doing so, you acted gallantly by worldly standards, but wrongly."

The hairs on the back of my neck come up and I bark, "I had a job to do! They killed Phil!"

He responds calmly. "Phil Tribby died because of your decision to involve him in your efforts. His death triggered an understandable reaction in you, but it was an errant one that prevented you from trusting our Lord. Your lack of faith led to more aggressive efforts to triumph through your own actions. These efforts led to more death."

"I was trying to save your life!"

Simon's relentless. "You used me as bait, Samuel, simply to defeat an unknown enemy. With selfish, vengeful motives, not obedient or sacrificial ones, you succeeded in preventing our Lord from doing what was necessary."

His truth pokes holes through my rapidly thinning veil of self-justification. Still, I resist it. "I didn't have a choice. They came to kill us, Simon. I had to act."

"Our Lord expects better from you."

His simple words crush me to my core. The weight of all that had happened, each friend I had lost and each life I had taken one by one, flood through me with devastating force impossible to hold back. Strength drains from me and any remaining resistance crumbles away into nothingness. My arms cover my head and it is my own sorrowful wail of soul-wrenching agony I hear.

Simon moves beside me and holds me close.

"He knows your love for Him, Samuel. He knows your heart. Know He forgives you, and know He will be with you always, now and forever."

Chapter 15

Cleanup

We make our way against the splash of early morning color bathing the small hill from where we had spent the last few hours watching the sun come up. Our path is a well-worn trail leading through a dense wall of surrounding trees.

I shake a warning finger at Simon. "You may not like it, but you're still in my custody."

His light laugh bothers me.

"I'm serious, now," I warn him again. We enter a path coolly shaded by the canopy of the treetops. "I've got to report all this and I don't plan on doing it all alone. You're staying to back me up, that's for sure and for certain. Don't make me have to beat you to death."

More light laughter. "Still so colorful, Samuel, even after all that has happened. How lovely."

"Lovely, my ass." I duck under a low-hanging branch. "I'm in deep weeds, my friend. When the chief gets done, he'll lock me up and throw away the key…"

Simon, trailing two steps behind, interrupts with an echo of my own words. "That's for sure and for certain."

"Funny."

The path widens and empties onto a road. To the right, asphalt pavement heads west up a small rise. To the left, the road turns to dirt and curves low to the east. I recognize it.

I turn to Simon and wave a hand down the dirt road to the left. "We're not as lost as I thought. That leads to the fork where we turned off to get to the Patterson place, remember?"

"Yes, I know."

It takes all I've got not to scowl. "I'm not a bit surprised you know. Anything else you know that you'd think I'd appreciate, don't let me stop you from sharing, okay?"

"Okay, if you insist, how's this: the Patterson cabin is now an official crime scene and the law enforcement community is well-represented. In fact, your chief is in attendance."

I do a slight double take. "I doubt that. He'd need a space-time curtain of his own to get up here that fast."

"You'll have to ask him about that," Simon says, falling in behind me as I lead the way.

"Too bad you can't pull back the old curtain right now," I mildly complain. "It's a bit of a hike back to the place."

Simon says nothing so I continue walking. The road curves and I turn to say something. He's not behind me. I quickly check my flanks and then scan the road back to where the packed dirt meets faded blacktop. Nothing. I peer through the surrounding trees and bushes that hug the road. Simon's nowhere to be seen.

A hollow aloneness immediately swallows me up and I curse out loud. I've lost another close friend, maybe the closest yet.

***

The Robin Lane fork is a parking lot loaded with Cass County Sheriff vehicles and media vans from Duluth, the Twin Cities' stations and two national networks. Where the road snakes through the huddled mass of gathered onlookers, uniformed officers and too many parked vehicles with flashing emergency lights, the lane itself is barely passable. The crowd faces away from me. On the other side of the yellow crime scene tape, access to the road leading to the Patterson cabin is restricted. No one notices as I walk up from behind.

I clear me throat and politely bother two people with their backs turned. "Excuse me, I would like to get through, please."

The taller guy to my right throws a careless glance over his shoulder to lay some "Minnesota Nice" on me.

"Yeah, you and everybody else, buddy."

Familiarly, I'm in no mood for rudeness. Through a tight smile and in a more serious voice, I ask again. "Pretty please?"

It must be the way I say it, because the guy turns more fully, cocks his arm back for a well-telegraphed punch, takes one look at my torn and blood-stained hunting clothes for the first time, and then freezes.

"Jesus! You're all shot to pieces!"

The guy on his left turns and steps back in surprise. "Man, you're him! You're the cop they're looking for!"

More people turn and a cacophonous echoing of "He's been shot!" fills the air. Other shouts of "Get a cop!" randomly join the continued rumbling through the mass of people now moving to surround me.

Too many voices come from too many directions drowning out my weak protests. Someone grabs my arm, quickly joined by other hands grabbing at me and I propel quickly through the crowd toward a pair of Cass County squad cars fronting the yellow tape strung across the road.

One of the two young deputies sees me emerge. In one startled look, he takes in my disheveled state to simply exclaim, "Jesus!"

Equally stunned, the other deputy triggers his radio mic. "We've found your detective, Chief Tomlinson. We're bringing him in."

I'm in the backseat. Like a strobe light the bright morning sun painfully flickers and flashes through the tall jack pines and into my eyes. The deputy makes quick work of the short trip, sliding to a sideways stop behind the black SWAT van parked on the dirt drive tucked just inside the Onawim sign post. He springs from behind the wheel as the van backdoor swings open with a loud bang. Tomlinson and Officer Shelesah Magan come running. Close behind are Rupert and the still too-tall Wayne-Baby Stephens of the FBI.

Tomlinson yells something unintelligible at the deputy and my door opens. I pivot, my feet hit the ground and I step from the car.

"For Christ's sake," Tomlinson yells some more. "Take the goddam cuffs off him!"

I turn to offer my wrists and the deputy complies. I smile my thanks and step around the car. Tomlinson looks pissed. Magan looks horrified. The FBI pukes simply shake their heads at me.

"You look like hell," the chief complains.

I nod. "Nice to see you again, too. How'd you find me?"

Tomlinson spit at the ground. "I didn't find you. I found Carter. When you stopped answering your phone, I figured sooner or later Carter would lead me right to you. I was right. Okay, I was a little late cuz he hopped on that helicopter at the Flying Cloud Airport last night, but I was right, just the same."

I'm surprised. "You put a tail on Carter?"

"You're damn right! He was easy. We knew every step he made. We even knew he had Toors when you guys were at the diner. After that, we lost you again. But we didn't lose Carter."

Wayne-Baby chimes in. "You weren't very subtle, Culhane. We got security video of you at the diner, the storage facility and the Wal-Mart. You've got a lot of explaining to do, Detective."

I know my disrespectful glance doesn't improve our relationship any. "I'll explain to my chief, Agent Stephens. You can take notes."

The agent takes umbrage. "You'll explain to me, Culhane, or you'll face Federal charges…"

The chief cuts it off. "Put a sock in it, Stephens."

Tomlinson turns to me. "Okay, we have a real slaughter house, here. Let's take a tour and you tell your side, okay?"

Over the next hour the five of us pace off the area, making our way inside the SWAT sentries positioned along the perimeter, carefully moving around the scattered CSI team working the crime scene for evidence and clues to what had happened, and visiting each sheet-covered body in turn. I explain what happened in each shooting; the overall operation I had undertaken, its strategy and my objectives, all the while confessing the taking down of each of the four bodies scattered between the road and the rear of the cabins. We stop at my shot-up Crown Vic. Pock marks dot the glass and the outer sheet metal of the ballistic door panels. The tires are pierced, too, but they're Run-Flat Goodyear's so the vehicle is still moveable.

"Too bad about your car," Tomlinson laments, adding, "sorry we have to hold it for evidence. You understand."

"Good car. It probably saved my life," I move to the driver's side and search the ground. "I dropped my rifle somewhere around this side…"

"We found it," Officer Magan says. "It's impounded as evidence, too, I'm afraid."

I accept this with a nod and describe how I used the rear of the car as a shield before the run to the cabin. We walk in that direction coming to where the fourth covered body lies behind the pine tree. I explain the circumstances of this kill again and how I had to get back to the Patterson cabin to make a stand.

As I finish up, Tomlinson summarizes things.

"So you take out the first guy by breaking his neck; then it's a single headshot three separate times while they're shooting at you with machine guns…"

"Assault rifles," I correct him.

"Yeah, okay, assault rifles. You're under heavy fire during all of this. I know you're good, Sam, but you can't tell me you came out of this without a scratch. That's bull and you know it. You look like you've gone through a meat grinder!"

I didn't need to look. "I didn't say I didn't get hit. I did, Mark, several times."

I proceed to expose the rips and holes in my clothing to show the scars of my wounds – the left and right sides, the back, and lastly, the thigh. The others lean in, observe and return only questioning looks.

"Amazing," Officer Magan allows. "You took four of them down by yourself. But how did you survive these hits?"

"I can't actually explain the injuries or how they were healed. All I can say is it's my blood on the clothing and my wounds are healed. I don't know how."

Wayne-Baby cracks something about a magic trick. Rupert agrees with his superior and demands a DNA test of the dried blood. Magan and Tomlinson say nothing.

"You can test what you want," I agree. "I didn't bring a change of clothes, so you're welcome to take these after I get cleaned up."

Tomlinson throws a thumb over his shoulder in the general direction of the slope leading to the lake. "What about the other six?"

"Six?" I'm surprised. "I thought there were only eight of them all together?"

"You're telling me you didn't do the others?" Tomlinson curls a figure in a follow me gesture. "You come with me, take look at this mess and tell me how I make sense of it."

We make our way around the Patterson cabin to the lakeside slope. Shattered glass from the riddled window wall, splintered wood from perforated framing, decking and siding, and destruction debris is strewn everywhere. The six sheet-covered bodies testify to a horrific firefight. Two bodies lie halfway down the slope from the rear deck. Three more l twisted in agony across the deck itself. One body lies upside down crumpled on the steps.

Tomlinson's arm sweeps across the carnage. "Did you do this too, Sam?"

"No," I admit plainly.

"I bet," Stephens scoffs.

Tomlinson ignores the FBI man. "Do you know where this small army came from?"

I survey the area once more before answering. "You may want to check out the Red River Consultancy."

Rupert is stunned. "The military contractor? You're saying the government is behind all this?"

"I don't know," I look up to the shattered window wall. "All I know is one of the last things Carter said before he was killed was that he believed these guys were from a group out of Oklahoma. If so, that's the Red River Consultancy."

"That's not possible," Stephens' vehemently denies. "Red River's exclusive to the U.S. military."

I wonder aloud. "Maybe not so much now that Iraq and Afghanistan have cooled down."

I plod up the grade to the body on the steps and pull the sheet back. Dressed in a black BDU, a ballistic ceramic chest shield and helmet, the body's face and exposed flesh around the neck is mottled and blistered with white seeping lesions, completely unlike the four bodies on the other side of the cabin.

Not surprised in the least, I state the obvious. "He's a crispy."

Tomlinson augments the observation. "On this side of the cabin, all six of them are crispies, Sam, just like what happened at the jail. What do you think did this?"

I look away from the corpse and answer plainly, "Truth."

I don't wait for a reply as I step past the body, take the stairs two at a time up to the deck, and move around another sheet-covered lump to what is left of the sliding glass door. I stride through the blown-out doorframe, my boots crunching on broken shards of glass as I walk into the cabin. Inside, another CSI officer is kneeling close to the staircase, flashlight in hand searching for anything that might be useful for the investigation. He looks up at me as I walk in, nods silently and returns to his work. To his right, Carter's body lies where I had last held it, covered by yet another white sheet. I look at the motionless shroud and my vision blurs with sudden moisture. The tears gather and I let them fall.

Behind me, I hear glass crunching again.

"You'll have to explain Truth to me," the chief says with more patience than I would have if the roles were reversed. "Maybe later, though. What can you tell me about Carter in all this?"

"He died trying to protect me. They nearly cut him in two."

"I'm sorry," he sounds sincere. "But can you tell me what happened to Toors?"

Unable to look away from Carter, I swallow hard and say, "I have no Earthly idea."

"But he was with you, right? In your custody?"

My small laugh emerges through the dull ache of personal loss. With the side of my hand I wipe the wetness from my face. "I used to think so, Mark, but Simon Toors has a unique way of coming and going as he pleases. Just when you know you've got him, that's when you don't."

I feel the chief's eyes bore into my back. I remain standing in silence over Carter. The torture twists in my gut and doesn't let go.

"Well, maybe later on that question, too," the chief finally says. "Until you're told otherwise, you're suspended with pay pending review. It's standard procedure when there's a shooting and God knows there's been a lot of shooting lately. Don't even let me see you anywhere near the precinct, got it?"

I wasn't in the mood to argue. "I'll need a ride."

Home Again

CHAPTER 16

"YOU'RE ONE OF US, NOW"

The sound of water rushing from the bathroom showerhead pulls me from a sour sleep – the kind of sleep where my tongue feels fuzzy and tells me I drank too much last night. I remember the ride sitting in the backseat of the Cass County Sheriff's squad car, but little else.

My bedroom is poorly lit and looks as fuzzy as my tongue feels. My eyes sting as I rub them and things begin to come into focus. A sliver of light slices through a narrow crack of the barely opened bathroom door, providing the only illumination in the room except for the pale blue readout from the digital clock on the nightstand that reads "7:27" and there's someone using my shower. Who?

Every muscle complains as I struggle to swing my legs from under the blankets and feel the familiar abrasiveness of the carpet on the soles of my feet. I sit naked on the edge and bury my face in my hands. There's a very real urge to lay back down, pull up the blankets and hide from everything.

The shower stops running. I hear the shower curtain pull back and someone's shadow moves from the tub to the vanity. Moments of silence are softly peppered with dainty sounds of a woman doing dainty things. I immediately feel the guilt of doing something I shouldn't have done combined with the embarrassment of not being able to remember what it was that I did. My breath catches in my throat as the bathroom door opens all the way.

Wearing my bathrobe, she scurries across the room to the small desk in the far corner where she retrieves her clothing.

"Shelly!" I can't help the surprise. I mean it's not like it hasn't happened before since our divorce, but it's remarkable that she should be here after all that had happened on Stony Lake.

"Don't distract me," she warns, tossing my bathrobe to me before fastening her bra with both hands behind her back. I marvel how a woman can do that. She adds, "I'm already late. Get cleaned up and I'll have coffee ready when you get out."

I slip on the robe still warmed by her body and enter the bathroom for a quick shower. About ten minutes later, I'm standing robe-less at the vanity with the electric razor grinding two days' worth of stubble from my face. The door opens and I see Shelly's fully dressed and coifed reflection in the mirror. Her eyes widen with horror from what she sees and the coffee cup in her hand begins to quake. Quickly, I turn and rescue the cup just in time. It loses only a few drops. I place it on the vanity.

She almost screams, "Those scars! What happened to you?"

I switch off the razor and place it next to the coffee cup.

"It's okay, Shel," I say as I reach to hold her.

She roughly pulls back from me. "No, it's not okay!"

I quickly put my robe back on and follow her into the bedroom. "I'm sorry, Shel, it happened yesterday at the lake. Everything's fine."

The confused words explode from her. "Yesterday? At the lake? What lake? This is exactly why I can't stay with you! Exactly what I mean!"

I've heard the words before and they hurt just as much now as they did then. "Shel, you can't mean that. After everything that's happened, you still came here to be with me."

She throws it back into my face. "Just because I need you sometimes, that doesn't change things!"

She moves back to the desk, scoops up her purse and jacket, and leaves the room. I know it's pointless, but I follow her anyway. In the front room she reaches the door and turns back to me. Her face is flushed with anger, embarrassment and maybe something close to real hatred. I'm not sure.

"It's your damn job," she says too familiarly, and it's déjà vu all over again. "I can't take it, Sam. I'm sorry."

This conversation is like a broken record and I resign to it with a surrendering shrug. "I'm sorry, too, Shel. It's okay. I'll be here when you need me."

She strains at words that do not come, only to turn and leave the condo, closing the door too firmly behind her.

A few moments pass as I wait there, watching for the door to reopen. She might think better of it. She might realize we need each other. My breathing slows with anticipation. Another moment goes by. Nothing. Just like before, I wait a moment more, give up and return to the razor in the bathroom to complete my shave.

A half-hour later, dressed in jeans, a sweater and sneakers, I'm at the kitchen table with a refilled coffee cup and slowly working on a bowl of Raisin Bran. The wall phone rings and I get up from my chair to answer it.

It's Tomlinson and he doesn't sound happy. "You coming in anytime soon, or what?"

I throw a questioning look at the receiver and return it to my ear. "Sorry, I was told not to, remember?"

"Not funny," is his clipped reply. "Never mind, anyway. I'm sending Magan down to get you."

"Why, what's up?"

"We've got a body. I need you at the scene, now. She'll be there in five minutes."

"Yeah, but you said..." Dial tone rudely interrupts my confused objection.

Outside the front of my building I wait with my hands shoved deep into my jacket pockets. It's an unseasonably cool morning and the sun is still too low in the sky to remove the chill. I curse myself for not putting on my heavier jacket as Officer Magan pulls up to the curb in a city squad car. I climb into the front passenger seat, mindful of the bracketed shotgun fronting the dashboard and the computer array where the armrest should be.

"Good morning, Detective," she says as I fasten the seat belt.

"Nice to see you again, Officer Magan," I reply, catching her questioning raised eyebrow. "Where to today?"

"Not far. Harrison Park," she says. "Off Glenwood near the Harrison Education Center."

"Glenwood Avenue again? I hope it's not another crispy."

She does a quick double take in my direction, and then checks behind her opposite shoulder for oncoming traffic. With a heavy foot on the accelerator, she pulls away from the curb as she flicks on her lights and siren. Within moments I experience firsthand her expertise with pursuit speeds.

She follows a zigzag route, taking Second Avenue down to Seventh Street, turning north across Hennepin to North Second behind the Target Center, then a hard left onto Glenwood. In mere minutes she pulls onto the short street west of the curved edifice of the Harrison classroom building fronting Glenwood, continuing to the rear where she skids to a stop just short of the rear parking lot that faces the open-air basketball court. The court itself holds two more police squads and the coroner's van. Several uniformed officers are in attendance, along with a few plain-clothes guys and several white-coated techs. It's an all too familiar scene and my stomach turns nauseous.

Magan exits the car and looks back in at me. "You comin'?"

Suddenly, everything about this makes me feel uneasy. I'm certain I'm going to throw up at any second. I've been here before.

"You know, Detective," Officer Magan leans in closer through her still open door. "You don't look so good."

"No, I'm fine," I lie. Releasing the seat belt buckle I move to leave the car. "It must be the Raisin Bran."

She nods and says something about raisins doing that sometimes. We walk together toward the trees on the far side of the basketball court and the good-sized crowd gathered there. We're almost even with the onlookers when I see the tall, top-coated figure of Carter Wolpren emerge from behind the suspended line of yellow tape.

My knees turn to water and I'm on the ground. Both Magan and Carter are on me in a blink while others from the crowd turn to see what's going on.

"Whoa, Sam!" Carter quickly stoops down to grab my arm. "You look like you've see a ghost!"

He catches my hand before I can touch his face.

"Just relax, okay?" Carter says. He turns to Magan. "Get Tribby over here, would you?"

Tribby? Tribby's alive? Carter's alive? The panic begins a terrifying swell within me and I feel Carter's hand tightens its grip.

"It's okay, Sam. Just take a breath, you'll be fine. Breathe in and out. It's okay, even short people need air."

I can't stop my shaking and it's quickly growing worse.

The unmistakable bald head and thick-rimmed glasses fill my vision as Phil checks my eyes, my pulse, everything he can.

"He's having a seizure," Phil says. "Careful now, help me get him to the van!"

Through the tremors, I feel myself being lifted from the ground, and then, it all goes dark.

***

I'm on a gurney in an ambulance painfully lit with florescent lamping. There's an IV in my arm and an oxygen mask over my mouth and nose. The ambulance rocks as it moves slowly through the traffic. The whoop-whoop of the siren is irritating and too loud. Each time the white-jacketed attendant checks my now open eyes with a small flashlight, I blink.

"I'm sorry," the attendant apologizes. "How are you feeling?"

I carefully remove the mask from my face. "What day is it?"

He raises a curious eyebrow. "It's Tuesday, why?"

"But what date is it?"

"March 18. Are you having memory problems?"

March eighteenth? That's not possible. March eighteenth was two months ago; the day the first Glenwood murder victim was found. Desperately, my eyes scan the interior of the ambulance while my mind struggles to make sense of what is happening.

From the front passenger seat, another attendant leaves the forward compartment and moves back into the rear of the vehicle.

"Let me take over," he says, changing places with the first man who leaves for the vacated front passenger seat. The new guy leans in close and in a familiar muddled British accent says, "It's a bit disconcerting, I know. You'll get used to it."

I look up into the man's face – Simon's face – and my mouth drops open. Now fully fearful for my own sanity, the only sound I make is incoherent mumble.

He gently pats me on my shoulder. "That's okay, don't speak; just listen. You, my friend, are not only colorful, not only chosen; you are greatly blessed among men, Samuel. Our Lord has blessed you beyond measure. Your timeline is altered. He has altered it, and by doing so, He has given you a second chance."

My words are distant and confused. "A second…? For what?"

"To start anew; to do things right; to follow His will so that those who must live do not die."

Simon is speaking, but I struggle to make sense of what he is saying. All that had happened hasn't happened yet? All that will happen can be changed? All my mistakes might be avoided or might be repeated? All who died because of me may yet live again, or because of me, may die again? The realization sinks in and the horror of it fills my soul.

I grab his hand tightly. "Simon, I cannot do this! It's beyond me. If I mess up again, if they all die again because of me, I couldn't live with myself…"

"You will do very little while He will do everything," Simon smiles. "You know Truth now. You know to rely on Him, not yourself. He promises you victory, Samuel. Trust in Him and let His peace fill you. You're one of us now."

The End

From the Author —

Dave, Paul, Larry, Ralph and I are having breakfast at T.J.'s in Edina like we often do on Tuesday mornings. I ask them straight-out:

"Suppose it's a normal day and out of nowhere God comes up to you, taps you on your shoulder and asks you to do something for Him. He promises you that, although there may be great risk and real danger in doing this thing, He guarantees you're going to be successful at it. All you need to do is trust in Him. Would you do it?"

"Which God?" Dave immediately asks.

"Yeah," Larry agrees. "I first wanna see His driver's license or something."

Paul, never at a loss for words when it comes to all things metaphysical, asks, "What are you, nuts?!"

Ralph, being Ralph, cautiously observes the reactions of the other guys before he says, "That sounds like that TV series cancelled a few years back – you know, the one with the *'What if God Was One of Us'* theme song."

Moaning, the painful realization of Ralph's simple statement hits me and I bury my face in my hands: there are, in fact, no original ideas.

FL

NORMANDALE COMMUNITY COLLEGE
LIBRARY
9700 FRANCE AVENUE SOUTH
BLOOMINGTON, MN 55431-4399